BROKEN OATH

A RAVEN THRILLER

by

JOHN D. TRUDEL

Broken Oath is a work of fiction. Names, characters, places, and incidents either are products of the author's imagination or are used fictitiously. Any resemblance to actual events or locales or persons, living or dead, is entirely coincidental..

Author: John D. Trudel

Cover Design and Art: Bruce DeRoos

Printed in the United States of America

DEDICATION

General Paul Vallely is the man you want to be with you when you get the call @ 0300 from a deployed asset or an ally reaching out for support. He is dead nuts honest and has an expert knowledge of geopolitics and military tactics. This is only a brief snap shot of his actual qualifications.

General Vallely has been a military analyst on television and radio. He is also a guest lecturer on National Security, international politics, strategic planning, the Global War on terror, and other threats to America. He and LTG Thomas McInerney authored the book, *Endgame – Blueprint for Victory for Winning the War on Terror*. He was the senior military analyst for the Fox News Channel from 2001-2008. General Vallely conducts an average of 4-6 national radio/TV show interviews per week and is well known for his published articles and talks on National Security and domestic issues.

General Vallely is the Founder of Nemo Arms Inc. of Kalispell, Montana and is the Chairman of **Stand Up America** and the **Legacy National Security Advisory Group.** Since retiring from the Army, he has served as CEO of three corporations. He has also travelled five times into the Middle East in the past three years with his Middle East Liaison team. He co-chaired two delegation visits to Cairo and meetings with President El-Sisi and his staff. He is also a member of the Citizen's Commission on Benghazi.

Paul is an exceptional American from the old school. I am proud to call him friend, honored that he says kind words about my Thriller novels, and delighted to dedicate my novel *Broken Oath* to him.

SPECIAL MENTION

We have been living through a crisis that is, effectively, a new type of war, one with 4D Warfare, Civil, Global, and extending well beyond nation states. We are suffering a test run for tyranny. America's elections have always seen a peaceful transfer of power, but 2016 was an exception.

We won. Hillary lost. Even so, since then, many have lost freedoms. Some have suffered abuse.

Doctor Jerome Corsi, a colleague, best-selling author, and critic of the left, was ensnared in a "Muller Investigation" perjury trap, like General Flynn and others. He was told he'd be left alone if he pleaded guilty to perjury, to lying to the FBI, a felony crime that he did **not** commit.

Jerry refused. That story is told in his book *Silent No More*. It will blow your mind. It will blow your mind. His recent book *Coup d'État* is even better.

I also want to acknowledge my long-time barber, Shirley. Some of my first book signings were in her shop. The youngest reader I know for my novels was her granddaughter, nine at the time.

What did Shirley do to be targeted? *Nothing.* She was unfortunate enough to live in a socialistic state. Governor Kate – then with only 23 cases, many in senior centers like in NY – shut Oregon down by a pandemic executive order, one since ruled illegal.

I was gone for over a month. When I returned, there was a "space for rent" where Shirley's shop used to be. She is gone.

The shut-down of our economy did more harm to America than any virus. Hitler did a shut-down too, on April 1, 1933. Both were test runs for tyranny. Both used the power of government to target non-supporters, crush freedom, and force compliance. **Shut it Down** in major American cities soon escalated to **Burn it Down, riots,** and calls to defund police.

ACKNOWLEDGEMENTS

"Keep buggering on. Courage is going from failure to failure without losing enthusiasm."

– Sir Winston Churchill

"A man does what he must – in spite of personal consequences, obstacles, and dangers – and this is the basis of all human morality."

– John F. Kennedy

"He who does not punish evil commands it to be done."

– Leonardo DaVinci

"No punishment is too great for the man who builds his greatness upon his country's ruin."

– George Washington, 1778

"There is a well-known saying that power corrupts, and absolute power corrupts absolutely. I disagree. It is not that power corrupts so much as immunity. That is, corruption results not from being able to wield power per se, but from being able to wield it without consequences."

– John W. Campbell

Ernest Hemingway said, "There is no such thing as writing, only rewriting." He also said, "You never finish a book, you just let it go." He was right.

I could not write at the level that I do without my team of critical readers, content experts, and editors who take the time to scan my drafts with eagle eyes, amazing insight, and brutally honest criticism. Each time they touch my words, my novels get better. Kay Jewett deserves special credit.

Finally, you, my readers, are most important of all. **Thank you for your support.**

DRAMATIS PERSONAE

Raven and Josie: The lead characters. He's a warrior. She's a paranormal.

"It is Raven and Josie who are at the heart of this story and who form one of the most interesting romantic pairings in the thriller genre.

Raven is a trained killer but also a patriot, a man on the order of the late Vince Flynn's character Mitch Rapp who will stop at nothing to destroy those he sees as a threat to his friends and country.

In contrast, Josie abhors violence and is even physically and psychically sickened by it. Even guns disturb her. Josie's contribution to the team is as a remote viewer, a person who can through extra sensory perception sense people, objects, and, in Josie's case, future events from a great distance.

Somehow the two manage to discover common ground, to blend darkness and light into a unique union in their relationship."

US Review of Books, Review for **Raven's Redemption**

RAVEN'S TEAM

- Rudy Rogers, jet black, bald, and six foot four. Helmsman for the Busted Flush.
- Terry Coston, a muscled up white guy just under 6 feet. Built like a weight lifter.
- Pat Barry, Six foot two, sniper, dead shot at over 1,000 yards.
- Vinnie Russelle, spotter, Italian, 5' 9", wiry, human monkey.
- John Black. Engineer. Sometimes goes operational. Chief pilot for TSG.

AMERICANS

President Peter Blager, ex-Military, ex-CEO of RenewTech in CA, and Former Governor of Wyoming.

Dr. Aaron Goldfarb: Retired CIA, NSC, trusted advisor to President. Old hand from the Cold War. Serves as Twenty Mike's control, and sometimes directly as Raven's control.

General Michael "Twenty Mike" Mickelson, CEO of Transnational Services Group (TSG). Serves as Raven's control.

William Patton Giles, Cybertech CEO. Subcontractor to Transnational Services Group, and board member. PhD in Quantum Physics, with a minor in information theory. Son of Iron John.

Colonel John "Iron John" Giles. Will's father. Intense, ice blue eyes, 6 foot. Former CEO of Cybertech, until he was captured by terrorists and imprisoned in Syria. Released only recently.

Gerry Patton Mickelson, Iron John's Daughter, William Giles' Sister, former NSA program manager, and a Senior Program Manager at Cybertech.

Millie Seymore, TSG surveillance expert, runs the "Watchers." Petite, 5 feet, wire rimmed glasses, intense blue eyes, and short white hair, 68 years old. Looks like a school teacher. Worked with MI 6.

Lieutenant Commander William Bromley. Weapons Officer, USS Gravely, lead escort for the USS Lincoln Battle Group, Fourth Fleet. Assigned to assist Raven's team.

Captain Karl Hipp, commands the USS Gravely.

Admiral Harold Perkins, commands the Fourth Fleet.

MEXICAN OFFICIALS

Public Security Minister Genaro Santaigo.

The President of Mexico is Obrador, and the previous President was Pena.

RUSSIANS

Patty Allgrove, code name Marie. Sparrow school, top Russian operative.

Anatoli Vasilev, Assistant Secretary for Trade, Russian Embassy in Mexico City.

Karlov Petrovich, legendary spymaster. Long time FSB counterintelligence. Reports directly to President Putin.

LOS SERPIENTES CARTEL

Sicario, Ramon Santos, started at 16, up and coming.

Sicario, Tito, 20 years old, quick, like a snake.

Chico, a boss, promoted to a new job. Becomes Ramon's mentor.

Miguel Trevino, Head of the Cartel. "You don't even talk about him...."

Pilar – Great Aunt of Trevino. Trusted Eminence. She keeps the books and knows the history.

Carlos Gomez – In charge of interrogations and runs the guards. Big man with a bad leg, and a scar on his face. Wounded saving Trevino's life. Had been his personal bodyguard.

CUBAN OFFICERS

Arnaldo Ochoa – Commands the Revolutionary Guard. General de División (2 star), based in Cuba.

Hernando Cardoza – Commands the Colectivos, the Cuban paramilitary forces in Venezuela. Coronel (Colonel), based in Caracas.

ACRONYM INDEX

APC: Armored Personnel Carrier

CBSA: Canada Border Services Agency

COMs: Communications

COMSEC: Communications Security

Covfefe: It literally means covfefe

CSR: Counter Surveillance Route

DOD: Department of Defense

DOJ: Department of Justice

ECM: Electronic Counter Measures

EMP: Electro Magnetic Pulse

ETA: Estimated Time of Arrival

EU: European Union (NWO, writ small)

FBI: Federal Bureau of Investigation

FEMA: Federal Emergency Management Agency

FSB: Replaced the KGB

HE: High Explosive

HVT: High Value Target

IED: Improvised Explosive Device

ISIS: Islamic State of Iraq and the Levant

JCS: Joint Chiefs of Staff

KGB: Soviet spy and state-security machine

MI5: Counter Intelligence (British FBI)

MI6: Secret Intelligence Service (British CIA)

NRO: National Reconnaissance Office

NSA: National Security Agency

NSC: National Security Council

NVG: Night Vision Goggles

NWO: New World Order

OP: Operation, a mission, usually covert

PSD: Personal Security Detail

Quds: Special Forces unit of Iran's Revolutionary Guards

ROE: Rules of Engagement

SAM: Surface to Air Missile

SITREP: Situation Report

SOCOM: Special Operations Command

TANGO: A target

TFR: Temporary Flight Restriction

TSG: Transnational Services Group

UN: United Nations

WMD: Weapon of Mass Destruction

PNR: Policía Nacional Revolucionaria. Cuban Secret Police

CHAPTER ONE
LOST IN HAVANA

Walking the Ground, Present Day

It was the details that got you, Raven thought. He'd been doing low profile surveillance in Havana for a week, learning the lay of the land, working up a mission feel, studying patterns, sensing the street, learning to blend in.

I had three of my team in-country. Me and the close-in half of my crew, Rudy and Terry. Both of them spoke Spanish.

Rudy was fluent. Six foot four, bald as a billiard ball, and jet black. He looked like a pro athlete or maybe some high-end muscle for one of the cartels. Terry Coston, a muscled up white guy, was just under six feet and scruffy. A big black guy and his seedy beach bum sidekick.

The Security Group (TSG) had gotten them bullet-proof legends as security for a well-known Mexican oil firm. If challenged, they would check out clean. Both had been Marine Force Recon. They were used to working undercover in Red Zones.

The original plan had been to develop a broad footprint, a reusable presence, including developing a base outside Havana in the country. It didn't work out.

Cuba is still in the 19th century. Many people walk, but in the country as many use horses, both to ride and pull carts. We saw wagons pulled by oxen on the highway. We traveled by open truck, stayed in crude motels, and ate in restaurants; all owned by the government. For the truck, hop on, 8 cents, and you stood.

Basic hygiene was an unexpected challenge. In the public restrooms, rare but there were a few, washing your hands was interesting. You need three things to wash your hands; water, soap, towel to dry. Well the towel was your shirt or pants, because there never were any towels. In a third of the toilets, there was no water, and in one case there was a lady standing beside the sink with a bottle of water to pour over your hands. In most places, there was no soap.

Toilet seats did not exist in Cuba. We never saw one. We toted our own water and did what needed doing in the fields.

There was one room we'd never forget. Rudy's dash for the shitter was followed shortly by a string of profanity. Terry bravely rushed in to defend his teammate from poison snakes, scorpions, or whatever.

It seems the "no toilet seat" theme was exacerbated by a "no toilet paper" crisis. In its place, somebody had carefully torn individual sheets of toilet paper from a roll and placed them on the back of the toilet.

Laughing, with tears running down his cheeks, Terry handed him a single square and beat a hasty retreat. *He claimed Rudy had just set a new standard for "dip shit."* Holding my nose, I passed Rudy in a small pack of Kleenex wipes. The mission went on.

So much for our rural base of OPs. It was ridiculous. Forget the "broad footprint." Well, maybe we could find some gaps to exploit in Havana.

Improvise.

I gave them the lecture and dispatched my team to what was once the finest hotel in town, the Riviera Classic. We met in a park a day later to debrief.

They were less than ecstatic: 20 stories with 3 elevators. Only one worked. That one had a government minder running it and a police station a block away.

The shower at the Riviera had hot water, the only one with hot water we found in Cuba. It was fondly remembered when we scratched it off the list, but scratch it we did. We never did find an acceptable safe house in Havana.

Terry, our beach bum, suggested basing at a marina. *Why not?*

I sent them off to find us a fast cabin cruiser with an acceptable registry and living quarters. Once they had it, they could scoot over to GITMO for a test run. They were to line up some kit, but to come back squeaky clean, running empty, and see if it triggered surveillance.

They might get to test their IDs. It was a dumb plan, but I didn't have a better one.

There wasn't a lot of downside, Terry said. The Cubans were tolerant of drug running into the U.S. so long as adequate bribes were paid to the right people.

We were learning that the best way to operate in Havana was on foot. Car rentals stood out. The ubiquitous tourist cars, mostly old American Chevys from about 1941 to 1957, plus an occasional Cadillac convertible, were driven by locals whose livelihoods depended on keeping their masters happy. A driver could make more in day with tips than a government approved medical doctor did in a month.

All these vehicles had long since worn out their engines. They were mostly powered by puny 4-cylinder Russian-made diesels. We'd timed the traffic in the country as averaging about 5 MPH.

The rural roads were terrible. They looked like they'd been carpet bombed.

What with potholes, pedestrians, and traffic, the tourist cars did about the same in the city. We figured maybe 10 MPH at best, and 20-30 in spurts. *Forget a fast getaway. It would be like trying to outrun the cops on a lawnmower.*

My job was roaming Havana on foot while my team was off on their nautical adventure, checking possible target sites and running counter surveillance routes, CSRs. I'd been doing it for days.

I had never picked up ticks. Other than verifying security was lax, neither did I learn anything useful. It was boring work, hot and sweaty. My feet hurt, I was tired, and it was now full dark.

This time I approached my hotel from the back, the blind side, down an alley that split the block between Tulipan and Conill. It was a good CSR path. A good place to check for tails. There were no lights and no illumination from buildings. You could easily see if anyone entered from either end.

I looked back. It was clear there, and clear ahead. And then it wasn't. A large figure emerged from somewhere ahead of me just as the moon came out from behind a cloud.

I saw a flash of white teeth. This one was huge. *Godzilla.*

Then I saw the knife. He held it low, blade up, at his right side. From there he could jab or slash. *Not good. This one is trained.*

Yeah, I'd had the training, but I hated knives.

Unarmed, the best bet is to run like hell, if you can. Next is to do something sudden that prevents the start of an attack. Third is to create distance and deploy a longer-range weapon. The last is to go berserk and hope not to get fatally cut going through and over your attacker.

I opted for number one, turning and fleeing. Two figures emerged in front of me, one from each side. The one on the left, smaller, was holding a pole or club.

I went for his buddy, target #1, brushed his defenses aside, and connected with a Muay Thai kick to his knee and a fist blow to the side of his head.

He sagged. I grabbed his arm and spun, just in time for his head to connect with #2's pole, now coming down in an overhead blow that shattered #1's skull in a dark spatter of brains and blood.

Messy. My mistake. It was a pipe, not a pole.

I stepped inside the arc of the pipe, gave him a Muay Thai fist to the throat, and another to the side of his head. He fell, limp. I'd not pulled my blows.

With my free hand I came up with the pipe before it hit the ground, highly motivated by the pounding of feet behind me. I whirled and saw Godzilla coming on like a charging buffalo, almost on me, knife extended, held low.

I needed to do something about that.

The words of a long-ago instructor came clear. *Jab at the soft, strike at the hard.*

Godzilla ran full-tilt into my pipe thrust at his stomach and doubled up. My strike, two-handed, and with everything I had behind it, shattered his right arm at the elbow. The knife dropped clear.

I could see terror in his eyes. In a moment he would scream. I raised the pipe, coming down hard from his right side, the side where he couldn't raise an arm to deflect.

Godzilla's skull shattered with a soft *thunk* and it was over. Silence. Three bodies on the ground in a spreading pool of blood.

I stood back, breathing deeply, looking around, thinking. Whatever this was, it hadn't been security. It was just some thugs seeking to rob a tourist.

I looked around, not seeing a soul, not hearing a thing.

Best to just leave them there. It would give the police something to do.

I wiped the pipe clean of prints, dumped it next to its owner, and started down the alley to my hotel. By the time I got there my breathing was back to normal. I was covered with sweat, but that was to be expected given the temperature and humidity.

I waved at the night manager, said nothing, and hopped on the elevator. I had a clean change of clothes for tomorrow. Tonight, even a cold shower would feel good.

Bella Habana-Aeropuerto, Havana, Cuba, Next Morning

I had gone out for a leisurely breakfast. Everything seemed normal. A new face at the desk, but no police presence. Apparently, thugs and thieves killing each other in the city wasn't enough to cause alarm.

I thought about last night. Cuba was turning out to be one of the most difficult targets I'd ever worked against. The Mideast was a mess, but Cuba was locked-down, hardcore, Soviet-Style Communist.

It was nothing like the halcyon paradise reported by the media. Well, *duh*....

Cuba was a surrealistic Twilight Zone, a cacophony of 1960s America, Stalin's USSR, and third-world squalor. What I saw was old American cars with tailfins and a subdued populace. The storied country of Hemingway had become a prison controlled by the gun-butts of political police.

No happy people cruising in their classic cars, dancing in the street to music of the Buena Vista Social Club, and thriving in an unadulterated simple life, with the benefits of free stuff and universal health care. That's what the nouveaux-tourists see and report.

Reality was dysphoria. Mexico's celebrated novelist Carlos Fuentes called it right, but no one believed him. "Perfect order is the forerunner of perfect horror."

Control was tight. People who put a foot wrong disappeared into prison or labor camps.

The hotel was my temporary safe house. The best of a list of crappy choices, it still sucked. The manager at the front desk could observe anyone entering. He wouldn't have that job unless he informed for, or worked for, the government. It would be the same, or worse, at any other hotel in the city.

In theory, the location was good. Ten miles from the airport, and the closest one to the Government buildings. It didn't help. There was no way to get close to The Palace of the Revolution, Cuba's Pentagon, with a kill team. A low chance of success, and a zero chance of egress.

A long gun wouldn't help. There was no high ground. Snipers were out, drones were out, and there would be no external support if it turned to shit. Using laser designators for smart bombs seemed was off the table. Without a major attack and a lot of suppression the cost would be too high.

Havana was a hard target.

The Cuban's had a few Su-35s, faster than our F-22s and arguably better in a close dogfight. They also had the Russian S-400 SAMs, only one system, but hypersonic with a 95% kill rate. It was the most capable and lethal long-range air defense missile system on the planet.

Effectively, my team was on its own. *Thank you, Bush, Obama, and Congress.*

Cuba was Plan B.

Plan A had been to target the new chessboard for an invasion, the new Syria, Venezuela. It was now a hard target, heavily defended.

Running weapons from Benghazi into Syria had spawned massive forced migration, which overwhelmed the nations of Western Europe. That was successful. The world had been "fundamentally transformed." Socialism, Communism, and Global Governance by unaccountable bureaucrats was ascendant. Nation States were in decline. Once proud Western Cities were starting to resemble third-world shitholes.

The new plan was for a repeat in the Western hemisphere, with the U.S. as the main target. Control of Venezuela was the key to success.

Hitting Venezuela had been my Plan A, but Goldfarb gave it a "Hell no." Venezuela was off limits. It was too lethal. There was too much downside. The Russians and Chinese were there as a tripwire.

Cuba's best forces were in Venezuela running armed *Colectivos*, 100,000 strong, crushing resistance, killing and torturing civilians. It was good training and sent a signal: *Cuba held the keys to Venezuela.*

That operational focus was a possible weakness. Cuba was subdued. Resistance was crushed, freedom was lost, and the population was docile.

Cuba had been under harsh Communist rule since 1959 and only a minimal force was on alert in Havana. No one expected America would dare try anything, not after Kennedy's legendary Bay of Pigs fiasco. Leftists in Congress would leak any inkling of such a plan and the media would rage.

Thus, the forces in Cuba slumbered, just as ours did at Pearl Harbor. CIA's contingency plan for Cuba said that covert teams might be able to operate there. They saw it as the soft underbelly.

The brief we'd gotten from Goldfarb was a rerun of Syria, where Hillary had tried to topple Assad using weapons from Benghazi, ISIS, and the Arab Spring. That plan failed when Russia stepped in to protect its own interests: Warm water ports and a presence in the Mideast. It did succeed at creating the most massive forced migration in the history of the world. Too bad for Western Europe.

Venezuela was the new Syria. All eyes were there, and on the invasion route on up to the U.S. border. In theory a small America force could prevail against a country in chaos. Just as the Russians had in Syria, we could protect our strategic interests without a major conflict and loss of American lives.

It was hopeful theory from analysts sitting behind desks at Langley, checking boxes. CIA and NSA were slimmed down and focused on the major threats like Russia and China. *CIA's plan was worthless.*

Sure, as long as my team stayed passive, didn't linger, didn't communicate, and followed Moscow Rules, it could avoid counter-surveillance. Security was sloppy. My hotel had no Internet or cell service. It checked clean for bugs and cameras. The phone on the front desk was rotary dial.

There was no hot water, but the refrigerator in my room worked, the toilet had a seat, and there was a hot plate to make coffee. The window air conditioner was rusted and probably hadn't worked for years. It seemed to be a home for some kind of small lizards that preferred to range outside.

There were no geckos in the room - perhaps a consequence of the liberal use of insecticides. I heaved a deep sigh, noting the cracks in the ceiling and the mold around the small window, mopping my face with a towel, and remembering GITMO. *It had been a steam bath.*

Havana was yet another testimonial that Cuba didn't have a climate. Through the summer, humidity ran 90% to 97%. Even the winters had over 60%. Over the course of the year, the temperature varied from 69°F to 92°F and was rarely below 65°F or above 94°F. It pushed the limits of "muggy."

My room would be a Hell hole in Summer, which was coming. *The joys of socialism.*

Cuba was becoming a backwater, fading in importance. Its socialist system could not provide even a minimal standard of living for its people. It needed subsidies to survive, but, after decades, Russia tired of that, and then-wealthy Venezuela took its place. Now the focus was elsewhere.

Despite Obama, Cuban communists saw the U.S. as a danger, not an opportunity. Which was why I was there as a Canadian socialist using my Digger Simpson identity, the one accepted by the Russians.

With Venezuela the focus, Russia fed up, Obama gone, and Hillary a bad joke, Cuba was facing disaster. The big dogs, Russia and China, had first dibs on plunder. The cartels were next. Cuba was left with table scraps, stuck being the hated enforcers, and sliding towards becoming a failed state.

That part made the CIA happy.

It did not help me a bit. My problem was targeting, access, and egress. In or near Havana, there were two airborne brigades, an artillery division, three infantry divisions, an armored division, a mechanized division, and more. Plus, of course, police and personal security details for officials.

No, they weren't on alert, but there were a lot of them. It was a police state with eyes everywhere. One with 19th century infrastructure, one where rapid movement was all but impossible.

A small team, once noticed, would be quickly overwhelmed.

We had been in-country for three weeks. I was still working on what to do, lingering in a Red Zone with limited options. Plan C was an abort. I was getting close to calling it.

I was packed, ready to check out, but we could reuse this hotel. It wasn't blown. It was the best local base we were likely to get.

We're still alive. Why not get out of here, get our act together, and come back to fight another day? The allies had several failed attempts before D-Day.

That could be Plan D. I just needed to give a plausible excuse for leaving early, easily done, and to tip well. It might be best to linger another day or two, to take some tourist tours, to do some tourist things, to look normal so we would fit in when we returned. *If we returned.*

Mostly, I needed to go somewhere that had secure COM. We needed better options.

CHAPTER TWO
IT WAS COMPLICATED

En Route to New York, Two Months Earlier

Josie had never been to TSG HQ before, despite several warm invitations from Gerry Patton, Twenty Mike's wife, to come visit them. The two women had hit it off, but Josie anticipated this event as like preparing for a first visit to a distant branch of the family.

This was the clandestine branch of the family, *Raven's people*. It was the only family he had, except for her and a lengthy trail of deceased agents he'd worked with long ago. Ghosts from the past.

It was complicated. To Josie, these were scary people, aliens from a different culture.

Gerry Patton was a descendent of the famous World War II General of the same name. Gerry's brother, Will, ran Cybertech, the company that supplied their exotic weapons and secure electronics. Gerry had been a top scientist at NSA.

Gerry's Dad, they called him "Iron John," had founded the company. Gerry's name, of course, was no longer Patton. She was now Gerry Mickelson, nee Patton.

She'd married "Twenty Mike" Mickelson, the retired Marine General, who for all practical purposes was now Raven's boss. Mike's company, TSG, the Transnational Security Group, dealt with security threats. Raven said it was sort of like the old Blackwater Company, except different.

Whatever that meant.

Dr. Goldfarb was close to President Peter Blager. He was an advisor to, but technically not a member of, the National Security Council. Effectively Goldfarb set their operational policy, through Mike.

Nothing was written down, of course. It was all classified, but the thing was these were good people. They were family. Josie was still alive because of them.

Josie knew these things, and more. She'd been a paranormal viewer for the CIA.

It had not ended well for her, but Raven's history was worse. It took Goldfarb, a faked death, and a new identity for him to get clear of that past.

Josie's powers included a strong sense of good and evil. In a previous life she'd been a Celtic Priestess. Good increased her powers. Evil shut them down. Josie was a creature of light and beauty. She chased rainbows. Violence could destroy her.

There was a lot of evil and violence out there. That was what Raven was about. Josie could *find* evil, but she dared not get close. Raven hunted monsters in the deep dark of midnight. He got close. *Too close.*

Raven was directed to bring her along to TSG. A first. Gerry's initial invitations had been social, not operational. This visit was commanded.

When she'd asked why, he just shrugged. They would find out when they got there. She tried her viewing talents, but saw only a gray fog of probabilistic uncertainty, trailing off into the future.

That part had happened before. *Whatever their future was, it had yet to sort out.*

Their airplane landed at Teterboro, taxied up to the TSG hanger, and shut down. A few minutes passed, then the cockpit door opened and John Black came out. He smiled at Josie, as always.

Once, she'd saved his life. In Durham, where he'd come in alone to help them against a *jihadist* kill team.

"They wanted me to come too."

Raven said, "Mike does?"

Black shook his head. "Goldfarb. He wants the three of us. My copilot will finish the shut down and paperwork. The TSG helicopter has a clearance on file and is ready."

Raven said, "Are we scheduled for a return flight?"

He didn't really expect an answer. *Where was Mike? Whatever was going on was unusual, but there was zero chance Goldfarb would discuss it outside of a SCIF: A Secure Compartmentalized Intelligence Facility, a shielded vault protected from all forms of surveillance.*

Black said, "I'm not sure. He said a working meeting with lunch. You and Josie are invited for dinner."

"Let's go."

Mike's assistant Crystal greeted them at the TSG rooftop helipad.

She nodded at Raven. "Don't upset the guards."

He grinned and winked at her. "Right. This is Josie. She doesn't do weapons."

Crystal said, "Good to know."

The two women looked each other up and down. Crystal was a tall blond, thin, flat chested, and athletic. She radiated physical fitness.

Josie said, "I heard you pulled a gun on him."

Crystal said, "Had to. He makes our guards nervous."

Josie smiled.

Crystal looked at Raven. "You got Iron John back. People are happy. Biggest thing that's happened since I've been here."

"We got lucky. How is he?"

"We're working on it. He's recovering. I'm helping with his physical therapy. He's weak, rusty, but improving. John used to be a Judo Sensei, a teacher. I want to get him back to that level."

"How's he doing?" Josie said.

"We'll get there. It takes time." She looked at Raven. "We are pretty much shut down here, what with everyone celebrating John's return.

Goldfarb is waiting for you. Gerry says dinner at seven, and she insists you stay at the house..."

"Right."

"What about me?" Black asked.

"I think you are going back out. Not sure. Mike left instructions. Doctor Goldfarb will brief you."

Raven gestured toward the elevator. "Let's go."

Goldfarb was seated behind Mike's desk, shuffling papers. He rose to greet us, came over and looked at Josie. "Thank you for coming."

"I don't understand why I'm here," she said.

"It will become clear. We've had some changes. I need to make sure you were okay with them."

I raised an eyebrow. He had never asked *me* that.

"What about me?" Black said.

He'd never been part of the policy meetings. He coordinated through me or Josie.

"You'll like that part." Goldfarb gestured at the side table. "Sandwiches, a lobster salad, cold drinks, water, and coffee. Let's catch up and relax for a few minutes. Everyone is very happy to have John back. Then we can go secure and talk."

Interesting, I thought. Relax and catch up. I'd not seen this side of him before. *Who are you and what have you done with Doctor Goldfarb?*

He looked at me. "Mike and his family are grateful about your getting John back. It's a big deal, Raven. The President plans to give you a medal. It will be classified, of course, but he wants Josie at the ceremony."

What could I say? "Thank you, Sir."

The lunch was good. New York was seedy in places, but their local food was still terrific if you knew where to go.

The main thing I learned was that Iron John was in good spirits.

He'd even managed to make friends with President Bashar al-Assad when he was under house arrest in Syria. *Amazing.*

Mike was with John and family, relaxing and debriefing at a compound upstate, but Gerry was going to attend our meeting later. The TSG helicopter had been dispatched to pick her up. When it returned, it would pick Black up. We were to stay for a few days.

In the SCIF at TSG Headquarters

Goldfarb started with happy news. Mike managed to get us a major upgrade in support equipment. He was retiring the speedy Citation X that John flew, trading it in for one of the first Aerion jets. It was civilian and legal to fly supersonic.

The cruise speed was Mach 1.2 to 1.4, about twice as fast as what we had been using, twice as fast as airliners, twice as fast as military transport, faster than some combat aircraft. At altitude, over land, it was legal for Mach 1.2, with no sonic boom on the ground. Over water, you could open it up.

The normal twelve seat configuration would be slimmed to eight, more than adequate for our team and their gear. Cybertech was going to add on some special equipment. DOD and the FAA had approved waivers.

The only catch was that Black had to get his ass to Reno ASAP to get himself and our Citation X crew qualified in the Aerion. They would be there tonight. We might have the new aircraft operational in a month.

Black was grinning from ear to ear, but Goldfarb insisted he stay for the briefing. We were going to have new rules of engagement. The old Covfefe Committee was no more. We were officially distanced from the government.

I was delighted. *They were finally letting us take the gloves off.*

Goldfarb gave us a presentation, including handing us all copies of this foil. It was the standard oath taken by all in Congress, traditionally sworn on a Bible:

Oath of Office

"I do solemnly swear (or affirm) that I will support and defend the Constitution of the United States against all enemies, foreign and domestic; that I will

bear true faith and allegiance to the same; that I take this obligation freely, without any mental reservation or purpose of evasion; and that I will well and faithfully discharge the duties of the office on which I am about to enter: So help me God."

History of the Oath

The Constitution contains an oath of office only for the president. For other officials, including members of Congress, that document specifies only that they "shall be bound by Oath or Affirmation to support this Constitution." While the oath-taking dates back to the First Congress in 1789, the current oath is a product of the 1860s, drafted by Civil War-era members of Congress intent on ensnaring traitors.

Josie and Black were staring at me, glancing at Goldfarb, their looks intense. Apparently, I was supposed to say something.

"Has anyone ever been prosecuted for breaking their oaths?"

"Many, many Members of Congress, from both political parties, have been convicted of various crimes related to their conduct while in office, but I'm unaware of any that have been convicted specifically for violating the oath of office."

"President Blager plans to enforce it?"

Goldfarb nodded. "He does."

"Seems reasonable. What's next?"

"That will be the topic of discussion for the next two days for you and Josie. We are making some changes. I wanted Gerry here too. You can brief your team when we get it all sorted out."

He looked at Black. "Here's the short version. You get a new toy to play with, and you need to have it mastered in no more than two weeks. Then you all get an expense paid vacation in a tropical paradise."

Black looked stunned. "Yes, Sir. What else?"

"You used to fly F-22s." It wasn't a question.

"Yes, Sir."

"When you are qualified in the aircraft, you are going to stop by Nellis AFB. I want you to practice engagements against some pairs of F-22s."

Black blinked, "Without any weapons, Sir?"

Goldfarb nodded. "Correct. You are flying a peaceful civilian aircraft. I don't expect you to shoot them down, but it would be desirable if you could survive."

Black looked at me.

"I'm with him. Do what you can. I have no idea what's coming up, but I'm going to vote for desirable. Highly desirable, you might say. It would be best if you came back alive, an inspiration to us all."

The grin faded from Black's face.

He looked at Goldfarb. "Yes, Sir. Sounds interesting."

Goldfarb said, "Best not to mention that detail to the others in your crew until you are all checked out and proficient."

"Proficient. Right. Understood. May I go now?"

"You may. The TSG helicopter is back and Gerry will be joining us in a moment."

On his way out, I stood and put a hand on his shoulder, "Break a leg, Kid."

Black paused, turned so his back was to Josie, and shot me the finger. Then he left.

CHAPTER THREE
NEW RULES

TSG Headquarters, in the SCIF

We broke for a few minutes, until Gerry joined us. Goldfarb escorted her in, but excused himself to take a secure call. The two women hugged, then sat down. They were both looking at me.

"Mike sends his apologies, Raven. He's with Dad. Thank you for getting him back."

"I got lucky."

"Has Goldfarb filled you in?"

I shook my head and gestured at the open door. "He was waiting for you."

We sipped coffee silently for a few minutes until Goldfarb returned. He pulled the door closed behind him with a solid *thunk*. The red light turned green and we were secure again.

"How's John?" Goldfarb said.

"Still recovering, but good. He's going to join us for dinner. You're invited too, but no business. Just happy talk and early to bed. He's been through a lot."

Goldfarb shook his head. "Send my regrets. I've got the duty. Someone has to be here."

Gerry nodded and made a gesture in our direction. "I came to brief them for Mike and my brother. Details. New Rules of Engagement, weapons, equipment, and keeping Josie safe."

"I like the last part."

Goldfarb said, "We need to have you good with the new ROEs. There are organizational changes and a mission brief."

Nice to know. The mission brief was expected. We'd had no warning about the rest.

He flicked on the projector and the screen lit up again with the Oath of Office. "This EO is new policy. It will impact your Rules of Engagement."

The Oath of Office is new? 1789? The 1860s? That made no sense.

Josie was looking at me questioningly. Gerry was smiling faintly. I said nothing. Waiting. *He'd tell us when he was ready. Goldfarb could be enigmatic, sometimes inscrutable. He was old school.*

"Raven, your last mission was a shit storm. You engaged a broad mix of enemies, both foreign and domestic. A former Vice President and likely candidate for the Presidency in the next election WHO died. High officials in a sanctuary state, senior officers in the National Guard, others along the procurement channels, and some in the State Department."

"Vice President Dunbar was collateral damage. We didn't even know he was there."

He'd not mentioned Islamists, Iran's Quds Force, other terrorists, crime cartels, and the rest, not even the Russians. People in DC loved to stew about scary Russians, but they'd been helpful to us this time.

"You need not worry. Dunbar died from his own Sarin gas. He will not be missed."

"I'm not sure where this is going."

"Treason has been committed. The Oath you see on the screen has been broken by some of our greatest domestic enemies."

Well, duh. No one has ever been prosecuted. What do you expect?

"Could that be why we haven't won a war since 1945?"

I did not attempt to keep the sarcasm out of my voice. We had traitors in Congress, including some known to be terrorists or foreign agents. They were untouchable. *Members of Congress can't even get traffic tickets.*

Goldfarb frowned.

For some reason, Gerry kept her smile. *She knew something I didn't.*

Goldfarb pointed a finger at me. "What did you just say, Raven?"

"Simply that we don't punish treason at high levels." I paused and added, "With all due respect, Sir."

"Why do you say that?"

"We've not executed anyone in my lifetime for treason, not since the Rosenbergs in 1953 when they gave our nuclear secrets to the Soviets. We've not hanged anyone for treason since the Civil War. Sure, some high officials, even a few in Congress, have resigned in disgrace, but...."

"Four senior Congressional Staff members enabled the massacre of FBI agents in California. The target was you and Josie, but you were both long gone. Eleven FBI agents died and three were injured.

"The biggest loss the Bureau has ever incurred...."

"Correct. Two of the staffers were tried by a military tribunal at GITMO, found guilty, and summarily shot by firing squad."

I blinked. "When?"

"Last Friday."

"Why?"

"There were other charges, but the death penalty was for treason. The other two staffers got to watch. They have since pleaded guilty and are now singing like canaries."

"You need to say more."

"You can watch that part on the News. The FBI took the hit, so they get to make the announcement. Federal charges are being filed against a number of California elected officials, including the Governor.

"After that settles out, the President will be giving a press conference. There have been extensive discussions about WMD threats to our national security. We could have lost much of Los Angeles, the second most populous city in America, maybe Sacramento too."

I nodded. It had been a near thing.

"The House and Senate Judicial committees agree that something has to be done. Broad public support is expected. The fact that VP Dunbar died when it backfired will help. Most of the deaths would have been from his own party. He didn't care."

"Okay," I said. "What does that have to do with the Oath?"

"Good catch, Raven," Gerry said softly.

Goldfarb said, "None of those people took the Oath, so it hasn't come up yet."

I frowned. Waiting.

"The part about Broken Oaths by Members of Congress being prosecutable as treason has yet to play out. The President took it to the Supreme Court. The Chief Justice supported it, but it will take an actual case and a court decision to make it stick.

The policy that mass attacks on U.S. Citizens will be considered acts of war and prosecuted by military tribunals is different. That will be announced. The rest, the part about the Oath, remains classified."

"Why?"

"Because it hasn't taken effect yet. Legal precedent has yet to be set. No Member of Congress has so far been charged, but there is a line of staffers seeking plea bargains forming to give testimony, a line that will grow as the executions proceed.

"A member of the House Foreign Relations committee may be the test case. Her passport has been pulled and her security clearances suspended pending investigation. She was up to her neck in the California mess.

"A few lives are balanced on one side of the scale. Thousands or perhaps millions are on the other side."

"This is the law?" I said.

He shrugged again. "At present it is policy by Executive Order, subject to legal review and going forward for as long as President Blager and his party stay in power, I'd assume. Hopefully longer. Until the world is a safer place? I don't know. Who can see the future?"

"We don't do law enforcement. We focus on preventing attacks by terrorists and enemy states."

"That has not changed."

"What has changed?" I said.

Josie said, "I need to know that too. What has changed?"

"Your primary mission is the same. It's changed only along the edges, only at the margins."

"You are going to have to be a bit more specific, Sir. What are you saying?"

"On your last mission, there was a WMD release that eliminated an underground Quds base. High Level American traitors died in that, ah, incident, did they not?"

"Dunbar. Like I said, collateral damage."

Goldfarb looked at Josie.

She said, "Dunbar died."

"Is America better off because an elected official behind this attack died? I say we are. It might serve as a lesson to prevent others."

She said, "How is it a lesson if it's secret? Our enemies won't know."

"Oderint dum Metuant." Goldfarb said.

Raven looked at him.

"They may not know, but they will fear," Goldfarb said. *"'Let them hate, so long as they fear,'* attributed originally to Lucius Accius, a Roman tragic poet in 170 BC.

"Dunbar's incidental death will be publicized. There will soon be public trials of major officials for treason. The disappearance of even one single Member of Congress, on top of that, would be a major news event."

Josie shivered. Her ancestral memories and paranormal powers let her sense things. Long ago, in a previous life, she'd been a Celtic Princess. She'd died when Roman soldiers under Gaius Julius Caesar destroyed her temple.

I touched her arm. "He's right. Our enemies will fear us."

"They will hate us."

"They already do."

She was frowning. I shrugged. "Spell it out, Doctor. Operationally, what's different? What should I do differently?"

"We are discussing adjustments in your targeting. In the course of preventing or preempting enemy attacks, you may, as in California, find American traitors in the mix along with your primary targets. What's new is that some high-level traitors may be specifically targeted."

"Kill orders?"

"There is precedent. Obama did it with drones in war zones."

"What about Seth Rich?"

"That was a crime."

One for which no one was ever charged or prosecuted.

"What does Mike say? He's been our control."

"Mike's good. You can ask him. You just rescued his father-in-law from seven years of Hell."

Josie was watching me intently, frowning.

I looked at Gerry. "Are you and Mike good with this?"

"There are issues, but, yes, we do, in general, support a more active role for your team."

Josie said, *"Who gets to play God?* If we don't have clear moral limits, we will become like our enemies."

"She's right," I said. "I don't favor the notion of casting lots or saying 'thumbs down' out in the field. If it gets down to killing assholes in Congress, it would be hard to know where to stop."

"Targeting approval needs discussion," Gerry said "It is why Mike sent me, why I'm here instead of with him and Dad. We'll be discussing that in my briefing."

"Discussing or debating?" I said.

"Both. You and Josie need to be comfortable with the new plans. We all do."

I looked at Goldfarb. "The Deep State and Hillary politicized the top levels of our Law Enforcement and Intel Community. At best, it was the biggest political scandal in our history. At worst, it was a coup. We want no part of anything like that. It must not happen again."

"The issue is treason, Raven. Specific targeting of Americans is a NO GO unless you and Josie are comfortable with the new ROEs."

"What else?"

"The administration is being distanced from your team. The old Covfefe committee will be dissolved. Your team is going to be more independent."

In some ways, that was good. "What does Washington get to do while we are wandering off in the dark on our own?"

"Regarding the matter of Oath violations being treason with trials of Members of Congress by Military Tribunals, the action will be in the Supreme Court. The focus will be on legal process and the Constitution. All will be classified until the first trial, but some in both parties will know it is coming."

Some will go apeshit, including leaks to the press. "Do you have a timeline?"

"My guess is years, but I don't know. Obviously, the first case needs to be airtight. It sets the precedent. There will, of course, be outrage from the left. Concerns from members of the President's own party is also likely."

"About morality and legality?" Josie said.

Goldfarb shrugged. "It will likely be framed that way, but in Washington you never know, do you?"

"It's usually about power," Gerry said. "The swamp protects its own. So does Congress, but logic need not apply. The same people who refuse to execute terrorists and mass murderers advocate infanticide and convicted terrorists voting. Washington fears farting cows more than EMP attacks...."

Goldfarb said, "Whatever happens, action to punish treason sets dangerous precedent, one like what was imposed during the Civil War, one well beyond anything we have done since, including even during the Cold War. Some in Congress were forced to resign for Communist ties back then, but none were ever hanged."

Gerry said, "Whatever the precedent is, it will apply to both parties. DC will never be the same."

All this was making my head hurt. "Will our briefing include specific targeting for our next mission?"

"Yes," Gerry said.

"Who decides the targeting?"

Goldfarb said, "We want your inputs."

"Josie and I need to talk privately after we are briefed in."

"Of course, but I need a decision," Goldfarb said.

"You said we'd be here for two days?"

"That's the plan."

I looked at Josie and held up two fingers. She nodded.

"You'll get a decision before we leave, Sir. If she says no, we are done. Is that acceptable?"

"After your mission brief?" Goldfarb said.

"Before we accept the mission. Is that good?"

"It has to be."

CHAPTER FOUR
THE COLD HARD TRUTH

TSG Headquarters, in the SCIF, Afternoon

I'd never seen Gerry in this mode. She was standing at the white board, speaking from notes. No canned presentation for this lady.

"First a show of hands. How many think America is currently facing the greatest crisis in our national history?" We looked at her, Josie, Goldfarb, and me. No one responded.

"What about the Revolutionary War?" Goldfarb said. "Rag-Tag farmers and volunteers against the greatest army in the world?"

She wrote **1776** on the board. "Ruled by a mad King and with a populace weary of wars. But, skip that one. We weren't even a nation then."

"Civil War?" Josie said. "Brother against brother, and more deaths than all our other wars combined?"

"Right up there," she agreed, writing **1861-1865**. "A huge mistake. One we won't repeat."

"How do you know?" I said.

"Neither side wants it."

"Really?" *I'd been fighting all my life, and the conflict was getting closer.*

"Think about it. If the radical left, the socialists and crazies, wanted a war, it would have started when Hillary crashed and burned, or later when the Deep State was attempting a Coup. If conservatives and patriots wanted a war, there would not **be** any liberals."

I smiled, "Maybe so. How about…?"

"World War II, unarmed and unprepared? The Cold War, Communists with nuclear weapons?"

"They both come to mind," I said. "Thank God for Churchill and Eisenhower, and that Hitler jumped the gun and attacked Stalin's Russia. God protects fools and Americans."

Gerry wrote **1941-1945**, followed by **1960-1990**.

"That is our nation's history. What do you conclude?"

Goldfarb took that one. "Like Reagan said, *Freedom is never more than one generation away from extinction.*"

"Exactly. Every generation," Gerry said. "And now it's our turn. Raise your hand if you agree."

Every hand went up.

"Worse now in some ways?"

Every hand but Goldfarb's went up. I smiled. He was a traditionalist. Also, he was older, and prone to saying that he missed the clarity of the Cold War. *Goldfarb thought the fact that the Cold War was worse actually made it better. Having 40,000 nuclear warheads aimed at you brings clarity.*

"It's not worse now, Sir? The Deep State, a third of the public clueless, and a large part of Congress and all the Fake News on the other side?"

He shrugged. "It's close. I wasn't hopeful we could win the Cold War. Just trying to not lose took all we had, including Mutually Assured Destruction, massive nuclear overkill. Then Reagan came up with Star Wars, and *poof*, the USSR was history."

Gerry interrupted. "Does anyone think that our response to current threats has been adequate?"

Goldfarb and I both said, "No."

"Josie?"

"I can't say. You **know** what I do...."

Gerry nodded. "I do." *Few people could say that. Paranormal viewing had tightly compartmentalized security.* "Why do you say that?"

"America has survived, so far, but I keep seeing nexus points and probability trails where **all** the options are worse. Some were horrific. Some of my colleagues have been traumatized."

I took her hand. *Easy,* I thought. *Josie had one episode that left her catatonic for months. We'd almost lost her.*

Josie said, "You lost your Dad for seven years, kidnapped by *jihadists* from a secure airport in peaceful rural America. Our cities have become crime-ridden havens for gangs and illegals. We have terrorists in Congress. Mexico, on our Southern Border, is now the most dangerous place on the planet. Do you think we've been doing enough?"

"I do not. That's why we are here." Gerry looked at me. "We want to loosen your ROEs. Put you on the offensive. Would that help?"

"It might," Goldfarb said. "We are so divided and entangled in legalist procedures we can barely move. So is Congress, our military, our law enforcement, our Border Patrol...."

"Raven?"

"We've been playing defense. We've been lucky so far, but you can't win that way."

"Keep talking...."

"There is no instance of a nation benefitting from prolonged warfare. Great nations don't fight long wars."

"Who said that?"

"Sun Tzu said it first, around 500 BC. Donald Trump said it in his 2019 State of the Union. The truth is that America has been at war constantly. We have not won one since 1945."

Goldfarb nodded. "Patton said, '*The immoral part of war is prolonging it.*' He had a point."

Gerry said, "What keeps us from winning, from ending it?"

"Some want to keep the wars going, to drain us, to profit themselves, or whatever. Some want our troops on the other side of the planet doing nation building, instead of here defending America. The threats to America are now close.

"We're here to brief for a mission on the invasion route up from Venezuela. My team just took out an Iranian QUDs base in California. A few years ago, such National Security threats would be unthinkable. Domestic politics gone insane. That enabled these threats."

"Yes. What other factors prevent winning?"

"Incompetence. Ignorance. These days, few in Congress have ever seen combat. Political Correctness. Corruption. Idiocy. Consider

McNamara in Vietnam, an accountant who managed the war as a way to communicate with the enemy. He thought a high body count would make the Communists stop. The truth was they didn't give a shit. They lost all the battles, but won in the media."

"What could make your team more effective at defending America?"

"Josie and I have been given support, but, like I said, we're defensive. We kill the fighters who come at us, but those sponsoring, leading, and funding the attacks on America stay well out of reach."

"You got VP Dunbar, a high-level kill, and a major setback for our enemies."

"He got himself. He died by his own weapons. I think Mike got one that way too, did he not? The Senior Senator woman?"

"Harriet Stiles," Gerry said. "A bad bitch with a lot of power in Washington."

"Stiles also died from her own bioweapons as I recall...."

"She did. Many of her coconspirators in Congress met the same fate. Too bad, so sad."

"Josie and I don't get that kind of luck. We're busy just trying to survive. Josie is not expendable and they keep coming for her."

"You saved the President."

"Goldfarb did. It was the same kill team that was after Josie. We were mostly defensive."

"You got Claus Vogel. The financial terrorist, wanted by many countries for decades."

I shook my head. "The Russians got him, not me. Last I heard, he was enjoying the pleasures of the Lubyanka. For all I know, they might turn him and he'll again be our problem."

Josie shot me a look. *I wasn't lying, but what I said was unlikely.*

"Enough discussion," Goldfarb said. "Let's get to the mission. Top level only."

"Right," Gerry said, looking at me. "Where do you want to base? You've been looking at the Intel."

"I'm not liking what I see. Venezuela is the chessboard, but it's a hard target. Plan B might be Cuba. What do you think?"

"Mike and I came to the same conclusion," Gerry said.

"We don't have good Intel on either," Goldfarb said. "I'll see if anything can be done, but I don't have a better idea. Do you have the target list?"

Gerry handed me a manila folder, marked with a red Top-Secret stamp. It was also marked SI, Special Intelligence in black block letters against a yellow background.

"SI," I said. "Who's on the list?"

"You, me, Mike, and Goldfarb. You can share what you deem necessary as needed with Josie and John Black.

"After we have a running mission, the list might be expanded to the President, the SecDef, and the Secretary of State. There is a dispute about that, so it could go either way."

"Some things are best not to know?"

Gerry shrugged. I looked at Goldfarb, but he made no comment.

I opened the folder and spread the contents out so Josie could see. All it held was six photographs, sharp, crystal clear, and full color. Each had a white data block with names and titles.

Two were Cuban: A General and a Secret Police official.

Two were Venezuelan: A General and a Secret Police official.

One was a well-known leftist, a former Secretary of State.

The last was a serving Senior U.S. Senator from Oregon.

Josie gave a slight shake of her head.

"Has the President approved this list?"

Goldfarb said, "He's not in the loop, Raven. I told you about the organizational changes."

"Who prepared it?"

No one spoke.

"Let me try that again. I'm assuming it was Mike. Am I right?"

Gerry took a deep breath. "Mike and I did."

"The U.S. Senator, did…."I stopped and waved my hand in dismissal. "Never mind. Scratch that."

Josie said, "We have a problem, Raven."

"We do." I put the pictures back in the folder, handed it to Gerry, looked at Goldfarb and said, "I don't want to ruin tonight's homecoming event, but we need to involve Mike. Is he available tomorrow?"

"I don't set his schedule."

Josie looked at Gerry. "Family matters. I know what you have been through. We can stay longer...."

"I'll speak with Mike after the party."

Goldfarb said, "We are on hold. Does that work for everyone?"

There were nods and the meeting broke up, leaving me and Josie looking at each other in the SCIF. She said, "I don't like these meetings."

"This one was odd."

Mickelson Estate, North Shore, Long Island, 9:30 PM

Mike sipped his brandy, looking out across the beach. It was a clear night, with a full moon and gentle breezes. The women were inside organizing things. Iron John had the guest cottage where he could sleep. Raven and Josie drew an upstairs suite with a comfortable King bed. They were still on West Coast time. The plan was breakfast at 10, with no interruptions.

"We owe you, Raven. I never spoke to Gerry about it, but after all this time, I figured Iron John was dead. We lost the trail years ago."

I shrugged. "I keep saying, we got lucky. John seems to be doing well."

"He tires easily, but his mind is sharp. The doctors are optimistic."

"His first few years with the *jihadis* were rough. They kept moving him. The country was falling apart. I kept thinking we'd see him in one of those beheading videos, but those who'd taken him defected or were killed along the way."

"Someone must have thought John had hostage value."

"Hard to say. It was total chaos. The bastards who took him were trying to save their own asses. The guy you traded to the Russians, Fuad?"

"Yeah?"

"His real name was Ahmed Mahmoud Muhammad. He was a Colonel, in charge of low intensity warfare, terrorism, in North America. Major bad guy. The Israelis were after him like a hound dog on a hot scent. Did you notice a scar on his left temple?"

"No."

"He used to have one. I put it there, a long time ago."

I sipped my brandy, waiting for a war story, but it didn't come.

"Heard you managed to piss Goldfarb off today...."

"It was mutual. We need to talk about that, Mike. I assume we're secure here."

"We are."

"I got handed a kill list you'd prepared. One of the names was a sitting Senator from Oregon. John was abducted from there. Interesting coincidence."

"Senator Wyatt. It's an old name, English origin meaning, 'brave in war.' Wyatt's never served. He's a political hack."

Mike nodded.

"The Broken Oath Executive Order. It was President Blager's idea?"

"Absolutely. Assholes will pucker. He's going to push it hard. Heads will explode."

"Wyatt is the perfect target."

"I disagree. The other party would fight to the death to save him. The Broken Oath as actionable will scare the shit out of many in Congress."

"Is Wyatt guilty of treason?"

"Of course, he is. I wanted you to shoot him."

"Is he legally guilty?"

"I expect so, if it could be proven."

"How do you know?"

"He's a traitor, Raven. *Senator Wyatt set up John's abduction.*"

"You know this how?"

"From the Russians, the ones who gave John sanctuary in Syria. They were blackmailing Wyatt."

I blinked. "No one is better at spy games than Russia, Mike. Why should we trust them?"

"We don't have to. President Assad and John found common interests. They became friends. *Bashar al-Assad personally told John about Wyatt being run by the Russians.*"

"Assad isn't America's friend, Mike."

"Not after Hillary and Obama created ISIS to overthrow him, he's not. But they are gone, and he **is** John's friend. If Russia has a public execution for Fuad, Assad is invited. He might invite John."

"So why did Wyatt show up on my kill list?"

"I put him there. He's dirty, Raven. Not just in Oregon, dirty in Cuba and Venezuela."

"I believe you. Encourage President Blager to have DOJ prosecute him for Broken Oath. He'll listen to you. Have him do it legally. Let the Supreme Court settle it."

"Based on the word of a hostile Dictator and hearsay from the Russians? Fat chance."

"What if we could get proof? What if instead of some looney, lefty, backbencher, the target was worth all the years of litigation? President Blager wants a Constitutional precedent. Why not go for big game?"

"I think they want to start simple. This oath thing will take hordes of lawyers and years to argue."

"There is no simple, Mike. This is about right, about American justice. Our founding fathers would have hanged assholes like Wyatt in a heartbeat.

"Do we care how much it costs or how long it takes? The longer it goes, the more people who will cut plea bargains and testify against Wyatt."

Mike shook his head. "We don't have enough legal proof to even get started, Raven."

"What if we did?"

"How?"

"Josie sees things. Across time and space, she can see everything, but paranormal viewing is not legal proof. It never will be proof, but it can lead to validation. You recall how America discovered Russia's new Typhoon SSBN submarine?"

"One of our remote viewers said a new type of submarine would be coming down a canal that had not yet been built, at specific coordinates, on a certain date that was over a year in the future. Everyone thought that was nuts, but it was high stakes, so we tasked satellites."

Mike nodded. "We got good pictures. It was years before anyone saw the Typhoon again."

"Exactly right."

"What are you suggesting?"

"Two things. First, there is no honor in being a Mafia hitman and not much future. Yes, we need to go on offense, but against enemies who are clear and present dangers. Second, no suicide missions. If we take out, say, the head of Venezuela's secret police, the hounds of hell will be coming after us."

"Keep talking."

"The invasion route is a hard target. The more I look, the less I like it. I need Intel, COM, and military extraction. I'm not aware of any friendlies in-country we can depend on. They've **all** been compromised.

"It's so bad I don't even want Josie doing viewings until we get our shit together. It would freak her out."

"What can you do to help advance the Broken Oath legal initiative?"

"We can feed you knowledge. Not proof, but where to **look** for proof. For starters, proof positive that Russia was blackmailing Wyatt and others around him. You can then send people who do that sort of thing, maybe the FBI or CIA, to go get it. Once that starts, they can roll on their own."

"You want me as your cutout."

"I do. There will be more. Josie remembered that Wyatt was involved in the Uranium One thing in Burns, Oregon. Americans died. Treason was committed. She can look into that."

"In return?"

"Better Intel. Full mission support for getting in and out. I don't care if Blager uses a Covfefe committee or a Ouija Board, but we need timely, adequate mission support."

"Say more."

"Were you briefed in on the first mission for Josie and me?"

"Total shit storm. Half of Durham was left in flames. Local police died."

"That upset people, but the problem was that our mission support got there just short of too late. We were up to our asses in gunned up *jihadis*. Everyone on my team were casualties. Josie almost died."

Mike was frowning. "Didn't hear that part...."

"Josie is a national treasure. My main responsibility is to keep her safe. Instead, we damn near got her killed on our first mission because of stupid assed ROEs. America didn't deploy adequate force in a timely manner."

"Does Goldfarb know this?"

"He damn sure should. He finally did get us support, but too little, too late."

"Should we take this to President Blager?"

"To Goldfarb first. He's on the NSC. He knows Washington. He can figure out how you can get evidence to the people who collect evidence so they can do their jobs. They can get it to those running Broken Oath. Once this is up and running, my guess is that Goldfarb can fade away."

"He fades good, for sure. Keep your team clear and keep Blager politically clear?"

"I'm more worried about the first."

"Say more."

"Blager knows how much of a shit storm will come down from his even *suggesting* the notion of prosecuting Members of Congress for treason. He's got the big picture. We need to remind him that this mission, my mission, is a NO GO unless we're in it to win."

"By backing you up…."

"Yes. If things go bad, we need support. We've been careful to stay off the grid, but kill teams keep coming for Josie. That's what got all those FBI agents killed."

"I can support that, Raven. We get Goldfarb on board and then the President."

"There is no Raven. I don't exist, but please keep Josie safe while I'm out hunting."

"You have my word." Mike paused. "One more thing…."

"Okay."

"The Russians. They were helpful in your last mission."

"They were."

"They are trying to reestablish contact. They want something."

Raven gave a deep sigh. He shook his head.

"What?"

"This is how it goes off the rails, Mike. This big picture political stuff may yet do us in. My team needs to focus on action in Cuba, Venezuela, and along the invasion route. I need you to stall Goldfarb and Washington until we get a handle on that…."

"I'll do what I can."

CHAPTER FIVE
OSA, RUSSIA, AND RAMON

En Route to Patrick AFB, Florida, Present Day

Raven was supposed to be working the Cuba problem. It held the keys to Venezuela, the new Syria, the chessboard for an invasion across our Southern Border. It was proving to be a difficult target. His mission was not moving forward and now there was a major interruption.

The Russians urgently wanted a meet and no one knew why. Goldfarb was on Raven's ass to get to California for a meet. It was something best approached carefully, like making love with a porcupine. Raven didn't like being rushed when the Russians were involved.

No one was better at spy games than Russia. The FSB was as ruthless and deceptive as the old KGB, but smoother, smarter, and better with technology.

The Cold War had been a dangerous time, one of two superpowers with enough massive overkill to turn the planet into a cinder at the push of a button. It was so bad both sides had agreed on safeguards and fail-safes: The famous Red Phone, special codes, keys, and two-person teams to launch nukes. Neither side wanted an accidental nuclear war, certainly not one started by a fanatic or maniac.

The strategy was MAD, Mutually Assured Destruction. Everyone knew that. People made movies and wrote books about it. Schools held drills for students. If attacked, you launched everything you had *while you still could.* Thankfully the MAD strategy worked, aided by nonproliferation agreements. There was no World War III. Instead, we had détente and the Space Race. Still later came Star Wars and the collapse of the USSR.

Less remembered is that there was an understanding, there were rules. Whatever happened – from Gary Powers and his U2, to the Hungary invasion, the Bay of Pigs, and Vietnam – we'd not kill or torture each other's agents. War was preferably conducted through proxies.

Direct confrontations between the Bear and the Eagle could escalate. Conflicts could easily get out of control with possibly horrific consequences.

The Cold War accommodations were old history, long gone, mostly forgotten. Several nations now had Weapons of Mass Destruction. Some were making them available to rogue states, perhaps also to terrorists. There was less fear and more corruption.

On June 19, 1953, the Rosenbergs, Russian spies who had sold American's nuclear weapons designs to Stalin's USSR, were executed for **treason**. In 2010, Hillary Clinton, then Secretary of State, sold 20% of America's Uranium – the scarce key ingredient to make nuclear bombs – to a Russian company in exchange for a $145 million "donation" to the Clinton Foundation. Concurrent with that sale were massive leaks of highly classified information from Hillary's unsecure email servers.

There were no consequences. Why not?

Broken oaths by those in power, a problem that had plagued mankind through all recorded history. Citizens were supposed to be equal under the law, but they often were not. Mark Twain once famously noted that, *"It could probably be shown by facts and figures that there is no distinctly native American criminal class except Congress."*

America had fought a Revolution and a Civil War over the issues of freedom and fairness. Our core values were framed in the Constitution and Bill of Rights, documents designed to preserve freedom. These set strong checks and balances to allow and encourage American Exceptionalism.

Still, no system run by man is perfect. Those with money and power got special attention. It could work both ways, positive and negative, but as high-level corruption spread it was clear that a two-tiered justice system developed, one that favored elites, threatened freedom, and drove 21st Century conflicts.

We'd regressed to Sixteenth Century ethics, the age of corrupt elites. History doesn't repeat exactly, but it rhymes. In this case, corrupt political elites were mixed with unaccountable bureaucrats and Cyber Oligarchs, but the fundamentals were the same.

As is oft quoted, "*Treason doth never prosper, what's the reason? For if it prosper, none dare call it Treason.*" In other words, if somebody commits treason and actually succeeds (overthrows the government and takes over), nobody will dare call the traitor a traitor because he's now the king or dictator and will punish anybody who says his actions were treasonous.

Hillary's major misadventures are called the "Uranium One scandal," the "Hillary Email Scandal," and "Benghazi." Her goals were basically achieved, and, at the time, neither political party objected. There was little public outrage, though the FBI's flip-flopping about guilt likely caused her to lose an election she was strongly favored to win. She would never be President, but neither was she held accountable.

Discussion of treason was lost in a fog of claims and counter claims, political spin. Hillary didn't "approve" the sale, she "failed to oppose" the sale. She didn't commit treason by leaking America's secrets, she was just "careless."

Soon there were myriad scandals, a "fundamentally transformed" world, a divided nation, and even a soft coup to depose a sitting President. The techniques of Alinsky and Goebbels were supercharged by social media and "Fake News" and used to rip societies apart.

One thing is clear: The world **had** been transformed, and it was now more dangerous. There were now other major players on the stage, not just the US and Russia. Many worried that Hillary's uranium might wind up in Iranian warheads, in weapons that could then be transferred to Hamas or North Korea by the IRGC, the Iranian Revolutionary Guard Corps, which was now designated by many, including the US, to be a terrorist organization.

Russia and America had both survived as nation states, but in a strange new world. Many groups could attack them with WMDs, and it might not be clear who they should strike back against. Their options for offense or defense were more constrained. Any action or inaction – even one by a third party, where they had no involvement whatsoever – could set off a firestorm of political rage.

Propaganda and emotion now overcome reason and statecraft. The UN, of course, is no help. It has never resolved a conflict, not even when times were simpler.

There are no rules now, just understandings between people in governments infested with oligarchs, corrupt bureaucrats, and worse, including high level traitors on both sides who would gladly sabotage mutual efforts between the countries.

In this strange new world, Raven, operating under a cover identity as being Canadian, one Digger Simpson, was meeting with a Russian agent, who has a cover identity of being French, one Patty Allgrove, but is working for a state-owned Russian energy company, Rosneft.

Despite common interests, the Russians could not be trusted.

It was all quite vague. The Russians seemed to be using Digger as a back channel to the CIA. Raven thought his Digger identity was still solid, but perhaps not. There was no pretense about Patty being a Russian asset, but it was hard to know what the Russians were up to and why.

Patty was being run by the legendary FSB spymaster, Karlov Perovitch. Raven prevailed against classic FSB tradecraft including overly aggressive kill teams, but barely.

Although their last encounter had resulted in a win for our team, Raven thought that was only because Russia **wanted** it to work. The exchange delivered someone Putin himself wanted. Raven delivered him, Doctor Claas Vogel a financial terrorist protected by allies in high places. Vogel's evil exceeded that of any James Bond villain.

Raven's side of the deal was fulfilled. The Russians still owed him – not money, something more precious, information from their interrogations of Vogel. That was the other thing the Russians did well: Interrogations.

The Russians were supposed to share the take from Vogel, but such an agreement was unlikely to sit well with them. Raven expected they'd delay and evade fulfilling their end of the deal. Instead, they wanted a meet.

Raven sighed, looking out the window as the courier aircraft, an aging DC-9, turned to land. The Navy called it a C-9B, one of only two left, both assigned to the Marines.

Raven had dispatched his team to get a boat. It seemed simple enough, but they'd not returned and he had no idea why. Nothing was working. His ability to communicate from Havana was essentially nonexistent. *Not with his team since they left to get the boat. Not with Josie since before he'd left for Havana.*

Raven did get a flood of urgent coded notes at dead drops from Goldfarb about needing a Russia meet. He'd not replied. He wanted his team based on the boat and back in Havana before he was pulled away.

Goldfarb had other priorities. His last missive was explicit. It ordered an extraction by submarine that took Raven to GITMO and put him on this plane. *To Florida?*

Rudy watched as the plane landed, turning to his teammate, Terry. "Raven's going to be pissed."

"No shit, Captain."

Rudy had been the buyer. It was his boat. He was the boat's Captain, with documents and a cover story to prove it. He turned to the third man. "You want to take this, Mike? You're his control."

"Negative. This is a technical issue. We have Cybertech's CEO himself here for technical support." Mike grinned and pointed. "We're going to blame you, Will."

Will Giles shrugged. He was smaller than the others, 5 foot 11, about 190 pounds, fit, but not professionally so, with a professorial look about him. "Blame me if you want, but just make sure I get paid for this. It's been a cluster fuck."

Mike chuckled. "It's not over yet. I've not yet shared our problems with Goldfarb."

Will said, "Who's paying me for this? TSG? Are you paying?"

Mike was the President of The Security Group, a private company. He was also the control for Raven. Increasingly, he'd been Raven's cutout for Goldfarb and official Washington.

Mike nodded. "The answer for now is, 'Yes.' Send me a bill. Call it equipment upgrades."

The group stood silently as the plane rolled up, the engines spooled down, the door popped open, and the rampers rolled up the portable stairs. Raven came bounding out carrying a small bag.

"Mike. Glad you're here. I need to get my ass to California."

"Slow down." Mike held up a hand. "You don't communicate worth a shit, Raven."

"I don't communicate? *What in the Hell is my team doing here in Florida?* I've been sitting on my ass in a red zone, waiting to get burned, cut off from COM, wondering what the Hell was going on, and why they didn't come back.

"Havana makes the old Cold War Moscow look like a playpen. It's fucking dangerous. I was the only asset we had left there." Raven looked around the ramp. "Do you want to talk about this here?"

"Here is good," Mike said. "The short version. Start with why you just bought an expensive yacht."

"It's our safe house and egress. We can't move freely in Havana. We lack COM and support. That place is locked down tighter than anything I've seen. I had to do something…."

"Told you," Rudy said.

Mike silenced him with a glare.

Raven said, "There are times you need to improvise in the field. This was one."

"You bought a very expensive yacht. Will and I have been scrambling to support you, but this one caught us cold."

"I bought a boat for the mission. Shoot me. We can sell it when we're finished with it. What's the big deal?"

Will said, "There have been some technical issues."

"Technical issues?"

"Large issues."

Raven looked at Will, then Mike, and finally at Rudy. "Did you get it? The boat. Did it pass inspection? I've been waiting for you in Havana."

Rudy nodded. "I have the title and papers, but was ordered to hold until you arrived."

"By whom?"

Mike said, "That would be me."

"Why?" Raven said.

"My fault," Will said. "Technical issues."

"More than technical issues," Mike said. "Operational issues. I had to get the Navy involved...."

Raven looked at Mike. "That's why we're here? In Florida?"

"Yes. You will need to personally be here for a few days of training. We had to make some upgrades to your boat. They are almost finished. You and your crew will need to be fully operational with the equipment before you re-deploy."

"What else?" Raven said.

"Budget issues. Large budget issues. We are busting our asses to keep these off the books."

Raven looked at Will. "Cybertech was in the loop."

Will nodded.

"I ran the specs and cost by you. I didn't hear any objections. It's just a boat."

"It was just a boat," Will agreed. "It's not anymore."

"I don't understand," Raven said.

"You know those cars and gadgets James Bond had in the movies?"

Raven nodded.

"That sort of thing...."

"More," Mike said. "Your operation has changed."

"What?"

"Your mission in Cuba has expanded. It turns out you have an Osa problem. Your team and Will came up with a solution, we hope."

"A what?"

"An Osa problem, Boss," Rudy said. "Osa is Russian for Wasp. Cuba has more Osa II missile boats than anyone in the world, except maybe for Yemen or Syria. They carry SS-N-2 anti-ship missiles, and two AK-230 twin 30 mm CIWS, fore and aft. One of those missiles sank the Israeli destroyer *Eilat*.

"The Osa is 127 feet long, has three diesels totaling 15,000 horsepower, carries a crew of 29, and will do 42 knots. They were the hottest thing in the water back in the day, expendable, designed to hunt and kill major warships.

"They are obsolete now, but still pack a punch. The pleasure boat we just bought, on a good day, running light, can maybe make 40 miles per hour, about 35 knots."

"Oh...." Raven blinked, thinking about it. Finally, he said, "Shit."

Mike said, "You need to reset and forget about Goldfarb's Russia issues for a few days. I'm going to scrub the Cuba thing unless we can demonstrate you can survive a hot egress."

"Against a warship?"

"Yes. Possibly."

"You're kidding...."

"We've made changes to your boat. We need you to understand them, to test them, to see if they help."

Raven was frowning. "How do you propose we do that?"

"You are standing on Patrick AFB. It used to be called NAS Banana River and there is a lot of water around, both shallow and deep.

"I've got the Navy standing by to play games with you. The Admiral who approved this exercise bet me a bottle of Scotch that he'd kill your sorry ass. If he does, he says your Cuba mission is off."

Raven's frown deepened. "What are you saying?"

"You can have your toy boat, but the Navy gets to green light your extraction."

"If they don't like it...."

Mike shook his head. "They **already** don't like it, big time. Now they are in the loop. If they don't approve it, your mission is scratched."

"Can they do that?"

"Maybe. I don't think we want to find out. The Admiral has made it crystal clear that the Navy wants no part of a 21st Century Bay of Pigs.

He says America doesn't either, not unless you can win me that bottle of scotch."

"You think the President will agree with him?"

"I think that he might. I **know** I might."

"So, we're all stuck in Florida until that gets resolved?"

"No," Mike said. "I'm heading to DC to get Goldfarb in the loop, and to make sure the President isn't blindsided. You're going to get your mission repurposed and operational."

"Then I go play with the Russians in California?"

"If I can hold that off for a few days, yes."

"Goldfarb is puckered?"

"Nervous as a whore in church. Not real comfortable with our having a team in Havana either."

"Is there any good news?"

"You don't have to respond to Goldfarb's messages. I'll say he can assure the President we have it all under control."

"Marvelous," Raven said.

Laredo Texas, Early Evening, twilight, just off of I-35

They were meeting in the back room of a small bar about a block from the Wal-Mart. No drugs tonight, not even beers. There was business to conduct.

Ramon had grown up a few miles away in a shack made of wood that was propped up on cinder blocks. His mother was an American, a hairdresser. His father was an illegal, an "undocumented immigrant" who worked on construction sites.

Three of seven children had survived. He was the oldest, now 24. An older brother had died with a bullet in his ear, a signal that he'd betrayed the cartel. Another died in a fight with a rival gang. He was given a church service and burial. Two younger sisters, 14 and 16 just disappeared, probably trafficked into Phoenix and up the corridor. No one knew. No one asked.

They weren't poor, poor. They had food every day. Growing up, Ramon played football, hung out at the lake, and played video games.

All his life he'd skipped back and forth across the border. Sodas and candies were cheaper and the nightclubs would let you in.

In some places, people wanted to grow up to be an attorney, a firefighter, or a policeman. Along the border, kids wanted to join a powerful gang, and so he did.

Laredo was one of the poorest towns in the United States, a border town. If you weren't a cop, you were a drug dealer, if neither, you worked for a cartel. Ramon had started at sixteen. He did not tell his parents what he did. He didn't tell anyone. If he did, they would be killed.

Ramon had been one of the expendables. You did what you were told to do, or you died. They'd given him weapons training. That was fun. When he was proficient, they tested him.

He was taken to one of the ranches the cartel owned. There were about thirty people tied up. Ramon was handed a gun, and the boss pointed at his first victim, who was kneeling, with his hands tied behind his back, lashed to his ankles. Some were crying, some were silent, but they all knew they were there to be killed.

Ramon took the gun and shot the man in the head. He never learned who it was. It didn't matter. If he'd not done it, someone else would have. It was a rush, like being superman. They tried to take his gun away, but he held on and asked to keep it. After that, he would volunteer for the shootings.

He did beheadings too. Sometimes the severed heads still moved. Sometimes they were frozen in a scream. Sometimes they went slack.

That was long ago. Now Ramon was twenty-four, a boss who gave the orders. The risks and rewards were higher. No one trusted anyone. If someone didn't like you, if you were at the wrong place, they would sneak up on you and kill you. The same people you were working with.

It was how he got to be a boss. He'd killed his predecessor by catching him off guard and shooting him in the mouth. When the cartel head asked why, Ramon said, "He talked too much." The response was laughter and a nod.

Ramon had been lucky. It could have gone the other way.

As a boss now all he had to do was snap his fingers, point, and say *kill him.* No one would object. Those above him, of course, had the same power. Random killing was discouraged, but doing what you needed to stay in power was rewarded. It was survival.

Being sent to butcher rival cartel members or their relatives was common. Unless you feared someone, it was the best way to get rid of him. Everyone knew that.

Laredo was the American side. It was quiet so far, but the rules for the gangs were harsh. You had to be so terrifying that no one would fuck with you. You had to be on your game. For Laredo, that meant whipping and shooting.

For Nuevo Laredo, the other side, it was beheading and burning. No quarter was given. The fights happened over there, across the border, out in the dusty desert. The winners would signal victory by dumping their trophies on the Mexican side within view when the sun came up.

Ramon's *Gruppo*, his posse, was going to raid the *Zeta's*, their arch enemies, of their human traffic. Tonight, he had eight men with him. All were armed, all had killed, and they would again tonight.

The streams of refugees were endless. Tonight, he expected the main group to be perhaps 40 or 50, with two or three guards making the crossing. Somewhere out there would be a *Zeta* sniper and a spotter with a radio. Ramon already had men staked out on the high ground. He had that double covered.

The refugees had paid money to get across. The going rate was $5,000 for children, less for women, and perhaps $1,000 for each combat age male. Get them to Phoenix or Portland and they were worth twice that, maybe more.

Ramon's prizes would be the Zeta's illegals, the refugees. Many would be plague carriers, perhaps a third to half. These were useful. It took two Border Patrol agents to baby sit each illegal in a hospital. He might let some infected men live if they showed symptoms.

The women and children were worth money, but the other goal was control. His raid would send a signal. Their decapitated heads would be left along the border in duffel bags. The women and children would be trafficked.

Rival gang members would be taken alive and tortured until they revealed everything – phone numbers, safe houses, who they worked for, what they did, corrupt police and officials, everything. Teams would then be sent to dispatch or convert assets.

The killing was important. cartels captured the market by violence and maintained it by terror. It was the same logic as demanded by prohibition. The bodies of rival gang members would be marked by messages. Each body was a billboard. Pictures would be distributed. A signal would be sent.

A few miles along the border there would be other Zeta teams crossing with other valuable packages, weapons, money, or drugs. Those mules were not Ramon's problem tonight. Other *Los Serpientes* teams would handle them, leave the bodies, and bring back their plunder.

To cross, only Los Serpientes could keep you safe.

Life was cheap, but there were treats. He once got $400,000 for killing an associate of the leader of a rival gang. He had a brand-new Mercedes. There were girls whenever you wanted them, and coke.

He was looking forward to raiding the Zeta's. They'd killed three of his posse a week ago. Tonight, was vengeance. *Ramon loved his job.*

CHAPTER SIX
SHOOT AND SCOOT

Patrick AFB, Florida, Present Day

They were meeting in a SCIF that had been provided by the Air Force, who did NOT attend. No notes were to be taken. The Navy had a brief presence from Admiral Harold Perkins, the local commander.

"Welcome to the operations area of the Fourth Fleet. On 1, July 2008, the Navy re-established the United States Fourth Fleet, based at Naval Station Mayport in Jacksonville, Florida, which then assumed responsibility for U.S. Navy ships, aircraft and submarines operating in the Caribbean Sea and the waters of Central and South America. The Navy again has a major role of defending the Atlantic, though now with a secondary constraint of not being, ah, overly provocative.

"During the Cold War we had a major presence in the Atlantic. It was greatly reduced when the Soviet threat faded. The Fourth Fleet had provided forward operating for the larger Second Fleet. It was dissolved when that mission was abolished. Second Fleet itself was dissolved in 2011, to, ah, 'save funds for more ships.' It was not reestablished until 2018. Second Fleet is still rebuilding, and part of our mission is to help them with training.

"Fourth Fleet is responsible for Cuba and this region. Our role is limited. Mostly we've been helping to interdict drug runners, providing hospital ships, and that sort of thing.

"Any questions?"

Mike nodded. "I have two. Let me translate, Admiral. You'll do what you can to help us, but you don't want us to cause problems for you."

The Admiral nodded. "Correct. I remember when you ran Marine Intel in DC, Mike. We'll help where we can, but please do not put a foot wrong. If you do, we'll disavow."

"Understood, Admiral."

"What's your second question?"

"Do you have a Carrier Task Force available?"

"We have two in the area. One is operational as a tripwire to keep an eye on the Russian and Chinese presence in Cuba. The other is here for training purposes. The USS Abraham Lincoln, commissioned in 1989, has just been through a major refit. She's based in Newport News, but is here in the process of forming a new Task Force. I can work you into that exercise."

"Thank you."

"Let me introduce Commander Bromley. He's the lead weapons officer for Lincoln's escorts and is somewhat of an expert on Osas. He has an engineering degree from MIT and I understand that he wants to talk with your Cybertech people. I'm going to loan him to you."

The Admiral gestured and a thin young officer with gold wire-rimmed glasses stood up.

"Is there anything else?"

Mike said, "We're good. Thank you."

Commander Bromley was standing at the white board with a pointer. He and Will Giles would occasionally lapse into geek talk and Mike would have to dial them back.

Raven said, "I don't care about frequencies and rep rates. You can get into those details privately. Can we talk operational, please? It's a simple problem. I have a small team to extract. Can Cuba's Osas prevent that?"

Bromley paused. "You are asking me if they can they kill your boat?"

"Yes."

"Easily. They were designed to kill my destroyers. The Russians calculated that three Osas had 100% chance of killing one of our missile destroyers, though they would likely not survive the encounter. They didn't care about that. Their Osas are cheap but deadly, designed to be expendable."

Will nodded. "Admiral Sergey Gorshkov said *better is the enemy of good enough.*"

"Correct. We messed his math up, mostly by shooting back. In a hot war, we'll shoot first."

Raven was frowning. "If these Osas can swat us like a fly, why are we even having this meeting? Why am I here?"

Mike said, "We're trying to improve the odds for you…."

"Cybertech has done work on that," Will said. "It's not hopeless."

Bromley said, "To get back to the Osas, they have weaknesses. What I'm going to say about them is unclassified. I think you might want to take notes."

Mike said, "Approved. Can we get some notepads?"

Bromley smiled. He pulled four pads from a small pouch and handed them out.

"The Osas are relics of the Cold War. They were half-ass slapped together.

"The weapons of most concern are their SS-N-2 missiles. Each Osa carries four. They are hard to stop once you are targeted. They fly low and fast, about 0.9 Mach and maybe 300 feet off the water."

"What can stop them?" Raven said.

"That's problematic. Our CIWS weapons systems do a pretty good job if they are not overwhelmed with targets."

"Define, 'pretty good.'" Raven said. "Also define 'overwhelmed.'"

"Sorry, all that is highly classified."

Raven started to stand, but Will touched his arm. "It doesn't matter."

Raven said, "Why not?"

"It's off the table. Say that we installed a Navy CIWS for you, which isn't practical in the first place because of size and weight, but skip that. If you had one and fired it, it would shake your fiberglass boat to shreds."

Raven and his team looked at Will, then at Bromley, who nodded agreement.

"We still use the Phalanx, which is euphemistically referred to as a demented sibling of Star Wars' beloved R2D2 droid. The Phalanx packs the M61 "Vulcan" 20mm cannon, a gun found on almost every modern American fighter aircraft since the F-104 Starfighter. Its six revolving barrels spray out a stream of tungsten sabot armor piercing rounds at a rate of over 75 rounds a second.

"The guns are autonomous, but we usually deploy them in pairs. The shells are about seven inches long, and a bit heavy. They kill by kinetic impact.

"You can see them in action in a lot of movies. It's a smart system. Turrets swing free, radar tracks the incoming missiles, our outgoing shells, and adjusts to put them in the same place."

Mike said, "Do you have anything that is, ah, a bit smaller?"

Bromley laughed. He paused and wiped his glasses.

"Well?"

"We are going the other way. The 20mm guns cause a high pucker factor. It's the last chance. Most of their kills are close to the ship being targeted. Hundreds of feet. Too close, most Captains think. We get kills most of the time, but the targets still take hits from shrapnel and debris.

The Russians tend to use heaver guns, 30mm. The ones you'll encounter on the Osas are the old AK-230s. They replaced manually operated 25mm guns which were pretty worthless.

Our larger ships now have The Raytheon SeaRAM CIWS. It takes the proven, self-contained, compact design of Phalanx and ditches the 20mm Vulcan cannon for a box launcher packed with 11 RIM-116 Rolling Airframe Missiles (RAM). The super agile RAM is now a staple on our heavier surface combatant fleet.

"Each missile costs hundreds of thousands of dollars. The RIM-116 hits extremely maneuverable and supersonic sea skimming targets at over six miles from its launching point."

Mike said, "What do you worry about now?"

"Some of the new Russian stuff is hypersonic. There is research into rail guns and beam weapons. Don't get me wrong, we worry about everything. A swarm of Osas is not a threat that we overlook for the fleet."

"Explain," Raven said.

"Osas can be ambush predators, dashing out of a cove or port. A swarm of missiles could overwhelm Phalanx. The best defense against that system is to attack the Osas, or any other missile boats, before they fire. My preference is to splash them as soon as their systems target you."

Will said, "We agree there is no hope of mounting a CIWS on Raven's boat, much less of firing one. That is not going to happen...."

"Right," Bromley said. "So, what...?"

Mike held up his hand. "Hold that, please. We need to know more about what weaknesses the Osas have. Can you speak to that? Then we can have lunch.

"We don't have a warship. Raven can't shoot, at least not much, but we need to scoot. Your Admiral wants us – that includes you – to see if we can come up with a strategy that allows Raven's team to make a hot egress out of Cuba if the shit hits the fan. We are not trying to win a battle, just to survive.

"It's a one-time deal. Can you help us?"

"Maybe. The Osas do have some weaknesses."

"Take notes," Mike waved an arm at Raven's team. "You too, Will."

Heads nodded. Mike said, "Go."

Bromley said, "We'll start with the missile. It's fast, small and hard to hit. It's also resistant to countermeasures, but that is due to a weakness you might be able to exploit tactically.

"The SS-N-2's arming and homing system cannot be engaged for targets closer than five miles to the ship. They point it at you, fire, and you can't jam it until it's up to speed and on the way."

"Electronic lock out?" Will asked.

"Old technology. A timer. They can't turn it off. Targets within five miles can't be engaged. Probably keeps Ivan from shooting up his own ships...."

"When they fire a missile, what happens?"

"The missile flies its programmed course to the target, until five miles out. Then its own radar homing goes active.

The missile's homing radar can't be relied upon to seek out the preferred target. If it has two targets, it's a crap shoot which one it goes for. It's only looking ahead for targets, so the firing ship is safe. It basically goes for the biggest thing it sees in the terminal phase."

"We're safe if we're close to an Osa?" Raven said.

"From missiles, yes. From guns, maybe.

"Osas have antiaircraft guns, two AK-230 turrets, fore and aft. They carry 2,000 rounds per gun. In theory, they can fire those in a minute at the risk of burning out or blowing up the gun. About 400 rounds per minute is practical. Big shells, 30mm, and a high fire rate, but not very useful.

"It's not clear that they could hit a small boat. In the engagements we are aware of, those guns have not done well against either air or surface targets.

"They use the old Drum-Tilt radar and it is basically crap. Vacuum tubes from the 1960s. Some fleets have better guns and radars, but not the Cubans. Inadequate."

"Might not matter," Will said. "We're gasoline-fueled in a fiberglass hull. Tell me more about the fire control radars for the missiles."

"The good news is that they don't do well against small and ECM equipped targets. The Syrian Civil war tested Osa-IIs. They were filmed firing their deck guns into the city of Latakia. It's easy to hit a city, but the missiles were a bust.

"The SS-N-2s have a long range, even over the horizon if the target is stupid enough to radiate. They can home on emissions. In the Battle of Latakia, the Osas fired first due to their long range. Unfortunately, their targets had ECM. They missed the targets.

"The Osas tried to flee, but most were not capable of escaping due to engine malfunctions. These were sunk."

"Say more about that," Mike said.

"It's the guns. They are worthless against a missile attack. Osas were not designed to survive combat against serious enemies, just to kill."

"No, the part about the breakdowns and the fire control radars missing the targets. In a major naval engagement, *breakdowns?*"

"The 'missing' part is two-fold. The targeting radar on the Osas is an old Russian model that NATO calls 'Square Tie.' It is pre-Vietnam. Basically, before the missile can fire, the ship must acquire the target. It is the ship's radar that finds and fixes the target.

While it's doing that, there has to be a lot of preparation. The gyros on the missile selected have to spin up and stabilize so its autopilot can work. That takes minutes. More important is that the Osa has to hold a steady course when firing a missile.

Sometime after that interval, the operators on the Osa decide to shoot. They switch the radar from 'search' to 'track.' It shifts to a narrow beam, a higher frequency, higher power, and a high pulse rate.

"That's a red flag. It would light up my battle board with a launch warning. If I saw an Osa doing that to my ship I'd blow it out of the water."

"Right," Mike said.

"The Square Tie is a dumb radar. It can be misguided by both chaff and active ECM, jamming, but there is more. When it goes to track mode, the ship's radar is precisely tracking the target, getting range, course, and speed data. It feeds that data to the missile's autopilot."

"And all this time, the Osa has to hold its course and speed?" Will said.

"Correct. That's the doctrine."

"How long are we talking about?" Will said.

Bromley shrugged. "Depends. A good crew, maybe four or five minutes. Could be longer if someone in their command chain has to approve firing.

"There is one other thing that might help. It's not usually a factor for us."

"Go ahead," Mike said.

"There is a gap to possibly exploit at the terminal end, too. The ship's radar is dumb, but the missile's is short range and it doesn't think at all. The ship fires down the bearing to the target and the autopilot flies that course at a programmed altitude. At 6 nautical miles from the target, the missile goes active."

"It turns on its own radar."

"Correct. It picks the largest target in its range gate and homes on it."

"Six miles. The biggest target six miles or less in front of the missile?"

"Correct. These missiles are designed to hit ships on the open seas. At that range it goes into a terminal dive, something over 600 miles per hour. It has infrared homing too. The IR kicks in after the missile radar picks a target.

"It is quite hard to hit with guns. What you see coming in head-on is about the size of a basketball, moving like a bullet.

"So, we're screwed," Raven said. "We don't even have guns."

"There is a chance. The missile's radar goes for the biggest target it sees. It has no velocity filter, so it can't differentiate between moving and stationary targets. And, by then, it is coming in for the kill. It's shifted to a conical scan, which is easy to jam."

Will said, "Can you get me the manuals for those radars and the IR seeker?"

"No problem. There are a few other limitations we can discuss after you've read them."

Mike said, "Thank you for the briefing, Commander Bromley. Are there any questions?"

No one spoke.

"Good. After lunch, we'll brief you on our boat. We'd like you to take a look at it and observe the first tests. Your opinions would be welcomed."

"That's why I'm here...."

CHAPTER SEVEN
GETTING REAL

Patrick AFB, Florida, Next Day

They'd finished breakfast and were back in the SCIF.

"I give. Where's Raven?" Rudy said. "I got him the damned boat."

Will laughed. "He'll be here. He's seeing Mike off. Said to start without him."

"He left you in charge?"

"Just for the upgrades. Running the boat is all yours, Captain."

"I'll get you a nautical hat," Terry said. "You'll love it...."

Rudy gave him the finger, just as Raven and Commander Bromley entered.

Raven said, "Let's get started. We need to get through this and get back to our mission.

"We're not mission-capable in Cuba, Venezuela is worse. We'll hear Goldfarb screaming all the way from DC if I'm not out of here by the time Mike gets done briefing him. We've got a cluster fuck and we need to get a handle on it before Washington melts down."

"Right," Will said. "The major upgrades to the boat are operational. I'll start with briefing you on what to expect."

"What major upgrades?" Bromley asked.

"The mechanical stuff. We'll need your guidance about having sufficient combat electronics and countermeasures."

"Sufficient for what?" Bromley said.

Raven shrugged. "You tell me. Sufficient to get your Admiral off our asses, for starters. Let's go secure."

Bromley latched the door and the green light came on.

Will walked to the podium and flicked on a computer. "We have new engines and controls. We'll start there. Please be seated." He looked at Bromley. "How fast do fleet warships go these days?"

"Our fleet was planned during the Reagan era. The magic number is 30 knots, about 32 miles per hour. That is fast enough to keep position with our carriers. The fleet escorts these days are *Ticonderoga* Class Cruisers and *Arleigh Burke* Class Destroyers.

"The *Ticonderoga* class was produced from 1980 to 1994. They are a bit larger. They were expensive, over a billion dollars each. The plan was to produce smaller less-expensive ships to replace them, hence the *Arleigh Burke* Class, introduced in 1991 and still in production."

"Were they less expensive?" Raven asked.

"Not by the time we got upgraded weapons on them."

"How much?"

"1.85 billion."

"*Billion?*"

Will said, "That is billion with a capital B. Congress shit bricks."

"What's the difference between the ships?" Raven said.

"Not a lot," Bromley said. The *Ticonderoga's* are older, larger, and faster, about 32 knots. There is an engineering rule. Longer hulls are faster. They also have two 5-inch guns, versus one.

"The *Arleigh Burke* Class, in general, has more advanced weapons systems for missile and air defense. That's the major concern these days.

Will said, "The plan was to replace them both with a new class. *Zumwalt* class ships. Very stealthy and high tech, but it didn't work out."

Bromley sighed. "We built three. $4.5 billion each, plus the development costs. There were a lot of problems. The Navy tried to divert the funds to more *Arleigh Burke Class* ships, but failed.

"My own ship is the **USS Gravely**, an *Arleigh Burke* ship commissioned in 2010. We're the screen lead for the Lincoln's task force. I'll put her up against anything in the fleet, anything our allies have. We got upgraded weapons systems when we were tasked with being Lincoln's lead escort."

"What about the Russians?"

Bromley shrugged. "They have problems of their own. The Chinese have a *Type 055*, not yet seen. It's reported to be a rip off of our *Zumwalt* class. Too bad for them.

"Shit happens. I'm here to talk about **your** boat. Tell me about it."

Will said, "How fast are the Osas, really? They look like fat barges. Can they actually do 40 knots?"

"They did in trial runs. *Reliably?* Not bloody likely. They tend to break down in combat after a few minutes at full power."

"Good," Will said. "We bought a 2008 Sea Ray Sundancer. 38 feet long, sleeps up to 6, quite fast, 40 miles per hour, relatively inexpensive, and not uncommon. You can snap them up used for $100,000.

"It came with two 370 horsepower Mercruiser engines with stern drives. Hard core boat people don't much like this brand."

"Probably because they can't outrun Osas…."

"Fuck you," Rudy said.

Will shot him a glance. "Sundancers don't excite civilian boat geeks. It's not the best fishing boat, the fastest boat, the best liveaboard, or the best yacht to impress rich friends.

We picked it because it's a good boat for our mission. It doesn't draw attention. If those aboard stay below, they are out of sight. It carries 200 gallons of fuel."

Bromley said, "It's too slow…."

Raven said, "Slow doesn't matter if it's tied up to the dock. It's our floating safehouse. My team is safer staying on a boat that we control than anywhere in Havana. Eyes everywhere. We're like bugs under a microscope."

"What if you're blown? What's the Plan B? What do I tell my Admiral if the shit hits the fan?"

Raven sighed.

"Well?"

"This is what we do, Commander. We go to nasty places and deal with bad people."

"If you get your asses killed there, it's a major political issue. If we have to shoot our way in with a military force to save your asses, it could trigger a war. We don't need a Bay of Pigs. We don't need a Benghazi either."

"Easy," Will said, "I agree. That's why we upgraded the engines. Stock was a 6.2-liter engine, but we dropped in a pair of 8-liter V8s. 430 HP each, stock, and a matched pair of Bravo Three XR stern drives, each with dual-counter rotating propellers. Those drives will handle up to 525 hp engines.

"Cuban waters extend for ten miles. At 50 knots, we're clear in under nine minutes. Can you protect a civilian American boat in international waters, Commander?"

Bromley nodded. "If we must."

Nine long minutes, Raven thought. "Can we depend on the boat?"

Will said, "Not sure. I'm going for fast. The main problem I'm worried about is controllability. Some of my engineers said that if an engine hiccupped it would all go ass over teakettle. The good news is that the drives have controllable pitch props, better technology than what people put on airplanes."

Bromley said, "Could be a wild ride in a moderate sea. My bet is that you still go ass over teakettle if you get a flameout on a fiberglass surfboard with 500 horses on one side and nothing on the other...."

"You underestimate technology," Will said. "Turns out that Mercury has electronic Joystick Piloting for novice captains in 'less-than-ideal situations,' people like, say, Rudy here."

"No shit," Rudy said.

"Read the brochure," Will said, handing it over. The cover said, Mercury: Go Boldly.

Terry read, *"Focus on a new feeling. One of total confidence. Confidence that comes from being effortlessly, intuitively, completely in control of your boat, thanks to Mercury's joystick piloting system."*

He passed it to Rudy. "Hell man, you have SmartCraft Digital throttle and shift, with electro-hydraulic power steering. It even comes with an engine-matched warranty for years to come...."

Rudy looked at it, shaking his head. "Finger-tip control, it says...."

"Okay," Raven said. "What are you suggesting?"

Will smiled. "We should all read the manual carefully. Then we and our good Commander go out on the water. We run the shit out of your boat and see what happens.

"One thing we **know** is working is the GPS. When you have the engines nice and warm, we'll make some long straight runs. Then we open it up, write down what we see, and get Commander Bromley to witness and sign off on it. Save the data. I'm expecting over 50 knots."

Rudy said, "Who is this 'we,' white man?"

Will flashed a grin. "That would be you, Rudy. Assuming you can keep the pointy end in front...."

Bromley had an odd look on his face.

Raven said, "What's wrong? Won't it impress your Admiral?"

"There are other issues. He'll ask about countermeasures. Your boat is not going to outrun a missile."

"That troubles us too. You and Will can discuss it while you're out enjoying the test drive. When you come up with a plan, we'll get it implemented and tested."

"You want me to go into harm's way on your hopped-up plastic surfboard?"

"SPEC OPS does this kind of thing all the time. Civilians like us do it for fun...."

"*Civilians?*"

Raven said, "It's a U.S. registered civilian boat. You ride in it, not on it, Commander. Perfectly safe."

"You're not going?"

"No."

"What will you be doing?"

"The hard stuff. Making secure calls. Getting my ass chewed.

"I've been stuck in a black hole. People in Washington want me in California. They are not happy. Mike's going back to smooth things out."

Bromley nodded.

Raven looked at Will. "What should I tell them if they ask what we've spent on our floating safe house?"

"Nothing."

"You got it for free?"

Rudy laughed. "Good guess. It's our cover story."

"You are shitting me."

Will said, "It actually is the cover story, but it's best not to bring that up. You tell them 'nothing,' if they ask. I'm paying for it. Mike and I will sort the money out. You have a mission to run."

I used to. Raven sighed. "Go do your thing."

Will nodded and looked around the group. "The boat should be ready. I'm running the tests. If there is anything you want us to do, Commander, just ask."

Bromley said, "I need a set of speed runs. I'll give you the headings when we get out in deep water and know the sea conditions."

Will said, "Rudy, you drive. You got the boat here. Terry runs the GPS and navigates. Commander Bromley is our observer and nautical expert. Is everyone good with that?"

Heads nodded.

"I want the tracking gear and radar off. We're going to run around for an hour or so. When we are well out of sight of other boats, the Commander will tell us where and how he wants the speed runs."

"Any restrictions?" Bromley asked

"Great question. Slow is smooth, and smooth is fast. I just spent a bundle on boosted, race-tuned, new engines. They want me to stay in a 75-90% power range till we get 25 hours on them. We'll start easy, get into that power range, and get familiar with the boat.

"Rudy, when you're ready and fully comfortable, let me know. We'll run the speed tests at 90% power when he tells us."

Bromley said, "Not above that?"

Will shook his head. "Not needed if my engineers are right. I do want the engines broken in before we reposition in Havana.

"We should be back in time for dinner. If we make 50 knots, Bromley pays. Okay?"

"You make 50 knots at reduced power and I'll gladly buy."

"Yee Haw," Rudy said.

They gave me a private office where I could make secure calls. I reserved the SCIF for 5 PM, hoping they'd all be back and my team could proceed with Navy approval for our boat. My first call was to Josie. In all the time we'd worked together, we'd never been out of communication for so long.

I missed her, of course, but it wasn't just that. Without her talents, our mission was compromised and our team was at risk.

Josie was a national treasure. She was a paranormal viewer, the best we had. She was able to see things, able to find evil across time and space.

My job #1 was keeping her safe. This time, to keep her safe, it wasn't possible for her to be anywhere near me. That had happened before, but never for so long. We were both a bit spooked.

Josie was convinced she'd long ago been a High Druid Princess and that we'd met in previous lives. According to her, we had died together in 56 BC when Roman soldiers under Gaius Julius Caesar destroyed her temple.

I had asked her when we first met if that was where her psychic powers came from, the Celts. Her answer, like so much about her, was unexpected.

"I like to think so," Josie said, "but I fear the dark side."

It was a core truth, one we fully agreed on. The dark side was much to be feared. The battle between good and evil is eternal.

I worked in the deep dark of night, killing monsters. It had made me enemies in high places. Josie could find evil across time and space, but was powerless to thwart it if it came for her. The least hint of violence shut down her paranormal senses.

Our worlds were vastly different. At times being near me had almost destroyed her. My world was one of violence and betrayal, one where the good guys all too often lost, sometimes betrayed by their own leadership. Over the years it had cost me too many friends.

Josie was a bright spirit. Her powers allowed her to sense realities far beyond what most mortals could perceive. Many were places of beauty, but some were dangerous.

It was on the sharp edges of reality where our worlds overlapped, a place where beauty met unimaginable horrors. The horrors were my job.

Josie picked up on the first ring. "Thank God."

I waited for the scramblers to kick in and the green light to come on.

"Love you, Babe."

Her sigh sounded hollow, what with the redundant encryption and time lag. Finally, she said, "You scare me, Raven."

"Yeah." It was that kind of a relationship. *What could I say....?*

"How many times did Goldfarb order you out of Havana?"

"A couple...."

"Nine. Twice after you'd sent your team away and were left there alone. Did you know there was a Cuban intelligence officer staying in your hotel?"

I'd wondered about that. The guy at the desk. "Did he suspect me?"

"No. She concluded you were an idiot tourist. I tend to agree with the first part...."

Oh. Whoops. Not the guy at the desk. A good time to change the subject.

"Are you safe?"

"Very," Josie said. "I'm in New York. Mike and Gerry are hosting me at their estate. He's with Goldfarb in DC calming the waters. When he gets back, the plan is to send me in the plane to pick you up. Did Goldfarb mention that he wants you in California?"

"I recall something about that...."

"Not funny. The Russians hit gold on their interrogation of Vogel, the Fascist billionaire you turned over to them. They need our help. Your FSB spy friend is wetting her Parisian panties."

I chuckled. *Josie was a sensitive, a bright spirit. She didn't usually speak like that.*

"What?"

"Does she even wear panties?"

"You don't want to know. You do need to set up a meet with her before Goldfarb has a heart attack."

"It's my next call, Babe. I'll set it for next weekend. We still have details about the boat to resolve."

"How's that coming together?"

"Marvelous. A textbook example of interorganizational cooperation...."

"You are so full of shit," Josie said. "I should to be there tomorrow night in time for dinner."

"I've missed you, Babe. It's better when we're together."

"I know. A lot better. Don't ever forget that."

"Never," I said. "I'll get it set up. Private. Just the two us. Candles. Fresh seafood."

"Good plan. I'll text my ETA."

"Love you, Babe."

"Love you too. Bye."

On Board the *Busted Flush*

Commander Bromley wasn't used to small boats. The smallest ship he'd ever served on was a destroyer. Small boats were, well, small by definition. More than that, they were low.

This one was very low. Visibility was obstructed. Except when they crested a swell, the water around them was higher than the boat.

Since the days of sail, naval vessels always had someone up high, in the crow's nest or on the bridge to see what was coming. This boat was built like a sports car, low on the water, with a rakish windscreen and an overhead canopy to shelter from weather.

The weather was strange, vaguely foreboding. No storm warnings, no ominous clouds, but a troubled sea, large rolling swells, and an unsettling light, pale and yellow. You might expect to see a weak sun like that in northern climes on the edges of winter, but not Florida in summer.

Florida sailors spoke of the "Dreadful Lemon Sky" as a bad omen. Local marine folklore was rich, dating back to the days of pirates, extending to the Bermuda Triangle and beyond. Tales of lost ships, planes, treasure, ghosts, and more.

Bromley made a mental note to ask about the sky when they got back to harbor. He forced his attention to the present. *Raven had passed on the test run. Everyone was acting as if he, who knew next to nothing about small boats, was somehow in charge.*

The boat was slender, a twelve-foot beam. It had a shallow draft, only forty-four inches. In the crossing swell it rolled like a fan-dancer's ass.

At speed it was mostly out of the water, up on plane, bow high. It was like a skipping stone, its weight predominantly supported by hydrodynamic lift, rather than hydrostatic lift. Rolling, bouncing, shaking, skipping, and slamming into chop, it was a rough ride.

Up front there were two captain's chairs, neither of which had any seat belts or restraints. Rudy was at the helm. Terry was working the GPS, calling out speeds.

Rudy had been trying different courses and power settings, getting ready for the speed run. The ocean was not cooperating. He'd finally gotten us up to about 25 knots, getting into the rhythm of fighting the helm to match the wave patterns. The boat was moving fast and riding well.

He looked at me, back over his shoulder. "This is the best so far. What should we do? Open it up and hang on, or wait for another day...."

Rudy said, "I can drive the boat, but you're the judge. I can give you 50 knots, but it will be a rough ride, Commander."

I was thinking, *A Ship in Harbor Is Safe, but that Is Not What Ships Are Built For....* We had to try. If I lacked confidence for even a test run, command approval was unlikely.

Rudy said, "I'm not asking for an order, just an opinion."

I sighed and made a decision. "Go for it."

"Roger that," Rudy said.

The boat accelerated. Will and I were soon bouncing around like loose cargo. We had two options. Neither was good.

Either we could sit in the rear looking forward, where all we could see under the canopy was the back of two heads. Back there, all we could hear at speed was the engines. Or we could sit sideways on the benches, under what was sort of a roll bar. It supported the canopy and had fixtures for fishing poles, tow ropes, and the like.

Sideways was a great way to get seasick. Also, with no restraints and the boat bouncing around, it took constant work to stay in place.

We exchanged a glance. Will said, "I don't like this...."

"It won't take long."

"You hope."

"Yeah."

We stayed where we were, sideways. We couldn't see much. After a time, it was exhausting.

There was a moderate swell, at least two-foot waves. Not the best for a speed run, but it was what it was. The book said to take a moderate swell at a 45-degree angle, but big waves head on. We were doing the former.

The boat was taking spray over its windscreen. Rudy was fighting the helm, but doing a good job at holding course. The boat was accelerating. Lord, we were moving. It was fiendish fast.

Terry called, "50 knots" as we started up another swell. *Impressive.*

Will, looking slightly green, asked, "Can we go to 90% and get this over. Commander?"

I nodded. The boat was plenty fast. We didn't need to prolong this.

Will called out, "**90% power. Hit it. Call your speed.**"

Terry repeated the order. Rudy hit the throttles, the engines roared, and we clawed our way diagonally up a big swell.

"Terry called, "54 Knots." Followed by, "**Oh, shit.**"

I stood up to see better just as we crested the swell. I found myself looking at a wall of a wave.

"Slow down," I screamed. "Power back. Take it head on."

White water was coming over the windscreen. It turned green. We were filling with water. The deck was wet and slippery. I was falling.

My head hit something and the world went black.

CHAPTER EIGHT
RUSSIAN COLLUSION

Fairmont Hotel, San Francisco, Morning, Next Day

Agent Marie had been running CSRs for two hours. She was positive that no one had her under surveillance, no ticks, no bugs, nothing unusual on the streets. As a sanctuary city in America's most populous sanctuary state, the local officials and police were too overloaded with problems to bother with a solitary, professional woman who was minding her own business.

She'd dropped the upscale clothing, dresses and pearls, she'd preferred in her Paris assignment. Now she dressed, acted, and looked like a native. Slacks, dark glasses, and comfortable shoes.

Iron Age Women's Black Leather she'd bought from Amazon. Feminist-approved safety walking shoes with high-impact steel toes.

You could never buy anything like that in Moscow. Probably not Paris either. Her cover name, Marie, was Russian, and it tracked back to her assignment in Paris.

She loved capitalism, but her Marie identity was Russian. She used that persona for her missions. It showed her as a legal immigrant from France. That cover, if checked, led back to a scandal. The details were murky. An affair of the heart with a foolish officer of the French military. Sadly, he'd committed suicide when his wife discovered his lapses.

Between missions in the U.S. Marie dropped from sight with a deep-cover cover name, Patty Allgrove. She'd been in place for over a year now.

Those documents were in order as a native-born U.S. citizen. She was fitting into local culture just as she was trained.

She had an official pre-2008 birth certificate, hand-recorded in a paper book at the time, and so noted in local newspapers in Hawaii. That one was secret, a special gift from her spymaster, Karlov. When he gave it to her, he'd said, "*No matter what happens to Russia or at the FSB, between missions you are an American, Patty Allgrove. No one knows this but the two of us.*"

San Francisco was crime infested, but Marie was prepared. She had MACE, a small, razor-sharp knife, and a full set of combat skills. Two of her lipsticks were single-shot weapons. She'd not needed to use them except in practice.

Mostly, Marie wasn't bothered on the street. She was fit, alert, and not a good target for thugs. Not a prostitute or a candidate for human trafficking or drugs.

Still, there were always fools. Once a drugged-out vagrant had demanded her purse, at night on an empty side street. All she had to do was click to put a fragmenting 7 mm bullet into his brain case. It would be good practice. She was tempted.

She'd have to report the use of a weapon. She might have to explain to *apparatchiks* at center. Her handler, the legendary Karlov, disliked such events. He would deem it sloppy. He chafed at interference from Moscow.

Still, why leave evidence? A single killing-strike to the throat crushing the larynx would suffice.

Marie left the body next to a trash can.

Most days saw the sun rise on several bodies across the city. One more would not attract attention, but a thug or vagrant killed with a gunshot might. FSB had an arsenal of covert weapons and poisons available, but the lipsticks were her preference.

She glanced at her watch, a faux-diamond encrusted Japanese Citizen model that fit her cover persona. It looked elegant, was relatively inexpensive, and had interesting technology. No batteries, nothing to maintain.

Mentally, she had been shifting her thinking from Patty to the Marie identity. She was being reactivated. She was half an hour early. She decided to run one more CSR. She was getting back into the rhythm.

It puzzled her why Karlov was so persistent about the need for her to schedule a meet with the Canadian who'd helped them with the Vogel matter. She'd find out soon enough.

I gave the code knock.

"*Введиme*," Karlov said in Russian. Enter.

Karlov Petrovitch was standing by the window, impeccably dressed, wearing a sublime two-button dark Brioni suit, with a Vivienne Westwood white dress shirt and silk navy tie from Marinella with tiny scarlet dots. He wore black Tod Gommino loafers over charcoal-gray socks.

He'd worn the same outfit at their first meeting. A meeting that had changed her life.

He smiled, "All is well my little Sparrow. May I offer Champagne?"

"Thank you, Sir."

He gestured at the small table by the window, then went to the computer desk, the only other flat surface in the room and poured our glasses. It had become our little ceremony.

Karlov held up his glass in a silent toast. They clinked glasses and he smiled. "Our masters are pleased with the prize we delivered."

"Herr Vogel is talking?"

"Singing like a bird. He might be the best source Russia has ever had. He's been a key player in high-level corruption all over the world. We've rolled up or liquidated a number of traitors. Slowly and silently, without attracting notice. President Putin is delighted. His enemies are panicked."

I nodded, waiting.

"I've been sending you orders to reactivate our Canadian contact on an urgent basis. He is golden, and we need his help. We might be able to use his influence and contacts with the Americans."

"We have a meet scheduled with him for Sunday."

Karlov set his glass down. "What took you so long?"

I took a deep breath. So much for the velvet glove.

"I don't know. He didn't respond to my communications until yesterday. His text said, 'Same place. Noon. Sunday.' Then he went dark again. I've not had any other contact with him since our last mission."

"He's your source. You can speculate."

I shrugged. "If you wish. It's been a long time since we abducted Vogel. Digger fulfilled his end of the deal. He might have assumed he was finished."

"There is no 'finished,' little Sparrow. What do you know about this man, your source?"

"Almost nothing. We wanted results. He delivered. My assignment was the results, which were, as you said, stellar."

"Be more specific."

"Digger Simpson, Aussie born. Aussie mother, Canadian father, now deceased. His father was a Captain killed in Afghanistan at Kandahar Airbase while serving with Canadian Military Intelligence in 2009 by an IED. Digger seemed to have contacts at the CIA, but I couldn't confirm that. There is nothing about him in their records."

"I presume you checked our Canadian sources."

"Of course. Digger has some sort of private security job. They know he exists, but the details are murky. The Canadians are not happy that we nabbed Vogel and extracted him on their soil. My relations with them are, ah, not as good as in the past."

Karlov nodded slowly. "Yes, the American media reported the Vogel disappearance. Pure speculation. Nothing was ever proven. The CIA denied any knowledge. Unfortunately, the extraction aircraft we used prompted discussion about Russian involvement."

"I was not responsible for that part of the operation, Sir."

"The CIA was supposed to issue smoke, to give us cover."

I frowned. Where did he get that idea? It was best not to speak.

There was a long moment of silence.

Karlov finally said, "What?"

"I had no impression that CIA had ever offered to cover for our snatch, Sir. Have they made any comment about it at all?"

"No. None that I know of...."

"My understanding, from Digger, was that we were to share the take we got from Vogel with CIA. That was how he got their cooperation."

"Do you know that, or just think that?"

"I know that's what he told me. Did we share the take?"

Karlov shook his head. "No. Not yet."

"I'm surprised that Digger returned my call at all. We made other blunders that might cause distrust."

"What blunders?"

"Your security people were clumsy and overzealous. There was a shootout. Do you think it's possible that Digger might feel that he can't trust us?

"The Vogel abduction – from Canadian soil, but on the American border – made the news. Vogel had American citizenship and major supporters in their government, did he not?"

"Vogel had high level connections with many governments, especially the U.S. He was a problem."

"It is understandable that CIA wanted as much distance from his abduction as possible, is it not?"

Karlov was silent.

"Our agreed protocols allowed lethal force if either side was followed from our meet. We violated the protocols by following Digger. I was not consulted about that."

"Yakov...."

"Yes. Digger's team could have killed him. They did not, but I think we may have developed a credibility deficit."

"What's your point?"

"This might not be the best time to be requesting favors from CIA or the Canadians."

"We got a major piece of information from Vogel. Something unexpected. A crucial situation is developing on the Mexico side of the U.S. border. It is something potentially adverse to both Russia and America. Unfortunately, Russia can't address it directly."

"Why should Digger, much less the CIA, want to help us?"

"An excellent question. Would it help if we gave the Americans full access to Vogel so they could interrogate him directly?"

"Is he in condition to be interrogated?"

Karlov nodded. "Perfect condition. Fully cooperative. In good health."

That surprised me. "Full access?"

"Yes, but in Russia, on our soil. We can run the logistics through their embassy in Moscow. Diplomatic immunity for a small number of CIA agents to interrogate Vogel."

"What about our records of his interrogations?"

"Tapes and transcripts, but only on matters that involve America."

I was impressed. Such authority could only come from Putin himself.

"Well?"

"I can make the offer. I have no idea if Digger, much less his CIA contacts, would agree."

Karlov said, "Good."

"What about the 'adverse situation,' the one you said Russia can't handle directly? Am I to raise that now?"

"Definitely not. It would make your negotiations much more difficult."

I thought for a moment. "Do I get to know what type of help we are seeking?"

Karlov was silent for a time. Finally, he said, "Yes, I think you do need to factor that in. You should know. You must hold the information in strict confidence."

"Of course."

"It is necessary to liquidate a small number of American traitors. This must be done in a way that gets international attention. We need bodies. Pictures in the Russian and Western media. It is imperative that there be no hint of Russian involvement."

"How many bodies?

"A small number. Two or three perhaps. No Russian presence."

"This doesn't sound overly difficult, Sir. What is it that you are **not** telling me?"

"This is just between us, my little Sparrow. We don't know the names of these traitors yet. We do know the parameters."

"I'm listening."

"They will be high level American officials. Some, perhaps all, will be members of Congress."

"Can we discover their names?"

"Not without a risk of leaving footprints or raising questions. It's not worth it. We do not need their names until after their, ah, unfortunate demise."

"How will Digger know?"

He smiled. I was seeing the Karlov of legend. "He will know. **It will become obvious to him.**"

"The obvious question is **why**. If you expect me to inspire action, what might get my contact, who is presumably dubious, to willingly take an active role?"

"You can be most persuasive, my little Sparrow. Digger and his CIA contacts are bound to be curious."

I shook my head. "Curious, yes. Access to the Vogel take will interest them, but I doubt it could inspire an assassination. It's not the CIA's style. It's certainly not anything the Canadians would sanction."

Karlov was smiling. He handed me a picture. "This will work magic."

The picture was dated May 3, 2016. It depicted several men in dark business suits and a dumpy older woman in dark glasses and a pants suit. The Hispanic man on the front right was vaguely familiar. He seemed to be the focus.

I shook my head. "It's an old picture. What am I looking at?"

"A payoff made in the runup to America's 2016 Presidential election. The person on the right front is Mexican President Pena. The rest are high-level U.S. officials. The woman was, at the time, the Speaker of The House, the third most powerful official in the U.S. government.

"The person offering the bribe is not in the photo. The sum paid was $100 million in cash."

"Who paid the bribe? One of the drug cartels?"

"Correct. The cartel run by El Chapo, formally known as a Mr. Guzman. It was the most powerful cartel at the time. Guzman is now serving a life sentence in a Super Max prison in Colorado."

"How do we know this?"

"El Chapo testified to it under oath during his trial. Technically that money was paid to President Pena, but it's reliably reported that at least $25 million went to the Americans in the picture. On top of that, American officials got campaign donations and other incentives."

"Why do we care?"

"We did not care at the time. Russia was investing with similar objectives. The common goal was to keep the U.S. border open and porous for drugs, weapons, human trafficking and the like. The KGB office in Mexico City was one of our largest. Under FSB, it still is."

"I don't understand, Sir."

"Under El Chapo, the Sinaloa cartel was the largest and most powerful in Mexico. Its dominance was fading even before his arrest – he was betrayed, of course – and there are now several competing cartels. His sons still run Sinaloa with an iron hand, but they have major competition.

"For the most part, his sons and their rivals have accepted Russia's accommodation with Sinaloa. We all want open borders and to weaken America. It has been no great cost to Russia to support the cartels, and there has been benefit."

I was paying close attention. "So, what's the problem? Why the need to assassinate U.S, officials?"

"Cuba. Most say it was Reagan and Star Wars that ended the Cold War and the USSR, but the reality is that Cuba drained us. Cuba bankrupted us. Star Wars was just the last straw."

That was hard to believe. "Really?"

"An embarrassing fact, but true. When Putin visited Cuba in 2014, he officially wrote off Cuba's $32 billion in Soviet-era debt. The debt was, in reality, much larger. We supported that dismal country for 50-plus years with little to show for it.

"We stopped our support when the USSR collapsed and Cuba turned to Venezuela. Now both Cuba and Venezuela are failed states. It's a mess, but Cuba holds the levers of power in Venezuela. Havana needs Venezuela to run Columbian cocaine to the U.S. and to Africa to supply Europe. It also depends on cut-rate Venezuelan petroleum.

"We've had an understanding with the cartels for decades. They can plunder and traffic all they want, damage America as they wish, but they need to respect Russia's interests."

"What specific interests are of concern to you?"

"It is crucial that Russia does not surrender our lead role in Cuba to anyone, not to the cartels, not to Venezuela, not to any locals. That has been our understanding with the cartels."

I nodded slowly. "Russia is concerned that our role is fading, that our influence is weakening."

Karlov said, "Yes, and more than that. Russia is constrained both economically and militarily. We walk a tightrope. President Putin does not seek war with the U.S. He does not want to provoke them to reassert the Monroe Doctrine that banned foreign influence in this Hemisphere for centuries. He does not want another Cuban Missile crisis."

"Of course not."

"Putin does not want to go back to the old status quo. Supporting Cuba sunk the USSR. We are weaker now. Russia's bearing the economic drain of Cuba plus Venezuela would be disastrous."

"Can you say that more succinctly?"

"Russia dominant. Cuba constrained and controlled. The same with Venezuela, plus Russian access to the revenue stream from its abundant natural resources to recoup what we've invested. No China presence. No political disruption of our interests or client states by the drug cartels. We want them dependent on us, not the other way around."

I took a deep breath. "That's a long list."

"Yes."

"I assume the action item, the reason we're here today, is to control the cartels."

Karlov smiled. "You are perceptive, my little Sparrow. The information we got from Vogel concerns a smaller cartel, one that is ascendant. Its operations have been limited to parts of Texas, but it is expanding. The golden plum is control of access to the Sanctuary State of California."

"What is the name of this cartel?"

"*Los Serpientes.*"

"I've never heard of them."

"They have been expanding. The most violent of the cartels was the Zetas. No longer."

"I presume *Los Serpientes* does not support Russian interests or the status quo."

"Not in the least. We sent an emissary to negotiate with them. *Los Serpientes* sent back his head in a box. They are animals."

I blinked. "What are your orders?"

"Simply this: To get Digger and his American friends to reengage with you, in return for access to the Vogel take and access to him for interrogation. That's the start, the tactical objective. Get them talking."

"That might be possible."

"Good. Along the way, when the time is right, give your contact a copy of the payoff picture. It's public information, available on the Internet. Mention *Los Serpientes*. Play it soft. Offer nothing. Ask them if they know anything."

I smiled. "A reluctant virgin?"

"Less," he said. "Softer. More like a helpful friend who is embarrassed at how poorly we handled things in the past. Tell him you might be able to provide the time and location of a coming meet with American officials to deliver a massive bribe to a cartel. Say we think history might be repeating."

"I can do that."

"One more thing. Keep your information soft. Make sure that under no circumstances Russia has any direct involvement with that payoff meeting."

"Yes, Sir."

"I need to make that part clear. Under no circumstances are you to take direct action. You will not attend the meeting with *Los Serpientes*, not under any circumstances."

"No hint of Russian involvement. I understand."

Karlov shook his head. "I'm not sure you do. No Russian involvement is the strategic imperative, but there are also tactical and perceptual issues. I don't want you or any of our assets anywhere near the meeting to deliver the bribe. If it goes wrong, and we intend to make it go wrong, retaliation from *Los Serpientes* is certain."

"You don't want to get my head in a box?"

"Let me put it this way," Karlov said. "Should your contact or any of his associates choose to attend that meeting, it's likely they won't be available to us in the future."

"You don't want us blamed if Western agents or assets are lost. There may be blowback. You don't want FSB or Russia implicated."

"Correct. You may lose some contacts. Such a loss is acceptable to me, but I don't want there to be any misunderstandings on America's or Canada's part. You can supply information and express a helpful attitude, but whatever happens – or does not happen – at that meeting is not Russia's responsibility in any way. You are under explicit orders to not go anywhere near that meet."

"If it comes up, may I express my concern about this operational restriction?"

"Specifically, what are you suggesting?"

"The simplest thing is the truth. I'll just say we are staying distant. I'll allude to getting our emissary's head in a box."

Karlov thought for a long moment. "Approved. That is clever. A cautionary remark like that would be repeated and remembered. It would be useful for helping to ensure that Russia is isolated and insulated from future consequences."

CHAPTER NINE
SORTING IT OUT

Patrick AFB, Florida, Private Office, Next Day, Late Morning

Yesterday had almost ended in disaster. An encounter with a freak wave swamped the boat during high speed tests. Commander Bromley and Will had been injured and evacuated to medical facilities. Rudy and Terry came limping back into port, with the boat minus its windshield, radio antennas, radar mast, and everything loose on deck.

Terry's iPad, used to document the speed runs, was somewhere at the bottom of the ocean. The huge wave put the boat completely under water. Somehow the engines kept running. The bilge pumps were still going when they pulled into harbor and docked.

Raven had been on the phone most of the morning sorting out details. Millie and her watcher teams in California, rumor control in DC, and trying get some clear space off the grid for time with Josie.

At present, he was talking with Goldfarb and Mike, calming them down, trying to get everyone on the same page.

Raven said, "The speed tests were successful. Terry and Rudy both saw 55 knots and accelerating before the incident. They were only at 90% power because they are still breaking in the new engines. Flat out in a calm sea, the boat should be good for 60 knots."

"You have an odd definition of successful...."

"The boat is fine, Mike."

"Define what that means. Is it operational?"

"No, of course not. Minor repairs are needed. So are upgrades. The engines and hull are in good shape. It was a test run. We learned some things. That's why we do tests. It's sorting out."

Mike said, "What kind of upgrades?"

"Restraints for the crew. Higher capacity bilge pumps. Antennas that won't tear loose. A shatterproof, bulletproof windscreen. Things like that."

"Electronics? Counter measures?"

I said, "We've not even started on the ECM. Will wants restricted items. The Navy wouldn't discuss it until the boat was a go."

"What does Will say? Is **he** operational?"

"I think so. He is on his way over here now. The doctors released him. He's bruised and sore, but no permanent damage. Do you want me to have him give you a detailed report?"

"No. Not if he's on it. What about the Navy?"

"Good question. My priority today, assuming I can get off the phone, is to get my ass over to the Hospital and talk with Commander Bromley. The doctors said I could see him this afternoon. He is off the critical list, but they're still running tests."

"Do you have any details?"

"Just from when he was admitted. Broken leg. A concussion. Some stiches. He hit his head and swallowed a lot of water. Will landed on top of him. That's all I know."

Goldfarb said, "Limited to the Cuba mission, what do you need?"

I gave a snort. "The big things? The obvious. A safe house, a presence in Havana, a target, and the approval to proceed."

"Is it really that bad?"

"Worse. Everything is watched. Everyone is a watcher. Not just the *apparatchiks*, secret police, security, and counter-intelligence, Cuba has been hard core Communist since the 70s. The most dangerous people are neighbors, workers, even the old women who sweep the streets.

"Want an example?"

Goldfarb said, "Sure."

"I thought I had a safe house. Just for me. Checked, double checked, and ran CSRs like the Devil himself was watching. Watched the place for days. I used all my skills."

"So?"

"When we finally got COM, Josie told me there was a Cuban intelligence officer I missed. A mistake like that when we're operational means I'm dead, my team is dead, and the mission is a total disaster."

"What are you saying?"

"This is a NO GO without poison pills and at least one safe house we can count on."

"Your safe house floats, Raven. If you go kinetic, a hot egress seems likely."

"I damn sure hope not, but taking a missile from a gunboat is a better way to go than being tortured to death by PNR security."

Mike said, "*Policía Nacional Revolucionaria.* Stasi was more ruthless than the KGB. PNR is more ruthless than the FSB. Interrogators for Communist client states tend to be more brutal then those of their masters."

I said, "It would be freaking wonderful if we had dependable support from the Navy."

Goldfarb said, "I agree. We're working on it. Is there anything else?"

"More Intel on Cuba. Better targeting. Deep cover agents in place, people not connected in any way with my OP, who know the ground, who have local sources. Can you check with the cousins?"

"We are. Given your cover, we reached out through Canadian Intelligence to our other Five Eyes partners. MI6 might have something. They won't discuss it with anyone but me, only in a SCIF, and in person.

"That should cover Cuba. We have a stalled OP. We need to fix that. Can we now talk about California and the Russians?"

"The Russians acknowledged my message. Our meet is on for Sunday. Is Josie on her way here?"

Mike said, "She'll be there with you in time for dinner."

"Thank you. How about I have Will call you after we talk? And that I call you after Bromley has spoken with his Admiral?"

"That works."

"One last thing. I may need to hang on to your airplane for a bit. We might be here for a day or two.

"The Russians want something. Whatever the Hell it is, I'll come to DC and brief you both when I know something. Just make sure my Digger legend is righteous with the Canadians. FSB excels at spy games."

"They do indeed. I've checked, Raven. You are solid at that end. Canada is keeping a low profile. They have their own issues with Vogel."

Interesting. "Did we agree to share the Russian take from Vogel with Canada?"

Goldfarb said, "Officially the Canadians, your unacknowledged masters, are irate about Vogel's clumsy abduction from their soil. You are not apprised of any agreements or understandings except for the CIA getting access. So far there has been nothing to share."

Goldfarb had cut a backdoor deal. One that would be denied by both governments. I had wondered about that.

I smiled. "Noted. I'll mention the tragic lack of communication when I meet with them."

"They will expect you to focus on that."

"Yes," I said. "Something else must have caused them to want the meet."

"Absolutely," Mike said. "The bear has a burr up his butt."

"Play it soft," Goldfarb said. "Your focus is on their unfulfilled agreement. Your Canadian masters and their Agency friends are less than happy. Let the Russians disclose their hidden agenda if they choose."

"And if they don't choose?"

Mike and Goldfarb both said, "Walk away."

"Wilco."

"We're all on the same page," Mike said. "Millie checked in. She will have her watchers in place well before your meet."

"The same protocols and locations as last time?"

"Correct. I'll personally verify that you have adequate security for your meet, including egress. Good luck."

Patrick AFB, Florida, Base Hospital, Early Afternoon

I eased the door open, not wanting to wake him if he'd dozed off. "Is this a good time?"

Commander Bromley was propped up in bed. He had the head elevated. White sheets, white bandages, and looking a bit the worse for wear. His right leg was elevated.

"Come in. I've been expecting you."

I came in slowly, studying him. He was sporting a black eye and his head was bandaged. He was squinting a bit.

"Can I get you anything?"

"I lost my glasses when the boat went under. They are getting my spares from the ship, but it may be a while. There is a pair of dark glasses over there in the drawer…."

Bromley gestured vaguely. I fetched his glasses, aviator style Ray-Bans, handed them over, and pulled up a chair to the side of his bed. We looked at each other for a moment. I was trying to think of what to say. My bedside manner was a bit rusty.

Finally, I said, "You look like Tom Cruise…."

"The day after he lost Goose?"

"Something like that. How are you feeling?"

"Pretty much like shit. No pain meds. They want to see if I'm alert."

"Are you?"

"I must be. It hurts everywhere…."

I said, "Do you want to talk about it?"

"Sure do. The first thing I want to say is that your team saved my ass. The boat pretty much went under. At first, I thought sure we were going to roll, but the big black guy at the helm made the right moves."

"Rudy…."

"Yeah. Rudy. He's got a lot of quick."

"He does. Was a star linebacker at U. of Texas. The pros were interested, but he did Marine Force Recon instead."

Bromley said, "I gave the order and Rudy yanked the helm over.

"I was airborne when we hit the wave square. We took it on the bow and it broke over us. We were taking white water down the whole length of the boat. I saw the windscreen tear loose. Rudy was still in the Captain's chair keeping us straight.

"About then I went head-first into something. That's the last thing I remember. The Doctor said that I'd stopped breathing. One of your guys got me going again, got me breathing...."

"Terry. He's our combat medic.

"He said the transom was barely above water. He laid you there, face down, and worked to clear your lungs. He said you'd swallowed a lot of water.

"Rudy and the bilge pumps managed to keep things afloat. He got off a Mayday and the Navy sent a rescue copter. They brought you and Will here."

"Will. Yes, we collided. I remember.... How is he?"

"Battered around the edges, but back at work." I smiled in spite of myself.

"What?"

"Will keeps talking about his engines and how well the boat performed."

"The engines were still running?"

"Yes. Rudy and Terry brought the boat back in under its own power."

"Is Will around? I need to speak with him."

"Are you up to that? He's out in the lobby."

"Yes. It's important. Please get him."

Will and I returned to Commander Bromley's room. The two exchanged a look and shook their heads.

"One Hell of a ride," Bromley said.

"It was. How are you feeling?"

"Sore, but I'll heal. The docs say I'm going to be out in a few days. How about you?"

"Pretty much the same." Will looked at Bromley's elevated leg. "Sorry about that. I came down on top of you. Went airborne when we slid off the swell down into the big wave. The whole front of the boat went under. We were buried back to the windshield.

"It broke over us. I wasn't sure we'd come back up."

Bromley said, "The engines and pumps kept running. How did you manage that?"

"A trick they use on aircraft. Alternate air doors. Rudy pulled the red lever before we hit. Good call on the helm order, Commander. Taking the wave head on saved us."

"Alternate air. Cute trick."

"We were lucky."

The two were silent for a time. I didn't interrupt. I'd not been there. This was their moment, not mine.

Finally, Bromley spoke. "I want to share some good news with you. Needed to see how your boat would perform first. It's fiendish fast. Probably 60 knots at full power and with a smooth sea."

Will nodded. "Yes."

"Given that, I think we'll get good support from the Admiral." Bromley looked at me. "How secure are we?"

I said, "Reasonably. It's a military hospital, plus the Navy put Marine guards on this floor. They checked our IDs."

"Here's the deal. No tasking yet, but probably the Lincoln battle group will be deploying to the Mideast to guard the oil lanes and keep Iran honest. That's the scuttlebutt. Keep it to yourself."

Will and I nodded.

"The Iranians use small boats to guard the Straits of Hormoz. An expendable little boat at close range can threaten one of our billion-dollar blue water ships. That sucks. The Admiral wants better options."

"I expect he does."

"I had one short conversation. I think we can get more Navy support for your project.

Bromley gestured at his elevated leg. "I'm not going be climbing any ladders or standing duty for a few weeks. I'm likely looking at two options. Medical leave, or a detached assignment to help militarize your toy boat."

Will was grinning. "Florida interlude. Balmy cruises with your civilian buddies...."

"Civilian my ass," Bromley said. "I plan to get some line warships to chase you around and give you some stress tests if you're interested. Training exercises. Working your asses off...."

"We're defensive only. Just trying to escape and survive."

"You'd be surprised," Bromley said. "We have some kick-ass smart weapons that can eat Osas and Iranian attack boats. I want to explore if boats like yours can help us target them."

Will looked at me. "This is a win-win, Raven. We need to break-in our engines, do upgrades, make repairs, and get some countermeasures working.

"I'll need your floating safe house along with Rudy and Terry for a few weeks anyway."

I looked at Commander Bromley. He nodded.

I said, "Sure. Why not?"

Will said, "You'll clear it with Mike?"

"Consider it done. Call him now. Tell him I'll be checking in. Anything else?"

"We have a name for the boat. It fits the cover story. *Busted Flush*."

"Huh?"

"The cover is that Rudy won the boat in a poker game. We have witnesses to back that up, including in the local paper."

I said, "Credible witnesses?"

Will laughed. "Not particularly, Raven. The tale fits Rudy's legend. Most will assume that a fast boat like this is used for smuggling."

"The story is bullshit?"

"Pretty much, but with a grain of truth. Perfect for the rumor mill. It's like creating a legend for an operative, it's layered to deflect attention. Boat people love sea stories like that...."

I frowned. "That's pretty thin if a Cuban intelligence officer digs into it, Will."

"The next level is better and true. The boat we purchased was already named the *Busted Flush*. It had belonged to a minor author who was a big fan of Travis McGee. That's a well-known character name in the publishing industry. It comes from a popular series of novels."

"Never heard of him...."

"Travis McGee is a fictional character, created by American mystery writer John D. MacDonald. Unlike most detectives in mystery/detective fiction, McGee is neither a police officer nor a private investigator; instead, he is a self-described 'salvage consultant' who recovers others' property for a fee of 50%. He lives on a boat, the Busted Flush."

"Never heard of him either."

"That's your loss, Raven. You need to get out more. John D. MacDonald was one of the top names in the industry. Sold something over 70 million books. He lived in Florida. MacDonald died years ago, but if you search for the name of the boat, you get endless pages about him, his boat, replica boats, and more."

"Boat people would fondly remember the *Busted Flush?*"

"Yes, they would. MacDonald actually had a boat of that name. He kept it at the Bahia Mar Resort in Slip F18, Ft. Lauderdale, Florida, just like in his novels.

"The marina has long since been remodeled and gone upscale, so all that remains is a plaque and a memory. The *Busted Flush* is a name that resonates with boat people. It fits right in."

I said, "What if someone checks the paperwork?"

"Rudy is the owner of this one. Funds paid from an offshore bank, taxes and fees paid, all squeaky clean. Part of the mission support we get from Mike's company, TSG. Have you ever had a problem with that?"

"No."

Bromley said, "Whoever can win a boat that way has a stupid opponent. The odds of filling a five-card flush, given you have four, are only about 19.5%. Rudy had an 80% chance of winning."

"Not a problem. It makes the story better," Will said.

"It probably does. Here's to stupid opponents. Let's see if you can get us better odds, Commander."

"80% is pretty good odds...."

I looked at Bromley and took a breath. Will was starting to say something, but he stopped at my hand gesture.

"You've had a rough day, Commander. I don't want to make it worse, but I do have a question."

Bromley nodded.

"Have you ever lost one of your people in combat?"

He shook his head. "No."

"Have you ever had to leave one of your people behind?"

"No."

"I have. It's something that you never forget.

"Cuba scares the shit out of me. Why I'm here, the **only** reason I'm here, is to do everything that I can to make sure my people get back safely from what promises to be a bitch of a mission.

"Some of the worst fights of my life have occurred during egress. Do you know why?"

"No."

I said, "It's the end game. *Winner take all.* If we do our mission and escape, we live. If not, we die, or worse. For the other side, it's similar. If the bad guys let us escape, their leaders will be shot, demoted, or punished, sometimes in creative ways.

"In such a situation, all you can do is to fight as long as you can and as hard as you can. We can expect to be vastly outnumbered and outgunned during egress, unless we are lucky, fast, or both.

"Do you see where I'm going with this, Commander?"

"Yes, Sir," Bromley said. "I do."

"Good. Your help would be greatly appreciated."

"We'll do our best."

CHAPTER TEN
COMING HOME

Patrick AFB, Florida, On the Tarmac, Late Afternoon

Until now, Raven had only seen pictures of the Aerion jet. It was beautiful in flight, but this one looked awkward, coming in slowed down and nose high on final approach. It was obviously on the ragged edge of its flight envelope.

The old Concord jets were so nose high on approach that the nose had to be drooped 12.5 degrees so the pilots could see to land. The droop snoot had four positions and was much discussed in aviation circles. *You had to hand it to the Brits, their engineers were, ah, unconventional....*

So were Aerion's. No droop snoot here, but it was also an unusual airplane. It looked like a sharpened pencil, 170 feet long, with a cluster of three engines and short, straight, stubby wings slightly to the aft of the middle. It was painted in Aerion white with a red accent stripe running the full length, a theme which was carried up into the engines and the top half of the aft fuselage.

Raven gave Mike's new plane an A plus for speed, but a D minus for blending in. Good for impressing people and repositioning assets, but there was no taking this one anywhere near denied access areas, at least not with him on board. *Best to stick to major airports and military bases.*

The normal trip time from NY for a jet was about two hours and thirty minutes. This one had just cut it in half, over some of the busiest airspace in America and into the wind.

Josie was here. God, he'd missed her. Raven wasn't used to missing people, except for the spirits of friends lost on busted missions. Ghosts came to him in the night, sometimes in dreams, sometimes in memories when he was out in the deep dark hunting.

Their relationship was uplifting, but complicated. He and Josie were a unique pairing, a situation where polar opposites complimented each other, where one plus one equaled something much larger than two. *They had never been separated for so long.*

They had bonded on their first mission together, alien creatures who each found that being with the other filled an empty void deep within them. Josie once said, "If two lie down together, they will keep warm. But how can one keep warm alone?"

The cold Josie spoke of wasn't measured in degrees. It was the deep, dark cold of the soul, a nightmare land where monsters hunted, an alternate universe far from the gentleness and structure that normal people knew, a harsh land that showed no pity for weakness, no softness.

The notion that good versus evil was an eternal conflict was fading from our racial memory. It was being erased. Few thought the dark alternate reality of yore really existed. Josie was unique. She **knew** it did.

She could sense evil. She could find monsters, know their plans, and see the horrific consequences of the wickedness that corrupted people and wrecked civilizations. All deals with the Devil traded wealth, power, and gratification for eternal damnation.

Josie wasn't alone, not quite. Those who studied history sensed that the customs, institutions, and religions that defended Western Civilization were failing. The difference was that Josie **knew** it wasn't normal or accidental.

Decline was purposeful. Humans were given free will, and some in power had embraced evil. There was a darkness on the land. Throughout history that cycle had repeated.

A few visionaries and writers argued Hell was empty and that all the demons were here. Josie didn't know if that was true or not. She did know that darkness was spreading. She'd seen it before in a previous life. She'd lived it millennia ago as a Celtic Priestess.

She could sense things across time and space, things that had happened and probability lines of things that could happen, but she was a gentle creature of light. Darkness and violence would destroy her.

Raven's world was a universe away from the love, warmth, and brightness of hers. His was a place that Western moderns and governments liked to pretend no longer existed except in echoes of ancient Western myth and the Old Testament. Josie could view it. Raven lived it. His was a world of monsters and violence, the place where good and evil collided.

His reality had razor-sharp edges. Orwell said, "People sleep peaceably in their beds at night only because rough men stand ready to do violence on their behalf," but that was only part of it.

Special operators are rough in the sense that they ruthlessly do what needs to be done, but they're also required to be extremely smart. Their survival depends on stealth, their ability to take calculated risks, and their knowing how to rearrange everything they've been taught.

In such a world, Raven was an apex predator. Repeatedly, Josie had found malignant evil. After Raven eliminated it, the future became just a notch brighter for those who loved peace and freedom. At least twice they'd saved the President's life.

They'd planned to come in out of the cold together, to share warmth, to have normal lives. Years had passed. They were still out in the cold, but not alone. Their being together made it better.

Being together helped to keep them sane. It gave them purpose, filled their empty spaces, and made them whole. It could also destroy them.

Sooner or later, it would. They knew that. Freedom wasn't free.

"Hi, Babe," Raven said, putting his arms around her. They were alone, sitting on the long couch that lined the left side of the Aerion, soft brown leather. John Black and the factory pilot who was training him had gone to get the rental car.

They were home. It wasn't a place; it was being together. Josie laid her head on his shoulder, hugging him tightly. "I missed you…."

"Yeah. Been too long…."

She remembered the long-ago night in Durham, the first time Raven had saved her life. Monsters hunted Josie because of her talents. He'd saved her, but he'd left a trail of dead bodies and a peaceful neighborhood in flames.

She raised her head, accepting his kiss. *She knew this man, not just in her heart, also in her soul. Two millennia ago, she'd watched him die defending her temple from Roman Legions under Gaius Julius Caesar, a lance in his side and his broken sword buried in the chest of a Roman Centurion.*

"Cuba was horrible," she said. "I couldn't be with you. I couldn't come to you. I saw danger everywhere. I couldn't even warn you, much less guide you."

"I knew it, Babe. Without you I wasn't sure what to do about it. I concentrated on keeping a low profile."

Josie said, "I know what to do."

I blinked. "You do?"

Josie nodded. "Yes."

I pondered that for a moment, surprised. Finally, I said, "Good."

Josie shook her head slowly. She heaved a deep sigh.

"When?" I said, feeling myself tense. "Tonight?"

"Tonight. We have a narrow path and a tight time line. We need to get a car for ourselves."

"Why?"

"We are going to have a nice Cuban dinner and meet some new friends. Tomorrow, you need to be in California."

I had never seen her so certain, so grim. "You're sounding like Goldfarb."

"I hate it too," she said. "I'll brief you after dinner."

"Is there danger?"

"Not tonight, but soon. I don't like the futures I'm seeing."

She's afraid for me. I didn't want to dwell on that.

I said, "When do we get some down time together?"

"Tomorrow at the Ranch. All day. All night. Maybe longer."

"Can't beat that, Babe. New friends, good food, and a hot date."

There was a sadness in her eyes I'd not seen before. *Best not to poke at it now.*

Cape Canaveral, Florida, Vargas Cafe, Evening

It was just off A1A, a little hole in the wall with a sign that said, "Home of Florida's Greatest Cuban Sandwich." No brag, just fact, as testified by the highest 5-star rating in the area.

We walked in. There were only four or five tables, plus some counter seats. The owner was singing, and the customers were laughing and telling stories. I felt myself relax.

It was a local place where everyone knew each other. They were happy. It was nothing like Havana. Good vibes. Freedom. Safety. A piece of the old America.

Still, I made sure we were seated in a corner, backs to the wall, where we could see the door. Old habits die hard.

Josie said, "The owners are Luis Estrada and his wife Rosa. Cuban refugees who made it out during the Obama years when travel restrictions were relaxed. Both are now American citizens and they thank God they made it out. They have two children, a girl in college and a boy in the Marines."

"Okay," I said.

"Rosa is *Santeria*. She is gifted."

"I have no idea what you're talking about."

"Think of Voodoo. Think of the Pagan religions."

I smiled. "Pagan like you, Celtic, a high priestess."

"Long ago. We worshiped intellect and nature, long before Christianity or Judaism existed.

"Voodoo is common in Cuba. It is centered in Haiti, quite close, where it is the primary religion. It's nasty. Sacrifices, curses, and the like. It came from Nigeria, imported by slaves who saw it as the only hope of freedom from their oppressors. It's dark, dangerous cult. Basically, they worship demons."

"If you can't beat them in battle, you can curse them into Hell or scare them into making mistakes…."

Josie nodded. The Celts had never been conquered, but they had been annihilated, their culture erased by Roman Legions.

"*Santeria* is a cult and it can be dark, but it's not Voodoo. The word means 'honor of the Saints' or 'way of the saints.' It's primitive, but was shaped by Spanish Catholicism. Those who practice it worship and honor Catholic saints. Spanish rule was harsh. It erased cultures that were more advanced, but lacked the weapons of guns, germs, and steel."

"Was *Santeria* also started by slaves?"

"Yes, by desperate people with little to lose."

"*Santeria* was their way to survive, to blend in, to appeal to the higher instincts of the slave masters?"

"In part, but also to be tolerated by the Voodoo cult. They were trying to survive, to live in peace."

"A little Voodoo, some Rosary beads, and maybe they'll leave us alone?"

Josie frowned. "Something like that...."

"Why are we talking about *Santeria*? What's your point?"

"Rosa is a paranormal. I found a way to communicate with her. She's been expecting us. She knew people like us would come to her, because her Saints told her."

"Why do we care?"

"I care."

"Why?"

"Because we need **you** to survive. I need you to survive."

"Keep talking."

"I can't go to Cuba with you."

"No, of course not."

"Can you operate in Cuba?"

"We can operate anywhere. We can get our mission done, Josie."

She was looking intently into my eyes. "Don't do that to me, Raven."

"Do what?"

"We are joined. We are one. If you die, so do I. I will not forgive you for committing a heroic suicide, no matter how noble. Not ever. You and I will have the rest of eternity in Hell to argue about it."

"I can get the mission done."

"We don't lie to each other either. I know you, Raven. Can you and your team, unsupported, hope to pull off a major attack in Havana and survive?"

Her eyes were burning me. I had to look down. I couldn't face those eyes.

"Your men will follow you. Do you plan to get them killed too? Along with yourself, us, and eventually me?"

Finally, I said, "No."

It was not easy being in love with a paranormal.

Josie said, "Rosa has an invisible network in Havana, deep down, so far down and so normal that the secret police can't see them. They have no weapons or technology, but they blend in. They can be your watchers, your eyes, the guides along your escape route."

I looked up. "Who?"

"Her family. Her aunts and cousins."

"Safe houses?"

Josie said, "What do you think?"

"I think, no. That would get them killed. We'll have to bring our own weapons and handle egress."

"Correct. You were planning on that anyway, were you not?"

I nodded.

"Will it work?"

"It could. That's the plan. We're trying to refine it."

"Good," she said. "Do you know why we're here?"

"Yeah. I do now."

"Good. We're going to have nice dinner. They will close at eight. Luis and I will clean up. You and Rosa will talk alone in the back room. What happens next is her call."

"You're the paranormal. Can you see the outcome?"

Josie smiled. "You're going to love the Cuban Sandwich. Finish it with an order of maduros and expresso and it will be a night you'll remember."

"My meeting with Rosa?"

Josie shook her head. "I don't know."

"What can you see?"

"Nothing useful. It's a nexus. All I can see is a gray probability fog. That outcome depends on you, my love."

"And if Rosa trusts me…."

"Yes. That too."

"What does she want?"

"The same thing that I wanted before I met you: to avoid evil, to live in peace. Now I know we have to resist it. She's coming to the same realization. Rosa has loved ones in Cuba at risk.

"She hopes you can make it safer for them, for Cubans. If not, she hopes we can at least get the loved ones at risk out of the country. Her mother needs health care that she can't get in Cuba."

I said, "Ain't socialism great?"

"Can we help her?"

"Maybe. If we can pull off a mission in Havana, there will be gratitude at high levels. America will owe those who helped us."

"But maybe not?"

I sighed. "Remember Durham?"

"Yes," Josie said. "We finally did get support. She'll know that too. She's a paranormal. Her Saints will tell her."

"So, what do I tell her?"

"The truth, as much as you can. Tell her that you and I will do our best to get what she needs. Can you promise her that?

I nodded. "Sure. Anything else?"

"Don't lie to her."

"I never lie to a paranormal, Babe. It would just piss her off."

Josie smiled. "It sure would and don't you **ever** forget that."

CHAPTER ELEVEN
DENIED ACCESS

The White House, Morning, Next Day

We were seated in the small SCIF, the one closest to the room where the National Security Council met. At present it was just Mike and Goldfarb. Waiting.

Goldfarb said, "They still have me listed as an advisor to the NSC, Mike. It gives us an excuse to be here without undue curiosity."

Mike shrugged. "Why are we here? Nothing on my plate is hot at present."

"Other than dunking an Admiral's weapons officer, a stalled mission in Cuba, and you getting ready to have Raven poke the Bear again?"

"We're trying to get our shit together. No crisis. No active OPS at present. We are assessing the situation. Preparing plans. Gathering intelligence about things that the White House and NSC specifically want to avoid.

"I have nothing to report. Do you?"

Goldfarb didn't reply.

I said, "You are the one who wanted the Bear poked. The Cuba OP may not even be **possible**. I was planning to report back when we knew something useful."

"Yes. All that is true."

"What are you not telling me?"

Goldfarb sighed. "The President wanted this meeting. Just the three of us. Alone."

"Oh," I said. "Did he say why?"

"He did not. This meeting is not on his official agenda, nor is it on NSC's. He's just going to drop by. It won't be in any logs."

We waited.

The door opened. One of the Secret Service agents, the tall blonde, stuck her head in. "He'll be here in ten minutes. Understood?"

Goldfarb said, "Affirmative, Sally. What else can you tell us?"

"He wants to ask you some questions. No notes. I don't know the topic. When it's over, he'll leave. We'll escort him out. When it's clear, we'll send an agent to escort you out the back way."

"Right."

We started exactly eleven minutes later.

President Blager was wearing a white shirt, no tie or coat, and blue slacks. He waved us down as we started to stand, then seated himself across from us. "I have a problem."

"We're listening, Sir," Goldfarb said.

The President said, "I promised to keep you autonomous, distant, deep black, and off the books. To not involve official Washington. That stands. This is personal, not official."

I said, "Understood. How can we help?"

"I'm not getting what I need from the Intel agencies."

Goldfarb said, "I've been in the game since the Cold War, Sir. Most Presidents I served under had similar complaints."

"Not to this level. I'm drowning in data, but starving for information.

"I get satellite images so clear you can see the serial numbers on aircraft and ships. Most every communication in the world is monitored in real time. But we still don't have useful actionable intelligence to help me make decisions along the invasion route up from Venezuela.

"Most of the people at CIA never leave the damn building. The leadership has recovered from the days of Brennan and Clapper, but we lack covert human assets in the field. The HUMINT I see is mostly rumors from embassy parties or taken from 3rd parties of dubious loyalty."

I said, "Our military Intel is better, Sir. Many of today's enemies used to be our allies. We still have some good sources."

"Very few in denied access areas. Effectively none in Cuba. Some in Venezuela, but all their military units have Cuban minders and we don't have access to that channel. Mexico is better for intelligence collection. We have an embassy there, but that is not where the key decisions are being made."

"True," Goldfarb said. "On top of that, we still have moles and leakers in CIA and State Department. At best, unaccountable Deep State people who don't want a successful America. At worst, traitors."

"It is taking years to clean that end of the swamp. Jimmy Carter created the Senior Executive Service, the SES, and it's all but impossible to fire those people. Also, we have the resistance in Congress. These people take oaths to support the Constitution. Too often the oaths are broken. For a time, even the FBI was corrupted. We're working on it."

Goldfarb said, "Until there is confidence that we can protect them, it's going to be hard to put human assets in the field. If they are blown, they wind up dead, in prison or tortured. Remember when the head of the Senate Intel Committee, Dianne Feinstein, had a Chinese spy for her driver and office manager? We lost all our agents there, he was allowed to retire, and she was never even censured."

"We are aware of the problems. I agree that it is difficult for a free society to run deep cover agents. It's why I've kept your efforts as distant from official Washington as possible. Speaking of that, is Raven's team operational?"

Goldfarb and I exchanged a look. I said, "We're running him through TSG, The Security Group, Mike's company. No government resources are involved. We've done some recon in Cuba, but nothing is as yet operational."

"So, the answer is, 'No'?"

"I've afraid so."

"I'm told we've gotten questions from the Navy. Something about a yacht being damaged. One of their officers was injured. Are you involved in that?"

"Yes. That was Raven's team. Their unarmed civilian boat was damaged off the coast of Florida down near Cape Canaveral. We've been doing some tests in U.S. and international waters. The Navy has been assisting us. There was an accident."

"Did you purchase a yacht with government funds?"

"No, Sir, at least not yet. The boat is owned, at present, by Cybertech, Iron John's company."

Goldfarb interrupted. "This is a fluid and complex situation, Sir. Raven is trying to find a way to go operational along the invasion route with a small team. It is proving to be quite a challenge."

President Blager nodded. "How bad is it?"

Goldfarb said, "Bad. Very bad."

I said, "Raven says it's the worst he's ever seen, Sir. Worse than the old Cold War Soviet era Moscow."

"Based on what?"

"Direct observation. Raven put a team into Havana. He says there is no hope of having a safe house. Everything is watched. He says attempting any kinetic action would be both suicidal and unlikely to succeed."

"How long were they down there?"

"A month. Totally passive. Low profile."

"That long?"

"Yes. Raven wanted to stay longer. We pulled him out."

The President frowned. "Please tell me you didn't put Josie at risk."

"Of course not, Sir," Goldfarb said.

I said, "Josie was nowhere near Cuba, Sir. That made it more challenging. Communications with agents in-country are all but impossible."

"How did they get out?"

"By water. Two of his team on a small fishing boat. We had a submarine extract Raven."

"How would you judge the risk level?"

"Extreme. One slip and we'd lose the whole team. We need to up our game a lot to operate there."

"How?"

"We need embedded assets in place, Sir. We need our own watchers. We need spies, human intelligence assets, in both Cuba and Venezuela.

The President was nodding. "Agreed. That is the problem I wanted to discuss with you."

"We're listening, Sir. Now that Raven and Josie are back together, they will be pondering that."

"First I have some bad news. It's why I made this a face-to-face meeting. I didn't want you to hear what I am about to say second hand, and neither do I want it to get out. I don't want to take any chance of it being leaked."

Goldfarb and I exchanged a look. *WTF?*

When I didn't speak, Goldfarb said, "How widely can we share this?"

"The two of you, of course, plus me, Raven, and Josie. That's all. You don't discuss it with anyone else, no matter what their need-to-know or clearance level. Agreed?"

"Yes, Sir," we chorused.

"I need Raven's team able to operate, able to go kinetic, in both Venezuela and Cuba, but we have an operational constraint, one that both you and they need to clearly understand."

We waited. Finally, Goldfarb said, "We're listening, Sir."

The President took a deep breath, letting it out slowly. "You'll be on your own. Totally."

Goldfarb was frowning. I was puzzled. Raven's team had always been operationally independent. Finally, I said, "I think we need to get this totally clear, Sir. What are you saying, Sir?"

"If you put a team into either of those countries, they will not have official support. If they get into trouble, no one is coming to help them. Raven needs to know that...."

Holy Shit, I thought. *He's not on board at all.*

There was a long silence. Even Goldfarb looked stunned.

Finally, the President said, "This boat thing, the incident that involved the Navy, I assume that has to be some off-the-wall plan for Raven's team to egress."

I said, "Raven expects that a hot egress may be necessary if he goes kinetic. It could be opposed by Cuban military assets. He and his team requested the Navy's advice on that one. The boat is a "live aboard." When in harbor, hooked up to power, you can live there. It's like a floating RV.

The cover is sport fishing. It might also serve as their safe house, at least temporarily."

The President frowned. "Raven's planning to run for open water in a floating RV with the whole damn Cuban military after him?"

"It's a contingency plan, Sir. We're still looking for better options."

"Is the boat fast enough that they have a chance?"

"Possibly. That's part of what they're working on."

Goldfarb said, "I'd like to know more about why we can't support our people when the shit hits the fan, Sir."

"Political constraints. I'm in a box, gentlemen. It's a bit like what Kennedy faced during the Cuban Missile Crisis, but more complicated. Venezuela is the new Syria, a high stakes chessboard for ambitious states. For all practical purposes, Cuba is an extension of Venezuela and vice versa."

We both looked at him.

"Obama set this up. John Kerry erased the Monroe doctrine. This was all a set up for when Hillary took power."

Goldfarb said, "Fortunately, she didn't, Sir. Obama wins polls for being the worst President in history. Kerry is long gone along with the John F. Kennedy Democrats. Post Trump, we are in a new era."

The President shook his head. "I wish that were true. It's not. The deep state is still with us. Broken oaths are common. We have domestic enemies.

"There are no term limits. Much of Congress predates Trump and the Federal Bureaucracies are worse, even after decades of Presidents trying to clean out Washington's Augean Stables. Only Hercules could clean the Stables of the Gods. Mere mortals don't have a chance.

Washington's dysfunctional bureaucrats are protected by **both** parties. Remember when they wanted to impeach Trump for sending an unkind tweet about a disastrous Ambassador, one that he'd **already fired**?"

"American military action in Cuba would inflame most of the opposition party, plus about a third of my own party, the entire Fake News media, the UN, China, Russia, and more. It would also panic many shaky governments in South America. They'd fear that'd we be coming for them next. Our being involved in an active war here could give a green light to hostile actions against us in the Mideast and Europe. Need I go on…?"

It was like the temperature of the room had suddenly dropped to that of a morgue. I made a mental note to refresh my memory of Hercules. Josie would know it. Centuries before the Greeks adopted that legend, the Celts saw Herakles as a God, the son of Zeus, the protector of mankind.

Goldfarb said, "We have zero chance of pulling off a mission if we can't get our assets out. If you lose Raven, you will also will lose Josie. Do you want to risk that?"

The President looked glum. He didn't speak.

I said, "Can you guarantee us any American support after we pull off a kinetic OP in Cuba? Assume that Raven's team takes out some of their key assets. Then they egress, running for International waters, with the American Navy waiting on station."

Goldfarb said, "Good question. Suppose they get clear. What happens then? What if the Cuban military targets American civilians, and perhaps even American military assets in international waters?"

"What do you want to happen?"

"I want us to kill them. If they target our ships or Raven's civilian boat in international waters, we hit them with everything we have. We cover Raven and his team like a blanket once they are clear."

The President was silent for a long moment. Finally, he said, "We warn the enemy *before* we shoot?"

I said, "Sure, why not? Broadcast it in the clear. Send a warning over the hot line. Record it. Then annihilate them and put the tapes up on the news."

"We might be able to do something like that. It's been discussed that we should have special Rules of Engagement for hot spots. Mostly Syria and the Straits of Hormoz have been the focus, but I can see we might want to extend such a policy to the Cuba and Venezuela."

"Can we get a decision and clear ROEs before we put Raven and his team back into Cuba?"

"Yes."

"We have your word on this?"

"You do."

"Thank you, Sir. I'll brief Raven and his team about this discussion."

"This one is a long shot, isn't it?"

I shrugged and looked at Goldfarb.

He said, "Very much so, Sir. It may not be possible."

The President sighed deeply. "One other thing. If Raven and Josie can develop covert support assets outside the agencies, such an effort would have my full support."

"Understood, Sir."

CHAPTER TWELVE
CALIFORNIA DREAMING

The Ranch, Private Estate near Mendocino, California, Next Day

Josie thought it was beautiful. She had fond memories.

The small resident staff called it "the Ranch." It was remote and rustic in the 1960's California style, nestled on the coast near the big Redwoods

The siding was straight-grain Cedar, the roof of low pitch, covered with shakes, and the construction solid with massive roof beams. Their unit was one story, tucked into the steep hillside, with most of its west wall consisting of the large sliding glass door leading to a sheltered deck overlooking the ocean and sweeping lawns far below.

From the soaking tub, they could open a screen and watch the ocean while still being shielded from the view of anyone on the grounds. Most of the main room was taken up by the king-sized bed, but there was a small couch in front of the river-rock, wood-burning fireplace next to the TV. Out on the deck, there were two wooden chairs and a small table to put drinks on.

The deck had a partial roof overhang and a waist-high privacy wall instead of an open railing. The sliding door had two sets of window coverings: translucent blinds for privacy, and opaque blinds for darkness. The glass had been upgraded. It was now bulletproof.

I said, "It's good to be back here."

Raven said, "Yeah. It's been a bitch of a day."

They were both exhausted. It had been a long night with their new Cuban friends, followed by a day that had seemed endless. The local airport was too small for the supersonic Aerion, so they'd dropped off Raven's team near San Francisco, got a car, and drove up. With stops and Raven running CSRs, it had been over four hours.

"Some of my best memories are of being here with you…. Don't you feel that?"

"They put me here right after Durham. It was a dark time for me, Babe."

"Why?"

"Back then, it was a rehab facility for agents with issues. I was one of their last patients. I was trying to heal, worried about you, and in deep shit with my handlers. You were dying and they wouldn't let me see you."

"Right after Durham? While I was in the hospital? *After I shot you?*"

"Yeah."

"You never mentioned that."

Raven gave a small laugh. "Probably not. Too much bad shit going down out there. I tend not to dwell on it."

"We came here together after you saved me. It was a good time for me."

"I have mixed memories."

"How so?"

He shrugged.

I said, "Talk to me. This is where we started. Where we fell in love. Before that, it was just about trying to survive."

"That part was wonderful. It was good. No one was shooting at me and you were safe. We bonded. We came together. You changed my life.

"The place didn't matter. It still doesn't matter. Too many places. They start to blur. This one actually vanished for a time after we left. *Poof.*"

I shook my head. "Vanished?"

"They shut it down, filed bankruptcy, and cleansed the records. A few years later one of the agencies bought the abandoned property. They reopened it under a new cover. Seems we're short of safe houses out here."

I laughed in spite of myself. "I can see why. The last one we had was totally destroyed."

"This one is safe. Low profile and safe. I think we're clean. Do you detect anything?"

"No. We're clean. It feels safe."

"Good." He took a deep breath. "I'm going to have a beer. Do you want anything?"

"You bet. Wine. White and chilled would be nice...."

Raven returned with a stand filled with ice, an open bottle in one hand, and two glasses. "It's from Oregon, a Gold Medal winner. To Hell with the beer, I'll join you." A minute later, he reappeared with a tray of crackers and cheese.

I took a sip. A Pinot Gris 2017 nicely chilled. It was smoother than a Chardonnay, a clean fruity taste, no oak. "Nice. Thank you."

Raven nodded. He put his feet up on the privacy wall, looking out over the sea. The sun was low, and the colors were starting to change.

"You seem distant."

"I'm right here...."

"Ever since Cuba, you've been distant...."

"I'm trying to sort things out."

"Talk to me, Damn it!"

Raven took a deep breath and looked at me. "Maybe we've been at this too long...."

"It's not over."

"No."

"Will it ever be?"

"You know what they say in Country songs...."

"Tell me."

"The road goes on forever, Babe. 'Down every road there's one more city....' That's how it works. It's the nature of things."

"I see things. You're a warrior. We both know that good versus evil is eternal."

"What do you see?"

"It's fuzzy, clouded, but we are making a difference. We make the world a little better, a little safer for normal people. Without what we do, it could get worse."

"For America?"

"For humanity. Most of the futures I see are worse."

"A lot worse?"

I nodded. "Yes. Some we prevented would have been catastrophic. Why?"

"I felt like a bug under a microscope in Cuba. Powerless. Waiting to be squished. One misstep would have been game over. I'm good at this stuff, but all I could do was ramble around and try to stay out of sight. No way we could run an OP.

"Goldfarb pulled me out. The boat plan is our final option, and it's a long shot. Do that or scrub the mission. Just testing it, we almost lost the whole team.

"For two centuries, America put a red line around this hemisphere. *Hands off. Kill each other somewhere else.* Our elected leaders erased that line. Too many in power don't honor their oaths of office."

"Treason," I said. "Broken oaths."

Raven said, "Yes. Exactly what they were talking about in our briefing. John Donne said, 'Oaths once broken, souls cannot be whole....' We suffer broken souls. We have met the enemy and he is us."

"The President took that issue to the Supreme Court. He got a green light...."

"No, Babe. He got an **opinion**. It won't be decided until they charge someone, try the case, win, and execute the bastard. That's a long process.

"Nothing has happened. We've not executed an American citizen as a traitor since the Cold War, not since 1953."

"So why did they brief us about it? About broken oaths?"

Raven shrugged. "Good question. I wondered that myself."

"Maybe it won't be settled by the courts," I said.

"What are you saying...?"

"The Russians want to meet with you. I think it's related."

"That's why Goldfarb pulled me out of Cuba?"

"Maybe. I need to do some viewings."

Campo Turistico La Joya, Maneadero, Mexico.

Ramon did exactly as he was ordered. Alone, paying cash, he took Aero Mexico to Ensenada and taxi #6 to this tiny little camp. The cab driver compared him to a photo on his cell phone, opened the door, threw his bag in the back, and dropped him off at this tiny resort.

They'd not spoken. The driver had refused the fare with a shake of his head.

Maneadero was a tiny, rundown, agricultural town. It didn't have the harsh look of the border towns. It just looked poor. The hotel was new, clean, and it had both power and water. His room was paid, and the desk clerk had a photo of him. The clerk checked it, then handed Ramon a key and a note.

The note said, "5 PM in the bar." It was already past four. Ramon went to his room, showered and put on a fresh shirt. As instructed, he'd brought no weapons.

Being unarmed made him nervous. Meeting the man made him fearful. Miguel Trevino. The boss of bosses. You didn't speak the name.

He'd only spoken with him four times. Once when he was accepted, once after a major fight with a rival cartel, once when he was made a boss, and last week when he been given the assignment to seize and interrogate the Russian, Anatoli Vasilev, in Mexico City.

It had not gone well. The only thing that gave Ramon hope was that he'd been brought to a meeting. If Trevino had been angry, one of his own group would have killed him. That was the way.

They met me in the bar. I recognized the leader, Chico. He'd been a boss before me, but had been promoted and moved to another sector.

Chico said, "It's been a long time, Ramon."

I nodded. "Yes, two years."

Many members didn't live that long.

Chico smiled. "Relax, my friend. We're taking you to a nice place. Get your bag."

That meant nothing. Neither the smile nor the words. *We both knew that what occurred next was entirely up to Mr. Trevino's wishes.*

It took almost an hour to get there, the last part on a dirt road. It was a walled palace with brick walls topped with razor wire, an ornate gate, and a guard post manned by two people with AK-47s. Even though they recognized Chico, we all got out and they inspected the car for bugs, and looked under it with lights and mirrors.

I looked at Chico.

He said, "Baja California has long been owned by Sinaloa cartel. It's changing. They put a bounty on Mr. Trevino. Those who enter are those we know. He keeps helicopters and boats here just in case he needs to leave."

"Along with a small army."

"That too."

Inside the gate it was a different world. There were three large pools, flowers, soft music, waiters with trays of drinks and food, and beautiful women in bikinis. Trevino himself came out to greet me, his hand extended.

I relaxed a bit. Not too much. When they want to kill you to send a message, sometimes they send a friend with a smile.

"Welcome," Trevino said.

He guided Chico and me to a small enclave with a table and comfortable chairs, then snapped his fingers. "Would you like anything?"

"A cold beer," Chico said.

"Me too," I said.

A waiter in white appeared magically with our drinks.

"Nothing for me," Trevino said, waiving him away. "Good. I need you with clear heads."

We held up our glasses, met his eyes, and nodded before taking a sip.

"I had the Russian's head delivered to their embassy. We've not gotten a formal response, but I expect neither they nor the Sinaloa cartel will welcome us to Baja."

I nodded.

"Tell me about the interrogation."

"His name was Anatoli Vasilev. We picked him up on his way to an event at the embassy. He had two security guards, plus his wife with him."

Trevino nodded.

"We killed the guards."

"Of course."

"The wife was a distraction. He wouldn't talk and she wouldn't shut up. She kept screaming. I decided to torture her."

"He kept saying, 'Let her go. She knows nothing.' It turned out he was right. She didn't know anything. It just hardened his resistance."

"So, you killed her?"

"Eventually I did. She was badly damaged by then. He was frantic, saying we were making a mistake. That he was just a bureaucrat, an Assistant Secretary for Trade."

"That was a lie?"

I shook my head, "No, it was true. He was the assistant Secretary for Trade for the Russian Embassy in Mexico City, 34, with a wife and two children. He was also an FSB asset. He did know that we, our cartel, was meeting with American Officials who were going to give us money to help our cause."

"Did he know the details?"

"I don't think so. He didn't even know the names of the Americans, except that they were elected officials in Congress and the Senate. He said five people."

"That is correct. Did he know where and when we were meeting them?"

"No, Sir."

"He'd passed what little information he had to FSB before we got him?"

"Yes, Sir, he did."

Chico and Trevino exchanged a look.

"Who at FSB knows?"

"Vasilev wasn't an agent for them, just an informer. He'd told a woman named Marie over the phone about our meeting. I called the number that he gave me for her, pretending to negotiate for Vasilev's life.

"A man answered. He wanted a code word, which I didn't have. He asked me twice, then hung up."

"Could the Russians trace your call?"

"No, Sir. I used a burner phone. Then I smashed it and threw it away."

Trevino said, "Good. I assume the line is now disconnected and we have no idea who this Marie is, except she might be FSB?"

"Correct, Sir. Vasilev said she was."

Trevino said, "I delivered his head to the Embassy as a message. They know that we killed him, but have not responded. Do you think we have a problem?"

Chico said, "Perhaps. FSB knows we are watching. Should I warn the Americans?"

Trevino looked thoughtful. He finally said, "No. I want their money. They might get cold feet and back out. If a few Americans die, it's not our concern, so long as we are not blamed."

"Yes, Sir."

Trevino said, "It might be useful to find out who this Marie is. She might be a problem. I have some contacts we can tap."

Chico said, "I'll put on extra security for the meet. What do you want me to do if the Russians show up?"

"Kill them, of course. Kill anyone who attempts to interfere."

"Yes, Sir."

Trevino looked at me. "You've earned a new job, Ramon. The Americans are bringing us $25 million dollars in nonsequential, unmarked, $100 bills. I want you and your posse to accept their gift for me."

I said, "Thank you, Sir." *I'd never handled that much money.*

Chico smiled. "Bring a vehicle and some help. One million in $100 bills weights about 110 pounds, my friend."

"If this Marie shows up, can I have her first?"

Chico laughed.

Trevino said, "Why not?"

CHAPTER THIRTEEN
RUSSIAN ROULETTE

Golden Gate Park, California, Noon, Two Days Later

Raven sighed.

It was the same set up as last time. A one-on-one meeting in a kill zone. One called by the Russians, who had picked the time and location, who had set the rules. No one was better at spy games.

The location was the Sweeney Observatory Site, a misnomer. There is no observatory there, not even ruins, just large stones from the foundation. The observatory was destroyed by the 1906 earthquake.

It was on an island, surrounded by Stow Lake. There were only two footpaths across the lake. I had to walk in and walk out. The location was on the high ground, a place called Strawberry Hill. There were a few trees, but it was mostly exposed. There was essentially no cover going in or out.

A good place to talk privately. A bad place to be ambushed.

I paused and stood quietly for a moment surveying the area after crossing the foot bridge over Stow Lake. I saw nothing hostile. I was clear of ticks. No one had followed me in.

All was peaceful. There were no visible threats and there were a lot of people around. A few young families, but mostly women and children on blankets in the meadow. Bright sunlight and a warm breeze. Same as last time.

Millie's watchers, a superb group of retired geriatrics and young mothers who didn't attract attention, had me covered, but it was still a danger zone.

Josie said it was safe. She was the psychic, but my mission sense was giving me alerts. Something didn't feel right.

Better safe than sorry.

I stretched, flexed my shoulders, and did one more scan. Then I reversed course. Moving quickly, I crossed back over the bridge, found a sheltered spot out of sight, hunkered down, looked back, and waited.

Nothing was moving. I tapped my secure COM. "How we doing, Babe?"

Josey's voice came back at once. "Same as before. No threats. They are eager to meet."

"What about after, when we egress?"

"Gray fog. Whatever you discuss with them changes the future in a big way."

"Same as before?"

"Denser. Opaque. I saw the two of you talking, then a fade to gray."

"Did either of us look alarmed?"

"No," she said. "Intense. Ernest. Not alarmed. What next?"

"I'll check with Black, then shut down COM and proceed. The meet is a go."

"Be careful, my love."

"Always."

Black picked up instantly. "The Watchers saw you turn back. Are we still good?"

"Am I clean?"

"Affirmative. Is there a problem?"

"Not sure. The Russians look good. Check the Watchers for anything unusual."

"Stand by."

He was back in 30 seconds. "They say clear. Less Russian security than last time. There is only one sniper team covering her. It's in the same spot as before."

I thought about that. *She's not worried about an American threat.*

We'd made the same call. The last meet wound up in a gunfight. This time our teams were less gunned up. It was a good sign. Tensions were lower. Detente was a good thing.

"Anything else?"

"A number of unaccompanied males walking around. Mostly Hispanic. That's not abnormal, Millie says. Sanctuary city in a sanctuary state. Do you want me to put a drone up?"

"Negative." Things were peaceful. No need to upset the Russians.

I took a deep breath. Show time.

"I'm going in. I'll call you on the way out."

"Roger that."

Pat Barry was the sniper. He was studying the Russian woman through his scope.

His two-man team was responsible for covering Raven. Six foot two, solidly built, and a former SEAL, his choice of weapons was a .300 Winchester Magnum, suppressed. It was overkill at this range, but had enough punch to penetrate body armor. He liked the weapon.

Pat said. "Raven's coming in now."

"Looking. No joy."

Vinnie Russell, his spotter, was a little guy who looked even smaller next to Pat. He was Italian looking, 5 foot 9 and wiry, small for an Army Ranger.

"We're his only support team. Stay sharp."

"I don't see any threats. There's a team covering her. We know their location, but I don't have eyes on."

Pat said, "I'll stay with the Russian. You keep scanning for external threats."

"Roger that," Vinnie said. "I've got Raven. He looks relaxed. Sauntering along like he's on a Sunday stroll."

"Hunker down and keep scanning. It's supposed to be friendly, but stay sharp. We'll trade positions every 15 minutes."

Vinnie said, "Roger that. Raven just waved."

"She waved back. So far, so good."

I spotted agent Marie, leaning against a large finished stone that bordered a grassy knoll. The same spot as last time.

The day was warm and sunny. This time she was dressed in working clothes. A light jacket, gray, white blouse, jeans, and the same shoes as last time. Practical shoes, white, some kind of modern high-end athletic shoes, not cloth, leather, with both laces and a strap. I wondered vaguely if they had steel toes.

Practical footwear. Useful for running or kicking enemies in the balls.

Marie sensed me coming. I saw her focus. One of her hands dipped into the bag at her feet.

I smiled and shook my head, keeping my hands open.

She smiled back. She leaned back against the large stone, relaxed, and put her open hands in her lap.

I approached her slowly, and we went through the pass phrases and counter signs. My part finished with, "… I was just practicing being rude."

She smiled at me. "Practicing, Digger, or rude for real?"

"I'm not sure. This is your meeting, Marie. I'm here alone. Why did you reach for a weapon?"

"I apologize. I've been a bit nervous. Are you really alone?"

"Always," I said.

It wasn't true, of course. I had a covering force, and so did she.

"Bullshit," she said.

"I've been nervous too, Marie." That part was true. I wasn't sure why.

She looked at me for a long moment. "Not about me?"

"No. Not about you. I'm here."

She thought about that for a long moment. *We were both pros. We were both skittish. That might mean something, or it might just be mission nerves.*

Finally, she said, "So you are. What took you so long?"

I laughed. "Gosh, let me think about that one…. Last time we met you violated your own protocols. One of your teams went rogue and followed me."

"Yakov," she said. "He made a mistake. Thank you for not killing him."

I shrugged. "Thank you for, ah, dealing with Mr. Vogel. My American friends are happy to have him out of their hair."

"The Canadians?"

My Digger identity was Canadian. It was robust, but there was no sense pushing it.

"Unhappy. Vogel was of little concern to them. You caused them embarrassment."

"Were they upset with you?"

"What do you think? You abducted Vogel from **Canadian** soil. It made the news…."

Marie sighed. "The operation was clumsy. Can you suggest anything we might do to appease the Canadian government?"

"Nothing. Please don't involve me in your diplomatic problems with Canada."

"Can you suggest anything?"

Marie was persistent.

Finally, I said, "Sure. One thing."

"What?"

"Leave me the fuck out of it, Lady. The Vogel abduction came from you. The Americans liked it. They helped. The Canadians were willing to look the other way, but FSB bungled it all to Hell and it wound up in the newspapers.

"Stalin would have had you killed. Does Putin know how badly FSB handled a simple abduction? Hillary Clinton could have disappeared him without a trace. Poof. Gone."

Marie actually laughed. "Let's just say it wasn't our finest hour."

"So why are we here?"

"We have some common interests with the Americans."

"Like Vogel? Like what got us into this?"

"Exactly."

She handed me a picture. I studied it. A small grouping of Americans with a swarthy Hispanic. Some looked familiar. It was dated May 3, 2016.

I said, "What am I looking at?"

"This came up at the El Chapo trial. Mexican President Pena took a $100 million bribe from the cartel. This is a photo of some of your politicians in Mexico City on that date, there to get their cut. The woman is your 3rd highest official."

"If true, so what?"

"It's an example of financial terrorism and political corruption. A payoff to keep the drugs and illegals flowing into your country. To keep your borders open. The person behind this was Vogel. You should be thanking us for getting him out of circulation."

"Your point?"

"Yes, some things went wrong, but Russia did America and Canada a huge service by taking Vogel out of circulation."

"May I keep this?"

She nodded. "Of course. Show it to your American friends."

"The Americans were promised access to the take from Vogel. That's why they supported his abduction."

"Yes."

"It's been over a year. They've not gotten anything. Nothing. Nada. Zip."

"Is that why you're here? Do they know that you are meeting me?"

"Some do. They wanted me to come, so I'm here. Most don't give a shit. They've written you off."

"You are to report back?"

"Of course."

"To the Americans, not the Canadians?"

"I don't think you are listening to me, Lady. The Canadians would be delighted if we killed each other, so long as it didn't attract media notice. My guess is that there are a fair number of Canadian Parliament members and officials who were on Vogel's payroll."

She smiled. "That's a good guess."

"So why am I here? Is Vogel even alive?"

"He's alive, cooperative, and singing like a bird...."

"Really? Prove it."

"I can. What if we gave the Americans full access to Vogel? Copies of all the interviews we conducted with him that touched on American interests?"

"Interrogations...."

"Whatever."

"In what form?"

"Tapes and transcripts."

I pretended to think for a long moment. Finally, I said, "They'd accept, of course. It would not build trust, but they'd accept. Why not?"

"What would it take to build trust?"

I raised an eyebrow skeptically and looked at her. "You need America's help?"

"Just answer my question. What would they need to move forward?"

"A lot, I think. Full access to all the Vogel interrogations and more."

"How much more?"

"They would want to interview Vogel themselves."

"In Russia? We are not going to release him. Might that work?"

"Maybe. What are you suggesting?"

"What if we allowed the CIA to question him, in Russia, on our soil."

I laughed. "In the Lubyanka prison? Dispatch some CIA agents and put them in FSB hands? Not bloody likely."

She shook her head. "Not there, obviously. We could run the logistics and protocols through the American Embassy in Moscow. Any agents who came to question Vogel could be given diplomatic immunity...."

"They'd still be compromised. Their covers would be blown...."

"What do you suggest?"

"First off, the Americans' major issues with Vogel are those of high-level corruption, the same as with you, the same as with any major nation. Vogel was a nexus of evil. America would want other organizations to interrogate him. My guess is that the DOJ and FBI would have more interest than CIA."

"That's possible...." Marie's eyes widened, and she yelled "Gun!" reaching into her purse.

Grabbing for my gun, I saw a figure rising. A Hispanic with a pistol. She was turning to face him, bringing her weapon to bear, firing a double-tap.

I saw another attacker behind her. This one had a shotgun. She was facing away, and I was going to be too late.

There was a whip-like crack as a supersonic round passed by my right ear. *Thank you, Pat Barry.*

The man with the shotgun jerked like a puppet with cut strings as a .300 Magnum round slammed into his chest. Target #1 was falling.

Marie put two rounds into someone behind me. I saw more figures behind her.

I'd never moved so fast in my life. My gun was coming on target. One was swinging a machete. He became Target #2.

I put one in his chest and one in his head. The third man had a pistol.

Target #3, but Marie was blocking my line of fire.

She ignored the friendly rounds passing by her. She was firing double taps at targets behind me that I couldn't see. She was standing firm, feet braced, in a two-handed shooting stance.

Totally cool. Icy calm. Like she was on a target range.

Another heavy round went by my ear, supersonic, catching Target #3 in the shoulder, spinning him. I heard the shot this time. A distant *boom*.

Pat was shooting suppressed. It seemed Marie's sniper team was finally getting into the fight.

I finally had a clear shot. I gave Target #3 a double tap in the chest, just as another round took most of his head off.

Marie's gun clicked empty. She dropped the magazine, grabbing a spare from under her blouse. I saw another figure behind her. Target #4.

I emptied my gun into him. The slide locked back. Her sniper managed to put a round into the falling body. Then it was quiet.

I continued to look past her, taking deep breaths, scanning for threats, putting in a fresh magazine. She was doing the same. Checking my back.

I called, "Clear!"

She did one more scan, then called, "Clear."

We stood for a moment, looking at each other. She carefully put her weapon in the bag at her feet.

I holstered mine, shaking my head. "What the fuck?"

She shook her head. There were sirens in the distance. "Not now, Digger. Time to leave…."

I took a deep breath. She was right. There were shell casings and dead bodies all over.

She said, "I'll find us a new meeting place."

"Good idea. I'll report what you said. Call me when you want to get together again. It's been real…."

Marie laughed. "It has, indeed. *Quand le diable s'en mêle ! Ça donne Vogel.*"

She gave a little wave, turned, and started off at a brisk walk, not looking back.

CHAPTER FOURTEEN
RUSHING THE RUSSIANS

The Ranch, Private Estate near Mendocino, California, Two Days Later

Raven and Josie were sitting in one of the conference rooms at the main lodge. They were in one of the prettiest locations around, but trapped in a small room with no windows. Inside, sipping coffee, waiting.

Things were still sorting out, both in California and elsewhere. Mike was down in Florida, fixing problems with their boat and the Navy, for a mission which had now been given a higher priority.

Goldfarb had arrived late last night. He was, at present, in a phone conference with Washington, tasked with positively engaging the State Department, Department of Justice, and perhaps the CIA with the Russians, none of whom much liked or trusted each other. He was a cut out between Raven's team and official Washington, one at the top of several layers.

He'd come with a single urgent purpose, to debrief Raven and return. So far that hadn't happened. Instead he was in a conference call, one ordered by President Peter Blager.

Raven was running a mission with the Russians. They thought he was a back channel to the CIA. He was not. The Russians had promised things of high value, promised to share key intelligence. So far, they had not.

The President was well distanced, but nothing else was working. My recent meet started off hopeful, but then it blew up. We were still trying to understand what went wrong.

There was a rap at the door. Goldfarb entered, a frustrated look on his face. That was unusual. The man had been in Black OPS most of his life, since the Cold War. He was normally a study in being enigmatic. Now he just looked pissed off.

He sat down, poured a cup of coffee, and said, "Good Morning."

Josie smiled and nodded.

I said, "Really?"

"No. Today would have to improve considerably just to make it to shitty."

I exchanged a look with Josie. "May I ask what happened?"

"Nothing. Literally nothing."

"Any discussion about what I should do next about the Russians?"

"No. I have to return to Washington…."

I started to speak, but Josie gave a small head shake. I waited.

"The shootout at Golden Gate Park is fading from the news. It's attributed to a turf war between rival drug gangs. San Francisco has a lot of that. Not as bad as Chicago or LA, but a lot.

"You and the Russians were not involved. There were no bystanders injured, nor have any witnesses come forward. The police will investigate the usual suspects. You are clean."

"Good."

"Do the Russians want to give us access to Vogel?"

"I think so. It was definitely going that way before we were, ah, interrupted, Sir."

"Interrupted?"

"Yes."

Goldfarb said, "There were thirteen bodies in a public park on a sunny peaceful morning. All hard kills. No survivors."

Marie had been busy.

"No comment?"

I shrugged. "The cartels are gunned up and violent. That's a normal day in some of our own cities. It wouldn't get notice in Chicago or Baltimore."

"No, it wouldn't," Goldfarb said. "That was my answer as well. It's now the official line. The media bought it."

I said, "Good."

Goldfarb shook his head. "Good in some ways, but not others. No more spy games, Raven."

"I don't understand, Sir."

"The President has decided that your mission with the Russians is now a diplomatic negotiation. Therefore, the State Department has the lead. He ordered me to transfer your Russian contact to Foggy Bottom. That is what my abortive phone conference was about."

Josie frowned. "Foggy Bottom?"

"The State Department."

I said, "God help us all. That's who you were speaking with this morning?"

"I was ordered to speak with them. Some assistant for international conflict resolution. He wouldn't talk to me."

That made no sense. Josie was looking at me. Finally, I asked, "Clearance issues and protocols?"

"Close," Goldfarb said. "He said we don't have an approved SCIF. I should go to Washington and meet them in their SCIF if I want to talk."

"The Ranch has a SCIF."

"It doesn't meet their standards. It's not in a Military or Government facility, doesn't have a white noise generator, lacks a GSA approved X-07 lock on the door, and, worst of all, we don't have TSG-6 approved STU-III telephones."

"What about our Cybertech phones? Totally secure. The best around."

"Cybertech never submitted their designs for State Department approval. They are proprietary, sole-sourced from Cybertech. Proprietary devices are not allowed, he said."

"Oh."

"We don't have an approved PCU either."

"What's a PCU?"

"A Perimeter Control Unit."

"You mean intrusion alarms?"

"I do."

"We have them. They turn them on at night."

"Not good enough. 24/7 and the PCU has to be inside the SCIF with its own backup power."

"Really?"

"Unfortunately, he was serious."

"What are you going to do?"

"Go to Washington. Tonight."

"To meet with the State Department?"

"To meet with the President. Mike and Will are to join me there."

"Did you call them from our substandard SCIF?"

"I did. On my Cybertech phone. Guilty as charged."

"What do you want us to do?"

"Continue. Meet with the Russians. Get me something."

"Yes, Sir."

"I have to leave, but can you give me the highlights of your meeting?"

"Vogel is talking. The INTEL he is providing is golden. The Russians appear willing to give us full access, only in Russia, but including diplomatic immunity for those we send over to interrogate him. Plus, recordings and transcripts. That's the good news."

"What's the catch?"

"They want something from America in return. Something big, I think."

"What?"

I shrugged. "I don't know. Like I said, we were interrupted."

"You have no idea?"

"We didn't get to that part, Sir."

Goldfarb looked at Josie. "Have you been doing viewings?"

She nodded. "Where I could. This whole interaction is wrapped up in the most sadistic violence I've ever been around. This is a nexus point, and that makes it harder. The future is foggy, depending on what happens now, or soon. I could view Raven going in, and his exit, but nothing during the meeting.

I said, "The drug cartels are animals."

Goldfarb said, "It's worse than the Middle East?"

Josie said, "Yes. Beheadings. Torture. Cannibalism. I can't get near it."

"Is there anything at all you can tell me?"

She was frowning, concentrating. "A name. Anatoli Vasilev, an official at the Russian Embassy in Mexico City."

Goldfarb looked at me. I shrugged. "No idea. That name didn't come up."

Josie said, "He's dead. One of the cartels delivered his severed head to the Russian Embassy."

"Do you know why?"

"No. Marie and her controller were talking about it. It was important. She was going to discuss it with Raven."

"Anything else?"

Josie was silent for a long moment. "Maybe. Vasilev had a special connection to Marie. They might have been lovers. The violence comes from the cartels, but somehow Vogel is involved."

I said, "Probably in the funding and setting of objectives."

Goldfarb nodded. "That's what he does. Financial terrorism, the Russians called it. That part might interest the President. Do you have anything else?"

"Marie said something odd as she was leaving. Something in French. I didn't fully get it."

Josie said, "I did. I could view that part. The violence was over and I know some French. *"Quand le diable s'en mêle ! Ça donne Vogel."*

"That's it. That's what she said. What does it mean?"

"When the Devil is involved. It is Vogel. He's behind whatever is going down."

"Does not surprise me," I said.

Goldfarb said, "We need to interrogate him first. Not the State Department, not the lawyers, someone involved in direct action."

"Yes."

Goldfarb stood to leave. "I've got to go. Anything else?"

I shook my head. We both looked at Josie.

She said, "Maybe. It's something I sensed dimly. Not a clear viewing."

Goldfarb froze in place. She had his attention. "What?"

"I might know what the Russians want to avoid. I'm not sure. It's just a feeling. Subliminal."

"Tell me."

"I sense dead Americans coming out of this cartel conflict. Dead high-level American officials. A political firestorm. The Russians don't want to be involved. They don't want to be anywhere near that."

Goldfarb looked stunned.

I said, "That might not be the best topic to discuss with the State Department."

"No shit." He pointed at me. "I'm going to Washington. I want you to get a private meeting with Marie. Find her, talk with her, and find out what the Hell is going on. Can you do that?"

I looked at Josie. She nodded.

"I can try."

"Call me when you have something."

CHAPTER FIFTEEN
VENGEANCE

Fairmont Hotel, San Francisco, Noon

Marie sipped her coffee, waiting for her master's wrath. The day was pleasant, the window was open, and the view was amazing. She could see the entire skyline, with the Transamerica Pyramid prominent and the Golden Gate Bridge off in the distance.

The Golden Gate. The near disaster in the park. A bad day for all involved.

Russia preferred its masters to be powerful, to be ruthless. Stalin had changed his name to exploit that.

Ioseb Jughashvili had earned the childhood nickname of Soso, a diminutive of Iosif (Joseph). After a long string of revolutionary aliases, *noms de guerre*, he came to power and changed his name to Joe Stalin – Joe Steel. He used nicknames like 'Man of Steel' to impress the Western news media.

It worked. Stalin started with a nation of bolt action rifles and horseback cavalry. He ended his career with nuclear bombs, missiles, jet aircraft, first-line tanks, a blue water navy, and a world that feared him. His Great Purge in the 1930s saw a third of the Communist Party dead or in prison and Stalin in absolute control.

Hitler killed at least six million of his own people, the Jews. It was nothing. Stalin killed more during the purges, and estimates for his World War II casualties ranged from seven million to over 43 million, more from starvation than by execution or combat.

In comparison, the U.S. population in 1945 was less than 140 million and its combat causalities for World War II were 405,399 recorded deaths.

Few in the West could comprehend the ruthless killing authority of Communist or Socialist states, or their lack of concern for the lives of their citizens.

The USSR came out of World War II at pretty much the top of the heap. Their citizens were used to horror and death. For them, the Cold War was next to nothing.

It was different in the West. Citizens wanted peace. War-weary leaders, eager to disarm and end war, were fearful. They let Stalin have most of the territory Hitler had conquered. He seized it with an iron fist, surrounded it with an Iron Curtain, and the world changed.

The UN came to be. The world pretended that it would prevent conflict. It did not, of course. It had never prevented a conflict. Wars and conflict, mostly proxy wars, became frequent, then constant.

The old KGB had wielded immense power. Once KGB, Putin was now Russia's leader, feared and respected. The new FSB that he created had more power, but it was more sophisticated, more subtle, more deadly. In a world with nuclear weapons, Putin used it as a rapier, not a bludgeon.

Karlov implemented Putin's plans and orders. He was FSB, but not accountable to it. He was a small man, five foot six, with thinning gray hair combed straight back, thin frame, wire-rimmed round glasses, and owlish eyes. If you saw him, unknowing, you might think him to be an accountant or a minor bureaucrat.

Those at the highest levels of the Russian government knew better. He was Putin's spymaster. It was best to not attract his attention. Oligarchs and *apparatchiks* who crossed him had a way of disappearing.

Karlov looked at her. "What happened?"

I said, "An excellent question, Sir. I hope you explore that thoroughly."

He frowned. "I'll ask you again. What happened?"

"I was betrayed. It was a trap."

"Who betrayed you? Canada? The Americans?"

"No." I shook my head. "I don't think so, Sir."

He looked thoughtful. "Who then?"

"You told me that our Embassy in Mexico City received the severed head of one of our diplomats in a box."

"Anatoli Vasilev. An assistant Secretary."

"Why did we tolerate that, Sir?"

"What are you saying?"

"Who killed Vasilev? How was he abducted? Has his killer suffered consequences?"

"The head came with a note from one of the cartels. It is still an open issue. You knew him, did you not?"

"I did. He was a friend, a colleague, and a source. Who killed him?"

"We don't know. We do know which cartel delivered the message, of course. *Los Serpientes*. It is run by a man named Miguel Trevino. That is part of why I pressed you to reconnect with Digger, your Canadian friend."

"Which I did. You sent me into a trap, Sir."

"Can you prove that? Those who attacked you were from a different cartel. They are all dead."

"Convenient, don't you think? I can't prove anything, but I do have a good mission sense. I was the target. We were surrounded. I could not defend myself from all directions. It was a preplanned ambush, well executed.

"Keep talking...."

"I did not pick the place for the meet, Sir. It had some advantages, but was an almost impossible place to defend. We were down out of sight, but surrounded by rocks and higher ground.

"Enemies on the high ground who got close could shoot down at us. To prevent that, we had to stand up and fire at them with our backs unprotected.

"Digger saved my life. I was fully occupied with those coming at me from the front. Multiple hostiles. Their target was me, not Digger. Not one of them fired at him. He was an easy target, but they all went for me."

Karlov frowned. He made some notes on a small pad. "Keep talking."

"Digger didn't take cover or try to escape. He stood there facing me with his back to my attackers, firing at those attacking from my rear. Totally cool. In control. Like he was on a practice range.

"His sniper team also targeted those behind me. The team that you dispatched to cover me was slow, late, and ineffective."

"Digger trusted you?"

I shrugged. "I don't think he had a choice. I was covering his rear and he fired to protect me. As I said, those coming at me ignored him. They wanted me, not him."

"Do you think we have a leak from the Embassy in Mexico City?"

"I think you need to find out. I suspect we have something worse than a leak. I think we've been penetrated and that I'm damned lucky to be alive."

Karlov was silent for a long moment. "You raise an interesting point. Some have raised suspicions about our Head of Station in Mexico City. It might be time to have him visit Moscow so we can ask him some questions. Do you have anything else to suggest?"

"Just a question, Sir."

"Yes?"

"Why is Vasilev's killer still alive? Why don't we know his name? That doesn't seem like us."

Karlov sighed. "It's a sensitive situation, my little Sparrow, one of the reasons I need you to get some help from your Canadian and his American contacts. Some dark things must happen and it is imperative that Russia is distanced from them. The blowback would be disastrous if we were implicated in any way."

"You are reluctant to have us dispatch the person who beheaded Vasilev?"

"Correct. I dare not leave any Russian fingerprints on the operation I'm planning. We can deal with Vasilev's killer later."

"What operation?"

"I'm not ready to reveal that yet. Except to tell you, in confidence, that it involves interdicting a massive bribe that American officials plan to give to *Los Serpientes*.

"Did you get any indication that we might be able to get some help with that?"

"We never got that far. I made no requests. We spent all our time discussing the fact Digger had delivered Vogel to us, and that neither the Canadians nor the CIA have seen any benefit from taking that risk.

"The Canadians, Digger's masters, have lost interest. They were embarrassed that the Vogel abduction made the news. They want to cut their losses."

"Is there any way to get Canada to reengage?"

"I doubt it. Certainly, none that he wants to be involved with. He made that quite clear, Sir."

"What about the CIA?"

"The situation is strained. Any further discussions would have to follow an agreement that allows them access to the Vogel interrogations. Digger made it clear that tapes and transcripts would not be adequate. They want to see him, to interrogate him directly."

"Would they be willing to do their interrogations in Russia?"

"We started to discuss that. It might be possible, with top level approval, diplomatic immunity, identity protection for the interrogators, full access, and things like that. He might be willing to present something to his CIA contacts, but he doubts they have the authority to approve it."

"I doubt it too. I have no such authority and there are other problems."

"Russian fingerprints?"

"Yes."

"What if the agreement was limited to a CIA interrogation of Vogel. Might we agree to that?"

"It's possible. I will speak with Putin. Is there anything else?"

"Russia dares not deal with Vasilev's killer or even the issue of identifying him. What if there was another way? One that didn't leave Russian fingerprints. One that didn't interfere with your interdiction operation?"

Karlov smiled faintly. A rare event. "You were sleeping with him, weren't you, Marie?"

"Irrelevant," I said. "The issue is dealing with someone who brutally murdered one of our diplomats, one who also happens to be an FSB source."

"No Russian fingerprints?"

"None whatsoever."

"You won't do it directly?"

"Of course not, Sir."

"There's no point in discussing it further then, is there? If an enemy of the state dies in the forest and no one is around, does anyone care? Of course not."

"Thank you."

Karlov said, "We need American help. You will get another meet?"

"Is there anything we can offer the CIA? They are less than enthusiastic and it's hard to fault their logic."

"What do they most want?"

"Full access to Vogel in Russia. The interrogation tapes and transcripts. Diplomatic immunity for their interrogators."

"The details and protocols to be directly negotiated between our appropriate bureaucracies?"

"I think that could work, Sir. It's worth a try."

"Tell them, Yes. Get the meeting."   .

"As soon as I can. One more thing…."

"Yes?"

"We may have other problems besides Mexico City."

"Local leaks?"

I shrugged. "Possibly. The location wasn't good. Meeting at the same place twice was poor tradecraft. My covering force was pathetic. Need I go on, Sir?"

He shook his head. "No. I'll look into it. Is there anything else?"

"Something is wrong. I'd like to keep our locals out of this. I'd prefer to make my own arrangements for the meet. Is that acceptable?"

Karlov nodded slowly. "It is. Permission granted. Soon would be good."

"Yes. Thank you, Sir."

CHAPTER SIXTEEN
CLARITY

The Ranch, Private Estate near Mendocino, California, Next Day

Josie got up early. She slipped out of bed, eased the door closed quietly, fixed coffee, and sat on the patio watching the rising sun behind her shimmer on the distant ocean far below.

She'd been careful not to wake Raven. He and his team had driven to Redding separately to dodge surveillance. It had been a long day. They'd been blown and it took some time to sort it out.

Only after watching the news and getting the "all clear" from Washington, Josie, and Millie's watchers did Raven call for the jet.

Millie's team of seasoned senior citizens were exceptional assets. They'd been fooled by the cartel gang bangers blending into San Francisco's burgeoning underclass of homeless, hopeless, street people, but it would not happen again. Only after conferring with them, Mike, and Goldfarb did he agree to stay in the area.

Raven and his team had arrived at The Ranch just before midnight, tired, still coming down from adrenaline highs. It had been a long day for them. Little River was well clear of San Francisco, but still close enough to easily reengage.

Josie met them at the airport. Raven had smelled of cordite and he looked exhausted. His only comment had been, "Rough day at the office, Babe. Never get into a gunfight in a rock quarry. Fortunately, everyone is okay."

Except for a Russian diplomat whose head came home in a box and a pile of dead bodies in a park....

Josie knew they were back at The Ranch only because Goldfarb wanted them there. The mission was still running.

Goldfarb wanted a piece of whatever it was that the Russians were seeking to share or planning to do, especially since someone had targeted their high-level FSB agent with a kill team of hired thugs. A nation-state would not have dared to take such action, but the cartels were crazy. Goldfarb had a stuck mission. He saw a common enemy, problematic but powerful allies, and a possible opportunity. It wasn't over. This was just the beginning.

Goldfarb was pushing pieces across the board. He'd just pushed Raven and his team into an unexpected kill zone. They had survived. Now he was getting ready to do it again.

I woke up alone.

Through the sliding door, I saw Josie out on the patio watching the sea. I stumbled out of bed quietly, shaved, and cleaned my face. Then I stood for a time in the shower, waking up, basking in the warm water, trying to plan. Nothing clever came to mind.

I needed her help. We'd gone in without it yesterday, into a trap. It might be best to start with an apology.

I took a deep breath, let it out slowly, dried myself, threw on a robe, dropped my little Sig 45 in the righthand pocket, grabbed a coffee cup, and went out to join her.

She knew I was coming of course. Josie didn't need to use normal senses. Without taking her gaze from the distant ocean she said, "You scare me, Raven. I was afraid for you."

"I know...."

She turned to face me. I kissed her softly, sat down next to her, and poured myself a cup of coffee. Hot and black. She had muffins on the small table. I tasted one. Blueberry. Fresh. It was excellent.

I said, "Are you angry?"

"A little, at Goldfarb. Mostly afraid for you, for us. I've viewed the attack. That damned Russian woman is going to get you killed, Raven. I'm not sure I could survive that."

"Did she betray me?"

"No."

"What then?"

"The Russians are compromised. She was betrayed. They didn't expect someone like you to be there. Watching you two in action was horribly violent, like a bloody Hollywood movie. You saved each other's lives."

"It turned out OK."

"This time. Goldfarb is going to send you back. He's sending his pet mongoose down the hole again to dance with the deadly cobra."

"It's what I do. It's what we do."

"I don't like your playmates. I especially don't like the monsters they attract."

"Did you see this coming?"

Josie was silent for a time, watching the sea. Finally, she shook her head. "I did not. Neither did you. Millie's watchers missed it too. That's what scares me. Maybe we're losing our edge...."

"You were having trouble with your remote viewings, but you clearly saw the attack. I don't understand."

"I didn't see the attack until *after* it happened. There was an uncertainty cloud of probability lines, a fog. We've discussed that before."

"You can see now?"

"Crystal clear. The future snapped into place. I could even roll back in time to watch the attack unfold, to see how it happened, and how her security team missed it."

"My team missed it too. Millie's watchers missed it. They are excellent and they missed it. She doesn't understand how that could be."

"The attack was well planned. They prepared the battlefield. California is a sanctuary state and San Francisco is a sanctuary city. They have a lot of homeless, a lot of illegals, and a lot of crime. The drug cartels pretty much run the big cities."

"Yes. So?"

"The attackers came in one by one over a period of six days. They drove the homeless and drug addicts out and took over their camps.

They scouted the ground and brought in weapons."

"No one noticed?"

"No one cared. The police have mostly been paid off, and, from their viewpoint, nothing had changed. A few beatings. A few drug overdoses. A death or two. Nothing unusual. If anything, the park was safer."

"They were waiting for us to arrive."

"Yes."

"Where are they now?"

Josie said, "You know where they are. Dead."

"All of them? Not likely. There would have been a scout. Someone to report back. I might be blown. He could have seen me, maybe he even had pictures."

"Yes, you're correct. One escaped. He was the runner, a child, a wannabe gangbanger named Adrian. He was only fifteen.

"He did not report back."

"You're sure?"

"Positive. The Russians are not happy. First the severed head of one of their diplomats, delivered to their embassy in a box by a drug cartel. Then the kill team going after an FSB agent. They caught Adrian and interrogated him intensely. He didn't know anything."

I frowned. "They didn't turn him loose?"

"No. This is getting very ugly, Raven...."

"You've done some other viewings?"

"Only two. I need you there before I go too deep. I stayed on the edges. I backed off from violence and horror."

"What did you see?"

"The Russians killed the kid. Adrian."

"They killed the kid? Did you view it?"

"I did not. I'm not sure his death was intentional. It may have been just a bungled interrogation. Does it matter?"

"No."

"Whatever operation is being planned by the Russians, it involves a different drug cartel, not the one that attacked you. Your attackers were hired. They were given the location, the time, and a picture of the Russian woman. They were contract killers.

"The cartel that the Russians are having problems with is called *Los Serpientes*. It is one of the most violent. It is growing and pushing into territories claimed by established competitors.

"It is run by a man named Miguel Trevino. His is a name you will never hear mentioned. He stays low profile, but is very wealthy and greatly feared. Trevino has safe houses all over Mexico. Probably in other places as well.

"One is in Mexico City, which happened to be where he was yesterday. When Trevino woke up this morning, the kid's body was on his doorstep, inside the walls of his heavily guarded villa.

"Two of his guards were dead and the body was there. No one had seen anything. No one had tripped the security sensors. Trevino fled with his entourage."

I blinked. "You viewed that?"

Josie nodded. "Just the aftermath."

"Who did it?"

"That part is interesting. A note was left. A false flag. The old El Chapo cartel has taken credit. It goes by several names, but is most often called the Sinaloa cartel. It's based in Sinaloa state, headquartered in the state capital, Culiacan. It pretty much controls the eastern edge of the Sea of Cortez, even down to Guadalajara and Acapulco.

It's the one that *Los Serpientes* seeks to displace. Guzman is gone. His sons are running it now. They are larger, more powerful, and eager to show their power."

"Did Sinaloa have anything to do with the attack on us?"

"Nothing that I could detect."

"With killing the kid?"

"Nothing. They had no involvement. The kid was captured and killed by the FSB, by the Russians."

"Who then went to some trouble to send a false flag message to *Los Serpientes*. One that panicked its leader, Trevino, who then fled Mexico City."

"Correct."

"The Russians are good at spy games. We talk now about 4-D war, about information being part of the battle space, but they've been doing it for centuries. Do we know why they are messing with Trevino's mind?"

"I don't know why you and the Russian woman were attacked, but I think *Los Serpientes* was behind it. I do know they are the ones who beheaded the Russian diplomat. The Russians hit them back. My guess is that somehow that made the cartel target your contact."

"You are certain of that?"

Josie shivered. "Certain? No, not yet, but it is likely. Somehow, the dead diplomat, Vasilev, and your Russian spy are connected. If so, the dots connect."

"Say more."

"I viewed the cartel leader, Trevino, discussing it with one of his gang, a man who reeks of evil, a stone-cold killer. The man was reporting on the death of the Russian diplomat he'd tortured and killed, one Anatoli Vasilev.

"He'd tortured Vasilev's wife to death, making him watch. Vasilev was crying. He revealed that *Los Serpientes* was meeting with American Officials who were coming to give them a large bribe. He kept saying that was all he knew."

I said. "Interesting. Anything else?"

"Vasilev didn't know the names of the Americans, except that they were elected officials in Congress and the Senate. He said it was five people.

"Trevino was pleased. He confirmed that the information was correct and promoted the man on the spot."

"Do we have a name?"

"A young cartel thug named Ramon Santos beheaded Vasilev. He's an animal, a dark, dangerous creature. He enjoys killing."

"Ramon Santos killed Vasilev?"

Josie nodded.

"Good. We now have something to trade the Russians. This is starting to fit together. Finally. Goldfarb will wet his pants."

Josie looked at me for a long moment. Finally, she shook her head.

"We know the cartels are dehumanized. We've known of the diplomat's severed head for some time. We've known there were corrupt officials in our Congress taking drug money and helping to run guns and human trafficking for decades. What's new?"

I smiled. "A name, a picture, a pattern, and a pending meeting of American traitors and cartel thugs. That's a lot.

"They say a picture is worth a thousand words. Our meeting was interrupted, but Marie gave me a photograph. I have it somewhere. Stand by."

I came back with two bagels, cream cheese, lox, a fresh pot of coffee, and the picture. I handed it to Josie.

She said, "What am I looking at?"

"Part of the take from the Russian's interviews with Vogel. A small grouping of Americans with a swarthy Hispanic, dated May 3, 2016."

"So?"

"It came up at the El Chapo trial. It's in the record. Mexican President Pena took a $100 million bribe from the Sinaloa cartel. This is a photo of some of our politicians in Mexico City on that date, there to get their cut. The woman was our 3rd highest official, the Speaker of the House."

"It's an example of financial terrorism and political corruption. A payoff to keep the drugs and illegals flowing. To keep our borders open. The person behind it was Vogel. I'd bet on it."

"Again, so what?"

"I think that's what Marie wants to discuss, and that *Los Serpientes* plans a repeat performance. The cartel will get a big bribe, and the Russians know about it because of Vogel. I think the FSB probably knows the time and place for delivering the money. That's the part of the meeting we didn't get to have."

"Unfinished business…."

"Yes. Do you know anything helpful? Anything I can trade?"

"Not much. They did mention the size of the bribe and how it was to be delivered. Cash. $25 million dollars in nonsequential, unmarked, $100 bills. It's to be delivered somewhere in cartel-controlled territory. Ramon Santos, the killer was promoted. His posse will take the delivery."

Josie said, "We don't know the names of the American traitors in Congress?"

"I don't. Marie doesn't seem to know. I'm not sure if her FSB handler does either. The main thing is that he does seem to want the transfer interdicted. It's why the Russians were pushing us to have the meet."

"That helps. It will take a truck to transport that much cash. It won't be easy to get it over the border into Mexico unless people have been paid off."

"You want to go back? To meet with her, with your Russian?"

"I do, but not where we met before and not with others involved. The Russians have a leak. We'll meet alone. I'll pick the place and time. A short public meeting."

"What's next?"

"We need to call Goldfarb today, to report back. My meeting blew up, but the Russians appear to have agreed to everything he wanted about American access to the Vogel interviews. That is a big win. We can pass it along to Goldfarb for action by others."

"Who? What others?"

"No idea. Not us. Do we care? Probably the CIA, perhaps with some involvement from State Department. My guess is that President Blager himself will make that call. We have happy news."

"I still have a feeling that Russian woman is going to get you killed, Raven. I don't like it."

"She just saved my life."

"To save her own."

"Admitted. That's how it works, sometimes. Did you view any threats to me?"

Josie said, "No, but I didn't look that far ahead, Raven."

"We'll check it out. I also want you to do some viewings to see if you can find names for our traitors in Congress. We can pass that along if we can find out."

"I'll take a look, but why are you so casual about this? I don't understand."

"I think we are wrapping up our part in this. The Russians are giving us what Goldfarb wanted. They probably just wanted us in the loop about our traitors and the bribe. FSB should be able to handle dealing with *Los Serpientes.*

"My guess is that they want to deconflict their actions. They want to make sure we don't blame them for our diplomats suffering consequences. Hell, maybe they'll split the money with us.

"It will probably take one last meeting with Marie to line things up. This is the easy part, Babe."

"When you are contacting her?"

"Today. After we report to Goldfarb. Why not?"

She looked dubious.

"We can have a nice afternoon and some down time before we go back to work. Maybe the Russians will even help us with Cuba. Who knows?"

Josie finally smiled. "Not me, at least not yet. Just be careful."

"Always."

CHAPTER SEVENTEEN
A BRIGHT RED LINE

The Ranch, Private Estate near Mendocino, California, Morning, Next Day

We got up early and had breakfast on our patio. They were to arrive at 10 AM, both Goldfarb and Mike, rushed in from DC after a terse secure text. *"Do nothing until we talk. Urgent. We are putting the Ranch on lockdown. Direct orders. No outside contact. Please acknowledge."*

Josie said, "So what do you think this is all about?"

I said, "No idea, Babe. My guess is something political back in the Deep State DC swamp is causing concern, likely prompted by my meet with the Russians being compromised. For sure assholes are puckered.

"I had to check with the guards to do my morning run. I was still on the grounds, just a run up and down the cliff to the beach, but they had me covered like a blanket. I've never seen sea patrols here before. Check it out."

Raven gestured. I saw a white ship in the distance with a diagonal red stripe. "What am I looking at?"

"Coast Guard cutter. She carries a copter. They had it up when I was running the beach."

"Nothing like this has ever happened before?"

"Not to me. You are the national treasure. Ever since you saved his life President Blager takes special pains to protect you. This is something else."

"How so?"

"We already had good personal security here. This seems to be about leaks. Controlling information." I looked at my watch. "It's about time. Let's take our coffee, go to the meeting room, and wait to be enlightened."

The room was secure, even including an armed guard at the door. I'd not seen that here before. It was set up with a conference table and six cushioned chairs on rollers. There was water, orange juice, and coffee on a side table. There were no electronics, and I noted that our new guests had left their phones with the guard.

Goldfarb and Mike had arrived on time. Mike looked irritated. Goldfarb was back to his professor persona, distinguished, unruffled, a bald man with a tweed jacket, rimless glasses, and goatee.

His jacket even had elbow patches. I saw the pipe he never smoked sticking out of the vest pocket. It brought back memories.

Mike said, "What the bloody Hell is going on with the Russians?"

Josie blinked.

I said, "I think they are being Russian, Sir."

Goldfarb actually smiled. "Russia is a riddle wrapped in a mystery inside an enigma."

"That was Churchill," Mike said. "I'm asking Raven. I don't need it historical, just current, concise, and actionable."

I said, "We were blown," and then proceeded to give him a short briefing.

He looked at Josie. "Care to comment?"

"They were blown. It was a near disaster. Raven and his Russian contact shot their way out. It was not her fault. For obvious reasons, they couldn't finish their discussions."

"You did viewings?"

She nodded. "I did."

I said, "You got the news about the Russians agreeing to what you wanted about sharing the take from Vogel?"

"Yes," Goldfarb said. "A positive result. President Blager shared that with the NSC. There will be appropriate contact very soon. It will start with a phone call today from POTUS to Putin to determine the proper contact points and protocols."

"NSC involvement set off a bit of a shitstorm," Mike said. "It's why we're here."

"They have their panties in a twist at NSC," Goldfarb said. "If I am to infer where this is going, Russia has two issues. Their beheaded diplomat, and what seems to be developing into a plan to block some traitors in our Congress who plan to fund one of the drug cartels with a large bribe."

Josie nodded.

I said, "That seems to be where it's going. I will know more when we finish our meeting."

Mike said, "This agent Marie is run by the legendary Karlov? He's a heavy hitter."

Josie said, "Yes. Karlov is her control. He reports directly to Putin."

Goldfarb said, "Assuming that the issue of the take from Vogel is handed off and under control, what do the Russians want from us?"

They were all looking at me.

I said, "We didn't get to that part of the meeting. I'm in the process of setting up another meet. This time I will pick the location and protocols. They will probably agree with anything reasonable. They know they have a leak."

They both looked at Josie. She said, "Raven is correct. We don't know what they want."

Mike said, "Do they know the name of the person who killed their diplomat?"

"They do not know," Josie said, "We do. A *Los Serpientes* thug named Ramon Santos beheaded Vasilev."

Goldfarb said, "It's odd the Russians don't know. Odd they've not taken action. Odd that Ramon is still alive."

I said, "The focus in the meetings seems to be on the *Los Serpientes* presence. Marie may have some personal issues. We suspect a connection between Vasilev and Marie. All that should become clear if we can ever finish our meeting."

Mike said, "Do the Russians know the names of the American traitors bringing the bribe?"

"Probably," I said. "My guess is that the Russians might tell us the names at our next meeting. I was planning to have Josie do some viewings to find out more, but, instead, we're locked down and here talking with you. Do we get to know why?"

Mike said, "In a minute. A question first. The focus of the Russians is on the cartel meeting with our traitors to obtain a bribe?"

Josie nodded. "A sizable bribe. $25 million in cash."

I said, "I think that's why they reconnected about Vogel after all this time. Why they are offering you what you wanted, access and interview notes."

Goldfarb said, "I think it's time to tell them."

Mike nodded. "Yes."

Goldfarb said, "Raven, in the past your missions have been off the books, under the radar, deep black, with risks, but without the political constraints that our Military and most of our agencies face. I'm afraid we've run into a tripwire that official Washington won't be able to ignore."

I blinked. "What the Hell are you talking about?"

"Bribes to cartels have happened before. Do you know that? Officials at our highest levels have been involved."

"Of course, I know. The Russians took the trouble of showing me a picture. One was our Speaker of the House at the time, Pelosi. It was a part of their briefing to me. High crimes. American officials involved in felonies and treason."

"Disgusting conduct, for which no one was ever convicted."

"Yes. Are you telling me that's okay?"

Goldfarb shook his head. "No. It's not okay, but it's not the Red Line that led to this meeting."

Mike said, "Why are the Russians sharing information about this meeting between a cartel and our traitors with you? Are they asking you to bring it to official American notice?"

"I don't know."

Goldfarb said, "Say the Russians do give you the details and names for the meet. What do you expect will happen next?"

"The Russians will handle it. They will block the transfer, seize the money, and probably kill those who interfere. If Ramon is there, and he likely will be, he dies. What's wrong with that?"

Goldfarb gave Mike an **I-Told-You-So** look. "Actually, nothing. They'd just be informing us to deconflict the issue. To prevent any possible blowback when they killed our traitors."

Mike said, "That's not why we're here. Nothing is wrong with such action."

"Then why are we talking about it?"

"What if the Russians want us to handle it? You to handle it?"

"That's crazy. If they expect me to handle it, I say no. If they expect our law enforcement or counterterrorism people to handle it, I take the message back to you, just like we did with the Vogel take. You can tell them no yourself. No problem either way."

Goldfarb sighed. "Sorry, it doesn't work that way. There is a big problem either way.

Mike said, "It's a Red Line. That's what NSC is all spooled up about. It's why we're here. Why you were locked down."

"Because NSC has paranoid fantasies about things they don't understand?"

"No," Goldfarb said. "We are here at President Blager's orders. I assure you that he does understand the issues."

"Can you define this Red Line? Keep it simple."

"Two parts," Goldfarb said. "The first part is that President Blager's administration wants no part of having our covert OPS people killing off opposing Members of Congress, no matter the justification. No way. No how."

"Agreed. I don't plan to do that. What's the second part?"

"The second part gets into complicated legal issues. Throughout our history, possibly excluding the Civil War, few if any traitors were legally prosecuted. After the Deep State attempt to remove President Trump, this is a huge deal, a raw wound. It was an historic high point for treason.

"Both the FBI and our intelligence agencies were weaponized. America suffered an attempted coup. Officials leaked and lied. Evidence was tampered with. There was even a fake impeachment attempt, all of which were started under pretenses of court-approved, legitimate, counterterrorism actions."

"Yes. What I don't understand, Doctor, is operational. How does this effect my mission now?"

Mike said, "You're the wrong person to deal directly with treasonous officials, Raven, no matter how justified or how egregious the crimes.

If we have traitors who have violated their oaths – and we likely do – President Blager wants them indicted, charged, and given due process by the DOJ and our courts before they are convicted and sentenced."

Goldfarb said, "He's been looking for a good test case. This situation might fit."

"That's it? That's our Red Line? Due process, and that I don't off these traitors?"

"Correct. You don't harm a single hair on their heads. This is why they have oaths of office. If we don't like what they do or did, it's a matter for the courts and DOJ."

"Can I recommend them for prosecution?"

"No, of course not. You don't exist. Even if you did, you would have to wait in line."

"Self-defense?"

"Always allowed, but it damned well better be righteous."

"And if the Russians whack them without any involvement on our part?"

"Not your problem. Not our problem. Might be Russia's problem. Just don't be anywhere near it."

"That's the Red Line?"

"Yes. Exactly."

"Mike?"

"That's it. Clean hands. Do you have a problem with it?" Josie looked at me and said, "We do not, right?"

"We do not. I agree. We don't ruffle the traitors."

Goldfarb and Mike looked relieved.

Goldfarb said, "Good. The lock down will be lifted as soon as we speak with the President. You can proceed with your meeting with the Russians. Share our Red Line concerns with them if you wish. How soon can you meet?"

"Soon. A few days. I'm waiting for a response."

Mike said, "Good. There is one other thing we need to discuss. Not a Red Line. Call it a Yellow Line."

I shook my head. "I can't believe it. They should not let people in Washington play with crayons. Not anyone, especially not officials at a policy level."

Even Goldfarb smiled. "It's more like a watch your ass. This one comes in from DOD. They are talking about it at the NSC."

"Okay, so we can't kill the traitors. What am I watching for now?"

Mike said, "Cartels on steroids. You haven't given us the location yet, but we are assuming that this issue with the Russians and the cartels involves the dominant Sinaloa cartel, the old El Chapo Guzman mob, versus this new one, *Los Serpientes*, which plans to push them out and take over."

"Presumably, the Russians prefer the status quo. To stick with Sinaloa, at least for the time being. The Devil they know, and all that?"

I said, "I think that's right. So?"

"It seems DOD may be developing a similar view. Are you familiar with Culiacan?"

"No. Why? Should I be?"

"Culiacan is the capital of Sinaloa State. In October 2019, Mexican Government forces captured two of El Chapo's sons. The older one, Ivan, was quickly freed by his men, who overpowered his captors. He then launched all-out siege of the city to free his brother, Ovidio.

"With military-grade weapons and driving custom-built armored vehicles, Sinaloa cartel henchmen launched over a dozen separate attacks on Mexican security forces. The ensuing scene was similar to Syria or Yemen, with burning vehicles spewing black smoke, dead bodies in the streets, high-caliber gunfire from belt-fed weapons, and more.

"Mexican soldiers and their families were taken hostage, and inmates were freed from prisons. The battle went on all day. It only ended when Mexican forces, outnumbered, outgunned, without reinforcements or a way to retreat, received an order from Mexican President Obrador to release their prisoner and surrender."

"The drug gang defeated the Mexican military in battle?"

"More than that. They achieved dominance. Obrador said, 'Many people were at risk and it was decided to protect people's lives. I agreed with that, because we don't do massacres.' This is the operative precedent in Mexico. It was a turning point in the collapse of the Mexican state."

I looked at Goldfarb. "No shit?"

"It's true. It's not about drug running, nor is it just an incident of organized crime. The cartels are into everything: smuggling, human trafficking, oil and gas production, industrial agriculture, offshore commercial fishing, and more. It's more like an insurgency or a shadow government. The last time this happened was when America had to invade Mexico, 1916-1919, back during World War I."

"Missed this in the news, I guess. I've been shifting my OPs down towards Mexico because Cuba and Venezuela are so bloody dangerous."

Josie was shaking her head. She looked at me. "*Oh, sinner man, where you're gonna run to all on that day?*"

"Huh?"

"It's an old Gospel song."

"Oh," I said. "Nice to know. What is DOD doing?"

"Planning."

"Does DOD care if our Russian friends get two of the cartels at each other's throats?"

"I doubt it," Mike said. "They already are. Homicides in Mexico have gone ballistic. They keep finding mass graves all over."

"Do I have a green light for encouraging the Russians to do what they want to do?"

Goldfarb said, "Could you stop them?"

"No way."

"I agree," Goldfarb said. "Let your Russian spy run. It's not our problem."

Mike said, "I agree. Let her run. It's not our problem and FSB is good at disruption and deception. Just keep America out of it, don't get caught, and watch your ass."

"Right," I said. "So, I'll have my meeting with the Russians, get clear, report back, and maybe by then we'll have a plan for handling Havana?"

"Yes."

I looked at Josie. "Any comments?"

"I'll do some viewings, but I don't see a problem in your finishing up with the Russians. Their enemies are our enemies, and all we're doing is being friendly. A meeting to talk can't hurt."

I said, "Good. Let's do it."

CHAPTER EIGHTEEN
A BAR TO REMEMBER

Rocky's Corner, San Francisco, Afternoon, Two Days Later

It was an old building, a local dive bar, but comfortable and dark. Back in the day, it had been a watering hole for mobsters, who probably got together to decide who deserved a cement overcoat and being dropped into the bay.

It had a lot of history, enough to answer Simon and Garfunkel's age-old question for Mrs. Robinson, "Where have you gone, Joe DiMaggio?" He used to come in, they said. To me, it had more of an old school vibe, like maybe the bar where Bogey came in looking for the Maltese Falcon of Hollywood fame.

These days it was a hangout for locals, who stayed close to the bar, maybe because the veteran bartender seemed to only bus the tables when he felt like it. That one took no prisoners, hurling insults at new patrons, especially foreigners.

I liked that. If you wanted to go somewhere where people are all the same and everyone knows everyone, but not you, this was the place. Hell, I didn't care if he bussed the tables or not. I picked a table in the back corner where I could see the door.

Marie showed up on time. I waved. She nodded, checked the room, came over, and sat down. This time she wasn't looking like a French Impressionist painting, just a working woman. Slacks, a blouse, and white running shoes.

She fit in. No purse or backpack. Nothing glamorous, nothing memorable. She'd probably cased the place. I'd allowed enough time for that as a professional courtesy.

She put her back to the wall, looking around, finally saying, "Hello Digger. It's been too long...."

"Hasn't it just? My friends were not pleased with our last meeting."

She was silent, checking the room. I wondered idly where she'd hidden her weapons.

She finally said, "Mine either. It was our fault. Please accept my apologies. The problem has been corrected."

I said, "There are four escape routes, four good ways out."

"Actually, there are five."

I raised an eyebrow.

"Ladies bathroom upstairs. Out the window. A fire escape."

"Oh." Good tradecraft.

I saw the barkeep working his way over. Finally. I'd gotten here a half hour early and was still waiting to order my beer.

She saw him coming. "What is this place? When I checked it out, the bartender was screaming at some Swedish tourist, calling him a fucking liberal idiot."

"Was he? The Swede?"

That got a short laugh. "Probably. We're not impressed with the Swedes ever since they let the Muslims in to rape their women."

"What about the goats?"

She looked at me. "I don't think they have goats."

"The Vikings did."

"The Vikings are dead. All of them. Ask the bartender if you don't believe me."

"Would you like a beer?"

"Sure. Whatever you're having."

I ordered two pints of Guinness. It seemed safe. The card on the table said they had a special. The waiter looked Marie over, scooped up the glasses, wiped the table, and came back quickly. He even brought a dish of pretzels.

She looked surprised. "Maybe he likes us."

"Maybe he's an old KGB agent. I think he fears you."

"Do you fear me, Digger?"

"You covered my back. I'm here. Last time was not your fault."

"Thank you. Do you have anything to report?"

"Good news. The Americans liked your offer of the Vogel take. I am instructed to thank you. It's working the way up their channels. Putin will be getting a call from their President to start negotiating protocols."

She nodded slowly. "That was quick."

"Not from their standpoint. They've been waiting for some time."

"Yes. Do they blame you?"

"Not for that, but they are impatient to know where our discussions are going."

"I have similar issues. Is there anything you wish to ask me before we get into that?"

"Perhaps. The death of Anatoli Vasilev?"

"His beheading by a cartel. What about it?"

"Is there something personal there?"

Marie shrugged. "It's nothing that matters now. Anatoli was a good man, a friend."

"I'm sorry. Those responsible should pay for his death."

She was silent for a long moment. "I agree. We need to get to business. What we are about to do concerns the cartel that killed him."

"*Los Serpientes.*"

"Yes."

"The Americans also see it as a threat. I studied the photo you gave me. Large bribes from American high-level politicians to the drug cartel. Corruption. Treason. Is that why we're here?"

She nodded.

"What can you tell me?"

"The interviews with Vogel put us on the trail. His information was out of date, but Vasilev had sources. He got us useful names. The bribe will be delivered in the next two weeks. High level officials in their government will deliver it personally. We have the approximate location and time.

"Are you familiar with Tijuana?"

"I've never been there, but I know where it is on a map. An easy run on Interstate 5, I'm told."

"It's not easy with a large cash stash, and it gets worse after you cross. Essentially, you will then be operating in a war zone. Tijuana has the distinction of being the most violent city in the world. Mexico has 5 of the top 6, and 15 of the top 50. Tijuana took the grand prize."

"Did Syria make the top five?"

Marie shook her head. "Number three was Caracas. Venezuela is at the other end of the smuggling corridor. The Cubans control that end. Through them, we have some influence.

"The cartels control most of the rest. No one has much control of them. The Mexican government controls very little. Some think Mexico is becoming a vast gangland controlled by warlords."

I thought about that for a long moment. *She was being truthful. Her information fit what I was being told.*

I pretended to be suspicious. It wasn't hard.

"You wanted this meeting. My American friends are asking if it is because Russia wants this bribe blocked?"

"Yes. We definitely do."

"Who gets the bribe?"

"We're not sure. Last time it was delivered to the President of Mexico and he dispensed it. That was the photo I gave you. This time American officials will use their political power and connections to get it over the border. The cartel will take over once it is across."

I said, "That fits with what the Americans told me. They discovered who takes it the next leg. The person who killed Vasilev has been promoted. He leads the group to transport it inside of Mexico. They trust him with the cash."

Marie's eyes got wider. Just for an instant. "Do you know his name?"

"The Americans do. Could you please give me the names of their traitors? They are most interested. I can probably work a trade."

She handed me a list.

Five names. I recognized three of them. One was the House Minority Leader of the opposition party. It must be some type of a tradition. I studied it, memorized it, and carefully tucked it away.

"I'll pass that along. It may help to get some people off my ass...."

"Tell me now. Who killed Vasilev?"

"You don't know?"

Marie shook her head. *Obviously, she did not know. That was surprising.*

"Ramon Santos, age 24, one of their hit men. A *Sicario*. He's been with the cartel since he was 16."

"The name. Are you sure?"

"It's what the Americans told me. He was just promoted by the cartel head, a reward for his work. He will lead the group that picks up the bribe. It is said to be $25 million in cash, in $100 bills."

"That's the amount we were told." Marie was staring at me intently. "The cartel leaders are elusive. Some just go by code numbers. Do you know who runs *Los Serpientes*?"

"Miguel Trevino."

She nodded slowly. "That's the correct answer."

It seemed things were wrapping up. She was happy. The Russians were informed. It was time to make my exit.

"It's been a pleasure working with you. If you'll let me know how this turns out, I'd be grateful. The Americans also want Los Serpientes stopped, or at least delayed. They think that having them come to power would make a bad situation worse."

"What are you saying?"

"Your path is clear. My American friends will be grateful when I tell them. They are happy to have Russia handle this mess for them."

"I don't understand."

"The situation is deconflicted. Americans officially know nothing. You can do what you wish with Los Serpientes and the money."

"What happens to the American officials when the bribe money they're bringing is hijacked?"

I shrugged. "Who knows? Who cares? Like you said, Tijuana is a shit hole. It gets ugly when drug deals go wrong.

"If some of America's officials choose to commit suicide by colluding with killers, it's not Washington's problem. Why should it be?"

"Don't the law enforcement people care?"

"The Mexicans? Surely you are joking."

"The Americans."

"American law enforcement didn't care last time, did they? The picture you gave me came up in evidence at the El Chapo trial. The bribe was well known, but no one was ever charged or convicted. For all I know it could have been legal. I don't understand political things."

"What about the CIA? Did they give you some guidance?"

"They did, off the record. They thought I was crazy. Drug enforcement is not their responsibility. They don't care if outsiders get into the middle of disputes between rival drug gangs, but they made it clear that if private American citizens did, they were on their own. CIA wants no part of this.

"They told me, Canadian or not, that if I even got close to high level American elected officials paying bribes to the drug cartels, I was looking at serious criminal charges. You'll recall the Trump witch hunt? All the corruption in US Federal Agencies? An attempted coup? America came close to a Civil War."

Marie nodded.

"Never again. No one wants to wake that monster. They made it very clear to me that law enforcement and the CIA were not getting anywhere near something so political."

"What if it was up to you?"

"Hypothetically?"

"Yes."

"Take the money, kill the bastards, and leave the world a better place for America and future generations. That would make a great movie. In the real world, it would result in a long prison sentence or execution. I'll pass, thank you."

"What should I tell my superiors?"

"All is well. Official Washington knows nothing. You can interdict the transfer, keep the money, and save the status quo."

"FSB has license to kill American officials?"

"Lord, no. Of course not. You're not planning on Russia's taking credit for something like this, are you?"

"No."

"If our corrupt officials go off on their own, and choose to get involved in the middle of bloody cartel wars, in the most dangerous place in the world, and suffer misfortune, why should it be Washington's problem?"

"There would probably be an investigation afterward."

"There always is. That's all the more reason to stay as far away as possible. I'm gone. I'm out of here."

Marie sighed. "FSB was hoping the Americans would handle this."

"Perhaps they will. Go talk with them. They are happy with the Vogel matter. Just leave me out of it. I'm just a messenger, a cut out. One who damn near got his ass shot off at our last meeting."

"May I call you again?"

I frowned, trying to think what Goldfarb would want. I finally nodded. "Sure. But with three conditions."

"I'm listening."

"First, you and your handlers need to understand I'm not getting involved in taking the bribe away from America's traitors. We've talked, you and I. That's what the American's wanted. It's all they wanted. If you want operational help, ask them directly."

"They will say no."

"Probably. It's not my problem."

"Second, I'm just a friendly messenger. I don't even exist. No contact with anyone but you."

"I agree. What's the third condition?"

"Next time, you buy the beer."

Marie laughed. "Deal."

"See you around."

I threw two twenties on the table, checked the room, and made my exit. No one followed me.

She was a big girl. She'd find her way home just fine. I hoped that Karlov could sort it all out. Mexico sucked. At this point, even Cuba looked good. What a mess.

CHAPTER NINETEEN
MOVING THE BRICKS

Safe House, San Francisco, Next Morning

Millie had found us a safe house. Josie and I settled in and enjoyed a restful night, but the logistics were getting to be a pain in the butt. I was afraid we were going to be split up again. For us to be effective, things worked best when we were together.

We were a team. Things went poorly when we couldn't communicate quickly and securely. I wanted to avoid that.

Josie was here, but half my team was now at The Ranch, the other half was in Florida, the Russians were here, and the next likely action was in Mexico. I'd tried my best to disengage with the Russians, but her viewings indicated that would not last for long.

Goldfarb was conflicted. He wanted me out here to keep a back channel with the Russians open until the money exchange between America's traitors and the cartels was completed. Paradoxically, he for sure didn't want me anywhere around when the Members of Congress delivering the bribe were attacked, no matter who did it.

That one was a hot potato. We'd been ordered "hands off." The Russians now held the potato, but I had a feeling they might try to pass it back to us. Worse yet, my Russian contact had been targeted by the cartels.

Mike mostly wanted me in DC to be interviewed about the Russians, Vogel, and God only knew what else. Other than that, I presumed he wanted us back on our original mission. That was Cuba. At present, we had no one there at all.

We had transport issues. Mike's new jet was supersonic, but it didn't fit the mission. It could land at Little River, near the Ranch, but, due to the short runway, it could only take off with partial fuel and maybe four passengers, counting the crew of two. It was good for running Mike and Goldfarb back and forth to DC, but not much else.

For short hops, the extra speed didn't help. It was too unique and high profile for my tastes. For longer flights, stopping for fuel took time.

Bottom line, we were not operational anywhere, there were loose ends, and a lot was happening. While we were waiting, Josie had been researching ways to snatch $25 Million in cash from under the watchful eyes of several governments, our traitors in Congress, and at least two ruthless, gunned up, cartels.

The Russians, at present, owned that problem. My own thoughts had turned to drones, airstrikes and napalm, but Josie seemed less than thrilled with my plan.

Josie came bouncing in, smiling, holding a folder. "I know what we can do. It's all about the money."

Well, duh. "Of course, it is."

"No," She said. "With most of our enemies, it's about geopolitics, power, or ideology, with the Jihadis being the worst. They kill, rape, lie, and enslave for Allah. Ideology. It's what their book tells them to do."

I shrugged. So what? *Evil comes in many forms.*

"The cartels are about money. That's all. The Russians just had a diplomat beheaded because he was watching the money flow, seeing it shift from one cartel to another. You and I are being warned not to interfere with traitors in Congress bribing cartels. The Mexican government is terrified of the cartels."

"Yes. So?"

She waved her folder. "What if we could just make the money disappear in a way that the cartels would blame each other? If they are busy killing each other, they won't be as much of a problem to us."

"Keep talking."

"It is astonishing how much money is involved. We are talking about a truck load. That makes it easier.

"I did a mix of remote viewings and Internet research. Our traitors got the bribe money in cash, all in one delivery, from the San Francisco mint. It's carefully packaged, all in $100 bills."

"So?"

"There are rules and procedures. You have to be careful handling, or even counting, large sums of cash."

"Too easy to steal?"

"Sure, because it's hard to count, and easy to miscount. They fixed that back in the 70s. Money now comes from the mint in ABA Standard straps, typically each with a bill count of 100. Each bundle has a tight, color coded strap. The bundles are called "straps." The strap for $100 bills is mustard colored. That's what we're looking for here.

"A strap of bills is about ½ inch thick. $10,000 per mustard colored strap."

"Straps are packaged into bricks. A brick is a tight bundle of Federal Reserve Notes. These are sealed with a heavy, color-coded shrink film, which is then heated to 450 degrees Fahrenheit. Four straps are one brick, 400 notes, $40,000.

"Four bricks are one cash-pack. $160,000. It gets its own color-coded, sealed package.

"Forty cash-packs is one skid. A skid is like what you pick up with a fork lift, a pallet. The value of a skid is 640,000 multiplied by the denomination of the notes contained."

I said, "So one skid of $100 bills is 640,000 times a hundred? $64 million dollars? We are looking for a bit under half a skid?"

She nodded. "Yes, just under 40%. They'd probably keep the pallet for easy loading. It would take up most of a van."

"How does this help us?"

"This cash is being delivered by Deep State elites. It's being moved personally by a small group of Washington bureaucrats and their top political staffers. Probably most of them have never had a real job. They deal with perceptions and spin. Right?"

"Sure. They'll probably be traveling with a few security people."

"Do you think they'll have their security doing the grunt work, loading or counting the contraband money?"

"No. They wouldn't trust them. Come to think of it, I didn't see any security in the picture Marie gave me, other than for the Mexican President who was receiving the money. The cartels are gunned up. They **are** the security. Having outside professionals or local law enforcement around as witnesses is unlikely."

"Do you think our political-elite high-level traitors are going to actually count the money?"

I shook my head. "No. That's beneath them. They probably won't even look at it."

She said, "Right. They might break open one pack, but maybe not. Even if they did, they might not examine the bricks. Why bother? Loose money causes problems, especially if you're trying to sneak it across a border. Better to keep everything sealed up.

"The Fed would follow its standard procedures to the letter. They'll have records and receipts. I'd bet on it. I want you to call Goldfarb. Maybe we can get the Fed to make up a duplicate pallet of counterfeit bills to substitute."

"To suggest your substitution plan? FSB probably has plans of its own that are none of our business."

"We can help them. If they don't like the idea, they can say no. Do you want to stop this transfer or not?"

I sighed. She was making sense. "I thought we were done, but we did set up a drop box. I can communicate with Marie. Let me do that before I stir him up."

She nodded.

I turned on my Cyber Tech phone. When it was off, it was electronically invisible.

Marie had sent me a message. The timestamp was 11:23 PM. Last night. I held it up for Josie to see.

Management concerns. We need another meet. Soon. Just you and me.
"Well?"

"No idea. You win. I'm calling Goldfarb. I'll see if we can get Mike into the call too."

I made it through to Goldfarb. He said they'd go into a SCIF and call back. DC was full of leaks. It would take more years to get that end of the swamp drained.

I did a scan for bugs, we made fresh coffee, moved to the small outside patio and waited. The call came in about twenty minutes later.

Goldfarb said, "What's happening? How are the Russians?"

"It seems they have management issues. They want another meet. We need something from you." I proceeded to give him a quick briefing.

Goldfarb said, "They don't have the time and location for the transfer yet?"

"Only approximately. They do know the names of our traitors, like I reported. You now have those names. Are we taking any action on that?"

Goldfarb said, "We passed it along. You are NOT to be there, Raven. Whatever goes down, you don't have authorization to kill our traitors. There is to be no American presence at the transfer."

"Yes, Sir. I made that clear at my last meet with the Russians. I stressed that I was just a messenger. I got out the silver bowl and washed my hands. Recall, they think I'm Canadian. My FSB contact is just using me as a channel."

"She did poke at that a bit at our last meeting. She said that, quote, 'FSB was hoping the Americans would help.' I told her to contact the Americans."

"Meaning the CIA?"

"Meaning whoever the Hell FSB wants to contact. She'd already said she didn't think CIA would help. I'd already told her that CIA didn't do drug enforcement. I'd already told her I'd likely be looking at criminal charges if I got anywhere near anyone interdicting the bribe money."

Mike laughed, "You got that part right *Kimo Sabe*."

I said, "Near or far, I seem to be somewhat stuck out here. It might be best to assume that our Cuba OP is on hold."

"No problem. We are still dealing with issues on the boat. You can plan a West Coast interlude for at least two weeks."

"That helps. I do have something we need from you. It has a short fuse. It's about the transfer. I need an answer before I meet with FSB again."

Goldfarb said, "Go ahead."

"Josie has a plan. I think it's prudent to consider it if you want the money transfer stopped."

Josie explained her plan. They asked one or two questions, then said, "What do you say, Raven?"

"I say, do it if you can. We'll need a fake cash pallet in 48 hours."

"Needed where?"

"Here in America. Domestically. Southern California probably. Wherever FSB chooses. For this to work, they'll need to do the swap before our little band of traitors crosses the border. We'll also need to ensure that local law enforcement isn't around while the FSB is making the swap."

"No problem with other Federal agencies?"

"Not for us. Getting the bribe across the border is up to the cartel and the traitors in Congress. They'll already have that set up."

Goldfarb said, "I'm going to have to get approval."

I said, "There is only one place you can get that. You saw the names. One is the minority leader in the house, and two of the others are minority leaders on other committees, including Foreign Relations. These are heavy hitters."

Mike said, "He's right. If that leaks, we're in worst shape than before and we'll sabotage the Russians in the process. Lose/lose all around."

"When you have the fake money and are sure we have no leaks, give me a heads up. I'll green light the Russians and get you an exact time and place for the delivery."

Goldfarb said, "Slow down. We haven't agreed to do anything. Does anyone have a better idea?"

"How about a 500-pound bomb, followed by a napalm tank? Problem solved. We lose the $25 million, but can save more than that on legal expenses."

Mike laughed. "Good point, but the President really does want to start prosecutions for Oath Violations."

Goldfarb said, "This might not be a good case to start with, Mike. Raven does have a point. It would be messy. The legal research would take longer than making up a dummy pallet.

"Treasonous or not, I'm not sure what laws our traitors are breaking, especially if we bust them before they deliver the bribe. We already know this sort of thing has been done in the past, perhaps by both parties."

Josie said, "I was only able to think of one downside, assuming that cartels and traitors don't detect the switch before the bribe is delivered. There is a war raging between these rival cartels. This would throw gasoline on the flames. It could turn into a bloodbath where cities burn and innocents die."

I said, "Once it is detected that the money is missing, it will escalate the Drug Wars. I don't think it matters."

Mike said, "Why not?"

"Tijuana, where the transfer will take place, is already the most dangerous city in the world. Mexico has five of the top six cities for violence. The cartels are already killing each other flat out. Civilians and police stay out of the way.

"So, what if the money is missing? Who gets blamed? Not us, we are nowhere near it. Our Congressional traitors? Perhaps. Do we care? I don't. The Russians? Not if they run a clean switch. FSB is excellent at deception."

Mike said, "Maybe that's what the Russians are pondering. Why they want to meet."

I said, "It could be. *Los Serpientes* is already gunning for Russians. I'd like some happy news to help motivate FSB. Right now, I don't have any."

Goldfarb said, "He's right. It's a question of degree. Latin America has about 8% of the world's population, and accounts for over a third of global murders. The murder rate there has been increasing since year

2,000. Tijuana is the worst. There is already a full battalion of soldiers there, just to protect government offices and infrastructure."

Mike said, "Seems like there is not a lot to lose."

I said. "Whatever is decided, all we are asking for is an official-looking collection of fake money to give to the Russians. Why not?"

Goldfarb said, "There is only one person who can approve what you want to do."

"I figured that, but I do need an answer before the meet. And, for God's sake, keep this from leaking or we will have a blood bath."

Mike said, "We need to meet with President Blager. Soon. Personally. Securely. In confidence."

Goldfarb said, "Yes. I'll see if we can get the fake packet started today. Raven, we'll get you a decision in 24 hours."

"Thank you."

"Remember what we discussed, Raven. You are to stay well clear of the interdiction of this exchange. You know where those orders came from."

Josie said, "I do. Whatever the Russians do or don't do with this bribe money, Raven will not be anywhere near it. You have my word."

I said, "Mine, as well. I do not want to get America into a war."

Goldfarb said, "I'll tell him that."

CHAPTER TWENTY
COMMON INTERESTS

Rocky's Corner, San Francisco, Noon, Two Days Later

I let Marie get there first. Poor tradecraft, perhaps, but one way of signaling trust.

I'd cheated, of course. I'd cased it last night myself. The bar didn't open until noon and Millie's watchers had it under observation. They were on their game.

Marie was sitting at the same table watching the door. The place was pretty much empty, just two people at the bar. One sipping coffee, and a seedy old guy with a gray beard enjoying his breakfast beer.

The crusty old barkeep was nowhere to be seen. Instead we had a solid looking blond woman with a Celtic tattoo on her right arm. Maybe she would bring me luck. I was ready for that.

Marie smiled and nodded. I came over and sat next to her.

"Sorry to be late. I wanted to make sure we were both clean."

She said, "I came alone. No one followed me."

"Same here. I think we're good."

The barmaid took our order. Two coffees. No chitchat.

I said, "What's up? Management concerns?"

"Yes. What did you expect?"

"I didn't expect anything. The last meeting was yours. My American friends insisted that I attend, so I did. They had me on a short leash. It's gotten tighter, I'm afraid."

"Can you explain that?"

"Sure. You are familiar with the problems the Americans have had with enemies within, Deep State traitors, and even a long running, failed, but still troublesome coup?"

Marie gave a short laugh. "Who could miss it? Russia was the home of Pravda, the historic motherload of propaganda. America has now surpassed us.

"America's media is dishonest and not particularly competent, but the world has never seen such an intense barrage of simple, persistent, political messaging. Different each week, not very coherent, but Stalin would applaud the passion and level of effort. America's Fake News will go down in history yet to be written.

"Western nations are training their citizens to see everything through the lens of politics. Russians know better than most how dangerous that can be. Better to see the world through the lens of reality."

Marie gave me a sharp look. "It's also better to liquidate or banish a nation's traitors before they can implement their plots. Is that what we're talking about here?"

"I'm not talking about anything. I just asked you a question. I passed your information about traitors in Congress bribing the cartels to the Americans. As expected, they are grateful. They voiced no objections whatsoever to your taking action to interdict the bribe. They were happy. Russia is free to act."

"Would they be willing to go on record about that?"

"You should ask them."

"I'm asking you."

"I told you last time. My guess is 'no.' We discussed this. Is my answer a surprise to you?"

"We gave you the names of the American traitors. We can give you the time and location for the delivery of the bribe. Will the Americans help us stop the transfer?"

"I doubt it. You are asking too much. My friends' position is clear. They don't want Americans anywhere near when the bribe is intercepted. They feel strongly about that. They don't want their fingerprints on anything that involves taking kinetic action against the domestic political opponents of the current administration."

"What about legal action?"

I laughed. "We won't live that long, Marie. The American legal system is ponderous. The good news is that it's fair, for the most part. The bad news is that it is slow. It works poorly if political issues are involved. The Americans have not convicted any citizens of treason since the Rosenbergs."

"Julius and Ethel. Electrocuted in 1953."

"Yes. They worked for the KGB, did they not? It's why they were convicted, sentenced, and executed."

Marie shrugged. "All that was a long time ago. The Cold War."

"Actually, the Americans did mention possible legal action on the matter we're discussing. It didn't help."

"Why not?"

I was watching her closely to see how she reacted to my next words. I kept my voice flat, trying to show no emotion, to let the content stand, not the tone.

"They told me explicitly that if I got anywhere near interdicting the bribe from their members of Congress to the drug cartels, I would be facing criminal charges. I am to have no involvement in that. None."

She blinked.

"Is that clear enough for you?"

Marie said, "I believe you."

"Good. Let's get back to your 'management concerns,' Marie. Why are we here?"

"These are America's traitors, not Russia's. Some in our leadership think this problem should be a joint commitment and that America should participate in the solution."

I said, "A valid argument, and one you might want to raise with the proper authorities. This is a high-level national policy issue. I don't want to lose my American friends or go to prison. I tested this as far as I dared. I can assure you that direct action is off the table for America."

"Did they say why?"

"Not explicitly. I presume they don't want to start a war over this. Can you blame them?"

"Do you understand what Russia's interests are in this matter?"

"Probably not. All I know for sure is that you don't want the transfer to occur, and that you keep insisting on meetings with me to warn American intelligence. I already warned them. I told them you favor a different cartel and prefer to keep the status quo."

"Yes. The Sinaloa cartel. Russia's objectives in having a presence in Mexico are limited. It was cheaper for us to pay them than to fight them. America made the same decision."

"Not to my knowledge."

"America paid them off too. The same cartel. I showed you the picture. High-level American officials delivering a bribe."

I shook my head. "You showed me American officials committing treason under a previous administration, years ago. They already knew about that. There were worse crimes being committed back then.

"Remember Fast and Furious? It wasn't about money. It was about America's Department of Justice under Eric Holder running guns to the drug cartels to destabilize the border. More treason. Americans died.

"These issues are still raw in America. They don't want a war. It's about broken oaths by their high-level officials. America almost had a coup and a Civil War."

Marie was silent for a time.

Finally, she said, "Russia will not act in the matter without American help. Our leaders don't want war either."

"May I ask you something? I know this is personal, but I need to know some things in order to help you."

She nodded.

"Your dead diplomat. The one who was beheaded."

"Anatoli Vasilev."

"You knew him?"

"I did. They tortured and killed his wife. Then they sent us his head in box as a message."

"Was he Russia's source for knowing about our traitors and the bribe?"

"I can't say."

He was.

"This is personal, isn't it?"

Marie sighed. Looking directly into my eyes, she gave a small nod.

This was huge. FSB agents didn't do personal. They'd been lovers. Marie was taking a big risk. She was telling me dangerous truth, but wisely, without her daring to speak the words. If questioned, she could deny telling me.

I said, "There is one thing the Americans could do that might be helpful to you. An idea that was raised by one of their analysts...."

Marie was looking at me intently. She didn't speak. She didn't ask. She waited.

"This is a bit off the wall, but let me bounce an idea off you. First off, I want to make sure we're on the same page.

"The Americans are assuming – and I agree – that the interdiction of the $25 million bribe is going to be high conflict, high profile, a significant battle. One that will get media attention, world notice, result in numerous casualties, and have adverse consequences. What is Russia's view?"

She looked at me strangely. "Pretty much the same, of course. It's why our leadership is reluctant to act alone."

"Good."

She looked at me strangely. "Why would you say that?"

"We now have a point of agreement. Both sides deem this important, see the benefits, want it done, and each has capabilities to get it done.

"Russia wants it done, but does not want to do it alone. American leaders want it done, but judge the political consequences to be unacceptable if they were directly involved."

"Assuming you have not gone mad, I still fail to see why this is good."

"What if...? What if, with some minor, off-the-record, indirect help, Russia could make this happen in a way that no one would suspect that either of our nations had intervened?"

"That's not possible."

"Sure, it is. Broaden your thinking. What if this interdiction went down in a way that the bribe money disappeared with no inkling of any involvement from either of our nations? *Poof.*

"What if the drug cartels blamed each other, and, enraged, then turned to slaughtering each other in an orgy of violence? What if Russia did the heavy lifting, but got to keep the $25 million? Would your leadership embrace such an outcome?"

"So now you work magic?"

"No, I'm hoping you can. FSB has the reputation of being clever and competent. Tell me if this might work."

I proceeded to explain Josie's plan to her, without attribution of course. Marie listened intently.

"Well?"

"Mexico is too dangerous. We'd need to do the swap in the United States."

"I agree. That's what the Americans thought too. They might be able to ensure that local law enforcement stayed clear, but they don't agree about that being wise. Some argue that a first-rate Black OPS team would prefer that no one else be informed."

"I'd argue the same. Secrets leak too easily in America. Could this pallet of fake money be created quickly?"

"Yes. They've already started getting it together, just as a contingency plan."

"How soon could we get it?"

"Domestically, perhaps 24 to 48 hours. Give me an address if you choose to move on this and I can get you a firm answer. They'd want a commercial address with a loading dock and a forklift."

"We'd want to specify the exact delivery time. Sometime after hours might be best. Such things are best done in the dark."

"No problem."

"I like it. I will present the plan."

"You do understand that if the packages are opened, the fake money will not stand up to scrutiny? If they've opened any to examine, you must leave it as you found it. It's game over when they start inspecting the load. You want it over the border and only the cartel members around when that happens. People will die."

"I expect they will. Can you get us the details of how the money will be packaged? Pictures would be best."

"In full color. Just give me an email address. I will have them send it from an account that does not accept replies. It will go dark thirty minutes after it is sent."

Marie said, "I think this just might work. Personally, do you support aggressive action to block the transfer?"

"I'm not sure what you're asking. You do understand that I can't personally be involved. Prison time. Remember?"

"Of course. I'll make it clear with my control that you are just a messenger, not to be involved in the operation. No one on the OP will even know you exist. I just wondered how you felt about the cartels."

"I think they are animals who suck the life and goodness out of civilization. If they all died in horrible ways, I'd be happy. If treason and betrayal can be punished as part of that, so much the better."

Marie blinked again. *She'd apparently not expected such a direct answer. She was watching me carefully.*

Finally, she nodded. "Again, I believe you. If you truly feel that way, enough to act on it, we do have common interests."

"I cannot be involved in any direct action to block the transfer, Marie. No matter how I feel."

"I understand, but there is nothing to prevent you from taking action against a cartel member before the transfer, is there?"

"I don't understand."

"My handlers have, ah, also put me on a leash. I am forbidden to do certain things that I feel are both prudent and necessary."

"I have no idea what you are talking about."

"We are running out of time. You presumably want me to go back, speak with my control, get the interdiction approved as a Russian operation, thwart the American traitors, and end your involvement. With the information and support you have just offered, that is possible, but not likely.

"I, on the other hand, want this done successfully. I want *Los Serpientes* crushed. I want Ramon Santos dead. I don't care how he dies or who kills him, but I want him dead."

I took a deep breath and let it out slowly. *This was more personal than I thought.*

I said, "He won't live long, Marie. Few *Sicarios* make it past their twenties. Others move up by doing them in. The cartels have a limitless supply of recruits. He'll be gone in a year or two, replaced by someone as bad or worse."

She shook her head. "Probably, but if we don't handle him now, I think nothing will happen. Even if I push for it, I probably can't get approval for a tricky swap like what you suggest."

"You don't like the plan?"

"It's the best plan I've heard, but it is risky. If things went bad during the swap, especially on United States soil, that would get media attention. It would be politically embarrassing for Russia. Failure would likely end the careers of those responsible. Russia doesn't tolerate failure.

"We generally don't risk what we have to get more. That's what ended the Cold War. Reagan made the stakes too high, so we stopped playing the game."

I was watching her carefully. "You are worried about your career."

"No, I'm worried about failure. I'm not going to throw my career away for nothing. But I might know a way to prevent that, provided that I can get your help."

"Let me guess: Killing Ramon Santos."

Surprise flickered in her eyes. "Correct. Before the transfer. His group is taking the delivery from America's traitors. His death will disrupt that and throw *Los Serpientes* into chaos for a week or two. A few selected leaks about a $25 million bribe shipment in cash will inspire their rivals, especially the Sinaloa cartel who owns that region, to hit them hard while they are disorganized."

"And the American traitors will be killed or held for ransom in the cartel wars...."

"Likely killed, I'd expect. A win for America. Treason doesn't pay. It's a win for everyone but the cartels."

"I assume that if Ramon is dead as part of the deal, getting Russian approval for the switch would be likely."

Marie nodded. "I'd not have to push too hard. It would be routine. The odds of approval and full support would be high, 80% or more. When the mission succeeded, we'd all be heroes. FSB is good at such things and we are only risking a small team."

"Great idea. So why not kill Ramon yourself?"

"Because I can't. I too have constraints, Digger. I'm under direct orders not to be involved in the interdiction. It's also been made quite clear that my mission is here in the United States, not in Mexico."

"Is this where I say, 'No way in Hell?' You must think I'm insane. You want me to go down into the most dangerous city in the world, a war zone, probably alone, off the grid, with no backup, and all that just to kill a cartel leader for you?"

She was shaking her head. "No, of course not. That would be suicide."

"Surely, you don't expect the Americans to start liquidating cartel leaders just because you have a personal problem?"

"No."

"What then?"

"Are you familiar with the *autodefensas?* They are becoming increasingly common in Mexico."

I shook my head.

"Some call them *policia comunitarios*, community police? In a nation where the police are corrupt, paid off by the cartels, they do self-defense, but the lines are blurred. Some *autodefensas* also have vigilante groups involved in *limpieza*, cleansing operations."

"I've never heard of any of that. What's your point?"

"The vigilante groups consist of murderers who kill murderers. They exist to seek out and liquidate cartel heads and cartel hit men, the *Sicarios*. The vigilante groups primarily exist to assassinate people like Ramon.

"They are very good at what they do. They sometimes capture cartel *Sicarios*. Most captives are killed, but a few of the most lethal are converted. These are used as trainers or turned back against the cartels."

"Interesting. How do you know so much?"

"I will answer that question only because I need your help and with an understanding that you did not hear this from me. Let me frame it as hypothetical."

I nodded. She had my full attention. "Agreed."

"What if my friend Anatoli Vasilev was running a small covert program out of our embassy in Mexico City to support the *autodefensas?* To help stabilize Mexico? To undercut the cartels?"

"I'd say he was a saint."

"Yes."

"Support how? What support did Russia allow?"

"Nothing that attracted any official notice. The *autodefensas* need money and weapons. The cartels are wealthy and powerful. Mexican law does not allow private citizens to own military grade weapons. The Mexican government allows *autodefensas,* but its support is limited.

Government support is limited and focused on community self-defense. Politically the local defense groups, the *autodefensas,* are called 'Community Police.' They are generally viewed as a police auxiliary.

As you might expect, local campaigns against the cartels, against organized crime, have caused violent responses. The *autodefensas* are outnumbered and outgunned. They get no government support for vigilante groups."

"They did get support and weapons from you? From Anatoli Vasilev?"

"Yes."

"What are you considering, Marie?"

"When I propose this to my superiors, I will suggest that we take, say, 20% of what we get and use those to cover the costs of this operation and to fund any counter OPS that come out of it in the honor of our fallen comrade Anatoli Vasilev."

"Do you think your superiors will accept that?"

"I think they might. We love our heroes.

"I intend to put Anatoli in for the Hero of the Russian Federation Medal. If Russia gets the cash and we crush *Los Serpientes* he just might win it."

"Where are you going with this? Why does it matter how I feel?"

"Making you aware of Vasilev's program supplies you with context. I need your personal help in dealing with Ramon.

"I can help supporting your takedown of Ramon. I don't need money. I have access to sufficient funds. I have the contacts I need and the risk to you will be quite low. The problem is that we'll need to move quickly. I need Ramon gone before the transfer."

"My takedown of Ramon?"

"Yes. I've seen you in action. I was impressed."

I was shaking my head. "Sorry, lady. You're going to unwrap that a bit. Let's start with the 'move quickly' part. How quickly? Before you do the money switch, like in 48 hours? I'd say that's not possible."

"We'll need to eliminate Ramon before your Congress members get to Mexico to deliver the cash. I still don't have a firm date and location for the transfer, but it should be several days out. Is that adequate time?"

I shrugged. "Maybe. There is another problem. I'm finding it a bit hard to accept your notion of 'low risk.' That's easy for you to say, but it's my ass on the line."

"That part is easy and your risk is minimal. One of Anatoli's top *autodefensa* operatives is in Tijuana. You don't have to kill Ramon yourself. Most likely you could not do so without high risk, not on his home ground. I'm not asking that. All you'll need to do is to do some research, then meet his agent and transfer some information."

"Tell me more."

"Are you in or not?"

"Not. At least not yet. What kind of information?"

"We'll need a picture of Ramon. Here's how the hit will go down. Anatoli's man will need a picture, a time, and a location. For this to work, he'll need to know where the target is and what he is wearing. It has to be a time and place where the target is not with a group or protected by bodyguards.

"Can you provide us with that?"

I said, "Probably. Keep talking."

"The hit man will work as part of a 3-man team that includes a driver, a scout, and the shooter, which will be him. They will engage the target from the back of a motorcycle. If they can't do it that way, the hit is off."

"Agreed. We'll have to find the right opportunity."

"If you can't get the target alone the hit is off. A gunfight in the middle of Tijuana would be messy. My superiors would not like that."

"I don't blame them."

She smiled. "Yes. Do you have any questions?"

I said, "A big one. Why me?"

"Several reasons. We are not going to leave any Russian fingerprints on the hit. We have enough problems down there. We don't want the cartels as enemies."

"That's why 'not you.' Again, why me?"

"That's simple. Anatoli is dead. He had this on a close hold. The FSB Head of Station in Mexico City knew, I knew, my control knew, and now you know. The circle of trust needs to be kept small.

"A personal meet with the hit man is needed. You are the best person. In fact, you are the only person."

"Why is a personal meet needed at all?"

"Here's how it works. I will set the meet up, inform you, and give you a *bonā fidē* for positive identification. You will meet the agent at a safe house. You will show up on time, present your *bonā fidē*, and explain that I can't be present and Anatoli is dead.

"Get that part right, Digger. If you don't, the meeting is over and we've wasted a lot of time."

I looked her in the eyes. "I suspect that if I fail that test it might end more than the meeting."

"It might. As you say, it's a dangerous place. No one is trusted. People are nervous."

"Okay, that's the protocol. What happens at this meeting? What is the purpose?"

"You are there for three reasons. First, to show the *bonā fidē*, which signals a running operation, shows him my approval, and signals that the hit man will be paid. Second, to deliver the photo we've discussed and any other information that assists in the targeting. You will provide the location, time window, and anything else that is helpful."

It made sense. "What's the third thing?"

"You will deliver an untraceable firearm with ammunition. This shooter prefers a 9 mm Beretta. He says they almost never jam."

I said, "I can get one. I will try for a Beretta 92 Elite LTT Compact. It's a nice weapon. He'll hate to throw it away. Tell him if this goes down clean, we'll get him another."

Marie smiled. "Gladly. I'll even pay for it."

"What else?"

"After you have delivered those items to the shooter, he will give you a burner cell phone. You have the phone to send a confirmation message the day of the hit, no later than an hour before, with any last-minute directions.

"If he doesn't get changes, and they will have eyes on the target location, the hit goes down as scheduled. You will get a text back confirming success. Then you destroy the phone, ditch the pieces, and get out of Mexico."

"That part I can do."

We sat silently for a long moment, both checking the room. The meeting was winding up.

Finally, she said, "Well?"

"Well what? It's been a productive meeting. Nobody shot at us. The coffee wasn't bad."

"Are you in or out?"

"I have to decide now?"

"I'm afraid so. There are a lot of moving parts."

"Contingent on your getting a green light for the money swap in the next 24 hours, and the deal's off if it doesn't go down well? If your swap team gets blown, we abort?"

"Of course."

I took several deep breaths. Goldfarb would shit bricks. Josie would not be happy with me.

"Well?"

I shrugged. "Sure. Why not? A Mexico vacation, how could I pass that up?"

Marie nodded. "Thank you. The shooter goes by Capache. It means 'trap' or 'trapper' in Spanish."

"How comforting…."

She took off her right earring and handed it to me. It was a small red star with a white jewel in the middle.

"Give him this."

"It looks Russian."

She shook her head, and we both scanned the room. "Nonsense. It looks like an earring. I will get you the location for delivering the funny money in the next 24 hours.

"I expect to have the location and time for the Mexico delivery in the next few days. It will definitely be in Tijuana. I'm assuming you prefer to make your own arrangements and pay your own expenses for the visit?"

"Absolutely. I'm not Russia's agent."

"Anything else?"

"Yes. You might still have a mole. Please don't screw this up. That could ruin my trip."

She smiled. "It could indeed. Would you like to make your exit first?"

"No. Ladies first. Have a nice day."

After she'd left, I sat there thinking for a full five minutes.

It gave Marie time to get clear. I was trying to imagine the rest of my day.

I was going to get my ass chewed and probably called back to DC to explain. Josie would not be happy with any of that.

CHAPTER TWENTY-ONE
CARTEL COUNTRY

Tijuana, Sunset, Two Days Later

The safe house sits on a side street in a barrio that looks out on the well-lit downtown and the dark foothills beyond. Tijuana is the largest city of both Baja California State and the Baja Peninsula.

It is part of the San Diego–Tijuana transborder urban agglomeration and the larger Southern California megalopolis. It is the most visited border city in the globe, sharing a border of about 15 miles with its sister city San Diego. More than fifty million people cross the border between these two cities every year.

San Ysidro Port of Entry is the busiest land-border crossing on the planet. The two stations between the cities proper of San Diego and Tijuana account for 300,000 daily crossings alone.

People call it The Gateway to Mexico. The economy is thriving and not just for tourism and farm goods.

There is a lot of industry. It is the medical-device manufacturing capital of North America. Many Americans go down there for their health care, and even more Canadians, due to their socialized medicine. Health care is famously "free" in Canada, but you can die or become permanently impaired while you are waiting to get it.

Tijuana is on the major route for drug and weapons trafficking, though Arizona is the leader in human trafficking, especially of young females. That traffic is still mostly through Phoenix, but with California now a sanctuary state, I expect that business is picking up.

A late-model pick-up truck is parked in the street and the surrounding alleys are scrawled with graffiti. The street is silent. Then the hit man steps from the shadows behind the parked truck and waves me on toward the safe house.

We sit at a bare table in the kitchen on the second floor. The tabletop is scored and oil-stained, as if machinery or heavy weapons are served there frequently.

I notice that the hit man has seated himself at the table in such a way that he can see out both of the room's windows at once. The curtains are open and the view looks out on the street below the safe house. A car approaching from either direction would be visible a long way off. He does not have his hands in sight.

The hit man says in Spanish to call him *Capache*. Yeah, right. *Trap or Trapper*.

I say in English, "I'm going to get something out of my pocket."

He nods. Using two fingers, I slowly extract the earring Marie had given me and slide it across the table.

He brings a hand from under the table, examines my talisman, and then nods again. "*Gracias*."

"*Capache*? Is that your real name?"

I have a little French. I studied up on my Spanish for Cuba, but my command of the language still isn't good. It is adequate for booking hotels and finding bathrooms, but not for serious matters. It was about what you'd expect in a tourist.

As in Cuba, that is my cover, but here it gave me more protection. Cuba, post Obama, had few Western tourists or businesspeople. Mexico has many and the cartels are paid by resorts and timeshares to leave them alone. Tourists still died, but mostly as bystanders or from mistaken identity.

"That is what you can call me," *Capache* said. He speaks good English with a soft voice.

"Marie said it was your name."

"It is what you can call me. What do I call you, *señor*?"

Marie gave me his background. *Capache* was once a *Sicario* for the Jalisco New Generation Cartel (CJNG), which had eclipsed the Sinaloa cartel—Chapo Guzman's old outfit—as Mexico's largest criminal syndicate. Then, about two years ago, Capache switched sides to oppose CJNG and its allies.

He currently served with an *autodefensa* in Tijuana. Probably a good move for him. Distant from CJNG, and a booming area with much need for his services.

I said, "What's in a name?"

"It defines who you are. I want to know who you are."

Apparently, he'd never read Shakespeare.

"Who am I? Why change things? I'm now your contact for Marie. You may call me *Anatoli* if you wish. He won't mind. He's not using the name anymore."

His eyes narrowed. "Where is he?"

"He's dead. The *Los Serpientes* cartel delivered his severed head to the Russian embassy in Mexico City. Marie wanted me to tell you that. They tried a hit on her as well. Do you know them?"

"Of course." *Capache* took his eyes from the windows and studied me for a long moment. "You are not Russian."

"No."

"Do you work for the Russians?"

"No. I am obligated to Marie. Her superiors have banned her from Mexico, so she sent me. She is your client."

"What do you want?"

"*Ramon Santos.* Do you know him?"

Capache said, "I know of him. Did *Santos* kill *Anatoli Vasilev?*"

"Yes. He tortured and killed him. Also, his wife. They sent a team from a different cartel after Marie, but failed."

"You are hiring me to kill him?"

"Not me. I'm not even here. Marie is hiring you to kill him."

"This is a job I'd do for free."

"No need. Marie wants to pay you. All that is between you and her, but I suspect it's probably best if you take her money."

"Is she paying you?"

I shook my head. "No."

"So, you are on the side of the Angels. Is that what I am to think?"

"You may think what you wish. Do you accept her assignment or not?"

"I feel good about the work I do," *Capache* said. "I kill murderers. Cartel members prey on society like vampires. Of course, I accept the job."

"Good."

It was an odd thing for a hit man to say, I thought. Strangely, it might even be true.

Capache scanned the windows. All was quiet outside. There were no lights from approaching vehicles. "Do you know what I require?"

"Yes. If you'll put both your hands on the table, I will pass you a weapon."

"Carefully, please."

"Marie said you prefer the Barretta. I think you'll find this one adequate."

Using two fingers of my weak hand, I extracted the weapon and placed it on the table.

"May I inspect it?"

I nodded. *This is where you earn the big bucks, Raven.*

He touched it gently and pulled it across the table to him. He nodded his appreciation. "A beautiful weapon, *señor.* May I pick it up?"

"Carefully, please. It is fully loaded with one up the spout. The safety is on."

Capache did a press check. He verified the safety was on and dropped it into a pocket. "Beautiful."

I relaxed slightly. "It's not tracible. Marie said she'll give you one just like it when you have to dispose of this one."

"That is most kind. Do you have the details that I require?"

"Preliminary." I proceeded to give him a small packet. A sketch of his target and a photo, plus two possible times and locations. A spare magazine.

"Will the target be in a group?"

"We don't think so. He may be in a vehicle with an armed driver, or he may be alone. Is that acceptable?"

"It is hopeful. We will validate it."

"We can give you an update the day of the hit. How much advance notice do you require?"

"An hour is sufficient. Both locations are close. No more than four hours, as things change. I will require descriptions of the colors and clothes he is wearing too."

"Understood."

I held out my hand and he gave me a cell phone. "My contact number is the only one in the directory."

"I'll text photos if I can."

"That would be helpful. You will dispose of the phone as soon as you get confirmation of the hit. Don't just clean it and throw it away. Smash it and the SIM."

"Understood. Is there anything else?"

"Not at this time. It has been a pleasure meeting you, *señor*. It would be best if you left first. Go with God."

"Thank you. Good luck to you, *Capache*."

Without a further word, I stood, nodded, turned away, and started down the stairs towards the back door.

A hit man with manners who spoke of God. Life could certainly be interesting.

Safe House, San Francisco, Later that Night

Josie smiled when her secure phone gave a soft "ding." Sometimes it was good to be a paranormal.

"You handled that well, Raven. I didn't sense danger. A meeting with a murderer turned vigilante, and with God on his side. Just when I thought I'd seen it all."

He said, "I think the earring did it, Babe. A Russian guardian angel. Who knew?"

"She's a dark angel, Raven. Marie wants vengeance and she is using you to get it. Do keep that in mind."

"Has she gone rogue?"

"Technically, no. She's banned from Mexico, but FSB won't mind if her efforts get *Anatoli's* killer."

"Understood. What are your viewings showing?"

"I don't see any imminent threats against you. How is your mission feel?"

"Bad vibes. Nothing specific. The entire city is a kill zone. We're doing good, but I'm glad you're not down here."

"When are you coming back?"

"Soon. I must stay here until our vigilante gets the job done. I'm to give him a targeting update shortly before the hit. I don't have to be close if you have clear viewings, and I'm trying to avoid close. Can you make that work?"

"That one is looking good. Crystal clear viewings for both the time-windows and locations you have. No changes in the clothing the target is wearing.

"His green 'Mexico' soccer jacket is distinctive. Vivid green, a red collar, and Mexico on the back as green dots against white letters, all caps. It looks brand new, and it is not in his current wardrobe. He is wearing it during both time-space windows."

"Where did he get it?"

"I'm working on that. I don't know. It's out of character for him."

"Do you have a preference for the hit?"

"The first time-window is best. It has stronger probability lines of success. I see that one as a primary, with the other as a backup."

"What about our friends interdicting the bribe transfer?"

"Highly uncertain, but unrelated. Right now, I'm seeing a hit that works in two days and the interdiction event about 24 hours later."

"Does the switch work?"

"It might. Flip a coin. Results will depend on the skill and luck of the FSB team."

"How about the hit?"

"The odds look good for both windows, but don't get too close. That one is a job for teams of locals."

"Yes."

"Stay safe, Raven."

"Always. I love you, Babe."

CHAPTER TWENTY-TWO
CIUDAD JEFE

Tijuana, Mid-Morning, Next Day

Ramon Santos was savoring his new life and learning how things worked. He was now in management, a side of things he'd not seen personally, only as an observer. The cartels had limitless funds and enormous power.

Chico is acting as my mentor and guide. His orders come directly from Mr. Trevino; the name no one dares speak. We are seated in the back of Chico's limo, enjoying the soft, comfortable, leather seats. The partition is up so the driver can't hear us.

Chico had just finished outfitting me at a fancy store called El Hombre. He had carefully selected my wardrobe. I didn't understand why this was worth such time and attention.

I said, "What are we doing?"

Chico said, "We have roles to play. It is important that you project the right image. The right clothes can help. Mr. Trevino wants you to be the face that we present to the local government officials. Do you like your outfit?"

"Of course. Elegant, and also comfortable. The Mexico soccer jacket is my favorite. I can wear it most of the year."

Chico smiled. "Tell me, have you ever been to a game?"

"No. I just like the jacket."

"What I thought. Appearances matter, especially so in your new job. *Los Serpientes* is part of Mexico. Soon we will become part of the government in Tijuana.

"All this is planned. It's why we buy from El Hombre and not a gringo place like Ralph Lauren or Tommy Bahama."

"I thought it was because they paid us for protection."

He laughed. "That too, my friend, but these clothes will become part of your new image. I will run operations and enforcement here, but few will know my name.

"You are collecting the bribe from the Americans. You will use that money to buy influence for us. You will use the money to protect us, help us grow, and to defeat rival cartels.

"Soon all those in local political power will know your name and value your support. Officials will know you as *Ciudad Jefe*. They will view you as a partner, a member of their team, a Spanish Santa Claus who dispenses gifts in return for good behavior. We are going to make you famous, Ramon."

"I don't understand."

"You will. Right now, the dominant cartel in Tijuana is the old El Chapo operation. The government lets them run free in return for helping them run the city, keeping tourists safe, and controlling street crime. Right now, we are getting the crumbs.

"We control less than twenty percent of the drug shipments, and we have to fight for those. A year ago, we had twenty five percent, but we've been stable at twenty for the past two months. It is taking a lot of effort to stay there and that eats into our profits.

"This conflict is costing both sides. Our plan now is to hold our share in drugs, to develop new revenue streams where we can have an advantage, and to gain more protection from the government.

"The most profitable business these days is human trafficking, women and children for sex, plus illegal voters to disrupt America and send money back to Mexico. Many groups will pay us big fees to get their people into America. Still, except for a few projects with Islamic terrorist groups that are friendly to us, we do little business in trafficking."

I said, "I assume Mr. Trevino wants to change that."

"That is my new job. It is his top priority for Tijuana. This is not just about making more money. It's also about denying money and power to the other cartels. As we gain power and protection, we will have more resources.

"Do you know that child trafficking is the fastest-growing criminal enterprise on earth? From Hollywood, to Washington, to Rome, and to all the capitals and playgrounds of the world, the elites in power turn a blind eye. Such crimes are seldom punished, but we are not even in that business. Yet."

"The big bribe coming in will let us fund that?"

Chico nodded. "That and more. You and I are going to do that, but there is a problem. All the cartels are run as businesses, with unwritten rules to prevent conflicts. Territories are assigned and protection is put in place. Conflicts are negotiated.

"The police are told who to raid and who to leave alone. To expand rapidly, we must break the rules or change them. We plan to do both. We will break the old rules, and put in place new rules that favor us."

"I'm listening. Tell me what to do."

"You will have a key role. We will use the bribe money to gain government support for our operations."

"By bribing officials in Tijuana?"

"By doing whatever it takes. Bribe them, kill them, coerce them, or replace them. Only the results matter. In one year, we plan to be the favored cartel for Tijuana. If not the largest, we want to be the most powerful, the most prosperous.

"The Sinaloa cartel is huge. They have a presence in seventeen Mexican states. Its main business is the distribution of marijuana, cocaine, methamphetamines and heroin from Colombia and Southeast Asia, to be delivered in the United States, Europe, and South America.

"Sinaloa is the largest and most powerful drug trafficking organization in the Western Hemisphere. They have activities all over the world, including better connections with drug suppliers than the ones we enjoy. They get better prices, and they move more product.

"We will slowly squeeze out Sinaloa. We don't have to beat them in head-to-head combat, we just have to make it more profitable to work with us than to fight us.

"Tijuana will become our bastion. We will control the land route for smuggling into the Sanctuary State of California, up into Oregon, Washington, and Canada."

I said, "There will be war."

"There already is, my friend. Now and forever. It is the nature of our world. Every night, both sides are putting duffel bags full of severed heads along the border. You know that."

"I've filled some of those bags."

"I know you have. The conflict here will become more violent for a time. That too is the nature of things.

"We can't beat Sinaloa in a total war. We will beat them by making it not worth the effort to fight us. That is why your efforts in gaining government protection are so important to us. Mr. Trevino is putting a lot of trust in you.

"When you sent the severed head of that diplomat to the Russians, it got attention. It stunned them to where they have not responded. The bribe money the Americans are sending us is a signal of support. That got attention too.

"You are helping us spread fear and gain respect. Most of Trevino's top chiefs support your new assignment. I recommended you to him and to them. Don't let us down."

"I won't."

"Good. Do you have any questions?"

"Just one. Can you tell me what you are doing in your new job?"

Chico said, "I can do better than that. We'll have lunch and then I'll show you. I also have a prize for you."

"What kind of a prize?"

"We captured the man who had the same job you have, except he worked for Sinaloa. We have been interrogating him. You'll find his information to be of use. We have a list of his contacts."

I heaved a sigh of relief. "Thank you."

Chico smiled. "We are family and you are now part of our family. I will help you succeed and so will the other chiefs."

After lunch, Chico's driver gave us a quick tour along the border. Not too close, as there were cameras and sensors, but close enough that we could see it.

He said, "The key distance is twenty kilometers, about twelve miles. Out of range of gunshots and surveillance, except for drones and for what I'm doing here we don't care about them."

"Why not?"

"Tunnels. I will show you."

We turned away from the border and came to an upscale neighborhood. Nice houses, not palaces, no walls, but large, and well kept. A few had security cameras, but the rest didn't seem to bother with them. That seemed odd to me.

Chico said, "Executives and officials live here. Protection is paid. This neighborhood is off limits for kidnapping and home invasions. The police and the cartels protect them. This is Sinaloa territory now, so we have to be careful."

I said, "We are driving around. Isn't that likely to attract attention?"

"Not if we don't linger or act in a suspicious manner. We are part of the landscape. I live here, or at least this vehicle does. It's registered to one of the homes. There is a sticker to prove that on the back window, a neighborhood association."

Chico called to the driver and we turned down a side street.

"We keep stash houses here. When active, we post lookouts outside to warn us. Everyone dresses nicely so they fit in. No violence is tolerated outside the houses. We will only move the women here after they have been trained to stop screaming and trying to escape."

"I discovered that myself. It is much easier when they are submissive."

He smiled. "That's why you are here, Ramon. The man noticed how you handled that runaway from Texas a few years back, the one who made it all the way out, all the way up past Phoenix. You got his attention. He told me to watch you, to see if you were qualified for management."

"The girl that we bought back from another gang?"

"Yes. It cost us almost nothing. I've heard the story many times. You lined up the other girls, and you beheaded her in front of them. Mr. Trevino liked that. It's now the standard policy for handling successful runaways."

"I remember. Her face was locked in a scream. I held it up for the others to see."

"We had no problems after that. Down here in Sinaloa country our policies are even tighter. Phone numbers are rarely used more than once. Phones are never used for calling out more than once. We change cars frequently. The safe rooms have locked doors and are soundproofed."

"It sounds expensive."

Chico nodded. "Yes. Each of these stash houses costs us over a million dollars."

I blinked. "How is that possible?"

He said, "I'll show you."

There were six stash houses in the community.

All of them were watched 24/7 by cameras, and the ones in use had stakeouts on patrol outside. The houses were linked by tunnels that had electricity and lighting. It was easy to walk through the tunnels, and there were pushcarts to help move drugs, weapons, and other supplies.

If any house were attacked, it could be quickly evacuated and there were explosives in place to collapse the tunnels. Each house had an interior room with a TV feed of the surveillance cameras.

There were two master stash houses, both larger. These had the big smuggling tunnels across the border. These tunnels had miniature rail cars that were electrically powered. The smuggling exits were well planned. They came up deep in the United States, well beyond the border.

The tunnel I toured was over thirty miles long. The exit was inside a large warehouse in San Diego. There were loading docks for large trucks. Chico told me it was close to light rail and a major freeway.

We did not exit the warehouse, but he told me there was security fencing and a main gate with a guard station that was manned by a team of four. Two remained inside the guard shack at all times, and the others were on a constant patrol of the perimeter. The guards were changed every eight hours.

I was told that the other large tunnel was even longer. That one came up in a rural barn.

Chico told me that all this was to go operational after the bribe money arrived, after I'd done my job to enlist the support of Tijuana officials. Not before. After.

I said, "Why are we waiting?"

"We dare not fail at this. Mr. Trevino does not want to launch this new business until all our protection is in place. I agree with him.

"For now, we prepare and test. As you see, the tunnels are working. They were constructed for us by Palestinians. They are the best in the world at building smuggling tunnels. Even the Israelis can't stop them.

"For payment, we are allowing them to use our tunnels on a limited basis to transport Hamas operatives, weapons, and other things of importance to them. It's been working well, and it helps cover our operating expenses.

"Hezbollah is interested in using our tunnels as well. We plan to renegotiate the terms and expand those operations when everything else is up and running."

Chico paused and gave me a direct look. "You have now seen the future, Ramon. How do you feel about your new assignment? This would be a good time to back out if you don't feel up to it."

I felt a chill. *We all knew the consequences of failure. One this big would never be forgiven. Would they even let me back out now that I'd seen all this?*

I took a deep breath. "I've never done anything like this before. It is key to our future, to the future of *Los Serpientes*. If it works, our future will be bright. If it fails, it would cause us great harm. It could even destroy us."

"We know that, Ramon. I need an answer. Can you do it or not?"

I lowered my gaze and braced myself. "I can't do it alone, Chico. I need help. I will need a lot of help, support, and guidance. There is no room for mistakes."

"Look at me," Chico said.

I did. He was smiling.

"That's the correct answer. You have passed the test. You will get the help you need, and your new job starts now."

I started breathing again. My heart was pounding. "What do we do now?"

"You are now a part of management, part of our family. So far, you've seen only the bottom of our organization. People down there are easily and quickly replaced. They are expendable.

"The average recruit comes in at about age sixteen and few live past their early twenties. They get to enjoy short, exciting lives with money, women, and drugs.

"It's different at the top. There, we are family. We support each other. We are brothers, Ramon, and you are now one of us. Do you understand what I'm saying?"

I looked at him. Realizing there was no turning back now. A new chapter of my life had opened.

I said, "Yes."

"I am taking you to meet our interrogator. The man who has been questioning the Sinaloa member who was doing that job, doing your new job, for the past five years. I'm told that we have drained him dry.

"Whatever you need, ask for it. Whatever concerns you, please share it with me. I will get you the help you need. If I can't get it, Mr. Trevino can. We need to get this done, Ramon."

I looked into Chico's eyes and discovered that I believed him. He needed this to succeed as much as I did.

"Thank you. How soon can I start?"

"Soon. Now if you wish."

"Do we have people good with the Internet, good at reading government documents?"

"Yes. What do you need?"

"I want profiles of everyone in the City Government for Tijuana. Their jobs. Their families. I want one or two-page summaries of each.

"I want to know who has the power. I want a special focus on those in Law Enforcement and Finance. I want to know all those being paid off by Sinaloa. Can we get that quickly?"

"When do you want it?"

"I'd like a briefing tomorrow morning, and a list of those who we think are on the Sinaloa payroll tonight.

"Can I work from here for a day or two, Chico? We don't have time to be driving around."

"Yes. I like your plan. I'll make it happen. How about a briefing at eight tomorrow? I'd like to attend."

"Of course."

"What about our hostage, the Sinaloa member?"

"Not yet. I want to get a briefing from our man who interrogated him first. I'd like a short summary of what he found, perhaps a page or two."

"Right after lunch?"

"Perfect. I'd like you to attend that one too."

"I will clear my day."

Chico called in one of his men. "Get Ramon whatever he needs. We'll be staying here through tomorrow."

He started making phone calls. I went with his man to find us rooms for the night, and a larger one where we could meet.

CHAPTER TWENTY-THREE
MEXICAN MADNESS

Tijuana, Next Day, Morning

The experts Chico summoned consisted of an accountant, two staffers, and the lead woman, old, imposing, and another name never to be mentioned. She was addressed as Pilar. She came with her own driver and a female attendant, both armed.

Chico had warned me to treat her with the utmost of respect. She was one of the founders of *Los Serpientes* and she was said to know everything that mattered.

When she entered the room, everyone stood. She looked at Chico. "I'm told that this meeting is important."

Pilar looked like an image from the days of the Conquistadors. Her skin was leathery and she spoke Spanish with a Castilian lilt, phrasing, and an accent from the old Spain, *castellano septentrional*.

I had heard that language before a few times. Not on the TV soap operas, but in major movies with Spanish translations. My mother told me it dated back to the time when Spain ruled the world. *This one had royal blood in her veins.*

Pilar wore her black hair severely pulled back into a bun. She had the most piercing green eyes I'd ever seen.

Chico kissed her hand and said, "Yes, Grandmother Pilar. We are honored that you came yourself. This is Ramon. He will be doing some important work for us."

She nodded at me and waved a hand. "Please sit. My time is limited and I've been briefed about Ramon and his new role. I found your questions interesting. I will share what we know. If you learn more, my staff and I would be interested."

"Thank you."

She had the woman with her pass out thin packets to Chico and me, saying, "You might want to take notes. I gather that neither of you know much about how the government works in Tijuana?"

She was here to brief me, so I spoke up. "We know very little. I think we must learn more if we are to be successful."

"A useful viewpoint," she said. "Ignorance usually leads to failure. Do raise your hand if you have questions."

Chico said, "Gracias, Grandmother. We need your wisdom."

Pilar said, "Frankly, we are puzzled that these American Congressmen want to spend so much money with a focus on Tijuana. The Mexican Republic consists of 31 states and a Federal District, the capital, Mexico City. Within the states, there are 2,377 municipalities. Tijuana is one, and it is far from the largest one.

"The nature of Mexico is authoritarianism. Policing and most public services are Federal. 'Mayors' in Mexico are actually municipal presidents. A different official, also called a Mayor, represents the city legally. The exception has been Mexico City, where the governor of the province is appointed by the President. Before 1993, so was the mayor."

Chico raised his hand.

"Yes?"

"You are saying that the mayors do not matter?"

"In the past they have not. The obligations of the mayors have been small. To chair the town council meetings, to execute the resolutions of the town council, and so forth. Mayors are also tasked with maintaining the public order and peacefulness, but they lack the resources to do much enforcement.

"This has been changing. With the murder rates being so high, local police forces are being formed and these are tolerated by the Federal Government. Tijuana, with strong ties to America and a major presence by American companies, is an example of this.

"In 2019, Arturo Gonzalez Cruz was elected mayor of Tijuana on a platform of open doors and an end to corruption. He is a business man who replaced a 'tough on crime' cop in that position. Some call him 'Mexico's Trump,' but that has been political speech.

"Not much has changed. We don't expect it will, though this sudden gift to us might signal something."

I said, "Why don't you think change is possible?"

Pilar flashed a quick smile. "Excellent question. With the exception of Mexico City, the mayors and city council members are limited to one three-year term. There are other constraints. For example, mayors are forbidden to leave the municipality without advance notice and their town council's consent.

"It would be difficult for mayor Cruz to collaborate with allies in America or even Mexico City. Some in the National Congress may support his positions, but they are not allowed to have staff. That limits any possible focus on power and action outside the Office of the President."

Chico raised his hand. "What is the President's position?"

"He is obviously fearful and insecure. President Obrador effectively allowed the cartels to establish sovereignty in 2019. It was Sinaloa that drove this policy change when it defeated the Mexican Army in combat. The new policy is 'abrazos, no balazos,' hugs, not bullets."

Chico said, "The government surrendered. We win. What's wrong with that?"

"It is good in some ways. The Federal Government will not resist the cartels, but neither will it intervene in conflicts between us. What's bad is that power has shifted from the Federal Government to Sinaloa."

I raised my hand. "So, the Federal Government favors Sinaloa?"

Pilar shrugged. "Not officially, but it is a concern. Sinaloa has more money and influence than we do. This is why I am extremely interested in why a high-level delegation from America is directing a large sum of money at the local level, which is to say, to favor us, not Sinaloa."

Our meeting continued for over an hour. We were given lists of elected officials, with photographs. Unfortunately, at the end, we had more questions than answers.

Pilar had no idea which officials were on the Sinaloa payroll, but she thought it was safe to assume that most were taking their money. That, she said, was the nature of things.

Pilar knew for sure that a fair number of officials, almost half, were taking money from us. She gave us a list of their names, with instructions to not copy, share, or discuss it with anyone but her.

Chico and I exchanged a look. It was a start.

After everyone left, Chico and I sat for a few moments, thinking.

Finally, he said, "You treated Pilar with respect. I think she likes you. That is a good sign."

I said, "Those green eyes look right through you. It's like she can see into your soul."

"She can read people. The first time I met Pilar, I was twenty. Someone betrayed us.

"We were raided by a rival cartel. We lost that fight and over a million dollars' worth of drugs. Only a few came back, myself and three others. One of our new members, a young kid, I don't recall his name, was strung out on uppers and angry at being sent into a trap.

"He cursed Pilar and called her a fool."

"What happened?"

"It turned out he was the fool. Pilar suspected something. She had him interrogated. It took him three days to die, but, by the end, he'd confessed about bragging to a girl about the run he was to make. It turned out she was the leak."

I said, "She's no fool, but the list of names on our payroll that she gave us is the main thing. I can access those people. I can control them."

Chico shrugged. "The list is useful, but better is that it shows Pilar trusts you. The problem is that we have no idea what these Americans are up to or what they expect for their money."

"That surprised me. We are lucky that we have the Sinaloa man who had my job. He will know."

"He should. When you recruit people at the city for us and give them their down payments, you can make them prove their worth and find out what they know. If you know how much Sinaloa has paid them, you can ask them what it got for the money, and what we can expect for ours."

"Yes," I said. "Did you have any other thoughts?"

"Pilar said she was unsure about whether the new policies made Mexico favor Sinaloa. But she **was** sure the new policies gave cartels more power. Correct?"

"Yes."

"No matter what Mexico favors, we know that Sinaloa is well connected. The American Congress is famous for leaks. I think Sinaloa might find out about the bribe. Do you agree?"

"I hope they are not that stupid. If they leak, we have big problems."

Chico said, "Even if they don't leak, we have problems. Just a rumor of a large payoff coming in will put Sinaloa on the alert. We need more guns. I'm going to ask Mr. Trevino for a covering force under my control with belt-fed weapons and RPGs until you can get the money distributed.

"Will you support me in that?"

I said, "Absolutely."

Tijuana, Afternoon

We met in the same room. This time there were three of us. Me, Chico, and the interrogator, a kid by the name of Enrique Miranda. He was small, wiry, and he looked terrified. His hands were shaking and he was holding a large white envelope.

We did not bother with introductions. Chico waved for me to proceed.

I said, "How long have you been with us, Enrique?"

"I joined at age 16. I turn eighteen next month."

"I understand that you questioned the Sinaloa man, the one running bribes into Tijuana?"

"I did. His name is Gerardo. I questioned him for over a week. His job was passing out money. He'd been doing it for five years."

"How did he pass out the money?"

"Cash. American dollars. Usually, hundred-dollar bills. He would just give them out in white envelopes."

"How much money in total?"

"He said about a million dollars American per month, this year. In the past it had been less, but he said it was getting more expensive to keep officials happy."

"Good," I said, making a note on my pad.

"Did he tell you what the bribes were for?"

"No, Senor. He said sometimes there were requests inside the envelopes, but that he never looked at them. He was told not to look, and he did not.

"There were quite a few different people. Most got paid every month, but some less often. It was money to get them to be friendly towards Sinaloa."

Chico could not contain himself. "How many people?"

The kid cringed. I shot Chico a look and gave him a small wave of my hand. *Easy.*

"A lot. A lot of people. Most were officials, and quite a few in the police.

"He recognized some of them because he saw them on the TV news. I have a list of names."

"Good," I said. "May I see it?"

"Yes. I brought it for you, Senor."

He handed me the envelope. I opened it and laid it out in front of me. It was the same list of officials that Pilar had given us, but shorter. Enrique's list had thirty-two names. Hers had sixty-three.

The kid's list was hand written in Spanish. Just names, with their contact phone numbers at work. No personal information. No cell phones. No home numbers, addresses, or family information.

Pilar's list had all his names, plus more. Hers had their office addresses and titles, while his did not. I checked it twice. There were no names on the kid's list that we didn't already have. Not even one.

"Do you know how much money he gave to each person?"

"No, Senor. He said it varied. He said that he made special trips and gave out bonuses sometimes."

"Did he know how much he was paying each one?"

"I'm not sure, Senor. I think that mostly he just got the envelopes and passed them out."

Chico looked at me. "Do we already have those names?"

I nodded. "Yes."

Chico said, "We need to speak with Gerardo ourselves."

"Yes. Where do we find him, and who runs that facility?"

The kid started to answer, but Chico interrupted. "I know where the facility is. The man who runs it is Carlos Gomez. I know him. He is responsible for interrogations. He runs the guards too. They have three shifts."

I looked at the kid. "Do you work for Carlos?"

"Yes, Senor. I do."

"Good. Tell him that we are coming over. We want to speak with the prisoner with him and you both present. You can ride with us."

The kid stood, but stopped like he'd hit a wall when Chico gestured.

"My name is Chico. Be sure to mention it. Tell Carlos that we're coming. He will know who to call if he needs authorization for our visit."

Remote Farm Outside of Tijuana

It took over an hour to get there, the last part on a dirt road in poor condition. Fortunately, Chico's vehicle had all-wheel drive. About a mile out, we passed a sentry with binoculars and a scoped-up rifle.

He waved us through, but the facility had tall double fencing, electrified, and there was a guard gate. There we were all made to get out of the car. One guard covered us with an American M-16, while the other searched the car, checking for trackers and looking underneath with mirrors.

He looked at Chico, obviously recognizing him. "Sorry, Senor. No exceptions are allowed. We must do the same on the way out.

"Once we found a prisoner hanging underneath. Carlos made an example of him."

Chico shrugged. "Just get it done."

They finally finished and we were directed to a large outbuilding in the distance. We pulled up in front and got out. Chico told his driver to wait in the car.

The building was old, with stone walls. Obviously, it had been a barn for cattle and horses, but the doors, barred windows, and security cameras were new. There was one guard, with a pistol on his belt, an American Colt .45, a radio, and a note pad, sitting under shelter by the door.

He made Enrique sign in, handing him a large key. "You know the way. You are responsible for the prisoner once you open the door. Understood?"

"Yes."

The guard looked at us. "Carlos is on the phone. He knows you are here and will be along shortly."

Chico nodded. I said, "Thank you."

The cell was at the far end of the building, behind a massive steel door. The key fit and the door opened easily. There were steps that led down and a light switch, which Enrique flipped.

The illumination was very dim. I could not see the bottom. I smelled dampness and decay. I could hear a faint scurrying, probably rats.

Enrique said, "Be careful. The lower steps are stone. They are often wet and slippery."

I said, "I'm eager to question the hostage. May he be moved?"

"I don't know. That is up to Carlos, Senor."

I said, "You never asked?"

"No, Senor. They gave me a flashlight. I questioned the prisoner in his cell."

The cell door was massive wood, and solid. There was no lock, but it was secured by two massive locking bars that dropped onto retainers on each side. Carlos had to help me lift them out of the way.

Inside was total darkness. "No lights?"

"I'm sorry, Senor. I should have asked for a flashlight."

Chico muttered a curse in Spanish. He held up his cell phone and we had light.

Enrique entered, followed by me. Chico stayed at the door. The smell was overpowering. I pulled out a handkerchief and held it to my nose.

I looked around the cell and saw nothing. Just a pile of rags on the floor, which was wet and slippery. The rags moved.

"There he is," Enrique said, poking the pile with his foot.

"I need your light," I said.

Chico said, "Come and get it, if you wish. I'm not going in there without a bio-suit."

I did, poking the pile with my foot. There was a man there and he wasn't moving. I shined the light on his face. I saw black hair, heavy beard, and a pockmarked face.

As I watched, he blinked. Once. One eye was blue, with a sightless stare, unfocused. The other was an empty, raw socket.

"Is that him?"

Enrique said, "Yes, Senor. That is Gerardo, the man I questioned."

Suddenly, the figure on the ground was pinned in a bright beam. Carlos had arrived. He was standing next to Chico, holding a large flashlight.

Carlos said. "You must be Ramon. I was briefed on you. Welcome to our humble facility. As you see, our prisoner is still alive."

I walked toward the light and handed Chico his phone back. Carlos was a big man with a bad leg and a scar on his face.

I faced him. Moving into his space. Making it a challenge.

"You were briefed?"

He nodded.

I pointed at Enrique. "This is the man you had question this prisoner?"

Carlos nodded again.

"Were you briefed on why we need the information, how critical it is that we know, and that my life probably depends on understanding the details of how Sinaloa has managed their relationship with the city?"

Carlos said, "You are boring me, Ramon. You've come to question my prisoner. Please do so, leave, and let us get back to our jobs."

I looked at Chico, then pointed at the pile of rags on the floor. "I can't question this man. He's dying or dead, and his interrogation was bungled. We have no useful information. That puts our entire operation at risk."

"Yes." Chico looked at Carlos. "We have a problem."

"I just got off the phone with Mr. Trevino. He did not share details, but he told me essentially the same. What do you propose? I am not in the business of resurrections."

Chico raised an eyebrow and met Carlo's glare. I was proud of him.

He said, "You raise a good question. We have major plans and your botched interrogation puts them at risk. What do you suggest, Ramon? You are closest to this."

I blinked. I had a feeling that what I said next would be the most important words I'd ever spoken. I took a deep breath.

Carlos laughed. "He doesn't know, my friend. He doesn't have a clue. Whatever you are doing, he's in over his head, and so are you."

I felt a surge of anger, but pushed it down. This wasn't the time. I looked at Carlos. "What do I suggest? We can't change history and bad decisions, but we can take action. We must take action."

Carlos looked surprised.

Chico said. "Indeed. The stakes are very high. What should we do?"

I pointed at Enrique. "Two things must be done. The first step is obvious. If this prisoner dies, if he can't be questioned, if we can't get the information we need, this man must die. He bungled the interrogation."

Chico nodded slowly. "That seems fair."

Carlos looked startled. "You think you have the right to kill one of my men?"

I shook my head. "Not at all. I think you have the right to do that. It might be best to have one of his friends do the execution. It would send a message."

Chico smiled and nodded. "A good solution. And if you don't choose to do that, my friend, there are Doctors. Hire them. Save this informer's life so that we can have professionals interrogate him. That way everyone wins. Do that, no matter how much it costs, and you can be a hero."

Carlos opened his mouth, then he closed it. He was thinking.

"What's the second thing?"

"I assume your interrogators have only had the basic training we give to recruits. Which cuts kill quickly. Which cuts kill slowly. Which cuts cause extreme pain and are useful when interrogating the captives that we've taken on raids?"

Carlos nodded. "That is basically correct."

"We are getting major opportunities to expand. Along that path, we will be capturing high value hostages whose information could make the difference between success and failure for our cartel, for our family, for our future, for our survival.

"There are some who are experts at interrogation. The Islamicists come to mind. We are already hiring their experts for tunnels. Why not hire them to train our interrogators?"

Carlos said, "How do you propose that I go about doing that?"

I smiled at him and nodded at Chico. "Do you want to tell him, or should I?"

Chico laughed. "I'll tell him. One word, Carlos. Do you want to guess, or must I tell you?"

"Tell me."

"Pilar."

There was no point lingering in the cell. Carlos said he would get medical help. He handed Enrique the flashlight, and directed him to stay with the hostage, saying he would send a woman to help clean him up.

Chico walked me back to the car. "There is no need for you to stay. I'll have my driver take you back to where we left your car. I need to speak privately with Carlos. We have things to discuss."

"What do you want me to do?"

"You did well in there. Start working on the money transfer. We still need a firm date and location. I'll pick you up in the morning at eight. We can have breakfast and talk then."

"Thank you for supporting me."

Chico shrugged. "We are all in trouble if we can't sort this mess out. Carlos most of all. I will be discussing that with him."

El Hombre Mall, Tijuana, Late Afternoon

Capache was sitting in a sidewalk shop a block from the planned hit, sipping coffee, and waiting. His cell phone was on the table. His spotter was in position, his motorcycle ride was waiting in a nearby alley, and half of a generous payment from Marie was in the bank.

This was his best team. They worked together well, and the targeting this time was superb.

He knew what his target was wearing. They even had a description of the car he'd arrive in right down to the brand, model, color and license number. Better yet the target would be dropped off to get his vehicle. There was only one spot that made sense for that. The curbside loading zone in front.

It was almost too good to be true. The target's vehicle was there in the parking garage, but they'd not touched it.

My phone gave a ping. The text said, "Positive ID. Two blocks out." I already had my text written. I hit send. "Go!"

I heard the cycle roar to life in the alley, tossed a bill on the table, stood, and strode toward the curb. The time had arrived. The trick was to move quickly, but naturally. To look relaxed, to not attract attention from witnesses who might be questioned later.

My ride pulled up and I hopped on the rear, putting my helmet on. I unzipped my pocket so I could easily reach my weapon.

"Stay a block behind. He'll probably get out on the curb side. I want you up on the sidewalk and moving fast when the back door opens. If he goes out the other door, stay in the street. Put me close."

"Got it." *It was exactly as we had briefed.*

The vehicle approached. A white Land Rover. Slowing. Two occupants. It moved to the curb, the left rear door opened, and I saw the green jacket.

My driver poured on the power.

Ramon was just straightening up when my first nine-millimeter hollow point took him in the rear of his head. I followed it with two more. One to the head, and one diagonally though his heart.

Ramon never knew what hit him. He never saw me. His body was still falling as we passed.

His driver was starting to get out, moving fast, reaching for a weapon. He did see me, so I gave him a double-tap through the partially open door.

There was no pursuit.

CHAPTER TWENTY-FOUR
THE FUTURE IS NOT WHAT IT USED TO BE

Tijuana, Next Day, Morning

M y secure phone beeped. It was Josie.
"I was going to call you. It's been a bit tense here. Didn't much like my ass hanging out down here with zero support, but we got it done."

"I know you did. I also know you need to get out now. Get out today, Raven. Our friends can have air transport for you in San Diego this afternoon. I can be there too."

"What do you know that I don't, Babe?"

"I know you scare me. You have quite a gift for stirring things up."

"Keep talking."

"You just caused the cartel wars to go nuclear. The gates of Hell just cracked open a notch. There is going to be a blood bath."

"Over one dead thug? The body count down here is dozens per day, sometimes hundreds."

"Should we discuss who sent you down there and why? That maybe you're being played?"

I sighed. "No. This is not a good time."

"Damned right it's not. Your target was a key player, a rising star. The cartel had big plans for him.

"There's more. Against the odds, everything worked. The funny money, payback for the diplomat's head in the box, treason and corruption soon to be exposed, and more."

"I'm done here, babe. I got validation, ditched my burner phone, and was going to call you."

"Yes, but more is coming. A sequence of small actions is adding up to change the world. What you just did was a trigger. Space-time is rippling with probability waves.

"I see chaos down there on the near horizon. Mexico is going to get ugly, Raven."

"It was ugly when I got here. Is someone targeting me now?"

"Not yet. What I'm seeing is cloudy, but it's more like a civil war between the cartels, with international players – like your friends – throwing gas on the flames. Burning cities. Dead bodies."

"When?"

"Hours. Maybe a few days. It turns hellish after the bribe money arrives. The swap worked. When discovered, it will cause a war between the cartels. One that will draw America in to protect our southern border, and others who will oppose us. You need to get out now."

"I can be at San Diego International by about two PM."

"They only have one runway and it might be closed. International flights might be shut down. Stay away from the Tijuana airport. The best bet is Brown Field. Can you be at the San Diego Jet Center by then?"

"No problem. Where are we going?"

"I was hoping for Florida. We can go on to Florida and get clear of the events out here."

"I need to go back to San Francisco. Unfinished business."

"Your Red Sparrow is going to get you killed, Raven."

"She's been getting shit done. More than that, she owes me. I need to collect."

"What? Are you saying this is about money? I'm disappointed in you, Raven."

"She actually got the cash? The bribe money?"

"Yes."

"All of it?"

"Yes."

"It's not about money. I wouldn't touch that money. It would compromise us."

"You got that right. That bribe will become the ground zero for a regional apocalypse. Mexico will soon be in flames. It will start in Tijuana and spread up and down the invasion route from Venezuela into the U.S. If the big players get crosswise, it could go regional or worse."

I frowned. "Can you assess the odds?"

"Not yet. If I had to guess, a near certainty for collapsing Mexico. Maybe a fifty/fifty chance of a regional war, one that could easily go global. The bribe money and its involvement with high level corruption in Mexican states is the trigger event.

"Don't blow me off on this one, Raven. These days we all remember how Pearl Harbor unleashed World War II and nuclear weapons. What we **don't** remember is that World War I, which may have killed more people, started off with some Duke that no one ever heard of being assassinated by a lone fanatic for a cause that no one ever heard of.

"It was one of the deadliest conflicts in the history of the human race. Over 16 million people died in combat. The total number of civilian and military casualties is estimated at around 37 million. Small events can trigger horrific outcomes."

"It's not about the money, Josie. I don't care about the money. That's not what she owes me."

"What then?"

"Cuba. I have a plan."

"That woman is dangerous, Raven."

"One short meeting and we'll go East. Can you clear it with our masters?"

Josie sighed. "I can get you picked up in San Diego. They want to meet with us somewhere off the radar. I think we go to the ranch next. Does that work?"

"It does. I think I can be over the border by noon, so step the flight up if you can. We can have dinner."

"Just get there. A plane will be waiting for you. Text me when you are out of Mexico."

"See you soon. I love you."

"I love you too. Just move your ass."

"Roger that, Babe. I'm coming."

Fairmont Hotel, San Francisco, Morning

Karlov seemed relaxed for once. He was casually dressed, brown slacks, a white shirt open at the neck, no tie, and loafers. It seemed we'd reached a new level of informality.

I watched him and sipped my tea.

"You seem happy, Marie. Have you avenged Anatoli Vasilev?"

I said, "Not me, Sir, but, yes, he has been avenged. The man who beheaded Vasilev, a *Los Serpientes* cartel thug named Ramon, was gunned down in Tijuana yesterday along with his driver.

"No witnesses came forward. No one saw anything and there are no suspects. The police are blaming it on cartel violence, which, of course, is common."

"There is nothing to tie Russia to this?"

"Of course not. Russia was not involved. I've been right here in San Francisco. I've not been to Mexico since I visited the embassy last year."

"What else can you tell me?"

"Just what's been in the media. It was a professional hit. An unidentified shooter on the back of a motorcycle wearing a helmet."

Karlov looked thoughtful. "There is an opportunity here. Most will suspect the Sinaloa cartel. The two are competing for power."

I shrugged. "Sinaloa would be the likely suspect. The groups are like savage feral dogs in a cage. Both are ruthless and they hate each other.

"Actually, Sir, I came to discuss something else. Thank you for approving the money swap. Our plan worked perfectly. I have the money."

Karlov blinked. "All of it?"

"Yes."

"Can we really be that lucky?"

I laughed. "It was a gift, Sir. The American delegation never even opened it. We just switched the pallets. I have the money. The American traitors will unknowingly deliver the phony batch to *Los Serpientes* in Tijuana soon, maybe tomorrow."

"Excellent."

"What do you want me to do with the money?"

"I've been thinking about that. I want to keep it off the books."

"Yes. That might be best for all concerned, Sir."

"FSB deserves some. The Americans provided the fake money, and on a tight schedule. They deserve some. You deserve some for operating expenses. How about a 40/40/20 split? I can give you a bank account number for the FSB part."

"My contact for the Americans is a Canadian. He didn't want to get involved."

"I could not care less about how it is handled so long as it doesn't trace back to where it came from, Russia, or FSB. Have him get the Americans to give us a contact point. He's the one who got them to send us the fake money. He can send their share back up that channel."

"Yes, Sir."

Karlov actually smiled. "You've done well, Marie."

He was silent for a time. I could almost see his brain churning.

Finally, he said, "I might even leak it that some major American bribe money is coming to the *Los Serpientes* cartel. Through appropriate cutouts and back channels that lead in harmless directions, of course. That would be fun to watch."

"I like the way you play chess, Sir. I'll get in touch with my contact and let you know what he suggests about the Americans."

Karlov nodded. "Do it today. It would be best to wrap this up before things explode down there. If the American delegation manages to get themselves killed in Mexico, it will be on the news for weeks."

"Yes, Sir."

CHAPTER TWENTY-FIVE
USEFUL IDIOTS

Safe House, San Francisco, Next Morning

Millie's safe house was adequate, but it was small and lacked perimeter security. It wasn't defensible, and egress was less than optimum. Its main attribute was the location, which was convenient for covert meets with the Russians. Trading off safety for convenience was a deal with the Devil.

Our safety here – tucked in the corner of a sanctuary city in a sanctuary state – depended on not being noticed, on not being followed. I sat on the small deck sipping coffee, thinking of the other places where we'd been burned in once-safe America, even Durham, Monterey, and Portland.

Josie was worried about my Russian contact putting me at risk, but my main concern was that I must not put **her** at risk. I made myself a mental note that if I needed another meeting with Marie, I'd come alone, try for a meet in a different city, and use a different legend, except with the Russians.

I'd had no problems getting out of Mexico. Then, just a short flight, and our being dropped off at Moffit Field, which was the most secure place I could think of nearby. One of the agencies stashed clean cars there and I'd borrowed one under my Digger legend. *Never trust a rental car. They all have tracking. Uber is worse.*

Meeting again with my Russian contact was necessary, but it raised some problems. I'd been using the Digger identity too much. My cover was wearing thin. Josie was nervous about my coming back and I couldn't blame her. I'd come to trust her paranormal senses, but, in the end, I was responsible for our security.

Caution was prudent. We spent more time running CSRs and making sure we were clear of ticks than we did getting here from the border. It was all relative. We'd had problems last time, but that was because Marie herself had been betrayed, not because she had betrayed us.

Somewhere, somehow, it seemed the Russians had a leak. I was confident that Marie would not take another chance on that. I was betting on it. She was a pro. She'd keep me safe to keep herself safe.

Compared to Havana or Tijuana, San Francisco was safe. Both of those were flaming red zones, with the latter on the ragged edge of turning purple. This one was just a failing American city, with corruption, shit in the streets, drugs, homelessness, and a lot of crime.

It was all relative. It was a short distance from *I left my heart in San Francisco*, to *They killed my ass in San Francisco.* I hoped to avoid both.

I didn't look back when Josie pulled the sliding door open.

She said, "It's just me. I'll give you hot coffee if you promise not to jump up and pull a weapon."

I turned, smiled, and she let me kiss her.

"I didn't even **have** a gun in Mexico, Babe. Cuba either, for that matter. Right now, back in the US of A with my little Sig close at hand, I'm like Linus van Pelt with his blanket."

"Who?"

"The scruffy kid in the Peanuts cartoons. Not a care in the world."

"You say the strangest things...."

"Not even close, compared to you. Does your magic still say we're good?"

"Yes," she said, "but let's not push it. I'm still coming down from my viewings of Mexico, but everything looks to be safe here for the next day or so."

"Want to go out for breakfast?"

"No. Let's not press our luck. Promise me we'll leave as soon as you get done with your Russian spy."

"Works for me. It should only be a short meeting. I'm expecting happy talk."

Josie came back with a small tray. Her cup, a coffee pot, and the bagels and lox we'd picked up while we were running our endless CSRs. She set it down, seated herself, and looked at me.

"What's the plan?"

I started telling her....

Rocky's Corner, San Francisco, Afternoon

Another broken rule. We'd gotten into trouble by using the same meet location repeatedly. Now we were doing it again.

I sighed. *Life was about tradeoffs. So was death.*

I watched Marie enter. She checked the room professionally, her eyes missing nothing, came over and sat down next to me. From our positions, we could both check the main door, the one from the alley, and the stairs coming down from upstairs.

Marie said, "How was Mexico?"

"Ferocious. I don't recommend it this time of year."

She gave a short laugh. "Good to know. I'll try to avoid it."

I said, "You were **ordered** to avoid it."

"True." Her look turned serious. "I was. Thank you for helping. I owe you."

"My pleasure. Actually, I do need to ask you for something, but ladies first. You called this meeting. Why?"

"I've been instructed to give you money."

I blinked. "Really?"

She nodded.

"How much?"

"40% of the bribe money. Cash. Non sequential bills."

Ten million dollars. "What do you want in return?"

"Nothing."

"Are the Russians giving away money now?"

"No. This was a windfall, a gift. We don't have to account for it. The Americans helped us resolve a difficult matter and this is their share.

They have earned it. In addition, the Vogel abduction was, as you pointed out, poorly handled by us. That caused public embarrassment. Sharing this gift might help the Americans think better of us in the future."

I shook my head. "Perhaps it will, but I'm Canadian, they are not involved in this, and I don't want the money." *Stick with your legend. Always.*

"Someone will." She handed me a piece of paper. There were two numbers and a date written on it in block print.

I frowned. "What's this?"

"Something for your American friends. The first is a phone number to call. It will accept messages. The second number is a code. Whoever calls must provide that code with a contact name and phone number for a call back."

"What's the date for?"

"The offer is void after that date. The contact number will stop working and this conversation will have never happened."

"And if someone calls?"

"A courier will deliver a package to the person named, to wherever they specify in the U.S."

I smiled at her. "To Mr. John Smith, care of CIA, Langley, Virginia?"

"I don't expect whoever you give this to would be that stupid, but it's not my problem. Let's just say that private addresses in the Western U.S. would be best. Yes, a signature is required for delivery confirmation."

"Why?"

She shrugged. "The normal reasons. We have our bureaucrats too."

"I don't know if that will be acceptable or not, Marie."

"Neither do I, but it is not my problem. Is it yours, Digger?"

I thought for a long moment. Finally, I said, "No. It is not my problem. I will pass your message along."

The barkeep was coming our way. This one was younger and probably better mannered.

Marie smiled. "Good. Can I buy you a beer?"

"Sure. Why not?"

She said, "Two pints of Guinness."

The kid nodded. He came back with two mugs, pretzels, and napkins.

"I told you I'd buy next time."

"Yes, you did." I took a sip and nodded thanks.

Marie smiled. "You said you want something more?"

"I do, but first a question. Off the record, what is your position about the Cubans?"

"My personal position? They are pigs. It was a happy day when Russia no longer had to support them. Those idiots were sucking us dry."

"What is Russia's position regarding the Cuban presence in Venezuela?"

"Our diplomats have been, ah, publicly circumspect about Cuba."

"What about privately?"

She shrugged. "They are our brothers, of course."

"Useful idiots, as Lenin said?"

"It's disputed that Lenin said that. In any case, we avoid saying negative things about them in public. They have been useful for controlling the cartels in some cases, but they can't be trusted for anything of importance."

"They cause problems?"

"Of course. For themselves and everyone else around them. After Obama served his term, they started bombarding your Embassy in Havana with some ultrasonic weapon that caused brain damage to the very same diplomats that he'd put there to help advance Cuban causes. They are idiots."

"I get it." *Not useful idiots. Just idiots.*

"Good." Marie pinned me with a look. "Can we get to the point now? What do you want?"

"The Americans have been asking me to find out something about Cuba for them. They brought it up again when I involved them in getting your counterfeit money."

She looked puzzled. "The Americans helped us. What do they want in return?"

"Information. A name. The name of a Cuban officer."

Marie was frowning and shaking her head. "That doesn't make any sense. The Americans have an embassy there. The Cubans publish rosters of their officers in the newspapers."

"I just know what they asked me. They asked me for a name.

"The Americans don't have a real embassy in Cuba. They do still have a small office tasked with supplying emergency assistance to their own citizens there, which are apparently very few. Clerical issues. Things like passport renewals, first time passport applications, notary services, authentication services, and Consular Reports of Birth Abroad."

"No ambassador?"

"No."

"Do any of their staff even read or speak Spanish?"

"I have no idea, Marie. They just asked me for the name of an officer. Well, two names, actually."

She was smiling. "That's just crazy enough to be true, Digger. What names do they want?"

"Who commands the Revolutionary Guard? Who commands the Colectivos in Venezuela?"

She looked stunned. "May I ask why they want these names?"

I spread my hands open. "I'm not sure. Something about humanitarian concerns in Venezuela. Apparently the *Colectivos* are an issue to some in their Congress. They are...."

Marie waved her hand. "Everyone knows who the *Colectivos* are. They are thugs, modeled after the Brown Shirts, violent groups to intimidate civilians. There are over 50,000 of them in Caracas. They took control of the city away from the local government and the cartels."

"That directly caused a humanitarian crisis and massive forced emigration?"

Marie said, "Yes, it did."

"Then it all does make sense, Marie. American politicians tend to get involved in such causes."

"That's all they want?"

"I have no idea. It is what they asked me for."

"I will give you the names, Digger. They are, as I said, public information. I cannot conceive that the Americans don't already have them."

"They might, for all I know. Silos of information and all that...."

She was shaking her head. "That's all you want?"

I nodded.

"General Arnaldo Ochoa commands the Revolutionary Guard. It is more or less modeled on Iran's Revolutionary Guard. Ochoa is a two-Star general, a *General de División*, based in Havana."

I was writing that down on a napkin. She waited until I was done, then said, "In Caracas, the *Colectivos* are commanded by Hernando Cardoza, a Colonel.

"He's hated by the populace. We're not fond of him either."

"Thank you." I wrote that name down too.

Marie sighed and finished her beer. "Sometimes I'm still astonished about the ignorance of bureaucrats."

"Me too. Are we done?"

"We are. You can leave first this time. I might have another beer and reflect on American ignorance."

"It's been a pleasure. Good luck in Mexico. I'm glad that we avenged the death of your friend."

"Good luck to you as well, Digger."

Marie gave a wave of her hand for another beer. I stood, nodded my thanks again, and headed for the door.

I did not look back, but I did take my time running CSRs and thinking.

Public information. They didn't even know that.

President Blager was right. It seemed that few in the CIA ever left their damned building and the State Department was worse. They didn't even bother to read the newspapers.

CHAPTER TWENTY-SIX
AN AWKWARD EXCHANGE

Safe House, Tijuana, Two Days Later

Chico was afraid. It had been a long time since he felt fear, but now he did. His life had been violent. He killed his first man when he was fifteen, just a kid, a novice trying to prove himself to the cartel. An older brother had sponsored him. Once you started down the road to being a cartel member there was no turning back.

Chico was clumsy back then, inept, and afraid all the time. The initiation victim kept moaning, flopping around on the floor, refusing to die. The older members laughed at him.

The boss made Chico kill all the prisoners that day. Three men, a woman, and two children. The ritual was repeated until he became proficient.

Weeks passed. The boss would point and say, "Do them all."

Chico would comply. Eventually, it was like brushing his teeth, no big deal. It didn't matter. The prisoners were going to die anyway.

He learned to both kill quickly and how to cause a lingering, painful death. Once proficient, he moved up the ranks quickly. He was now family, and, under normal circumstances, no longer disposable.

Unfortunately, circumstances were anything but normal. Ramon Santos was dead. Sinaloa cartel was in control of Tijuana. It had them outnumbered and outgunned. The money the Americans was bringing was no longer an opportunity for *Los Serpientes*, it was a survival issue.

Failure was not an option. Failure would not be forgiven. Failure meant death.

I looked across the table at Pilar. "I need to meet with Mr. Trevino."
She shook her head, "That's not possible. He sent me."
"I need to speak with him."
"No."
"This is important, Grandmother."
"I agree, but there is no time. Our security has been compromised. Until we find out who did it and fully interrogate Ramon's killer, we are taking no chances. Trevino will not come to Tijuana."
"Then I will go to him."
"No. He sent me. The Americans arrive tomorrow.
"Five officials and a pallet of money. You are responsible for the transfer, for security, and also for getting money promptly to the local officials. We urgently need their protection."
"I've never done anything like this before."
"You know how to do security, Chico. Help is coming. Twenty people, a team leader, belt-fed machine guns, and RPGs. They will be here tonight. They will be under your command."
"I'm not a diplomat. That was to be Ramon's job."
Pilar looked at me critically. "Ramon had no more experience at diplomacy than you do. Less, if anything."
I met her eyes. If she thought I was making excuses, I was doomed. Orders were to be followed. I chose my answer carefully.
"I can only be at one place at a time, Grandmother. If we lose the money and the American officials, we lose everything."
She thought about that for a time. Finally, she nodded. "You make a good point. We would, and we won't get another chance.
"It took considerable effort to get them to side with us. The Americans have been supporting Sinaloa. The money they bring is needed, but it's even better to have the support of their high officials."
"We can hire lawyers to distribute the money to government officials. That's just a detail. I can handle that myself, if needed."
"Do we know why the Americans are switching sides?"

"We do not. I personally doubt they are. One faction has chosen to support us. We will find out more when we take the delivery."

"Why are they making the transfer here in Tijuana? This is Sinaloa territory. They have us greatly outnumbered. If I'm not mistaken, the council last year decided this was their territory, that we were allowed to do business, but must give them half."

Pilar shrugged, "The Americans chose the location. We are in compliance with the council ruling."

"We are? How can that be? You know about the tunnels. You know about the money."

She was silent for a long moment. Finally, she nodded.

"Another good point, Chico. Having you run this operation requires a promotion. You have more responsibility and you need to know the protocols. I will share some information with you, but you are not to discuss it with anyone except me and Mr. Trevino. Do you understand me?"

"I do, Grandmother. Clearly." *If I leaked, I died.*

"The council must be obeyed."

"That's what I thought…."

"Do you know why?"

I shook my head.

"In the end, it is about making money. No one wants a total war between the cartels. A war would hurt us all. That's the main reason we have a council, why we obey their rulings.

"Any cartel that violates a council ruling would see every hand turned against them. All the other cartels, international rights organizations, governments, law enforcement, the UN, the news media, and on and on. The good news is that none of that matters for this transaction. It is not a concern."

"Why not?"

"Because we do not violate the council ruling, Chico."

"I don't understand."

"There was a dispute between us and Sinaloa, one that drove the council ruling last year. The council decided that Tijuana and all of Baja

California State was their territory, but ruled that we could operate here if we gave Sinaloa half our drug trafficking revenues.

"It was a harsh ruling. Half of our gross revenues removes most of our profits from drugs."

"Why did we agree?"

She waved an arm. "It's complicated. Mostly, because they are strong and we want a presence here. There have been arguments about the accounting at every council meeting ever since. There have also been periodic skirmishes between us and Sinaloa."

"They don't know about our smuggling tunnels?"

"Of course not. They will eventually find out, but by then we will have data to show our tunnels are used for human trafficking, not drugs. The council ruling only applies to drugs."

"We run drugs down the tunnels as well."

"A small amount. Right now, it's in the test phase. We are just getting started. If discovered and challenged, we can do the accounting needed to comply with the ruling. We can apologize and pay what is needed."

I nodded. *It was complicated.*

Pilar said, "That's what's so nice about the Americans coming to support us. Do you understand why?"

"I can guess. Bribes to officials are not part of the council ruling?"

"Correct. Nor are they ever likely to be. Everyone gives and takes bribes. Only the Americans call this a bribe. This is *La Mordidita*, the little bite. It is a normal part of our doing business.

"*La Mordidita* is everywhere. None of the cartels would be willing to disclose the details, not even to the council. No one wants them disclosed, not the cartels, and not officials or law enforcement."

This was bigger than I'd imagined. "It would be a major disaster for us if this transfer failed."

Pilar laughed. "Of course, it would. Did you think that I am here because I didn't have anything else to do?"

"No."

"What are you most worried about, Chico?"

"Politicians are fools. They talk. They brag. They leak. Someone killed Ramon. That can't be a coincidence."

"I agree. So?"

"What do you think the odds are that Sinaloa has been tipped to the transfer?"

"Better than even, if I had to guess."

"What should I do if Sinaloa or someone else shows up and attempts to interfere?"

"Ask them to desist, of course. Speak clearly. Use your cell phone to record it. Get that on record."

I frowned and shook my head. "Desist?"

"Get them to back off. To stand down."

"And if they refuse?"

She shrugged.

"If someone tries to block the transfer or tries to take the money, what are my orders?"

"Try to save a witness. Try to save a recording to prove that you warned them. Kill the rest. The main thing is to get the money."

"Kill them all?"

"Yes, if needed. It's your call. We can sort it out later at the council if anyone complains."

"Is that what Mr. Trevino has ordered?"

"It is. He told me that personally, face to face, looking into my eyes. Can you do that?"

"Is this team you are sending me good at what they do?"

"It's one of our best, Chico."

"Tell them to bring a lot of ammunition."

CHAPTER TWENTY-SEVEN
CUBA LIBRE? OR NOT....

Patrick AFB, Florida, Private Office, Next Day

It seemed like old home week.

Everyone was there. Me, Josie, Goldfarb, Mike, Commander Bromley, and my support team for Cuba. That was Rudy, Terry, Vinnie, and Pat, our sniper. Plus Will, who ran Cybertech and had been stuck with paying the bills to get our boat, the *Busted Flush*, operational.

I had just finished briefing everyone about Mexico, the other end of the invasion route. It had been a short discussion.

Mike looked at me, shaking his head. "I was hoping for good news, Raven. Inspiration. A new approach. Bottom line, you just told us that trying to mount an OP at that end of the invasion route is a no go."

I shrugged. "Reality sucks. For now, I suggest we stay clear. It's the wrong end of the dog to wag, in my opinion. Mexico is a war zone and we are back to square one."

Goldfarb said, "Explain that."

"Which part?"

"Start with the 'back to square one.' I presume that means Cuba."

"It does. Cuba holds the keys to Venezuela, the open end of the invasion route."

"We knew that before, Raven. How is this progress?"

"I now have specific targeting, we've done a recon and know the ground, we still have an intact team, and I'm told we now have an operational boat and an egress plan."

Goldfarb looked sharply at Mike. "Is that true?"

"Probably. We are here to discuss those details. Rudy will report on the boat status, and Commander Bromley will tell us what the Navy can do to support us."

"Cut to the chase. Do we have an operational boat and a covering force, yes or no?"

Rudy said, "The *Busted Flush* is a go. It does 62 knots in a flat sea and all systems are operational."

Bromley said, "The boat is operational. If they can make it out into international waters the Navy will cover them."

"You got that from Admiral Perkins?"

Bromley nodded. "I did, Sir."

Goldfarb eyed Bromley critically, looking him up and down. "I see that you have a cane and a walking cast, Commander. Would you care to comment on the crew status?"

"I'm still on limited duty, but the boat crew is operational. Some of our best helmsmen have been training Rudy. He's good."

I said, "Egress is a key risk, Rudy. Tell him."

Rudy said, "What Commander Bromley said is correct. They put me through the wringer. I'm Navy qualified in small boats. They had me practice evasion in the *Busted Flush*, including in rough seas and against fleet warships."

"Admiral Perkins is good with our plan?"

"Provisionally."

I said, "What the Hell does that mean, Commander?"

"It means we don't **have** an operational plan yet. The boat can scoot, but it can't shoot, Sir. How much force can we use? Do we have the authority to violate Cuban waters or airspace to protect your boat? Can we use lethal force? If so, do we need eyes on, or can we turn our weapons loose?"

"You are asking about ROE's?"

"Yes, but more. What is our mission scope? We need guidelines. When we go weapons hot, the Rules of Engagement will involve decisions that need to be made in real time by the local commanders."

Mike and Goldfarb exchanged a look.

I said, "My team is hanging out on this one. You have heard of the Bay of Pigs?"

Mike said, "We had a fleet in position off Cuba with orders to do nothing. It did not end well."

"That's the one...."

Goldfarb said, "It helped to topple a Presidency, as I recall. I do need your egress plan."

I said, "A plan is a piece of paper. If we have to haul ass out of there with the whole Cuban Military after us, we'll need the fleet prepared to do more than watch."

Bromley said, "That's why I'm here. To make sure we're all on the same page."

Goldfarb said, "Your plan is that page."

"It's still coming together, Sir. That's our next item. I can't firm up all the details until we're on the ground and active in Cuba, but I can give you a baseline in an hour for approval, assuming we're all good with the concept."

"Do it."

"What I can give you right now, if you wish, is not a plan, but an opinion. Why Cuba?

"I need to share why I think we should stay clear of Mexico for a time. Cuba is a tough nut to crack, but it's our best option from a short list of shitty choices."

Goldfarb was scowling. "Give me the short version."

"Expect a major shit storm, starting in Tijuana, and soon."

"Why?"

"Traitors in Congress. Recall the talk we got about broken oaths? This shit is turning real."

"Keep talking."

"A contingent of American Congress Members from the opposition party is taking a sizable bribe down into Mexico to benefit a particular cartel. A significant pile of cash in unmarked bills is coming in."

"That's happened before, Raven."

"Sure, but it's usually been laundered through popular government programs with layers of cutouts, labeled as foreign aid, military aid, humanitarian aid, and so forth.

'The money comes wrapped in high purpose, but it's dirty. Corruption is deep, everyone is paid off, and the fix is in. Both parties feed at that trough, often with low profile family members who are not government employees being gifted with lavish jobs, fees, or other perks."

Josie said, "It's the dark side of civilization, Raven. Today, both parties do it. Tribute to rulers is as old as the human race. It's how the Romans crushed the Celts.

"Money is power. Power is control. Power corrupts, and, in the end, the dreams die and there is tyranny."

I shut my mouth. She was right. *She knew.*

She was our group's bright spirit who always looked for the good in people. *Even me. I was blessed.*

Finally, I said, "This time it's different. This time it's stupid. This time it shines crooked in the naked light of day for all to see."

Goldfarb said, "This time it's a flat-out bribe paid directly to a cartel? A truck full of cash?"

"Exactly."

"That's stupid. Why did they go that way?"

"No idea. What I do know is this: If detected by an opposing cartel, and it probably will be, there will be violence. There will be a blood bath. It could set off an all-out war between the drug cartels. They are already killing each other."

"How soon?"

I shrugged. "Good question. Watch the Fake News. They often leak and spin such things for those who favor open borders. It's time to put the Intel community on alert. It's their job to know these things.

"My guess? Soon. The inciting event is maybe tomorrow. Likely this week. When do we see a shitstorm on the news and government reactions? I'd guess within a month."

"You are talking about State Department stuff? Warnings? Travel restrictions?"

"Yes, and more. These bad actors from our Congress might be killed or taken hostage. Major wars between nations start over things like that."

"They are bringing money. No one shoots Santa Claus."

"I don't know the *quid pro quo*, but for sure the money isn't a gift, Santa's not involved, and drug deals go wrong all the time. There's a lot that could go wrong with this one.

"The cartels kill for fun and hijack each other regularly. It's what they do. People die, disappear, or get taken hostage, including police, messengers, officials, and innocent bystanders."

Goldfarb said, "A cartel recently defeated the Mexican military in a battle for control of a city."

"Correct. That was Sinaloa. They control Tijuana, which happens to be the most dangerous place in the world and is also where this money is going to be exchanged."

"The bribe payment is going to Sinaloa?"

"No. Actually, it's going to one of their enemies. A rival cartel."

"We have high-level traitors delivering a large bribe to a drug cartel, doing the transfer on the contested home turf of its major enemies?"

"They are planning to. Yes."

"How large a bribe?"

I shrugged. "What we're hearing is $25 million."

"Sums like that have been moving back and forth. We know then-President Enrique Peña Nieto of Mexico took a $100 million bribe from El Chapo back in 2016. That was admitted at El Chapo's trial."

"Officials from our Congress were involved in that too?"

"Likely so. We had a high-level delegation visiting Mexico at the time. Speaker Nancy Pelosi and a few others, including then-Congressman Beto O'Rourke. They were photo'd at the time with Nieto. A coincidence, I'm sure...."

"Right.... What else?"

"More coincidences. We know that then-President Nieto openly endorsed Beto, and that he donated to Beto O'Rourke's campaign for the Senate.

"Beto lost both the election and his seat in the House. Nieto lost his election. Trump became president, and none of that was ever investigated, much less proven."

"Do you have any idea where you are going with this?"

I said, "The word was that $25 million of El Chapo's bribe was laundered through the Mexican government to benefit sympathetic political candidates in the United States."

"So?"

"It's interesting to me that the sum coming back into Mexico is the same amount. $25 million. What's more interesting is that the Mexican government isn't involved this time. The money is being paid directly to a cartel."

"But not Sinaloa?"

"Correct. The new cartel is called *Los Serpientes*."

"A possible loan payback, but one made to a rival cartel? Our traitors are switching sides?"

I shrugged. "Or it's a new game. All the players have changed...."

Goldfarb's eyes narrowed. "Are we involved with this cluster fuck, Raven?"

"No, Sir. At the time I left Mexico, it hadn't yet happened."

"Are the Russians involved?"

"It would not surprise me. Ask the State Department. Have our CIA ask Russia's FSB. They like to chat about such things."

"I'm asking you."

"The Russians are involved with everything. They just had one of their own diplomats killed in Mexico by one of the cartels. Someone shipped his severed head to their embassy in a box. They don't react well to threats. Russians are not known for being as gentle and accommodating as we are.

"Like I said, it's a war zone in Mexico. CIA and FSB could have a 'Come to Jesus' discussion about unpleasant events of mutual interest. Who knows? It might make the world a notch better."

Mike smiled. Long ago, he'd been responsible for Intel at Marine HQ in DC.

Goldfarb said, "What the Hell were you doing mucking around down there, Raven?"

"Looking for a safe place. It's more dangerous in Mexico than what we saw in Cuba. That surprised me, but it's true. It's a war zone, and it's going to get worse."

"I need you to be more specific about just what exactly you were doing."

"I was scouting around, learning the lay of the land, low profile. I was looking for an alternative to our trying to run an OP in Cuba. I did not find one."

Mike said, "I spared you those details, Doctor. We've been stuck. Raven's been looking for a way to insert his team at a choke point along the invasion route. That's what we're here to discuss."

Goldfarb frowned, "Do you know about these problems in Mexico?"

"I know Raven went into Mexico to check out that end of the invasion route. He went in alone and unsupported, low profile. He told me it's a scary place, and I believe him.

"I've been watching the body counts and stats for some time. I've crossed Mexico off my list. Raven says it's a bad go. I agree. It's a tinderbox, with several groups of crazies running around striking matches.

"We are staying well clear. We are back to square one. I'm here to be briefed in so we can plan the Cuba OP, just like you."

I said, "This might be happy news, Doctor."

Goldfarb frowned and shifted his gaze to me. "How so?"

"If major chaos erupts in Mexico, it is a perfect time for us to quietly insert my team into Havana."

Mike said, "Unless you have a better option, we do need to get back to talking about Cuba."

Goldfarb did not look happy. "President Blager is going to want to know what's going down in Mexico."

I said, "We've just decided to refocus on Cuba, have we not?"

Mike said, "We don't know any more than what Raven just reported to us. If there is a Congressional delegation visiting Mexico, surely the State Department would know about it. It would be their problem. He can ask them. Right?"

Goldfarb nodded. "Yes, in theory, that's how it works...."

"Good to know," I said. "So, maybe you can give Mike your approval and we can get on with business?"

"Maybe. I need a clean OP, not an international incident."

"That's the plan, Sir."

Mike said, "Egress and targeting were what stopped us. These seem to now be coming under control."

Goldfarb said, "Josie, do you have anything to add?"

She shook her head. "Not really. I agree that Mexico is about to explode. We should all be relieved that Raven got out safely. I know that I am."

Goldfarb sighed deeply. He looked around the room. No one spoke and the silence lengthened. "Analyzing this more won't help. We need to decide."

I said, "We do. I think of it like D-Day. Cuba is a difficult target and we have a limited window of opportunity."

"D-Day was considered an impossible target, Raven. There was no choice."

"We've looked at everything, Doctor. Difficult or impossible, Havana is the best shot we have with a small team."

"You want a Cuba tasking?"

"Yes."

"When?"

"Approved now, but to go active when world attention is elsewhere. I want it timed when the chaos we've been discussing erupts. Seeing Mexico in flames, a regional crisis, would be the trigger event."

"What happens if this money exchange goes down smoothly?"

"Nothing dramatic. I suppose we'll then hold for Cuba and have another meeting. The key thing is we need a decision now."

"I like it. I'll need a plan everyone can agree with today. All in favor of activating a Cuba mission raise your hands."

All the hands were up except for Josie and Commander Bromley.

Goldfarb said, "Problems?"

Bromley said, "Not on my part, Sir. It's not my call. We're support. Do what you need to do. Or don't. The Navy will be there for you either way. Just get me an approved plan for the Admiral."

"Josie?"

She shrugged. "All I can see now is a gray fog of uncertainty. I'm hoping it will clear after you make a decision and we get started. If it does, I'll let you know."

"President Blager is going to ask me. Can you say anything now?"

"I already did. Mexico is bad news. Having high-level traitors funding the cartels makes it worse. It's a tinderbox."

Goldfarb took a deep breath. "Okay. Cuba is now a running mission. The code name is '**Square 1**'."

Mike said, "This might be a good time for us to take a break."

Bromley said, "I need to get to a secure phone and update the Admiral. This thing might move faster than we expected."

Goldfarb said, "It seems that I will need to make some secure calls as well. Let's take an hour. When we return, I want to know how quickly we can have a team on the ground and operational in Havana.

"I'll also need a draft plan today. One page."

"Can do," Mike said.

There were several tables on the deck outside the building where we'd been meeting. We had umbrellas and an awning for shade and there was a cool breeze. My team was sitting at the big table under the awning.

They were having some intense conversation with Bromley. Talking, laughing, and making hand gestures. I caught a few words. *Boats and missiles.*

I waved and kept walking. Rudy gave me a nod. He was wearing a nautical cap with skull and crossbones.

Josie was down at the far end of the deck at a small table, gazing into the distance. Alone. Some distance from the others. She liked aloneness. Meetings not so much.

Too many people creeped her out. Violence and conflict shut her down. We were on the edge of both.

I sat down next to her and handed her a frosty glass.

"Lemonade, Babe."

"Ummm...."

"Are you OK?"

She nodded and looked at me. "Yeah."

"I know you have concerns, but we finally have a mission. Thank you for supporting me."

Josie said, "Always. Mexico scares me, but so does Cuba. Neither is a good place for running and gunning.

"This is your world, Raven, not mine. I can sense evil and find monsters, but I can't do anything about it myself. Sometimes I think my talents are more of a curse than a blessing."

"Don't think that. You are magic. Dealing with evil is my job, Babe. It's what I do. We're a team."

"I'll be glad when this is over."

"Me too. It will be soon. That boat is a life saver. Are we set to meet with Rosa?"

"Tonight. Her mother isn't in good health. Remember, she hopes that if *Santeria* helps us, we'll help get her family out. Her Mom and her oldest aunt especially. They want to live free before they die."

"I know. How well can you communicate with *Santeria*? With Rosa?"

"Not well at all. Rosa comes to me in dreams sometimes. I can see her in my remote viewings. She's praying for you. Her relatives in Cuba are praying too.

"She's afraid, Raven. The Castro government killed her father and uncle."

"I know that too. We'll try to get her out after this is over. Anything else?"

"No. I'll do a viewing in the morning. Rosa's going to give me some personal items from her mother and aunt. That will let me do targeted remote viewings like what we did for Antarctica back when we first started together.

"Remember that old book that took us across history and half way around the world? I saw beauty."

I nodded, took Josie's hand, brought it to my lips, and gently kissed her fingers.

"I remember, Babe. It changed my life. You changed my life."

Her eyes teared up, but she was smiling. "I love you. Now get over there with your team and get a plan together. I know you're going. I want you back safe."

I started to say something clever and comforting to her, just as Will walked over carrying a coffee cup.

"May I intrude?"

Josie nodded, wiping tears away. "Sit down. Raven was just about to give me some bullshit about Cuba being safe, and I was going to pretend to believe him. Instead of that, I want to ask you a question."

"Okay."

I slid a chair out and Will sat down. "Shoot."

"We have civilians who might be able to help us in Cuba. Nonviolent. Noncombatants. Peaceful. Unfamiliar with covert OPs. They fit in. They've lived there all their lives."

Will looked at me. "Can you trust them?"

"Yes, up until when they are caught and tortured. It's a generational family thing."

"Mothers talking to save a child?"

"That sort of thing. Grandmothers. Whole families. Close families."

"Suicide pills?"

"Not an option," Josie said. "They are Catholic. Suicide would damn them to Hell."

I said, "We were only planning to use them for low-risk, high-value assignments. Like Millie's watchers."

Will said, "So what's the problem?"

I said, "We need a bigger boat...."

"Huh?"

"A line from an old movie, don't worry about it. Here's the deal. My team can slip in easily and we have a plan for a survivable hot egress."

"*Busted Flush*."

"Correct. The boat gets us out, but there's no room for anyone else. Likewise, bringing in any but a few weapons might get us blown before we even start."

"You want to go in clean?"

"I do. Other than two of my team on the boat, I want us to go in squeaky clean, on airlines, and through security checks. That way Cuban security knows how safe we are.

"On our test run, that's how Rudy, Terry, and I got in. Naked. They are my close combat team. We're already in their records."

"Rudy's your boat Captain."

"He is now, for combat. Coming in will be easy. Vinnie and Pat can drive the boat in. They'll play Rudy's crew. They **are** Rudy's crew. We can conceal their personal weapons on the boat somewhere."

Will was frowning. "Civilian Watchers should be safe. By nature, they are invisible. What's the problem?"

"I'm not worried about that part, but we need local logistics support. We'll need to get weapons in for our own use. We'll need to stash them somewhere convenient, so we can use them for our OP. Pat's not going to be walking around Havana with his long gun."

Josie said, "I also need a way to communicate with partisans in Cuba, something simple and covert. They are naive about technology."

"What kind of weapons, Raven?"

"Suppressed pistols for me, Rudy, and Terry. Pat needs his sniper rifle. It will be sighted in. The first shot counts, so it needs to be treated gently. Vinnie needs his range finder and spotting scope. Ammo.

"Grenades and RPGs would be useful. I'd love a belt fed machine gun. Maybe a landmine or two. A few other special items."

"Are you planning to fight your way out?"

"I hope not. Just a quick OP and we scoot. The best option lets us leave what weapons we can't carry behind."

"For use next time?"

"Let's just say to pave the way for better options...."

CHAPTER TWENTY-EIGHT
THE SAINTS COME MARCHING IN

Cape Canaveral, Florida, Vargas Cafe, Evening

It was a Monday, so the Café wasn't open, which allowed us to slip in unnoticed and speak at leisure with Luis and Rosa. I checked for trackers, ran CSRs on the way in, scanned for bugs, and made sure there were no smart phones or computers active.

All clear. We were clean. No threats.

Mexico had been scary. San Francisco hadn't been much better. Where I was going was worse.

I needed time to calm mission nerves and be with Josie, and this was a start. Oh, I still had my Sig locked and loaded in its paddle holster, but this was a respite, an interlude with people she judged to be trustworthy and safe. I trusted her talents and judgements regarding people more than I did all the official, meticulous background checks and security clearances.

Congress lied and leaked with impunity. For a time, we had a member of a Somali warlord family, the Black Hawk Down people, on the House Foreign Affairs Committee. Congress had unpunished debacles ranging from the Awan brothers, Pakistani ISI spies, running the IT department for one party, to a Chinese spy being the chauffer for the head of the Senate Intelligence Committee for many years.

When exposed, the Chinese agent had retired on an American government pension. Over his tenure, CIA lost every agent it had in China, either jailed or executed. Too bad for us.

The bureaucracies in DC were worse. John Brennan – an *admitted* Communist when the CIA hired him during the Cold War, a time when we played hardball – was eventually given the highest clearances we had. He later ran the CIA and weaponized it for political purposes. Comey at the FBI had similar issues, and a long history that reeked of corruption.

High officials had family connections to foreign governments, including hostile regimes. The swamp was a dangerous place, a cesspool of security breaches.

My world suffered from a severe deficit of "safe." In general, those of us who worked deep black had a small circle of trust, one that we kept tight for our personal survival.

Unfortunately, most of the interactions with those within my circle of trust were professional. Josie and I had a personal relationship, but it wasn't easy. It separated and stressed us.

My recent missions into danger zones, places where I dared not take Josie, exacerbated matters. Cuba was not only a danger zone, it was also "denied access," a spot where timely secure communications were simply not possible. I had Cybertech working on that one.

Tonight was different. This meeting was almost social. Almost safe.

Rosa was happy to see us, or, at least, happy to see Josie. The two had a connection through their unique gifts, or "talents" as Josie termed them.

We'd not ordered off any menu, instead we had some Cuban dish Rosa made from her mother's recipe. Mostly pork and black beans, it was delicious.

The Vargas Cafe menu was 5-star. This meal was a six, and the coffee was excellent.

The women were relaxed. I was in stand-down, but Luis looked nervous.

Nervous people made me apprehensive. Josie knew that, of course, and she knew that I knew. It didn't matter here, relaxed and safe in Florida, but small things could make a difference in Havana.

I sipped my coffee and waited. The women were chatting about small things. I started paying attention when their talk turned to Rosa's family in Cuba. She'd somehow alerted them that friends from America were coming and might need help.

The women stopped talking. They both looked at Luis.

He said, "What?"

"You know what, my love. Our friends are going into danger. They will be depending on us."

He nodded. "That's what you told me. I didn't like it. I still don't like it."

"Tell them your concerns."

"*Quiero a mi familia.*"

"In English."

Luis looked at me. "I love my family, Mr. Raven."

"Of course, you do. That's natural," I said. "What else?"

"There is a sense of death about you, Mr. Raven. It concerns me."

"I visit dangerous places, Luis. I just returned from one. Soon I'll be visiting another."

"Cuba."

"Yes."

"Have you been there recently?"

I nodded. "I have. It's a police state. The people are afraid. Freedom is dead."

"Do you seek to change that?"

"People with bright spirits, time, and courage may seek to change that. Me, I work to prevent evil from spreading. We do what we can."

Josie and Rosa were watching us intently.

Josie said, "I'm the one who seeks light and beauty. I look for butterflies."

Rosa said, "I doubt you will find any butterflies in Havana. It's not a happy place under Communism."

"When I find *el murciélago vampiro*, Raven handles it. That's why I'm still alive."

Rosa blinked, then started laughing.

I shook my head, puzzled.

Josie said, "Vampire bats...."

Luis said, "My father was an officer at the Bay of Pigs. Americans armed him, trained him, and sent him to take back his country, to regain our freedom from a Communist dictator. They were landed in a swamp with no support and only one road out."

"The first day their ammunition ship was sunk before they could unload it. Castro had Migs that blew the few old bombers they had from the skies. An American fleet was close but it did nothing to help. They had no choice but to surrender."

"I know that history, Luis. I can't change it."

"Castro had my father shot."

"I'm sorry."

We sat in silence for a time. *Sorry didn't cut it, but I truly had nothing else to say.*

Finally, Rosa looked at Josie. "Tell him about Durham. About how you met."

"You know?"

Rosa nodded.

"Our story is similar. Durham was our Bay of Pigs.

"We were put together and tasked to resist evil. I found it, but was detected and followed. Terrorists sent a team to kill me. Raven resisted them. The help we were promised did not come. It was a bad time."

Luis said, "But here you are ...."

"Yes. We were almost overwhelmed, but we had friends, and help finally came. Raven was wounded. I almost died. Police were killed and a nice neighborhood was left in flames."

"It sounds like you were lucky."

"I was blessed. Raven killed most of those attacking us. His friends killed the rest. We thwarted evil."

Rosa said, "So now you come here to help us?"

Josie said, "Perhaps. This is my doing. I found you, and we came to help. I hope that you can help us."

Luis said, "Why would we do that? Involvement with you could put family members in Cuba at risk."

I nodded. "I won't lie. We are in a war. It's not about Democrats versus Republicans or Country A versus Country B. At the core, it is about freedom versus tyranny.

"Involvement with me puts Josie at risk. Freedom isn't free. It requires choices. That's how it works."

Luis said, "We made a choice about Cuba. We fled. We are now Americans. We are here. We are safe. Every day I thank God for that."

"Only temporarily," I said. "Cuba is a danger zone, and you know it. 'They who can give up essential liberty to obtain a little temporary safety deserve neither liberty nor safety.'"

Luis said, "Yes, I know Ben Franklin said that. You say we are in a war. My father felt the same and it killed him. 'The most successful war seldom pays for its losses.' What do you say to that?"

"Thomas Jefferson. You have studied our history, Luis, but Jefferson also said, 'Endeavor to avoid war; but if it shall actually take place, no matter by whom brought on, we must defend ourselves.' You chose to run, but Rosa's mother and many others couldn't do that."

"I was a child. I chose nothing. My father chose to run so his family could be safe."

"I will stick with Ben Franklin. Is your own family safe in Cuba? They are not.

"Rosa's mother can be punished or killed at any time, for what she has done, for what she hasn't done, or for nothing at all. Perhaps for simply getting old, for not being of value to the state. Surely, you know that?"

"They are alive...."

"But not free."

"My family, our people, they are not fighters, Mr. Raven. Rosa's mother is sixty-five. She runs the family and refuses to leave until the others are safe."

"I don't want to mislead you, Luis. From what I saw in Cuba it will be a long time before anyone is safe. People there live or die at the whim of the rulers, whom I doubt are ready to relinquish power."

Rosa said, "Mother has a heart condition. She needs care that she can only get here."

"Can she visit the United States?"

"No. Permissions and visas are required. They are hard to get, and simply asking puts you under scrutiny from both governments."

"Can you visit her as an American citizen?"

"Under constraints, it may be possible. I've never tried."

"Do you know the details?"

"You need a license to visit Cuba. There are two types of visits. The most hopeful is to get a P2P license.

"Support for the Cuban People (SCP) is the general license. SCP trips are meant to enable travelers to support Cuban people. They are for tours to shop, to buy goods or purchase services.

"People-to-People (P2P) trips are intended to foster educational dialogue between Cubans and Americans, while SCP trips are meant to enable travelers to support Cuban people."

I said, "Orwell warned us. Isn't socialism wonderful? Tell me about the restrictions."

"On both types of trips travelers are required to stay in casas particulares (local guesthouses) instead of hotels and have a "full-time" schedule of activities. These activities must support Cuban people in some way. This may include shopping in independent markets, attending dance classes, meeting with local artists or tobacco manufacturers, exploring independently owned museums and more.

"On the SCP trip, you must keep a daily journal of your trip and a record of your expenses. You must buy a diary for travelers to track your activities and interactions with the Cuban people, and must build time into the trip in the evening for journaling.

"On both trips, you'll have a local leader to guide you through Cuba and introduce you to its friendly people, rich culture, and fascinating history."

"No shit?"

Rosa smiled, "I love your quaint American expressions, but I don't think excrement is involved. The people are friendly, but the government is not."

"Tell me about the 'local leader,' the minder."

Luis shrugged. "They are licensed tour guides. Some are probably Cuban intelligence agents. I thought you'd recently visited?"

"Yes. I visited Cuba as a Canadian citizen on vacation, working for a Mexican oil company. I got to stay at a hotel. I didn't have a minder, but the hotel where I stayed did."

Rosa said, "What else did you notice, Raven?"

"Everything is watched. Everything. It's like the spy novels about Moscow during Stalin and the Cold War, but on steroids and with modern technology."

"That is what my mother says. She doesn't want me to visit, because she fears I would not be allowed to leave.

"There were some loopholes in the law, back when Obama was President. I suggested that my daughter, then sixteen, could visit her grandmother for summer vacation. Mom started crying. She said I was lucky to get out before Castro, that they had tightened their grip, and that it's too late now."

Josie said, "That was a few years ago?"

"Several years, and it was the last time I spoke with her."

Luis said, "I agree with your mother. You recently visited Cuba, Mr. Raven. Would you care to comment?"

"I suggest you not visit or try to call, Rosa. Cuba is locked down tight."

"I expected that. It's why I asked Josie to come here. Mother will need care soon, and I'm afraid to go to her. Can you help us get her out?"

"Not anytime soon. I can't think of a way that doesn't involve breaking laws and possible international incidents. Have you thought about using a lawyer or a bribe?"

"We've more than thought about it. We've had discussions with smugglers and lawyers. Nothing looks promising."

"At least they're being honest with you."

"Can you add anything?"

I shook my head. "Nothing of value, I'm afraid.

"For sure, it would not be easy. I need to go back, but getting access for myself and my team has been a major problem. That's hopefully resolved, but, once in, we could use some local help with our mission."

"If we helped you, then you could help us?"

"I can't promise you that, Rosa. My own mission is high risk. No one will be coming to save us. No one will risk a war to rescue us."   .

"Can we revisit this after your mission, after you are home and safe?"

"Sure. If you help us, I'd try to help you. Do you want to know our biggest problem?"

"Getting out?"

"We think we can get my team in and out safely, but I could use some local help, people who live in Cuba, help that I can trust, to assist me while we are there. It would make things easier."

"I understand."

"Good. Here is the time when you need to decide. I need help in Cuba, but there will be zero direct contact in Cuba between your people and mine.

"We can't lead them to you. You can't lead them to us. We plan a total cut out. If someone is caught and interrogated, it doesn't bring the whole network down.

"I have a logistics problem, Rosa. There are some equipment items I'd like to get in without their being noticed. It would be best to have them in place before we go in."

"What kind of items?"

"The first is that we need secure, undetectable communications. I need to be able to communicate with Josie quickly. We have the technology. I'd like to get some small electronic devices into Cuba and test them before we arrive there."

"Why?"

"I need to communicate with Josie and my boss while in Cuba. Our secure phones can be detected, so we need something better. That part isn't your problem, it is mine.

"What becomes your problem is that I also want to use these devices to have support equipment in place for my team when we need it. These would be smuggled into Cuba by third parties, people that we'll not have any direct contact with."

"What kind of equipment?"

"Best to not talk about that. Let's agree to call these items 'biscuits.' Is that a good name?

"As good as any. In Spanish that would be '*galleta*.' It's not a name that would alert anyone."

"Good."

"We will first provide some covert communications devices. There will be one for me and one for Josie. I'll get one, or maybe two, for your people in Cuba, plus one for you here as well. I want you to be able to communicate with me or Josie.

"You will need some way to hide these items. The worst case is to have one captured, so we'll have internal self-destructs."

"How large are these?"

"Small, about the size of a cell phone or pack of cigarettes. I don't want them buried in the woods or hidden in remote locations. Whoever you have for communications in Cuba, will need to keep them close when my team is in-country. I will want them checked once a day when we go hot."

Luis and Rosa exchanged a look.

I said, "Are you in or out? I need to know."

Rosa said, "I say 'in,' but we'll be safe here in America. In Cuba, it will likely be my mom."

Luis said, "Yes. After we get communications, I assume more 'biscuits' are coming?"

"Yes. We'll need some things smuggled in and cached for our use. The largest will be perhaps two feet long and weigh twenty or thirty pounds. Most will be half that size and weight. Some will be smaller and heavier."

"What's in those boxes?"

"Do you really want to know? People can't reveal what they don't know."

Luis looked at Rosa. She said, "I want to know."

"Weapons. I need your Cuba agents to hide them in precise locations that we'll give you. It might be best if they wear gloves to not leave fingerprints or DNA."

"What other help do you need?"

"None. There will be no direct contact between your local agents and my team. If we get blown, you don't know us. If we don't make it out, these items are yours."

I stopped and looked at them.

"Like I said, it's decision time. If you say 'no,' we're done. We'll thank you for the dinner and go away."

Rosa looked at Luis. "I want to do this."

Luis said, "It's people like your mom in Cuba who we're putting at risk."

"She'd want us to do this. So would your dad."

Luis took a deep breath. "We're in."

Josie said, "Thank you."

Rosa looked at me and said, "We're in. I have an idea."

"Okay...?"

"How many of these, ah, Cuba agents are you thinking that we'd have?"

"Not many. Your mom, plus someone with a vehicle or donkey cart to reposition and hide some boxes."

"How about more? Cuba is divided into fifteen provinces and a special municipality that is not included in any province. Given good communications, we can put agents in all but the special province. It's an island, run by the government, isolated, and hard to access."

I blinked. "An island?"

She nodded. "It used to be called Isle of Pines, but Castro renamed it *Isla de la Juventud* in 1978. It is now the 'Island of Youth.' Children are removed from their families and, ah, educated there."

"How would you put agents in the provinces?"

"We know who we can trust. The people you need are already there, they just need training and support. The saints would help us."

"What kind of people?"

"We are *Santeria*. My family has been in Cuba since before the United States was a country. *Ochún* would protect us. The government allows that. Even Castro permitted it."

"Lady, I don't have a clue as to what you are talking about."

"I'll show you."

Rosa got up, went off to the back of the restaurant, and came back with a statue, a woman in a white dress and robe. She set it on the table in front of me. "She's a saint."

"Is this saint the *Ochún* you are talking about?"

Rosa was smiling. "We came long ago as slaves from Africa. Our *Ochún* was black and she was the youngest of our saints, the god of beauty, love, prosperity, order, and fertility."

"Sounds like she had a lot to do...."

"She is also the protector of the poor and mother of the sick, as well as the queen of the rivers and freshwater. We do not trust a God. We trust saints, actual people who've protected us, not unseen entities. To save us, our *Ochún* transformed herself into a Christian saint.

"The Spanish used to persecute us as heathens. They were Catholic and didn't tolerate old Gods, so our *Ochún* evolved from the one we'd worshiped in the 1600s. This image is of her as 'Our Lady of Charity,' from the shrine at the Basilica of El Cobre in Cuba.

"This worship is permitted. The statue in the Basilica is about 16 inches tall, made of baked clay. It dates from 1801, when King Charles of Spain decreed that Cuban slaves were to be freed from the El Cobre copper mines.

"We *Santeria* tend to have small shrines honoring her in our homes. My mother does.

"Pope Benedict XV declared her the Patron Saint of Cuba in 1916. Pope Pius XI granted her a Canonical Coronation in 1936, making her an official Catholic Saint. Subsequent Popes have reaffirmed that, including Pope Francis in a visit to Cuba in 2015."

I was shaking my head. "I rather doubt the Communist rulers of Cuba care about that."

"You'd be wrong. They do care. Her statue kept disappearing and then reappearing. It is cherished in Cuba. Your Ernest Hemingway donated his Nobel Prize in literature to the people of Cuba, and it was placed in the shrine next to her statue.

"Someone stole his medal in 1986. That was the last straw. It was returned days later after Raul Castro said that thieves would suffer the consequences. Since then, no one has bothered either the medal or her statue."

Josie said, "What are you proposing?"

"I'd like to loan you my statue. My mother has one that is identical. I'd like you to make a copy with a hidden compartment to conceal her communicator. *Ochún* will keep her safe.

"I am also suggesting that you should place at least one in each province with a trusted Santeria, and teach them to use it. Surely you have the resources to do that?"

They were both looking at me. "We'll get some made up for the mission. If the idea floats, I'll suggest that we should do more."

Luis said, "How does that help your mission?"

"It doesn't, but it may help future missions. The best way to hide a needle isn't in a haystack, it's in a pile of other needles that look just like it."

Luis and Rosa exchanged a look. She said, "Why not?"

Luis shrugged.

I said, "I'll borrow your statue and take it with me. As soon as the communicators are available, I'll get someone out here to train you. If we're around, Josie and I can take the class with you.

"Once you're proficient, let me know how you want to get your mom equipped and trained. For her safety, I don't want direct contact with my team, but we can work something out.

"There may be some government people around to get you to sign things, take fingerprints, and maybe hire you as consultants or something. If so, Josie or I will personally do the introductions. Okay?"

They both nodded.

I finished my coffee, looked at Josie, and stood up. "We'd better go. We have work to do."

The mission clock was running.

CHAPTER TWENTY-NINE
BADDOG

Patrick AFB, Florida, Private Office, Next Day, Late Morning

The group was smaller and more relaxed today, just me, Josie, Mike, and Will, who'd dominated the morning's discussions. It was show and tell time.

Will brought in one of his Cybertech geeks to show off his new, denied-access area, communications units and train us in their use. Goldfarb was off to the swamp, back to DC, to update the President and a few others.

The geek Will brought, named Scott, was what they called an operational tech, a trained engineer who knew you couldn't sneak a listening device into an office if it came in ten pieces and weighed five hundred pounds.

He understood operations and his technical solutions reflected it. We needed more people like that.

Even so, I felt like I was James Bond meeting with Q. I was needing to get on with things, but knew that my life and that of my team – James typically didn't have a team, of course, he was macho, at least until they recast him as a female – might depend on these gadgets and being able to use them in the field.

The units came in two versions, but both types used the same protocols. Anything loaded into the device would be stored until it detected an authentication code from the BADDOG telemetry satellite in a geosynchronous orbit over the equator.

The units were interactive, multifunctional, personalized, and protected from tampering by a retinal-scan permissive action link. Each unit was assigned to a unique user.

My team would get the full functioned version allowing 2-way communication. The others were a stripped-down version that had only the receive capability, plus a panic button.

Those units were basically for friendly civilian use, and they fit what we needed for logistic support. You could send, "Go here at this date and time. Get this. Take it to this location," and know the message would get through.

The system would even log when your message was received. The "Oh, Shit," button would warn that what you expected wasn't coming, not when expected, and maybe not ever.

These units were keyed to work in the western hemisphere, covering North and South America, plus the Caribbean. When the full functioned units were queried by the BADDOG code, all stored messages would be uploaded. The process took from 2.3 to 5.8 seconds, depending on the size of the message. The stripped-down units had only one message, and it took 0.25 seconds.

The uploads came first, and, when finished, any incoming messages for the agent would be downloaded at a slower rate. Uploaded messages would go to a central location, in this case a SCIF at Cybertech. The operator there could forward the messages as per instructions.

I said, "When we're in-country, operational, and down in the belly of the beast, I want all the messages to go to my full team, plus Josie. Can they be automatically rebroadcast like that?"

"Sure," Will said. "No problem."

"Add me," Mike said. "No pillow talk, Raven."

Josie said, "Lately, there has been no pillow talk, Mike. None. We barely get to see each other."

Mike blinked. He looked at me.

"Yeah, that was on my list of things to discuss with you too. We've been running on empty, boss."

Josie interrupted, "I did a viewing this morning. The Mexico crisis has been delayed. You are going to have a revolt if we don't get some down time."

Mike put his hands up defensively. "Whoa, Lady! A delay is fine by me. I'm getting the same message from Gerry. That's great news. When we get done today, I'm not going back to the swamp.

"How much delay do you expect?"

"Several days. Maybe a week. We'll know when it breaks, it will be all over TV."

"Why the delay?"

"Some political thing in DC. Congress is not in session, but Reps in the opposition party are being called back for some 'must attend' meeting."

"Brief us today, and I'll brief Goldfarb tonight. I'll tell him we're repositioning Busted Flush, I'm going home, and that Raven is standing down until the Mexico shitstorm breaks in the news."

I was smiling. "Do I get a vote?"

"Sure."

"Great plan. There's a 5-Star Sandals in Grenada, their luxury All-Inclusive Resort in St. George. If you can drop us off there, I can route back through some place that won't red-flag – no, not Mexico, thank you – into Cuba on an airline under my Digger legend. It will be better that way than my coming in from the US."

"Agreed. Now let's wrap this up. Do you have any questions?"

"I'm not worried about the download, but I've heard that transmissions to satellites are vulnerable to radio intercept or direction finding."

Will said, "You mean triangulation. Not with this system. The power is low, but, more important, transmissions are diffused. It's like the difference between tracking back a searchlight beam in the night sky, and stuffing fog in a gunny sack."

"If you say so. It doesn't seem like much training is required."

"That was a design goal. You press the ON button twice, look into the sensor, don't blink, and it knows you. It's like setting a password in a computer. When it goes 'beep,' you look in again, it goes 'beep beep' and it's your unit.

"It's paired to you. No one else can use it. Once it knows you, just look in to turn it on. Tap the button to turn it off.

"The satellite will have the codes for all the units we've issued. After the 'beep beep,' your unit is registered and active. In theory we'll know that, but it's best to identify yourself in your first transmission each time so the system can verify or update.

"To clear it so you can give the unit to someone else for use, hold the on button down for a minute, and it will clear. It doesn't matter if they speak the same language or not. The system will figure it out.

"If you want to destroy a unit – advisable if you are about to be captured and tortured – just tap the button five times quickly and it will never work again."

The case was plastic. "How about I just smash it with my gun butt or something?"

"Sure, but I'd trash it first, if it was me."

"Are they waterproof?"

"The production units are specified good down to freezing and up to about 120. Good for hot tubs and cold showers. Steam baths and toilets are best avoided.

"The ones you're getting will be what we call A-Phase. No guarantees. It might be best to not test the environmental limits in some denied-access hellhole where you don't have a spare.

"If you must hide one under water, I'd use a prophylactic. Buy American, not Chinese. If our unit crapped out and got you killed, I'd feel real sad."

I grinned. "Me too. I'll take nine of them. Five for me and my team, one for Josie, one for a Cuban asset here that you'll be meeting, and two for field use in Cuba."

"No problem. I brought a dozen. I've also checked out that saint statue you brought. It's beautiful. Looks old. Handmade, not mass produced."

"Yes."

"We can copy it with a hidden compartment for the units, but it will look mass produced. Is that a problem?"

"No. How soon can you get these done?"

"I'm not sure. Probably several weeks, maybe longer."

"Can't wait that long. We'll have a running mission by then. Just do your best, and try to get one to us in the field when you can."

"We borrowed the statue from the lady you'll be training, Rosa. It's a family heirloom. You'll need to return hers in good condition and give her one of the new ones."

"It has a few little scratches. There is one place were the glaze has faded a bit, probably from exposure to bright sunlight. We could make it look like new if you wish."

Josie was my best hope for questions like that. I shot her a questioning look.

"I don't know. Ask Rosa. It's a personal thing."

"Right."

I said, "We're getting tight on time, Mike, but I promised to train our locals before we left. If you're good with that, I want to ask Rosa and Luis to come here.

"We'll introduce them to Scott. You can clear them in, get what paperwork you need, and have him check them out."

Will said, "I was thinking about how to do that. Keep it simple. We'll just make them, ah, field reps, for Cybertech. If Mike wants to change that later, he can.

"No need to brief them all the way, just for support as needed in Cuba. Who will be their contact?"

"My vote is Josie. The two women have a rapport. Okay?"

Josie said, "Yes."

Mike said, "I'm good. Goldfarb may want it changed, but let's go that way."

I said, "Can you get us to Grenada tonight without using your fancy supersonic jet? I want us to be low profile."

He laughed. "You are sitting on an Air Force base, Raven. They shuttle in and out of GITMO all the time. We can probably locate something."

"Nothing military, and nothing that has been seen around GITMO or Cuba."

"Right, something with a civil registry and a boring history. I'll work on it. We'll get Digger and his woman the most secluded King suite they have available. It's only money."

Josie smiled and her whole face lit up. It had been a long time since I'd seen that smile. Too long.

Sandals Grenada, St. George, Evening

Mike had somehow gotten us the South Seas Honeymoon, One Bedroom. He said it was preferred, and that we'd like it. It was small with no view, but private and quiet.

He was right. That was what we needed.

Privacy and walls. To Hell with the ocean view. I'd seen lots of oceans.

The hotel picked us up at the airport and took us directly to our room. It was prepaid and we were traveling light. No weapons of course, just casual clothes, bathing suits, and jogging outfits.

Josie had never looked more beautiful. Her clear blue eyes with gold flecks still seemed to look right through you, and the truth was, she actually did. Not just with her eyes, but also her mind. Her special talents could see things across time and space.

She was the best paranormal we had, a national treasure, someone to be protected at all costs. Mike figured that good security, that was me, and our short notice trip would keep her safe.

I wanted to try my new COM unit and now was as good as ever. It locked in immediately and off went my message.

"Arrived G. Plan 3 days. Advise status."

"All quiet. Check bathrobe. Out."

Josie had washed her face and was brushing her long brown hair. It was still silky and shiny, but I knew there were some concealed streaks of gray. We'd been together for a long time.

I had some gray too, along with a few scars. Thankfully, she'd avoided that. Despite several attempts, none of the assassins had gotten to her. I wanted to keep it that way. So did President Blager.

She had some kind of sarong on with a flower in her hair. I bent down and kissed her.

"You have too many clothes on, Babe."

She smiled. "Are we still interested in that?"

"Hope so…."

She gave a provocative wiggle. "We don't want a scandal at Sandals, do we?"

"No worries. We have a wall, a hot tub, and a pool outside."

I kissed her again and helped peel her wrap off.

"Your nipples are getting hard…."

"Not the only thing," she murmured, touching me. "Yummy…."

"Let's christen the hot tub. I'll get robes."

The closet held two, heavy white cotton, each with a sash. The larger one was heavy.

I checked the pockets. I found a .45 Sig in one, and an extra magazine and suppressor in the other.

"Gifts from Mike." I dropped them in the drawer by the King-sized bed.

"Don't hurt yourself, big boy…."

Josie started for the patio, rolling her hips slowly. I stripped and followed her out with the robes. It was warm. I didn't think we'd need them, but you never knew….

On the Third Day, Noon

It was a delightful set up. We had two white lounge chairs and could set them on a little ledge where I could dip my feet in the pool.

I was sitting on the patio, sipping coffee, waiting for Raven, and listening to music.

The Wi-Fi was playing old American music, the Eagles, *Take it to the Limit*. What did that portend? I was trying to find out.

I'd done my morning viewing. All was still quiet, so I'd been doing them solo. In the bad old days, I needed someone to support me, and more than once I'd wound up in an ER when things turned ugly.

The future remained foggy. It was as if the universe was waiting for actions that would drive change. I knew this was the lull before the storm, so I was careful. I'd peek into the future, but use Raven for support as soon as I glimpsed chaos on the far horizon.

Our pattern was to have a quick snack for breakfast. Raven would go do his workout, I'd do a viewing, and then we'd talk.

Mostly we'd spent our afternoons making love, followed by showers and walking to one of the restaurants on the grounds. My favorite was the Italian one, Cucina Romana. It was right on the beach.

They started serving at 6:30. We usually helped them open, ate on the patio, and then walked the surf a bit before returning to our room. It gave them time to clean the room, and put mints on our pillows.

Since we'd arrived, we'd spent most of our time in the room. I guess that was why they called it the honeymoon suite. We'd never left the grounds.

I was coming to like this place. It was our refuge. It gave us a safe place to discuss the things we'd long avoided. It is hard to think about a future, much less marriage or children, when you're running for your life.

Ever since we met, we'd been running. People kept coming for me. We'd stayed a step or two ahead, but I didn't like to think about the bodies strewn along our backtrail.

In the early days, we'd been playing defense. Now Raven was going on offense. That was safer for me, but I feared for him. Take it to the Limit, indeed.

We spent too much time there, on the edge. One step beyond and he might not come back. This was one Hell of a time for my powers to shut down. We needed to know the future, but all I could see was a gray fog.

I heard a sharp rapping. Someone was at the door.

I stood, put on my slippers, cinched my robe, stepped inside, and went to answer, calling out to Raven, "I'll get it."

I opened the door a crack, leaving on the chain. It was one of the hotel staff, smiling, holding a tray with snacks.

He said, "With our compliments."

How nice.

They'd done that before. I smiled back. "Just a minute."

I closed the door and took the chain off. It burst open, pushing me into the room.

The staffer dropped his tray and pushed me further inside. There was another man behind him, tall, Hispanic, not a staffer, flowered shirt, dressed like a tourist on holiday.

I saw a gun.

Suddenly, Raven was there. He was yelling, "Down! Down!"

I dropped for the floor, just as two rounds snapped past my head. *A double tap.*

Raven was shooting suppressed and that saved my hearing. I heard the pop of the rounds going by, but not the muzzle blast.

Time seemed frozen.

The tourist with the gun dropped his weapon. I saw a red spot appear on his forehead and blood gushing from his chest. He was falling, but the staffer grabbed Raven's gun arm.

Raven hit him twice with his left hand, incredibly fast. A chop to the throat, followed by a fist strike to the temple.

The staffer was falling. Raven's gun was free. He put it to the staffer's head, fired once, and it was over.

Raven kicked the door shut and locked it, not bothering to drag the body inside.

I put a new mag in my gun and took a few deep breaths.

How in the Hell did anyone find us here? Had I missed something?

Josie was leaning on the counter, taking deep breaths, shaking. I went over and hugged her until she stopped trembling.

I stepped back and looked into her eyes. "Are you okay?"

She nodded. "Yeah. It just scared me."

"Me too. We're out of here, Babe. Get your stuff together."

CHAPTER THIRTY
BACK TO SQUARE 1

Sandals Grenada, St. George, Early Afternoon

Josie was ready to go. I'd run quick recon of our perimeter. It was clear, so I dragged the body inside along with the weapon he'd dropped.

None of their pocket litter was helpful, but I did find a set of keys for a rental car. Thank you, Sixt Rental Car. It even had the license number and a note saying where it could be dropped with the keys. A green Toyota.

Sixt was the only car rental on the Maurice Bishop International Airport so it should be easy to find. I vaguely remembered Bishop had been the Prime Minister who'd been killed when a Cuba-supported People's Liberation Army had taken control.

Exciting times, back then. The Russians had wanted the island under their control as a fuel stop into Cuba. President Reagan took Grenada back by a risky daylight low altitude parachute assault onto the airport. *God Bless America.*

We were scheduled to leave today anyway. I'd better check in. I pulled out my new COM unit. It locked in immediately and off went my message.

"We're busted. Two Tangos down. Have transport to airport. Need egress and cleaners."

"Checking. Say status."

"Clear. We're good."

"Any ID on Tangos?"

"Negative. Both looked Hispanic. One had a 9mm Walther."

Then Mike was on the net.

"I've got this. How soon can you be at the airport?"

"30-40 minutes."

"You live lucky. Bug out. Square 1 is running. Rudy and Terry will be landing at GA terminal about the time you arrive. We'll extract you."

"Understood. I'll dump the rental."

"Screw that. Just get your asses on the plane. Leave the Tango's gun. Don't leave prints."

"Understood."

"Confirm Josie is good."

"She's a little shaken, but doing okay at the moment."

"Any questions?"

"Negative."

"Move your ass. You were blown."

"No shit, Sherlock. Raven out."

Maurice Bishop International Airport, Grenada

Mike had sent the Citation to pick us up. It was already on the ground refueling when we arrived.

John Black was the pilot. He greeted me with, "You have a real knack for getting in trouble, Raven."

"Shit happens, Bro. What's the plan?"

"Not sure. Not even sure there is a plan. All I know is that we're on our way to Costa Rica. My orders are to get you out of here pronto."

"Costa Rica. Why?"

"No idea. Mike's orders. He keeps saying the 'T' in TSG is for transnational. My guess is he's trying to get more distant from the swamp, but that's just a guess. I think he has some contacts there."

Back when I was being chased around California, John helped save my ass from a kill team of misguided Russians. Before that, coming to rescue us, we'd almost gotten him killed in Durham. He was a good guy, more than adequate in the field, but flying was his first love.

He'd flown F-22s for the Airforce, and was now the Chief Pilot for Mike's company, TSG. John's copilot, a young kid named Graham, appeared. John introduced him and sent him off to deal with paperwork and flight plans.

"Tell them we're trying to do a quick turn. I'll get everyone on board and do the preflight."

"Roger that, Boss."

Josie gave John a hug.

He said, "Hop aboard and kick back. I figure maybe twenty minutes to engine start if we're lucky. I've got to figure out where the place is and get the magic boxes programmed."

Rudy and Terry were in the plane, slumped loosely into the posh cushions like a pair of lounging leopards. Rudy at six four, bald, jet black, and looking like the NFL linebacker he'd been briefly, didn't fit normal furniture. Terry was shorter, but he was built like a weightlifter, square, wide, and solid.

They looked up and smiled at Josie when we boarded.

I said, "Black is trying to figure out where we're going. He said twenty minutes."

"Costa Rica," Terry said.

"Yeah, that's what he said. You don't want to get off and stretch your legs?"

Rudy said, "What's the point? You just broke our hearts. All airports look alike."

I looked at him, puzzled.

Terry said, "I always wanted to see Grenada. Have an uncle who dropped in there with Delta Force in 83, back when Cuba tried to take it over. He said it was beautiful."

"Huh?"

Rudy said, "I had a buddy who loved it. Beautiful women. Fantastic beaches. Good rum and great food. A little piece of heaven, all expenses paid. Some down time. Now we're leaving in twenty minutes.

"What the Hell, Raven?"

"Not my fault," I said. "External factors."

Josie said, "Some Tangos came for me. Didn't anyone tell you?"

Rudy said, "Nope. Just the abort. No explanation. Are you okay?"

"I'm fine."

Terry looked at me. "So, are you going to tell us about the Tangos, Raven?"

"There were two of them. They faked a delivery and pushed their way in. No IDs. Nothing to identify them. Mike figures we were blown somehow. I didn't see it coming."

"Did they say anything?"

"Not after I shot them in the head. Do you know anything about Costa Rica?"

"The airplane has Internet, but John shuts it off when we get into busy airspace. I did a quick look. It looks like Switzerland so far as geopolitics."

"How so?"

"It's a tiny country, with good banking, a highly educated workforce, and a strong presence of finance and pharmaceutical companies. Most speak English. It has free trade zones, good financial access, and strong tax incentives.

"It has a good airport and unbelievable air connections. You can get direct flights to Toronto, London, Zurich, Frankfurt, Madrid, Amsterdam, all major US cities, and most everywhere else you'd want to go."

"What else?"

"Two things stand out. First off, it has no military. Secondly, it's a long-standing and stable democracy. That despite general chaos in the region."

I said, "No military?"

"None. Costa Rica permanently abolished its army in 1949."

"So, it's safe, not a threat to anyone, and powerful people with a lot to lose, especially including cartels and dictators, like to park their money there? Like the Nazis, Communists and others did in Switzerland?"

"Bingo. Safe and good access, what's not to like?"

I grinned. "Hey, you're the ones bitching...."

San Jose, Costa Rica, Early Evening

Mike arrived after dinner. We all stood to welcome him.

"How's the swamp?"

"Still there. I'm glad to see everyone got here OK. How do you like our safe house?"

I said, "No complaints. What's the deal?"

"I made an executive decision. We've been stuck for too long. Costa Rica is the safest place that I could find along the invasion route. A friend owns this villa, we were talking, and I snapped it up. It comes with some severe operational restrictions, but I think it can work if we behave ourselves.

"First off, tell me what the Hell happened in Grenada. I want to share it with the team so we're all on the same page. You had no warning?"

I shook my head. "None. We came in clean. No ticks. No surveillance. Josie and I never left the grounds."

Josie said, "My viewings haven't been clear. Just a fog. I've been concentrating on Cuba and taking peeks at the Mexico end, trying to see when things are going to blow up. For some reason, I can't.

"I don't see much out there. I did verify both targets Raven identified are in Cuba and planning to be there for some time. They are having meetings.

"I didn't sense an attack coming this time. I don't know why I missed it. That's a first. It worries me."

"Anything else you want to add?"

We both shook our heads.

I said, "Is our mission compromised?"

"No, I don't think so. I've been in touch with the police in Grenada. We put smoke out to divert attention.

"The cover is that you two are in witness protection. It's a nation friendly to us and they are helpful. There won't be anything in the news, and no one will be looking for you.

"The records of your stay are sanitized. They prove you'd checked out before there was an incident. You were not involved. That seems to be half true. How long before you bugged out?"

I shrugged. "About ten minutes after we communicated. Maybe twenty or thirty beginning to end."

"It seems the two Tangos are not associated with any of the threats we've been watching."

"So, who were they? What were they doing there?"

"Private detectives. The Walther was registered, so we could track it. The police know them."

"That doesn't make any sense."

"It didn't to me either. The Royal Grenada Police Force appears to be quite competent. They get investigative training from MI5. Turns out, they had these detectives under surveillance. They had been hired by some oligarch from another country."

"Why?"

"They weren't after you. The client suspected his wife was cheating. Her family is powerful, he's Catholic, and he needed proof to get a divorce."

"She looked like Josie?"

"Apparently they thought so. They were there to get proof. It was supposed to be an easy job, but you'd disabled the hotel's security cameras, hadn't you?"

"Would you respect me if I didn't?"

"Did you find any bugs in the room there, Raven?"

"Sure. Small, but nothing fancy. Audio and video. It was the honeymoon suite. I thought maybe hot new couples sometimes wanted to capture that stuff. No one complained."

"Not to you, but I assure you that your watchers were complaining up a storm. They didn't tell their client, of course."

Rudy and Terry were grinning ear to ear.

"They were quite frustrated that the two of you never left the room long enough for them to do a good search or plant new bugs.

"The Royal Grenada Police taped their bitching and the check in calls to their client. He was pissed that all that action was going down in your suite and they didn't have proof or photos."

Josie was bright red. "You didn't tell me?"

"I didn't want to break the mood. It was a special time. Our private time. No one was watching us."

Terry had tears in his eyes. Both were trying not to laugh.

I said, "Okay, I give up. So, why'd they storm our room?"

"You were scheduled to check out. It was their last chance. They were going to take pictures, question you both, and get a big pay check."

Josie said, "Too bad for them. It was all a big assed mistake? We have a happy ending? No one is after us?"

"Dear Lord, would it be that were so. Let's just say these detectives found it to be career limiting. I'm sorry, if that helps any. Are you okay?"

She took several deep breaths. "No, but I'm alive. I can't blame you. They shouldn't have invaded us."

I said, "Mike, shit happens in the field. Are you good with this?"

"Bet your ass. Anything comes at Josie, job #1 is we take it down. Which is one reason that we are not letting her go into any access-denied places. I expect President Blager, if he knew, would classify the details and give you a medal.

"In this case, we'll spare him that. An attack on Josie was thwarted. Period. End of story. Understood?"

In unison, we said, "Understood."

Mike said, "That's important. You need to put down a Tango, you do what you have to do. I'll back you up."

I said, "We got it."

Mike looked at Josie. "That goes for you too. I don't want you losing your confidence."

"I don't understand."

"Your viewings have been blocked for a while now. I don't want you losing trust in your talents, Josie."

"Why do you think I would? That's happened before. It's just how the universe works. How my universe works, anyway...."

"You didn't see the incoming threat, did you? The one Raven took down."

"No. I did not."

"Do you know why?"

She shook her head. "I've been missing things lately. This was just one more. It worries me."

"Wrong. You probably didn't see it because there was no threat to you. Raven saw it differently. You both did what was appropriate. Promise me you won't worry about it."

Josie was quiet for a long moment. She looked at me.

"He's right, you know. Don't sweat it, Babe."

The rest of our team chorused, "Hoorah."

Josie looked at Mike. "Thank you. That helps."

Mike said, "Great. Glad we got done with that. Now let's talk about Cuba.

"Here's the deal. We now have a safe house here, but we can't run OPS from here. No trail leads back here. Never. Not ever."

"Cuba is close, and so is Mexico, but when we go in or out on a hot OP, we'll have to route through somewhere else, somewhere that fits our cover. That's a hard rule."

"Why?"

"Costa Rica is like Switzerland. It's a haven for powerful people, some of whom are dangerous, a few of whom are genocidal. The rule is that no hostile actions can be tracked back to here. That's how it works.

"During World War II and the Cold War, Geneva was crawling with agents from almost every intelligence service in the world. There was a lot of spying and intrigue going on, but no violence, no warfare, no sabotage, no wet work.

"That's the iron rule. Unwritten, but understood. Switzerland is neutral. You leave it alone, and it leaves you alone.

"All the players agree, and God help anyone who puts a foot wrong. If someone puts that neutrality at risk, those responsible will suffer consequences."

I said, "What's the big deal?"

"Switzerland is a stable, wealthy country in a turbulent world. Why?

"Except for finance, it lacks industry. It lacks natural resources. It lacks geographic advantages. It lacks military power. It's been neutral since 1815.

"It avoided WW I, WW II, and the Cold War. It had a short and almost bloodless civil war in 1847, but, other than that, war hasn't touched Switzerland since Napoleon."

"So?"

"What's the obvious question, Raven?"

"Why does everyone leave them alone?"

Mike shook his head. "That's one, but there is a better one."

"Why are the Swiss so wealthy and powerful?"

"Bingo. It's in everyone's interests to leave them alone. You do not kill the golden goose.

"What do you think happens with all the gold and wealth deposited by centuries of dead Nazis, Communists, Kings, dictators, despots, corrupt officials, and defunct corporations?"

"The Swiss keep it?"

"Yes. What do you think might happen to a person, nation, or group who threatens to screw that up?"

"A shit storm of monumental proportions."

"Exactly."

"What about accidents?"

"Don't have them. Stay clean. During WW II, a few combat aircraft from both sides came down in Switzerland. The survivors were impounded until the war was over.

"This is important. No exceptions. If you screw up, I can't save you. The existence of Costa Rica as a Nation State and the stability of the entire region depends on keeping it neutral and pristine.

"Violate that, and, best case, you are looking at impoundment or jail time. The other options are worse."

Mike pointed at us in sequence, saying, "Do not fuck this up. Do you understand me and agree?"

We each said, "Yes, Sir. I understand and agree."

Josie started to speak. Mike held up his hand.

"You, I don't worry about. If you ever do feel a desire coming on to run around shooting people and blowing things up, please check with me first, okay?"

"Yes, Sir."

CHAPTER THIRTY-ONE
SO IT BEGINS

Safe House, Tijuana, Industrial District, Next Day

Chico got the call from Mr. Trevino himself. "The Americans are coming."

"Yes, Sir. Do we know when?"

"They are on the way. The excuse is that they had problems in Washington and lost one of their members."

I looked at my list. We had names, and Pilar got me their pictures. "Which one is missing, Sir?"

"The one who got them the money. Representative Jayne Whiteway, the one on the finance committee. The others have our cash and are now in a rush to deliver it. Have you seen any unusual activity from Sinaloa?"

"Sinaloa cartel is all over the place. We're waiting for the transfer, trying to avoid notice."

"Pilar is nervous. Sinaloa's cross border traffic is up 200%. They killed four police officers and an American Border Patrol agent last week."

"We are nervous too. We are badly outnumbered and outgunned."

"I am going to change your orders. Sinaloa has more votes on the Tijuana council than we do. The others might vote with whoever has the money in their possession.

"When you get the payment, don't delay, bring it directly to me in Maneadero, to Campo Turistico La Joya. We can defend this compound against against an army. If anyone interferes, kill them."

"Yes, Mr. Trevino."

San Jose, Costa Rica, Midmorning

The Villa was a poor site for remote viewings. Josie preferred pastoral settings, places miles away from other humans. Trapped in a dense city, she was struggling to compensate, sitting on the terrace alone, trying to focus.

She finally found what she was seeking. Flashes on the far horizon in Tijuana, and soon, less than a week in the future. She started sketching and taking notes.

Mike and Raven were sitting at the kitchen table, planning, crosschecking. Trying to make sure that they'd not overlooked anything.

Turned out, the problem wasn't so much about overlooking things. It was about not knowing.

Mike was complaining that we knew a lot about enemy capabilities, but almost nothing about timing and intent. I'd asked Josie to try one more remote viewing.

Josie came in. She was smiling and holding her note pad. I looked up and smiled back. "Good news, I hope?"

"Good and bad. Which part do you want first?"

I said, "Give us the good news. We're ready for some."

"I finally managed to do some viewings and see where it starts. The transfer occurs in the southeast corner of Tijuana, in an industrial area with warehouses, at about 11 AM tomorrow. Our traitors arrive with the money, a rival gang tries to hijack it, and that sets off an intense conflict between the cartels.

"Soon there are firefights from there South along the roads to the coast. It spreads. By the next day, much of Tijuana is in flames and all the border crossings and airports around there are closed. The day after that, Martial Law is declared, refugees are trying to flee, and America is deploying troops along the border."

Mike said, "That's the good news? Chaos?"

"The good news for me is I can do remote viewings again. I can see the future. The gray fog is gone.

"The good news for you is that the Airport in Mexico City will not close down until local noon, two days later. You have a time window."

I said, "We can stage Rudy and Terry back through Mexico City into Cuba on the airlines. Squeaky clean, and unnoticed outbound in the wave of people trying to flee a war zone. Right?"

Josie nodded. "Yes. I'm functional again and you have access. In your case, with your Canadian legend, I suggest you route in through Canada, maybe somewhere east, perhaps Toronto."

"I like it."

Mike said, "How, exactly, did this war start? Who triggered it? Where are our traitors?"

Josie said, "That's the bad news. I don't know. I can't see any of that. It gets worse, I'm afraid."

Mike started to speak, but stopped when I held up my hand. "Wait."

I looked at Josie. "What's wrong, Babe?"

"I can't do my remote viewings from here, Raven."

Mike said, "Why not?"

"Noise. Psychic noise. It's hard to explain. I've not experienced this before."

I said, "Have we seen it anywhere else?"

"Maybe. Remember Kaimi?"

"Of course. You and he saved President Blager's life."

"He is Huna. He was my Kahuna and advisor. His powers are much greater than mine, but they come with a cost. He can't stand to be too near people. Living in a city would kill him.

"Kaimi sticks to remote islands. It stressed him just to make a few short visits to the Presidio of Monterey, to help cure the President, just to visit in his private room for a few minutes."

Mike said, "How did he get into...."

I held up my hand. "A long story, one totally implausible and now classified and on a tight hold. If you want to know, ask President Blager. As far as we are concerned, it never happened...."

"Except it did...?"

"We're getting off the subject, Mike," I said. "How does this effect your viewings, Josie?"

"My talents are small, compared to Kaimi's. I will never be at his level, but my powers have been getting stronger. I've been able to see things increasingly better over the years. Mostly, this is a good thing, but now I'm seeing the down side."

"I'm trying to understand. Can you tell us more?"

"San Jose is a dense city, and, by its standards, the Escazú section is one of the best places in the metro area. It is a premium location, but there are still 15,000 people going about, doing what people do. That is about 3,400 people per square kilometer."

Mike looked at her sharply, "No way."

She frowned. "I didn't count them, but that's what their website says, Mike."

I said, "It's dense. This Villa you leased for us is legal for 35 guests. Right now, we have eight people here, counting the pilots. If we were full up with 35 people, we'd be falling over each other. There are only nine bedrooms and bathrooms."

Mike said, "I figured it would be OK for your team, plus me and Goldfarb. It is adequate, physically. You can barely hear the street noise. We have 24/7 security and Internet."

"She's not arguing that, Mike. You found us a safe base for OPs. She saying it's shitty for remote viewing."

Josie said, "It is psychically noisy in many languages. Escazú is an expatriate enclave. Several embassies have their residences located here, including the residences of the US Ambassador, Dutch, British, German, Canadian, and South Korean Ambassadors.

"Violence and danger shut me down, it always has, but that isn't my problem here. People here are safe, happy, busy, and active. Too active. This place is an operational disaster for remote viewing."

Mike said, "You can't work here?"

"I can just barely function. Oh, I found the disaster Raven tasked me with all right. It was like seeing a nuclear explosion, off in the distance, over the horizon. Hard to miss."

"You couldn't see the details?"

"No, I could not. It's like listening for whispers and looking for shadows in a room full of clamoring people flashing strobe lights. I'm not going to be of much use to you here."

Mike was silent for a long moment. "We have a problem, people. We need to slow down and think this one through, Raven."

I said, "Why?"

"What did you accomplish in Havana last time? We risked your team and came up dry. You concluded it wasn't possible to operate there. What's changed since then?"

"I have targeting."

"You don't know shit. You have names, two people, high value targets. What little you have is public knowledge. It turns out those names were in the fucking Cuban newspapers which Langley and our consulate people apparently don't even bother to read. We have no sources inside."

"We know who to hit."

"When and where can you best hit them? Can you get them both at once? If that doesn't work, do you have a Plan B?"

"We have local embedded resources. Deep cover."

Mike sighed. "What you are trying to get set up is local support, some partisans, and this in a total surveillance police state that puts the old Stalin era Moscow to shame. Cuba ain't like Paris, Raven.

"Your so-called 'embedded sources' consists of a loose band of witches, *Santeria*, Voodoo people who worship saints. Right?"

I nodded. "Yes. Pretty much."

"How many of them have military training?"

"Not many."

"How about zero? The Communists have been in power for seventy years."

Josie said, "They are locals who blend in. They are deemed harmless and tolerated by the government."

I said, "We have a secure way to communicate with them. They would help us."

"How? Suppose I send your team in now. They have no training or operations experience. To the best of our knowledge, they have no connections whatsoever inside the government?"

"It doesn't matter. We are not planning on getting anything from them except minor logistics support."

"How many are you in contact with?"

Josie said, "I think quite a few. The *Santeria* are all over Cuba. There are hundreds of them, maybe thousands."

"They see each other in dreams, Josie. They pray for freedom and have been doing it for centuries. How much freedom do they have?"

"Not much. It's why we can count on their help. We can answer their prayers, Mike."

"Or we can get them killed. Realistically, if we get them COMs and go this week, how many in Cuba might help us operationally with the logistics?"

"A few. Two or three."

Mike said, "Maybe. The key contact is the mother of one your friends. How old is she? Maybe seventy?"

"She's in her late sixties."

"She won't be helping us hump ammo and guns, will she?"

"No. That's why I said two or three. We'll need some muscle."

"So, at best, Raven might be in direct contact with one person, who has a few helpers?"

Josie nodded.

I said, "I have a backup plan. If this doesn't come together in time, we can supply by submarine or an air drop in remote area."

"With a higher probability of detection."

"That's how these things work, Mike. It's about tradeoffs. Can I ask you a question?"

"Sure."

"We've worked together for years. We have a damned hard target and a use-it-or-lose-it time window. The clock is running. We have a top team ready to go. We know the ground. We've been there."

"What's your question?"

"Why are you going chickenshit on us now, Mike? These things are always crap shoots. No plan survives contact with the enemy. We'll have to improvise."

Mike was silent for a long moment. "Maybe it's time for some straight talk, Raven. You need some command oversight."

Josie was giving me **The Look**. I shook my head and said, "Go right ahead."

"If you go blundering around Cuba with zero INTEL what happens? Nothing good."

"We don't blunder around in bad guy country, Mike. We run CSRs. We recon. We get mission feel. We look for opportunities to exploit."

"You were in-country for a month, all over the place, looking hard and deep. You concluded you couldn't even operate there. That it was too dangerous. Right?"

I nodded. "So, we do it again. We'll have the Mexico distraction."

"It will be worse with these leaders having meetings. Security will be tight."

"Could be. Or maybe their security teams don't coordinate well. Maybe they get sloppy. No one would dare hit them there...."

"We go in and take a look. All we need is a seam or gap in the security coverage."

"I don't like the odds, Raven. At best, we risk good people, our best people. Likely we get them hurt or killed, including you, but that's only the start...."

"We do that on every OP, Mike."

"This time there's a lot more downside. If you get your asses killed in Havana that might be the end, but you're good. Even if you miss, maybe your egress plan executes and you make a run for safety with the Cuban military after you. You might or might not survive it.

"Work out those odds. I did. They are not good."

I started to speak. Mike held up his hand.

"Say you beat the odds, Raven. You have before. Maybe you do escape. It doesn't end there."

I said, "Why not? Game over. We fight another day."

Mike said, "Cuba is a tripwire, Raven. Maybe on top of a failed OP, we get an international incident, a political crisis, or even a war, and not just with Cuba. All of a sudden, others are at risk. Good people. Leaders who trusted us. Important people."

"Who?"

"Fleet officers, for sure, everyone in the chain of command. Congress feeds on stuff like that and so does the media. That's bad enough if we'd accomplished something major for God and Country. If you get our high value targets, we could call it the cost of victory. A high cost, but shit happens. Like when Trump took out Qasem Soleimani and Fake News and the opposition party were raging about World War III."

"If you miss the high value targets and get caught, it could turn into another Bay of Pigs. It could set off major shitstorm. Without cutouts, a mission failure could reach all the way to the President."

I said, "You're worried about your ass? It that this is about?"

"No. If I approve this, I'll take responsibility. I'm one of the cutouts, Raven. I'd write my resignation, sign it, and hand it to the President before the mission."

Josie and I exchanged a look. We looked at Mike. *He was deadly serious. I'd never seen him so grim.*

"It's our best shot. We can do this, Mike."

"No. You can't. Not without top notch INTEL."

"My team got in and out clean before. Whatever happens, we can improvise."

"Negative. I'm going to cancel your mission, Raven. It's a bad go."

"God Damn it, Mike...."

I stopped speaking when Josie held her hand up. We both looked at her.

"Is this a private fight, or do I get to say something?"

Mike said, "Of course you do. You're the one with the special talents. All this started because America needed to protect you. It all started defensive, centered on protecting you. It's because of you that we have President Blager's support."

She looked at me. "Should I speak, or do you want us to just bag it?"

I said, "Speak your mind, Josie."

"First off, I'm going to request we take a break. I need you to settle down and stop screaming at each other. You both make some valid points. Okay?"

Mike nodded. "Sure."

I said, "Why not?"

"Good. You both have ghosts. I think we need more thinking and less macho.

"Raven, I want you to ask Mike about Yemen. He lost most of his unit there and was badly wounded himself. They were going to invalid him out of the military, but some photographer took a picture that won a prize, rehab worked, so they gave him a medal and promoted him instead. Now he does cloak and dagger geopolitics from behind a desk instead of leading combat troops."

Mike blinked. "That is very old news. You looked it up?"

"I did, and then I went back and remote viewed it. It's my job to know these things."

"What do you want me to ask Raven about?"

Josie said, "I expect he'll tell you. Kill teams keep coming after me. We've been running and hiding for years now, barely surviving one attack after another.

"In between these attacks, we don't get to have much of a personal life. It's not getting better. We finally got some happy time in, just to wind up running from some idiot detectives who got the wrong damned room. Me, I wound up watching people die. Again.

"The last real attacks came down the invasion corridor from Venezuela, the one we're now trying to block. Raven, badly outnumbered, recently survived a gunfight with a drug cartel. He wants us to preempt instead of defending."

"I can understand that."

"Good. Also, understand that I am going to freaking quit if something doesn't change. This sucks."

Mike said, "A thirty-minute break. Then what?"

"When we get back, you both shut up, listen, and let me talk. You want better odds. You want better Intel. Raven wants a mission while we have a time window. He wants to improvise.

"I have a suggestion, a plan. It will require decisions from both of you and we don't have a lot of time. Can you keep the mission running? Can you come back prepared to reassess and decide then?"

Mike said, "If you wish. Square 1 is still running, Josie."

"Thank you."

We settled back in at the kitchen table. As elegant as these digs were, it was the best place for a meeting. We were tight on space.

Josie looked at us. "Decision time. Are we ready?"

Mike and I nodded.

"Here's the deal. The head of the Revolutionary Guard, General Arnaldo Ochoa, is meeting next week in Havana with Colonel Hernando Cardoza, who commands the *Colectivos*, 100,000 strong, in Venezuela.

"We already know where the official meetings will be held, in the Palace of the Revolution, which is heavily guarded. It's a fortress. In 1957 a force of fifty commandos supported by over a hundred other forces in surrounding tall buildings tried to take it and kill Batista. They failed. It was a hard target then and it's probably worse now.

"Fortunately, the Palace is a bad place to discuss sensitive operational plans. It's the official residence of the President, the Council of Ministers, the Communist Party, etc."

Mike said, "Right. So, there will be a sequence of small private meetings elsewhere with just these top officers and a few of their staff. Maybe twenty people."

"Yes. Each would bring their own security. A few bodyguards. Do you agree?"

Mike said, "I do. They'd keep it small and private."

I said, "They will be staying at separate places and coming in small private convoys. Communists don't trust each other. Right?"

Mike said. "That would be my bet."

Josie said, "What if I could get you the times and places of the key meetings which both would attend, plus where each of them was staying? Is that the 'good INTEL' you seek?"

Mike nodded. "Your viewings are golden, Josie."

I said, "Would that information, plus having my team already in-country, positioned and provisioned to target those meetings, be enough for you to approve this operation, Mike?"

"Sure. It would be if we had it. Do we have it?"

Josie said. "No, not yet. Hold that question, please. Now, let's assume they will be shifting some of the meeting locations and times, not just for operational security, but also to make sure individual schedules are accommodated and political opponents are excluded. Is that reasonable?"

"It is."

"Right. So, we'll need not just good initial INTEL, but a real time stream of information to Raven's team in Cuba. We'll have to improvise, both for our intelligence collection and his attack plans. Our new COMs will let us coordinate in near real time, even in Cuba. Agreed?"

They both nodded. "Yes."

"Good. Here's the decision I'm requesting.

"If you want good viewings, I need to get clear of this noise." I looked at my watch. "To do that in time to support this OP, Raven and I must be on a 2:00 flight to Carate, Puntarenas, today."

"Where?"

"It's in a remote area on the Osa Peninsula."

"I've never heard of it."

I said, "I think this is the improvise part, Mike."

"It is. Costa Rica is big on eco-tourism. This is a small domestic airport, just a strip of concrete in the jungle surrounded on three sides by tall trees with water on the end. They run scheduled charter flights from the big airport. If I call in the next hour Raven and I can be on one."

Mike said, "What's there?"

"Nothing. That's the point. Birds, wildlife, jungle, and blessed quiet.

"The airport has no lights or facilities. It's just a small strip of concrete and a shelter to get out of the rain. There are a few small, secluded, romantic hotels that will pick us up. If we fly in, it's an hour. Otherwise, it's a few days and a 4-wheel drive."

Mike said, "What exactly are you proposing?"

"This comes in two parts. First, Raven and I go there. I do some detailed remote viewings. If I connect, I give you the meeting information, plus what more I can get. Based on that, you get Raven's team headed for Cuba so they will be in position."

"What if your information isn't adequate?"

"You do nothing. We come back. Mexico burns, Venezuela remains occupied, and Havana is off limits."

Mike said, "I can agree to that."

"Excellent. The second part is harder, Mike. I will need to **keep** doing good remote viewings. Raven needs logistic support in place, and he needs a stream of good real time INTEL. Right?"

I said, "Yes. With that level of remote viewing support from you, we can do this."

Mike said, "How can we assure that?"

"You tell me. That's where you get to improvise. One way would be to let me go to Cuba with Raven."

"President Blager will never authorize that, Josie."

I said, "I'm not fond of the idea either."

Josie shrugged. "Fine. You have some time to sort that out, Mike. Do we go now, or not?"

Mike said. "You go. We all go. I'll head for DC tonight. Your team goes to Cuba. Goldfarb and I need to meet with the boss. Keep your COMs close and your secure phones."

"Thank you."

CHAPTER THIRTY-TWO
MEXICO MADNESS

Luna Lodge, Carate, Next Day

Josie never fails to amaze me. This place she found was, literally, at the end of the world.

I've been to the ends of the world many times, but my destinations were generally nasty, harsh lands with hostile people, gunfire, and bloodshed. My trips must have been to the wrong ends.

Josie's world is a place of sunlight and rainbows, and this trip reflected it. We were finally going to a place that she picked, and, so far, it was looking good.

The lodge was in sixty acres of tropical wilderness. Most of the lodge's property was "primary" rainforest, original old growth, undisturbed. It was on the border of Corcovado National Park, voted as the #1 park in the world, a full 164 square miles of beautiful, primary, pristine wilderness.

We were up in the mountains, looking down. Luna itself was a mountain, while the park itself was down near sea level. Which was fine by me. Down there were things like twenty-foot crocodiles, big snakes, and even a few jaguars. Up here we saw the non-predators, mostly monkeys and birds.

The deadliest predators are people. These were few, and the ones we encountered were friendly. There were only sixteen rooms in the lodge. Half of these were safari tents on platforms out in the jungle.

We had a bungalow, lucky #7, with walls and outside doors we could close. Getting to it was a steep climb on a trail with close to one hundred steps. It had a King-Sized bed, one of only two at the Lodge. Best of all, it had an inside bathroom with running water. That was a big deal.

The steep trail was the only way to our room. The deck in back overlooked a sheer cliff, which featured nesting snakes and a long drop. Up here it was safe. Down there, not so much.

The snake mentioned most is the Fer De Lance (Terciopelo), by far the most common and most dangerous one in Costa Rica. Its growth rate is exponential with up to 90 snakes being produced per litter. It is known for being aggressive.

Yes, per litter. I went to snake school.

Some snakes lay eggs, but the poisonous ones often give live births. The venom the little guys have is just as deadly. In either case, the newborn or newly hatched can fend for themselves and receive no parental nurturing.

Bushmasters or Matabuey were down there too, the largest viper in the world, up to 4 meters in length, similar to rattlesnakes, but larger and without the rattle. There were others, of course, including coral snakes, vipers, and rattlesnakes. One viper lives in crevasses and could strike its full body length.

Fortunately, we had groups of 30-40 Coatimundi everywhere, roaming the trails and trees around the lodge, about the size of large house cats and better at climbing trees. They were omnivores, like racoons. They ate small snakes. Big snakes ate them.

It was like sharks and dolphins. It you saw Coatimundi, snakes were not likely around. They didn't fear humans and we were warned not to feed them.

The monkeys, also omnivores, ate snakes too, but mostly the snakes ate them. They got loud if any snakes were around. There were four species, and the howlers went off at 5 AM, snakes or not.

Josie liked that, something about local sidereal time, and it being a good time for remote viewings. Right now, she was inside. She'd pulled the mosquito netting around the bed, and was sitting there remote viewing up a storm, taking notes, happy and relaxed.

She'd said, "Total clarity."

It all made me feel safe. Who needed a security system when you had troops of howler monkeys in the trees surrounding your room and a remote viewer on full alert? Not me.

I was gazing across a deep river gorge watching the rays of sunlight crowning the canopy of the primary rainforest across the valley with a hue of gold. I was relaxing in a lounge chair, taking sips of fresh pineapple juice on the deck.

The mists below were beginning to part, offering me glimpses of the blue Pacific in the near distance. I could hear the rhythms of the waking rainforest, an orchestra led by the howler monkeys only a few hundred yards away.

All in all, not bad. It was a Hell of a lot better than Mexico. Or Cuba, for that matter...

Tijuana, Industrial District, Afternoon

Chico was now responsible for the entire operation, for both the money transfer and for getting it delivered safely. Trevino had called together a large team, but Chico didn't know most of them.

When he expressed concern and suggested someone else might be better suited, Pilar had assigned two people to assist him. He wasn't happy with either of them.

Carlos Gomez had run the guards, the interrogators. He was trusted by Trevino, but he was old, slow, had a bad leg, and hadn't seen combat in years.

Tito was the other extreme. A young kid with the eyes of a killer, often coked-up, but fiendish quick and accurate with a gun. Tito had been recruited and groomed by Ramon Santos. Ramon was gone, and even he said Tito was crazy. This one was a loose cannon.

I said, "The Americans are coming soon."

They both nodded.

"Mr. Trevino sent us support teams. I don't know any of them. Do you?"

Tito shook his head.

Gomez said, "Only by reputation. These are the key teams he has guarding his compound in Maneadero. Presumably, they are good to be trusted with that responsibility."

"Presumably. Since we are all going to be held responsible if this transfer goes bad, forgive me if I must question that. Do you have any evidence to prove that?"

Carlos shrugged. "A year back we had a confrontation with *Sinaloa*, down south. These teams were used as fire support with sniper rifles, .50 caliber machine guns, and even small mortars. The conflict ended inconclusively and the dispute was later resolved favorably by the Council."

I'd heard of that one. "We were badly outnumbered, as I recall?"

Gomez said, "Two or three to one as I recall. We lost about twenty people. They lost more."

I said, "Good. We have new orders from Mr. Trevino. We are no longer just accepting and guarding a money transfer. My orders are that we are to hijack the vehicles. We are to bring the money immediately to him in Maneadero."

"Did he say why?"

I said, "He is concerned that the Council might vote with whoever has the money in their possession."

"He could be right."

I nodded and proceeded to outline my plans. I wanted Carlos to manage the support teams, and for him to ensure that we were protected not only when we met, but also along the way to his enclave.

I wanted Tito's body in front of me when we hijacked the shipment. If anyone threatened me, he was to kill them.

If the Americans objected, we would apologize and tell them we feared an attack, that this was for their own protection, and that we could sort all that out with Mr. Trevino when we got to the compound.

When I finished, they were both looking at me. "Do you have any comments or suggestions?"

Tito said, "No."

Carlos said, "It sounds reasonable. I don't have a better suggestion."

I said, "Good. I think you both know the consequences if we fail to deliver the money to Mr. Trevino. Do you think he will forgive us?"

They both said, "No."

I said, "Correct. Get everyone into position. It would be best if this goes down quickly and we get on the road. I want us rolling five minutes after they arrive. If anyone tries to follow us, kill them."

There was an open square in front of the warehouses. Except for ours, most were dark with only a few security people there. Ours was lit, with the inside lights on and the main doors open, front and back.

We could be out on Highway #2 in five minutes. This time of evening, traffic would be light. We'd run down that and then take Highway #1 south along the coast. Our support teams would block the road behind us in several places, and lay covering fire down on the road as was needed.

The trick was getting out of Tijuana if the Americans had been followed. We expected a convoy of four vehicles. Three SUVs and a van. It was the van that had the cash on a pallet.

We had a password and counter sign arranged. I'd stand at the front door with Tito and handle the protocols.

Carlos had a radio so he could communicate with me and our covering forces, and I had an earpiece. We had two snipers covering the front door, and one on the back.

The Americans arrived on time.

Carlos said. "Two black SUVs, a white Van, and a black chase SUV. Lead car has two people. Looks like a woman and maybe a security guard.

I clicked to acknowledge and said, "Understood. Did you detect any activity?"

"No. So far, it's just them. All is quiet."

"Same here. I see them."

I stepped forward and signaled "Come here" with my arms.

The Convoy rolled up. A woman got out of the right front of the front vehicle, followed by her driver. He looked like hired security, not secret service. The gun on his hip was too obvious.

The woman approached me. She was short, with glasses and a serious look.

She said, "Zimmerman."

I replied, "Telegram."

"Correct," she said. "I'm Nicia Volpe, do you know me?"

I shook my head.

"I'm the house minority leader. I represent California. May I ask your name?"

I smiled. "Just call me Chico. I represent Mr. Trevino. He sends his welcome, and he sent me to advise you of a slight adjustment in our plans."

She frowned. "We deliver our package to you, and proceed to some meetings with your government."

"I'm sorry, there have been some changes. Tijuana is not safe these days. Your mission may have been compromised. My orders are...."

Tito said, "We've got a problem, Boss."

A large man, stocky, with a bushy beard, and dressed in black stepped out of the shadows. He looked vaguely familiar.

"Do you know him?"

Tito said, "No."

"Do you, Ms. Volpe?"

She shook her head. "No. He's not with us."

I clicked my radio, "Carlos?"

"I can't see him clearly boss."

The man approached us, walking slowly, exuding confidence. "You must be new, Mr. Chico. You don't know me?"

"I do not. Whoever you are, you have no business being here. This is a private matter."

"You are mistaken. My name is Che and everything that happens in Tijuana is my business."

I heard Carlos in my earphone. "Oh, Shit. Che Escobar, Pablo's elusive cousin. Bad news."

The little American woman had spunk. She bristled and faced the man. "Mister Che, this is a private matter, and it is one of no concern to you.

"My name is Nicia Volpe, I'm an elected representative of the United States Government, I am the...."

"I don't care who you are Gringa. You are not in America, or are you too dumb to know that?

"What I do care about is the money you brought across the border. I'm going to take it, and you are going to let me...."

"Like Hell, you are...."

Che pointed a finger at her. Volpe jerked, looking down at her blouse. A dark stain had appeared. She collapsed just as we heard the shot. Her driver was falling as well.

Tito had his gun out. He fired three shots into Che. Two in the chest, one in the head, and he was down.

Tito was screaming, "Down, down, down...."

I hit the ground, crawling behind Che, then frantically toward the shelter of the vehicles. My radio came alive. People talking on our net.

Tito was firing at something, but I dared not raise my head to look.

Carlos was yelling on the radio, "We have targets."

"Shoot, shoot, shoot. In the name of God, engage them."

All Hell broke loose. There was a long volley of rifle shots. A heavy machine gun opened up, firing green tracer. Russian ammo.

There were rounds bouncing off the tarmac around me. I slithered towards the empty vehicle. I knew I was going to die.

Then I was behind it, sheltered. It was taking rounds, but they didn't seem to be penetrating. Thank God for armor.

Counter fire was going the other way. Our own machine guns, two of them. Red tracer, and then the crump of mortars, screams, and buildings in flames.

Three men were running towards me. Not ours.

I fired, hitting one. I put two more into him as he collapsed.

Tito dropped one. We both hit the third one, he dropped, and then Tito was down.

Carlos somehow arrived out of nowhere with a rifle, limping, but making good progress, and leading two other men. One had a rifle, the other a grenade launcher.

All of them were shooting. I couldn't see what they were hitting, but there was no return fire.

Carlos said, "We gotta go, boss."

"Right. I'll drive the lead car. Give me one good man for shotgun. You get in the van with one of your men and make sure it follows me.

"Tell the others to follow us if they want to live."

Off we went into the night. We made it to Highway 1 in under four minutes. If there was any pursuit, I did not see it.

I looked behind, and saw the white van on my bumper, with Carlos at the wheel. *Thank God.*

CHAPTER THIRTY-THREE
INTERLUDE

Bungalow #7, Luna Lodge, Morning

J osie was wrapping up her remote viewing, triggered again at 5 AM by the unholy cries of the howler monkeys. I thought it odd. The natural sound of loud monkeys didn't interfere, but psychic noise from a bustling, crowded city overfilled with humans limited her abilities.

I was out on the deck again, enjoying the vista. Yesterday had been a good day, peaceful and productive.

Mike was back in DC making sure the t's were crossed and the i's were dotted. Goldfarb was happy. We'd gotten them the INTEL he needed to justify a go. Our new COM units were flawless, so long as we let them have a good look at the sky. They didn't work at all through the thick thatched roof.

We had no phones, no power, no Internet, no television, and no communication except for our small units. Our friends in DC seemed to be suffering under the impression that we were roughing it in the wild, presumably eating grubs and nuts and bathing in jungle streams. I'd not dissuaded them.

We had propane lanterns, flashlights, and solar powered lights outside on the steps, but why spoil the image? Our whole mission was off the grid and this was the good part.

We had hot water for our shower, thanks to solar heating. It was much appreciated. Josie had even brought shampoo. There was a radio back in the lodge, but it didn't matter. We had no plans to use it, and it would blow our cover as a honeymoon couple if anyone attempted to contact us.

There was a Land Rover Defender to shuttle folks around – mostly to the airport or beach – but it had driven itself out of its "garage" the night we'd arrived and down into the jungle. They were still working to haul it back, but a neighbor was reportedly filling in for the afternoon flight. That didn't matter either.

The truth was we had three gourmet meals per day. Chicken, meat, vegetables, and fruit last night, and it was all fresh and delicious. We'd made a deal with the lodge to tote our breakfast up the steep steps so we could relax on our deck and enjoy the spectacular view.

Today it was eggs, rice, and beans. It would arrive soon. I heard the shower cut off. Josie and I were already settling into a rhythm.

The dining room had electricity, ice, chilled wine, and beer. It was fine at night, and, by then, the heat and humidity had backed off. Reportedly, two rooms in the lodge had air conditioning. We didn't care. There was a nice breeze at our bungalow and we left the doors open during the day.

This time of morning, there were swarms of colorful humming birds all around. They were silent except for clicks to communicate and the buzzing of wings when they disputed territory. Fun to watch.

This was as close to heaven as I'd ever been. Sharing it with Josie made it perfect.

The breakfast was perfect. I stuffed the remains in the little hamper they'd left us. Josie took the towel off her head and shook her hair loose.

"It feels almost dry. How does it look?"

"Looking good, Babe. Did you pick up any messages?"

She shook her head and started brushing her hair. "Quite a few. I didn't look at them carefully. Scary stuff out of Mexico. It's started, it's bloody, and I didn't want to ruin our breakfast.

"I did the upload for my viewings, focused on Havana. You'll get a copy."

"Anything major?"

"Mostly good news. We're ahead of schedule. Mike's back with Goldfarb. They are going to brief President Blager today.

"Rudy made it through Mexico City with no problems and he should be landing in Havana about now. Terry's flight is finally in the air, but it was delayed. There are a lot of people trying to get out of Mexico."

I said, "You sure called that one."

Josie sighed. I could see the pain in her eyes.

Best to change the subject.

"Why don't I look though my messages while you're getting even more beautiful?"

"What are we doing today, Raven?"

"Recreation time together is precious, and we don't get enough of it."

"It's nice here. I did some viewings. Crystal clear. No threats. No one is coming at us."

"The folks we met at dinner were mostly enjoying photography. There are guided hikes into Corcovado, kayaking in the lagoon, basking on the beach, sport fishing, and swimming in the pool."

"Not in the ocean?"

"Swimming is not recommended. Sharks. Big ones, feeding in close. This is the Peninsula de Osa. Spanish for shark."

Josie said, "Right. Bad karma. Let's avoid the ocean, but why would the Russians name a class of warship in Spanish? Was it to honor Castro?"

"Hard to say. It's the only time they did it. I doubt there are any sharks in Russia, as they are a bit short on warm water ports.

"Crazy Ivan sometimes does weird stuff like that. Russia named the crappy washing machines they sold to Cuba after a porn star.

"Cuba got the last laugh, because they never paid Russia for them. I actually saw one when I was there...."

"Did it work?"

"That's hard to say too. Maybe. The one I saw, nothing worked but the plug."

Josie shook her head and made a face. "Ugh. No comment."

"Yeah. Maybe we should get back to our plans for today. I think we may have a superior choice...."

Josie was smiling. "Which is?

"How about do **nothing**. Would that work for you?"

"It sure would. I'd like that."

"After we check our messages."

She sighed. "Yeah…."

It turned out there were a lot of messages. Washington was paying attention, our two guys had arrived safely in Havana, and the *Busted Flush* would arrive there in two days. Mexico was in flames already, sooner than was expected, and with a higher body count than anticipated.

Goldfarb wanted Josie to update her viewings to include Mexico.

I gave that notion a strong veto.

"Request refused, Mike. No way in Hell. We have a running mission. Cuba viewings only until our OP is done and we're well clear."

That got an immediate reply from Mike. "State Department needs help. It's on the news that we have Members of Congress being held hostage. One is reportedly dead."

I sent back, "No shit. Do you want me to scrub our mission? In the name of God, please keep our OPSEC pristine. Do not share anything with State. Or anyone.

"I need to keep Josie and my team clear of the shitstorm in Mexico. The plan, which you approved, was to use that mess for a diversion. You are scaring me."

The answer from Mike was immediate.

"Easy. You get to make the call on your team, Raven. State's concern is over Mexico. Your OPSEC is tight on all fronts. No one outside our team is read in on your mission. Yes, the Navy is standing by, but that's flagged as a training exercise.

"My orders to you are NO SCRUB and carry on. I will, however, send your position and question all the way up the chain for confirmation."

Excellent. *All the way up was President Blager.*

I acknowledged and immediately got a question back.

"My pilots can't find a Carate airport. Nothing in the data bases. They want a 5,000-foot runway."

"Rustic, quiet, and low profile is part of the appeal, Mike. We're a couple on honeymoon. No extraction needed. Let's stick with the plan we have."

"Just asking. Where did you land?"

"Carate. Thin concrete. Same color as the beach. It might not show up well on satellite. 2,362-feet."

"You are kidding me. Source?"

"Source is Glen."

"G-L-E-N?" He spelled it out phonetically and said, "Please repeat."

"That's all there is, Mike. Glen. Speaks English. Claims to be Canadian. Frizzled gray hair with a ponytail. No phone number, no email, declines to give his last name, but did say that he gets sporadic mail."

"Did you identify yourself?"

"Absolutely. Digger. Canadian. We were like brothers meeting in the jungle."

There was a long pause. "How do you plan to get back?"

"Same way we got here, Mike. We left our gear at the Villa in San Jose.

"Our plan is to make our own way back, clean up, do an overnight, and egress on the airlines. It might be best if I routed though Canada. We're still working on the details and timing."

"Where will Josie be going?"

"One of the details. Can we get back to you on that?"

"Cuba is not approved for Josie."

"Understood. We are working on support issues."

"Avoid Mexico. Are you watching TV?"

"What's a TV?"

"Never mind. Independent return to San Jose is approved. Carry on."

"WILCO. We'll check in once a day, and also from San Jose. Raven out."

I turned off my COM and sighed. "I fucking hate the DC swamp...."

Josie's powers came at a price. Viewing trauma and violence could destroy her. It could literally destroy her mind.

Before we'd first started working together, before we'd even met, she'd saved my life. Her viewing the consequences of an Iran with nukes had put her in intensive care and almost killed her.

CHAPTER THIRTY-FOUR
INSURRECTION FEVER

Trevino Complex, Campo Turistico La Joya, Mexico. Next Day

Pilar was finishing her briefing to Mr. Trevino.

"The fighting in Tijuana has been constant and escalating ever since the money transfer. We lost Tito and the Americans lost their leader, Nicia Volpe, at the beginning of the fight. She was the US House Minority leader, a very powerful person. Her death made international news."

"Yes. Did we kill her?"

"We did not, but we are being blamed for it in the media."

"Who killed her?"

"We don't know who fired the shot, but it was a *Sinaloa* sniper. We know who ordered the kill. It was Che Escobar himself. We have it on video. We have two witnesses, Chico and Carlos. They both told me the same story."

"How can we prove that if it was a long-range shot?"

Pilar said, "Che gave a hand signal. He pointed at the American and a sniper immediately cut her down. We reacted by killing Che. It was only then, after Chico's command, that our people started shooting.

"Are you sure that we got him? Che, Pablo's cousin? That is huge news."

Pilar nodded. "Che is dead. It's been reported on the news. A large funeral is planned. We are responsible for his death. The news neglects to mention that *Sinaloa* fired first.

"Tito shot Che at close range on orders from Chico. Tito's dead too. Chico watched it all unfold, up close. Carlos saw it too. When Che went down it set off a melee. Lots of gunfire. Total chaos. We evacuated."

Trevino said, "Did you see the Americans' vehicles? They all took hits. It was fortunate that they had armor and run flat tires."

"Yes. I counted 137 bullet holes in one. Two had their back windows shot out. How are the Americans?"

"Unwounded and happy to be alive. They were terrified when they arrived. The Senator is elderly. He was incoherent and had soiled his pants."

Pilar shook her head. "What?"

Trevino said, "The Senator literally shit himself. We put them all in guest cottages. At present, they are confined to the grounds for their own safety.

"I've not met with them yet personally. Chico said they were happy to get out of Tijuana alive, and glad to be here safe in my compound."

"Are they grateful to us or just happy to be alive?"

Trevino said, "Hold that question for a moment, Pilar. How many people did we lose?"

"Three at the exchange site, counting Tito. The total we lost getting here was nine, and another two wounded. Most of them were lost at the roadblocks we set up behind the convoy.

"It is hard to get a good body count and totally impossible to know who's doing the killing. We are losing twice that every night in Tijuana now and more along the border. *Sinaloa* is probably losing twice as many, maybe more.

"All this carnage has been getting far too much attention. I think other cartels and groups may be using it to settle scores, possibly the police too. I assume you've watched the TV news? It is claiming over 800 dead or wounded yesterday, violence is increasing, and several neighborhoods are in flames."

Trevino said, "I watch the news. They are blaming us for destabilizing the region."

"Yes. They say if we'd just given *Sinaloa* its fair share of the money, this would not have happened."

"That's pure propaganda, Pilar. It is false. It is Fake News. Are the Americans blaming us?"

"Not yet, but they are making general statements about the unfortunate surge of cartel violence."

"The Mexican government?"

"No. Not yet."

Trevino said, "So, other than *Sinaloa*, who is driving this?"

"The Russians have been the most vocal. Perhaps we should not have sent that diplomat's severed head to their embassy? They hold grudges and it's well known that one of our people killed him."

"Ramon killed him. That's old news. Ramon is dead, probably killed by *Sinaloa*, in another attack on us."

Pilar shrugged. "Mostly, so far, the blame on us comes from *Sinaloa* and the Russians, but as you know, these things have a way of gaining traction. The UN and other globalist groups will pile on if we don't do something. We need to stop this, to shut it down."

Trevino said, "I agree. That's why we are talking, and why I have not yet met with the Americans. I need to know how to play it before I see them. What are the main talking points in the press?"

"Tell me that. Advise me how we can best counter this information war. We need to do something."

Pilar said, "The talking points in the news are simple. They say we attacked the Russians by killing their diplomat, that we attacked *Sinaloa* by first cutting a corrupt deal with the Americans to give us an advantage and then by killing Che when he came to get his fair share. Finally, they say we attacked the Americans by taking their officials as hostages."

"Those are all lies, Pilar. Unfortunately, clever lies, demonic lies that all contain partial truth."

"Please explain slowly. I want to take notes."

Trevino said, "The severed head and the Russian embassy have nothing whatsoever to do with Tijuana. It's old news. They were running a spy ring, an illegal operation, and it went bad for them. If anything should be investigated, it's the Russians."

Pilar nodded. "Noted."

"Next, this transaction, this money exchange, was set up by the *Americans*. They chose to invest in us. We did not solicit it. Their giving us money didn't break any of Mexico's laws. There are many precedents.

Sinaloa has taken much more in donations from the Americans over the years."

"That is documented?"

"Well documented, but seldom discussed. Usually the money is run through various aid or foreign assistance programs administered by the government. This time the Americans chose to do it directly."

"Why?"

Trevino said, "I have no idea. It wasn't discussed when we set it up. A delegation of American officials came along with the money. They offered me cash. I accepted. Only a fool would say no to free, unaccountable money."

"What else can I tell the media?"

Trevino said, "The biggest thing to say is that the fair share that *Sinaloa* is entitled to is exactly **zero**. It was a private arrangement between us and the Americans. It is none of their business. *Sinaloa* has done many such deals over the years. They have never given us or the other cartels a single peso. That is what the Council will be ruling on next month. It is already on the agenda."

Pilar paused in her note taking. "Are you sure the council would rule in our favor?"

"Absolutely, if it came to a vote, and for many reasons. The problem is that we may not want to allow a vote. I'm thinking of tabling it, of delaying the vote."

She put her pen down. "These are difficult arguments, Sir. The stakes are high. Tensions are high. The government is considering martial law. Do we want to fight both Sinaloa and the Mexican Army?"

"I don't want to fight at all, Pilar. I just want the cash. We have a problem, a big one. If I share it with you, you will be only the third person to know. The information is quite sensitive. You must tell no one."

"What?"

"Swear on your mother's grave that you will tell no one without my specific authorization."

"I swear it."

"There is no money, Pilar. None."

"How is that possible?"

Trevino said, "I do not know, but I can show you the evidence with your own eyes. This is why I'm having such a hard time deciding what to do with our American guests."

"They don't know?"

"I don't think that they do, but I've not spoken with them directly. What they know or do not know will become apparent, given time. I intend to make finding that out a part of your job. If needed, Carlos can support you. He is in on the secret and his methods can be most persuasive."

Pilar said, "You are more interested in our getting the money than you are concerned about escalating a war with *Sinaloa?*"

"Exactly. Conflict between the cartels is inevitable, but all of us are mainly interested in profits. War is costly. That is why the council exists."

"What would you have me do?"

Trevino said, "Two things immediately. First, get out the message to the media that it was *Sinaloa* who murdered this high level American official, the US House Minority leader, and that we tried to defend her and were fired upon by *Sinaloa*. Tell them some of our people were killed defending this innocent American. We are on the side of the angels."

"That is easily done. It is all true."

"Good. Hit that hard. Spend money as you deem necessary. When the media begins to take notice, I want you to make a second announcement. Write this down precisely and make it explicit."

"I'm ready, Sir."

Trevino said, "If *Sinaloa* does not admit their guilt publicly, I plan to target the funeral for Che and to kill all their leaders who attend."

"Will we actually do that?"

Trevino gave a shrug. "Possibly. It's why your use of the words 'plan to' is key. Don't say we will, just that we plan to."

"That's very clever. What would you have me do long term?"

Trevino said, "Interview our American guests. Make friends with them, if you can. See if they are willing to make public statements to aid our campaign for justice. Get your staff up to speed on Alinsky tactics. We will blame our enemies for what we do ourselves.

"Get me an actionable plan and budget for our public relations. Make sure it includes the United States media and their Congress. Then advise me as to what we should do next."

Pilar was jotting down notes. "Do you plan to set any limits as to what actions I should consider?"

"None. If our American guests should become hostages, or if we need to escalate this war, so be it. The stakes are very high.

"I view this as the most significant crisis that *Los Serpientes* has ever suffered. Make sure that your people know my view on this."

"Absolutely. I agree with you, nephew. We are blessed to have you as our leader at this time."

CHAPTER THIRTY-FIVE
THE CHIPS ARE DOWN

The White House – In the Bubble, Two Days Later

There were just the three of us there, me, Doctor Goldfarb, and the President. He was looking at us intently, frowning.

He said, "Mike, we need to speak candidly. We are still using the Trump protocols. The visitor's logs for the White House are classified. They will be sealed for at least 5 years after I leave office.

"No one but the three of us in this room will be privy to this discussion. You will not keep notes. I will take some for my own purposes, but I will not share or preserve them. I need everyone to speak freely."

We both said, "Yes, Sir."

"It's all over the news that a delegation of American officials was abducted in Mexico while in the process of delivering a large sum of money to a drug cartel. One of them has been killed, the House Minority leader, one Nicia Volpe, a most irritating woman from California. Have you seen that?"

We both nodded.

I said, "I saw that on the news and read the articles about it. It's a nasty business."

"More than nasty. It's a state of war. Tijuana is in flames and it's spreading. Mexico is becoming a failed state. Have you been running an operation down there with Raven's team?"

"Not running, but considering. We've been exploring an operation, but not necessarily one in Mexico. Our general mission was to interdict the invasion route up from Venezuela across our Southern Border.

"The hope has been that we could take small, focused, local actions that would change the geopolitical situation without involving the United States and risking a regional war. We did take a look at Mexico. The situation down there is volatile."

"Damn it, I know that. Give me a straight answer, Mike. Did you have any assets involved in this Mexico debacle or not?"

"No, we did not, Mr. President. Raven did go down into Mexico recently. He went in alone and unsupported to do a recon. He's been back for over a week.

"Raven advised us that Mexico was much too dangerous for his team. We accepted his judgment. He predicted that chaotic violence was soon to erupt. It seems that he was correct in that assessment."

"You pulled Raven out?"

I sighed. "No, Sir, technically, we did not. Raven has been operating independently. He went in on his own initiative to assess the situation and he came out the same way. Alone."

The President stared at us critically. "You two look as nervous as a pair of whores in Church. Is there a reason that you've not been keeping me informed of your activities?"

Goldfarb said, "I'd better take this one, Mr. President. As a general policy, we've always been operational in a low-profile manner that distanced Raven's operations from your office, and, hopefully from anything official that involved the United States.

"That's what the old Covfefe committee was all about. It was a fig leaf of dubious value, and one that proved increasingly problematic as you shrunk the size of the NSC."

"I told you to drop all that, Aaron."

"You did, Mr. President. We did drop it, and that was a good thing. The oversight was cumbersome. Raven's operations in the past have all been primarily defensive. This one is not.

"The focus at first was to protect Josie as a national treasure, a valued strategic resource. That expanded to protecting you from unconventional threats. Along the way, some operations involved protecting the United States from unconventional attacks."

"Yes. Like WMDs."

"This operation is not like that, Sir. We were tasked with helping to shut down an invasion route. That is not defensive at the core. It is offense, and that was the mission you gave us."

"Where is Raven at present?"

"On his way to Cuba, Sir. He and his team spent weeks doing a recon there. They had judged Cuba to be an impossible target.

"So, on his own, Raven took a look at Mexico. He judged that to be even worse. Josie was ringing alarm bells, and he got out."

The President was shaking his head. "Let me get this straight. Cuba was impossible. So, Raven looked at Mexico, deemed it to be even worse, and then he refocused you on Cuba?"

Goldfarb said, "Pretty much. He and Josie got better targeting information. They reevaluated."

"Have you gone mad?"

"No, Mr. President. Opportunistic. We seek to exploit the chaos in Mexico."

"Raven saw it coming?"

Goldfarb nodded. "He did. So did Josie."

I said, "Cuba holds the keys to Venezuela."

"Yes," the President said. "It does."

I said, "Cuba is a high risk, high return situation, Mr. President. We all favored doing an OP. Raven, his team, Josie, and, yes, me. We talked Doctor Goldfarb into it."

The President looked at Goldfarb. "Tell me about it, Aaron."

"We call the operation **Square 1**, for obvious reasons. Technically, it has been live for a few days. Nothing operational, and nothing kinetic so far. We've just been positioning our assets and support resources. We were coming to see if you wanted to be briefed in."

"Do I want to be, Aaron?"

Goldfarb said, "When we take out high value targets in Cuba, Mr. President, it will provoke a violent reaction. Events will then occur that we can't control. The trick is to stay ahead of them."

"Raven's team will be running for their lives with Cuban forces in hot pursuit?"

"Let's just say that pursuit is likely. Mission success gets down to surprise, execution, speed, and timing. If things go wrong, others may become involved."

"Including me?"

"That is unlikely, but, yes, it possibly could go that way if things went wrong.

"I can't say if it is best for you to know what Raven plans, or politically better for you to be able to honestly deny knowing that, Mr. President."

"What can you say?"

"Egress is high risk. It poses troublesome issues."

"I can imagine. Brief me in, Aaron. How long will it take?"

"Just you? Not long. Perhaps an hour or two."

"I will clear my schedule. Let me put it this way. Neither of you is leaving Washington until I'm fully in the loop. Were you planning on having military support available for egress?"

"Raven has made some informal arrangements with the Navy, Mr. President. He has a fast, civilian boat. We'll include those details in your briefing."

"Damn right you will. Let's take a fifteen-minute break. I'll get us some coffee. You might want to book rooms for tonight."

We'd been going at it for hours. A full briefing, one without notes and based on our best recollections, took several hours. The main thing we decided was that we needed to decide now.

The chips were down, the mission was running, and we had an unknown, but short, time-window. We had resources on the ground, and we could either let it run or scrub it. There was no third option.

We'd made our call and now it was up to the President. We fell silent and let him think. Finally, he said, "Is there any important aspect of this that we've failed to discuss?"

I said, "I don't think so, Mr. President. Cuba is a denied access area. Raven's team was there, on the ground. They are there now back in-country to get up to speed, to rebuild their mission sense.

"We have Josie and good COM to give the team real time information we'd never get elsewhere."

The President looked at Goldfarb. He shrugged. "We've covered the key points."

I said, "There is a short list of things we know, and a longer one of things we don't know."

The president gave a thin smile. "Does that include the 'don't knows' we don't even know exist?"

Goldfarb said, "That one runs out over the horizon. I'll start with what we do know.

"We'll never get an opportunity like this again. The two best high value targets we have will both be there, meeting together, in Havana. Taking either out would be a win. Getting both would be huge.

"The best team we have will be there at the right time, prepared and ready. We have good COM, and potentially world-changing events are causing a level of chaos that the region has not seen since Castro made Cuba a Communist State."

The President said, "Anything else?"

I said, "Safety is not far away. We have a fleet off-shore and GITMO is close."

The President said, "Kennedy had a fleet offshore for the Bay of Pigs, as I recall."

"One with orders to do nothing. It was a disaster."

"Yes. A fact worth remembering."

The President held up his yellow notepad. It had short list of talking points, and all those we mentioned were covered. "Good. We seem to be in agreement."

"Now comes the hard part. I am going to ask you each to write down four numbers. I will ask you estimate some odds. Initial the sheet and hand it back to me. I will do the same, then we'll discuss it.

1. Will Raven expose his team without taking kinetic action?
2. If they engage, can they get at least one HVT kill?
3. If successful on one, can they get both targets?
4. If they engage, what are the odds they can escape?

That's all. Four simple questions. Four numbers. No discussion. Your best judgements."

The President handed out sheets of paper, and we took a short break. When we returned, he collected the sheets, and scanned them for a time.

Then he stood up and said, "Interesting. Thank you, gentlemen, for your time and expertise. The Cuba mission is approved."

Goldfarb and I exchanged a look. He said, "Mr. President, wait a minute. What were the answers?"

"Oh, they were pretty much in agreement. The odds of Raven's team getting blown are near zero. The odds of them getting one target are better than 60%. The odds of them getting both, if they can get one, are better than 80%. I would not expect less of you or Raven's team."

I was frowning. "What about the last number?"

"I didn't like that one. It is too low, but I don't want to jinx your mission. I don't like sending brave Americans into harm's way, but it is a part of my job."

Goldfarb said, "Do you plan to do anything, Mr. President?"

"Nothing official, Aaron. I promise you that.

"High level people muddling in operational matters often makes matters worse in my experience. Too much attention might risk exposing Raven's mission, or, worse, getting America into a war. Please keep me informed and call if you need anything."

"Thank you, Mr. President."

"Wait," I said. "What about privately?"

The President gave a faint smile. "My wife and I will be praying. I may have some words to share with friends about the important job Admiral Perkins and the Fourth Fleet are doing for our nation.

"I'd love to be able to spend more time with you, to have dinner, but people are insisting on a meeting. Something about problems in Mexico. I expect we'll be hearing about it in the news...."

Goldfarb said, "Perhaps after the mission."

"I'd like that."

CHAPTER THIRTY-SIX
GIRL TALK

South Patrick Shores, Florida, Five Days Later

J osie was having a new experience. As a paranormal, she learned not to share or get close to normal people.

Witches were no longer burned, but she understood that people might think she was eccentric, possibly crazy. Even at the Rhine Institute, the psychics worked independently and those studying her were distant.

Separation increased when her work intersected with national security, things to not be discussed except with those within tight circles of trust. After the kill teams started coming for her, she and Raven were guarded, isolated, constantly vigilant, moving from one safe house to another. That is life as we knew it, life as I knew it.

I was getting to know Gerry Patton better, an amazing woman with an interesting history. Patton was her birth name, and she'd hung on to it for security reasons. Her driver's license carried her married name, Gerry Patton Mickelson. She was married to Twenty Mike, who was, these days, pretty much acting as the controller for Raven.

Gerry's younger brother, Will, was the Mad Scientist who ran Cybertech, and this house was one of several the company had acquired while doing the work to upgrade the Busted Flush. It was convenient that the house backed up to a dock with a shed large enough to conceal a boat.

This is where they'd parked me. Gerry was my personal security detail. She packed a gun in her purse and technically was still a subcontractor, through Cybertech, with NSA. She had been a program manager there when she and Mike met.

We were alone in the house. Mike and Raven left last night on one of the Cybertech airplanes. First to drop Mike in DC – the swamp as he called it – and then to take Raven to Canada, where he'd fly on the airlines to Cuba under his Digger legend.

Gerry looked at me. "Is Raven in Havana yet?"

"His airline ticket said he should be."

"You don't know?"

"He hasn't checked in with me yet and I'm not going to bother him. It's a denied access area. He says it's worse than Stalin's Cold War Moscow. The whole team is spooked about that.

"He won't communicate until he's sure he's clean. Maybe tonight, probably by tomorrow."

"Whoa." Gerry held up her hand. "Easy, girl. I was just asking…."

I took a deep breath. "Sorry I snapped at you. Two days ago, Raven and I were at peace, safe, serene, as happy as Adam and Eve in a remote rain forest. Since then, it's been a bustle. Everyone is tense and no one is talking about it."

"We've been there, Josie. Mike and I. It's a damned helpless feeling watching an OP from a situation room. It has to be worse if you see it in your head."

That wasn't what made it worse. I needed to be closer. We were missing something and I didn't know what.

I chose my words carefully. "Raven is fine right now. If something bad happened to him, we'd both know it. You might be rushing me to an ICU."

Gerry said, "They briefed me on that. One is fifteen minutes away. It serves the Cape and is one of the best in the country. I've got the number and names in my phone. Has that happened before?"

I nodded. "I wound up in a coma, and the government and doctors didn't know what to do. Raven was wounded himself, but he came to see me and wound up saving me."

"You want to be with him, don't you?"

She did understand, at least a little.

"Not with him. I couldn't handle that. I'd be in the way and I might get him killed. Violence shuts me down, but I do need to be aware.

"I need to be closer. I'm part of this mission, Gerry. I'm not a shooter, but I see things. Things that can make a difference."

Gerry was watching me intently. "This was the closest safe place we could find. We have direct orders from the President. You are a national resource, to be protected at all costs.

"It's why I'm here. This isn't social. I'm part of this mission too."

"What are your orders?"

"To get you what you need. To get you as close as possible. And to keep you from being captured."

"That's all?"

"I'm your personal security as well."

She'd take a bullet for me.

I said, "That's asking a lot of you, Gerry."

"Support is close. There is a boat on patrol out in the Indian River Lagoon with a SEAL team on board. Another team is ready to deploy from the Air Base. Both are only minutes away."

I was trying to read her feelings. "What are you most worried about?"

"Not a lot here. This is a safe house. If anything happens, we hunker down and shelter in-place.

"We're more at risk when you're moving, especially if we have patterns, places we return to."

"You're talking about my Cuban friends. I trust them."

Gerry nodded. "They check out clean. Local help is useful.

"Your friends are located North of both Patrick AFB and the NASA facilities at the Cape. When we go to meet with them, I want you to drive. I'll have you run CSRs. If someone tails us, that's a good thing."

I blinked. "Why?"

"We have gate passes for both facilities. If we see anything suspicious, we'll just duck into a secure facility, scrape the ticks off, and alert the FBI. They will tag the Tangos and neutralize them."

"Kill them?"

"If needed. More likely, they'll either arrest them or put them under surveillance."

"Thank you."

"People are being careful with you, Josie. You're safe here."

"I don't mean to sound ungrateful."

"You just sound scared. Relax. Raven knows what he's doing. He won't hit the dangerous part for a few more days. We still have to get provisions in place for his team."

"That's why I need to meet with the Cubans."

Gerry nodded. "What would you like to do tonight?"

"I think a hot shower and an hour alone. I can de-stress and do a remote viewing. Then I'll leave a message for Raven to let him know I'm all right. Is that okay?"

"Of course."

"You will like my Cuban friends. You are going to get a dinner to remember...."

Bella Habana-Aeropuerto, **Havana, Cuba**

The best I could say is that nothing had changed. Cuba was still the grim, gray, third world, 21ˢᵗ century, version of Stalin's Russia. The populace had been crushed under four generations of hardcore Communism. They were docile.

Any who had resisted the Castro regime were in prison or dead. Hope was gone. No one dared to resist. Cuba had passed from being a failed state into a Gulag.

Mexico was earlier along that road to a socialist Hell. Venezuela had just started its descent. Both were war zones. Here in Cuba there was peace, but it was the peace of the grave.

I'd sold Goldfarb on the notion that Cuba was the best target, but that was mostly because just being in Mexico or Venezuela put my team at risk. So many violent groups were fighting each other that any presence there, passive or not, was potentially lethal.

In Mexico or Venezuela, anything you did could get you killed. Just being in the wrong place was dangerous. The body counts proved that.

What I'd not mentioned – Goldfarb probably knew – was that the instant we went kinetic in Cuba we and our allies would be the only target in the country. Every hand would be turned against us.

Cuba was safe as long as we did nothing. Once we acted, it would go off the scale dangerous.

It was remarkable that Josie had managed to somehow link up with an indigenous group – one viewed by the Castro regime as harmless kooks who worshiped dead saints – that might actually be able to provide us with operational support. They were nice people. I hoped we didn't get them killed.

The same manager was at the front desk. He did no work that I could detect, except to observe and report everyone. The updated hotel register would be in the hands of Cuban Security by tomorrow.

A lowly desk clerk handed me my key and said, "Good to have you back, Sir."

My legend seemed to be holding. A harmless Canadian guest who worked for a well-known Mexican oil firm was returning for some down time. Something to be expected, given the chaos in Mexico. Most businesses were closed. TV news showed few on the streets.

"Can I have my usual room?"

That stretched "usual" a bit, as I'd only been here once before, but I doubted the manager bothered to keep up with such details. It wasn't a lie. And, what the Hell, the refrigerator worked, the bathroom had a toilet seat, and the room might still be free of geckos. I could do worse.

The clerk nodded and smiled. "*¡Sí Señor!* The hot water, she is working now. Do you know how long you'll be staying this time?"

I smiled back and shrugged. "Perhaps a few weeks. There is much confusion in Mexico. They've given me time off. I can let you know when my employer tells me."

"That is good, Sir. Stay as long as you wish. It's good to have you back."

I handed him a 500 Cuban peso note, about $20.

His smiled broadened. It was probably a week's pay if the manager didn't take a bite out of it.

I shouldered my tote bag and headed up to my room. The elevator was still working.

I decided that was good sign, a signal for me to get off my tired ass and spend a few hours wandering the city running CSRs so the assigned watchers would remember how boring I was. I was exhausted, but the clock was running and I wanted a day or two of that before I tried for a meet with my team.

Havana, Cuba, Morning, Next Day

I checked the messages on my COM.

Josie was safe in Florida. Rudy and Terry had made it in with no problems. They'd been keeping a low profile, waiting for me to arrive, mostly running CSRs, refamiliarizing themselves with Havana.

Josie had given us a short list of possible spots for hitting our targets. The Palace of the Revolution was where most meetings would be held, but it was a hard target.

The three of us were separately running CSR routes that let us check these hot spots out in detail. We were playing tourists on vacation, trying to bore our watchers with monotonous regularity while becoming familiar with the terrain and environment.

Our sniper team, Pat and Vinnie, were living on the boat, hanging around the harbor, acting like bored fisherman. They reported only a low level of surveillance. Vinnie, now our number two helmsman for the Busted Flush, was practicing his Spanish and scoping out the best fishing spots.

It was thin cover, but that didn't matter. The locals mostly assumed, based on the fast boat, vague backgrounds, and generous tips, that they were running drugs.

No one cared.

CHAPTER THIRTY-SEVEN
RANGING AND ROAMING

Sunrise Café, Havana, Cuba, Morning, Two Days Later

The room was mostly empty, the breakfast crowd gone. Our CSRs overlapped here and we'd each been dropping in at random times to check it out.

Rudy was sitting at a corner table drinking coffee, his back to the wall, watching the door, wearing a bright flowered shirt. It was hard to miss him, jet black, bald, well-muscled, and six foot four.

He flashed a smile, bright white teeth, and gave me a wave of recognition. Left hand. All clear.

I sat down next to him. He said, "The huevos are great."

"Let's eat, my friend."

Another sign and countersign. No bugs. No surveillance. The mission is running.

I let Rudy order for us, then I slipped him a hand-written map under the table. "I have some goodies for you and Terry. You can pick them up as soon as it's dark and you're clear."

"The weapons are here?"

"Not yet."

Rudy's smile faded. "We've been here damned near a week, boss. Did someone screw up?"

"There have been some complications."

"This shit hole creeps me out. The Tangos are here. I put eyes on them yesterday at the hot spot Josie flagged. I could have popped them both with an M4."

"I believe you, but getting your ass killed isn't the mission. This isn't the Alamo."

"We need to get this done and haul ass."

I nodded. "I'm aware. You've seen the Tangos. How did they arrive?"

"Two convoys. Three cars each. Two in each vehicle, with our targets in the middle car. They came in from opposite directions.

"It was well-timed. Our main target came out first. Number two exited his car about the time number one got to the building. Each walked with one security guard.

"The big guy took his guard inside. Number two shed his at the door. The security guards in the other cars stayed inside. That was a bit sloppy."

"Pretty much as Josie predicted?"

"Yes."

I was thinking. "The total time exposed was about two minutes?"

"A bit longer. No one was rushing. Slow and relaxed. They feel safe here. Hell, maybe they'll stop and chat."

I gave a small laugh. "We should be so lucky."

"What about our weapons?"

They are coming. The first items are here, cached locally. I need you and Terry to pick them up and put them to use."

"What's here in Havana?"

"Three rangefinders, a pair and a spare. Most of our other gear is in-country. Two special items are still coming. I want more firepower because we're only going to get one chance at this."

"No guns?"

"Not yet, but our sniper team's gear came in on the boat. Pat's rifle and Vinnie's spotter scope. They are not to be touched until we prepare the battle space. You and Terry have some work to do."

"What kind of work?"

"Between now and Sunday night, there are four hot spots where we might be able to hit both targets. Two are in daylight. The sweet spot is Sunday, mid-morning, for several reasons. Focus on that one.

"I want you and Terry to range and mark those four hot spots. Find good hides for our sniper team.

"Ask Pat what he prefers, but my guess is sniper placement should not be out too far. Maybe between 300 to 600 yards. I'm hoping for under 300. We need Pat to be able to make two separate head shots in under a minute.

"Assume our targets will be well separated and walking. None of this thousand-yard stationary target bullshit."

Rudy said, "600 or closer. Under 300 if possible. Sure kills. Secure hides."

"Yes."

"What will the rest of us be doing?"

"You and I will handle things up close. We hit the Tangos first, and suppress their security as is needed. We'll both start shooting as soon as Pat drops target number one."

"Interesting. How do you expect we can do that? Do we get invisibility cloaks?"

I smiled. "I'm hoping for local support."

"The same local support that hasn't gotten our guns to Havana?"

"I was the one who delayed that. I wanted heavier weapons. We'll probably need to leave them behind. I want them sanitized so as to not compromise our locals. Mike and Will are working on it."

"Sanitized?"

"False flags. Best to not discuss the details. This part is tricky and I don't want to jinx it."

"What kind of weapons?"

"I want Pat's team to have a mortar. You and I will be in close. Too close. I want Terry to have a belt fed machine gun to cover us. We trained on that."

"No nukes or air strikes?"

"I wish. Alas, not possible."

"That sucks."

"It does. Let's talk about transport. Can you steal us a motorcycle? If not, two bicycles."

Rudy gave me an odd look. "I've never even seen a motorcycle in Havana. Would you settle for a donkey?"

"Would you?"

"No, but we have a bigger problem. There is going to be a shit storm when we hit those guys."

"We have serious transport issues," I said.

"We do."

"I want us to all be on the boat and headed out twenty minutes after this goes down. That means we'll need to have two vehicles positioned. One for us and one for the sniper team."

"What about Terry?"

"We'll either pick him up on the way, or we need a third vehicle."

"Right."

"Pass the word to look around, but don't attract attention. Josie has our locals looking too."

South Patrick Shores, Florida, Same Day

Gerry looked at me. "You saw the COM messages? Raven's team is still waiting for weapons."

I nodded. "We have a problem. I did a remote viewing. He's right. Rosa's Santeria have set up caches in Havana, but they don't have some of the items Raven wants. They've not arrived in Cuba."

"I think it's time we called Mike, Josie. Something is wrong."

"You call him. Tell him if this isn't fixed quickly, we'll miss our time window."

"Right." She picked up her Cybertech secure phone and hit the call button.

I said, "Can you put it on speaker?"

She nodded.

Mike picked up immediately. "I'm in the middle of something. Are you guys OK?"

Gerry said, "We're fine. Josie is with me. **Square 1** is in trouble. If you can't fix it fast, we are going to have to abort."

"Put her on."

"I'm here, Mike." I gave him a quick rundown and finished with, "Are you on top of this?"

He said, "I hope so. I'm at Andrews now. The problems are at this end. There are disconnects with paperwork and bureaucracy.

"Goldfarb will be here in about 20 minutes. President Blager is on Marine One, inbound. We have a SCIF reserved."

I said, "What's missing?"

Mike said, "It's complicated. Raven wants a lot of firepower. The standard stuff is there, but some special items got stuck. It's about approvals and protocols. We're working on it."

"I can communicate with our local support. If you can give me place and time for the delivery, we can have someone waiting. Do not go near Havana. It's too hot."

Mike said, "Understood. The last drop was made at a remote beach after dark. How long from there into Havana?"

I thought for a long moment, remembering the details of my viewings. "Four or five hours. Get it there by 3 AM local Sunday and figure we can have it in place and cached by ten. I'll validate that with Rosa and Raven."

Mike said, "Do that. I should be able to get you a drop time for Rosa's people. The missing hardware is in the air and inbound to me here. I've got a jet waiting on the ramp and a team waiting at GITMO to make the drop."

Gerry was frowning. "Is that good, Josie?"

I said, "I'm not sure. There are a lot of moving parts, Mike."

"Yes."

"Just keep it moving and let me know when you can schedule the drop. I'll check with Rosa and Raven when you have something definite. We'll let Raven make the call."

"Acceptable," Mike said. "Stand by. I'll call back as soon as I have a drop time."

"Thank you."

CHAPTER THIRTY-EIGHT
PROTECTION

Joint Base Andrews, Maryland

Doctor Goldfarb arrived about five minutes after I did. He looked disheveled, which was unusual. He was my link to the President. I was now the *de facto* control for Raven and his team.

He plunked down in a chair, glanced to see that the secure light was on, and said, "Mexico is a total cluster fuck, Mike. State Department is in a panic. DOD is rolling out plans and planning for a major troop presence there. CIA is once again caught with its dick hanging out. All they have is satellite images.

"It goes downhill from there. Not just in Mexico and along the border. All along the invasion corridor, and with a major cartel presence on this side of the border."

Over the years we'd moved Raven's team more distant from the government. Goldfarb was still on the downsized National Security Council, his position there as unconventional science advisor preserved in part because no one had a clue what that was, but mostly because the President wanted his advice. There had always been tension between the need for kinetic action and geopolitical reality. Recently it was extreme.

I said, "Yes, Sir. I agree with you."

"Is that all you are going to say?"

"It's the reality, Doctor. Raven saw it coming. We reported it."

"I passed that along. What's the problem?"

"Raven's mission was to interdict that invasion route. We've poked at that every way we know how, and the only option that might work is to disrupt Cuba. Is the President current on that?"

"Not fully briefed in, but I told him that **Square 1** was active a few days ago."

"What did he say?"

Goldfarb said, "Nothing. He just nodded. You got approval. So, what's the problem?"

"The problem is Cuba. Raven's weapons didn't get there. His team is in Havana. He has local support with logistics. We have a time window that is closing. His team doesn't have the weapons he needs.

"Raven's mission is dead in the water. He will have to abort if this can't be resolved. This is a list of what he needs."

I passed Goldfarb a piece of paper. It was a short list:

- Two MXT135 Rifles with Ammo
- One SIG Belt fed-MG 338 (With 338 Norma Mag ammo and SIG new generation suppressor.)
- China End-Use Paperwork for one DIS-Tech Ultra-Lightweight 60 MM Mortar (With ammo.)

He scanned it, frowning. "Those are exotic weapons. Does Raven plan to start a war?"

"Cuba is a bad place. Raven's team can make the hit with a sniper rifle and hand guns, but they'll need more than that if they have to shoot their way out."

Goldfarb nodded. "The problem is egress. I did tell the President that."

"The problem is getting the team out alive. Raven's solution is Sun Tzu."

"You are going to need to explain that…."

"*Appear weak when you are strong, and strong when you are weak.* Sun Tzu's, *The Art of War*. Raven wants his force to appear as strong as possible. Think about it."

Goldfarb said, "I get that part. When Raven goes kinetic, he and his team are exposed. They will have massive forces in pursuit. He needs firepower to slow them down."

"Correct."

"What I want to know is how did this get so screwed up? And why in Hell is it just coming up now?"

Just then the door opened and President Blager entered. We both stood to greet him, but he waved us back down. He sat at the end of the table and looked at us.

"Raven was spot on about Mexico. Our Intel community was blindsided and it's turned into a shit storm. This better be both important and urgent."

"It is, Sir." Goldfarb said, signaling that he was going to take the lead.

The President pulled a small note pad out of his pocket, "I can spend thirty minutes and then I need to get to the White House. I want you along with me, Aaron. You can ride on the helicopter with me."

"Yes, Sir."

"Good. Brief me in."

"Raven's team is hot and on the ground in Havana, Sir." Goldfarb proceeded to give a quick briefing. He hit all the key points.

The President was frowning. "Cuba is the only spot along the invasion route that isn't a problem right now. It's peaceful."

Goldfarb said, "Cuba is the key, Sir. We've discussed that. *Ubi solitudinem faciunt, pacem appellant.*"

The President smiled faintly. "I love your briefings, professor. 'Where they create desolation, they call it peace.' Right?"

"Correct, Sir. Tacitus, about AD 100. Rome had peaked and was sliding into corruption. He could not prevent it."

"Cuba is peaceful at present, Sir. It won't be when Raven goes kinetic."

"Yes. It's a hot spot. Cuba holds the keys to Venezuela, to control of the invasion route. I approved your mission. What's the problem?"

Goldfarb took a deep breath. "I'm afraid some of Raven's weapons didn't make it in, Sir. The opportunity window is about to slam shut. We may have to abort."

The president set his pencil down. His eyes narrowed. "You have got to be shitting me, Aaron. Raven's team is in Cuba without weapons? That's not possible."

"He has some weapons, Sir, but he doesn't have all that he needs. Here is what he's lacking."

332

John D. Trudel

Goldfarb handed him the list. The President set it down on the table.

"I don't want a fucking shopping list, Aaron. I want to know how we managed to deploy key assets into a hot zone without the basic equipment needed to get the job done."

"Yes, Sir. Mike and I were just discussing that. He was about to explain."

"Good. I'm listening." The President looked at me. "What's the problem, Mike? Make it short."

I took a deep breath. "I'm afraid you are the problem, Sir. We didn't realize it until just now."

"You are going to need to explain that."

"Yes, Sir. As you know, Raven warned us of the impending problem in Mexico. We planned his mission to exploit that opportunity. That's what activated the Cuba OP."

"Tell me something I don't know."

"Whatever is going on in Washington is apparently causing assholes to slam shut all over DOD and beyond. We had the weapons for Raven's OP lined up. They were promised to us. Now we're told that we can't have them."

"Were you told why?"

"We were not told anything, Sir. When they didn't show up, I asked why. I was told that they are unavailable."

The President turned his gaze to Goldfarb, who said, "I'm just hearing this now, Sir."

I said, "No one is telling me, shit, Sir. It's why I called this meeting."

The President picked up the list and studied it. "Does Raven know about this?"

"Not yet, Sir. We had concerns about getting local support for logistics, but that worked out. The Cuba team is waiting for a drop. They think it's coming."

Goldfarb said, "Should we discuss the list, Sir? I'm not familiar with the items."

"We damned well need to, Aaron."

I said, "The MXT135 rifle is owned by the Army. They have only a few. They cost about $35,000 each, and the rounds cost about $45."

"For a bullet?"

"A smart bullet, Sir, with a range of about 7,800 feet. These are 35-millmeter HE rounds that have a computer chip that talks to the gunsight to get range information. They can be set to explode over or alongside the target. They can even be set to hit targets hiding behind walls."

"How does it do that?"

"You push a button near the trigger, and it goes one meter past the target and explodes, Sir."

The President said, "That's not a rifle, Mike, it's a cannon."

I shrugged. "It weighs twelve pounds and is twenty-nine inches long. Raven wants two of them with ammo."

Goldfarb said, "I've actually heard of that. Didn't have a clue what it was. They called it a Counter Defilade Target Engagement System."

The President sighed. "What about the next one. The MG 338. It's a machine gun. Surely, we have machine guns."

I nodded. "We do, Sir. We even have a few of these. They are owned by the Marines and by SOCOM. Apparently, they won't give theirs up."

"Do we know why?"

"I can guess. It weighs in at under twenty pounds, packs more punch with less recoil, and it also has an excellent suppressor.

"Our standard weapon, the M240, is 60 years old, quite a bit heavier, and has less range and lethality. A better comparison might be to our M2, a .50 caliber. It's been in service for 110 years and is four times the weight."

"Why does the suppressor matter, other than for keeping it quiet?"

"It greatly reduces toxic fumes and signature. That makes the operator less vulnerable."

"What about the last one, this DIS-Tech Mortar. I assume it's also much lighter?"

"Ultra-light weight, only twelve pounds and of US production, but it had problems. We do have one of these. Raven plans to leave it there as a red herring. It's a piece of shit."

Goldfarb said, "I've never heard of DIS-Tech."

"Disruptive Technology. They went out of business. It was set up as a subsidiary by a Swedish firm to do US manufacture for our military. They had high hopes, but it turned out that no one wanted it."

The President said, "Why not?"

I shrugged. "SPEC OPs and Marines didn't favor it. Even if it was light, so what? 60mm mortar rounds weigh about four pounds each, and no one wanted to lug a bunch of them around in the field."

Goldfarb said, "What about the Army?"

"The artillery guys laughed. They saw it as a toy and chose to stick with their M224.

"The M224 is crew-served and can fire 120 rounds in four minutes. A three-man crew can have 15 to 20 rounds in the air before the first-round impacts. If you are burning through tons of ammo, you could care less about having a lightweight cannon."

The President said, "Why is this on the list if you already have one?"

"Raven wants cover paperwork for it. He wants an end-user license that links that specific weapon to China in the files. The State department can do that."

Goldfarb said, "So can the CIA."

The President said, "Why China?"

Goldfarb said, "Do we care?"

There was a long silence.

Finally, the President said, "I don't think that we do. Increased confusion along the invasion route is unlikely to do us more harm, and it might do some good."

He looked at me. "Do you have an aircraft here on the ramp?"

I nodded.

"Keep it ready, Mike. The weapons that Raven needs will be here today. The documents you want will be in the files within a week."

Thank you, Sir."

He looked at Goldfarb. "I will have a short conference in the Oval before the meeting tonight. The SecDef and the Secretary of State will be there. You will attend.

"I'd prefer not to involve the CIA. I want this to look like routine bureaucracy, not cloak and dagger."

"Yes, Sir."

"If you encounter any problems or delays, you are to call me immediately. If you have to do that, please get the names and numbers of those involved."

"Yes, Mr. President."

"What about Josie. Tell me she's safe."

Goldfarb and I exchanged a look. "She's in Florida. She's with my wife and they are covered by good security."

"Good. Is there anything else?"

"One thing, Sir. Josie keeps saying that she needs to be closer to Raven."

"Not in Cuba."

"No, Sir. None of us want that. I don't think even Josie wants to be in Cuba. We can't protect her there. Worrying about her would hinder, not advance, Raven's mission."

"Correct. Why does she need to be closer? Josie can see across time and space."

"I don't know, Sir. She's not been able to explain that, but she keeps saying it."

The President said, "The woman has incredible talents. I trust her intuition and abilities. As a nation we count on her."

"We do, Sir."

"Call Admiral Perkins. Get Josie closer to Raven, make her happy, and keep her safe. Work it out, but make sure she agrees."

"Thank you, Sir."

The President looked at his watch. "Five minutes early. Let's go Aaron. Back to the swamp."

"I wouldn't miss it for the world, Sir."

The President pointed and winked at me. "Thank you, Mike. 'Proper armament is the surest guarantee of peace.' Theodore Roosevelt said that."

They both walked out and left me sitting there.

CHAPTER THIRTY-NINE
LOCK AND LOAD

Havana, Two Days Later, Unknown Location

Raven had been running CSRs all afternoon, moving repeatedly though a sequence of choke points where Rudy and Terry had eyes on. So far, he looked to be squeaky clean.

He moved into a park, settling down on a rock under a tree. Out of direct view. He slipped his COM out.

"Still clear?"

They all replied, "Affirm."

"Excellent. We'll do this one at a time. Vinnie first. Are you on, Vinnie?"

"Affirm."

"Did you find the package?"

"It's all there."

"Go to point XRAY. I want you to verify. We'll overwatch. Be ready to abort."

"Wilco. Moving."

We all waited for Vinnie to reposition and check out XRAY, the spot chosen for their sniper hide. He needed to make sure it was good for spotting, shooting, and egress.

I was pretty sure that it had a good view of the kill zone, but our locals were civilians. We needed to be positive the site was good for two separate head shots in a minute. We'd fire a few rounds from our Chinese-licensed mortar and leave it, but that was window dressing to divert.

Today was also a stress test for the Cuban surveillance. When we went kinetic, there was a lot to do in a short amount of time. There were too many moving parts to take any chances. We needed to go directly to our key locations, ready to shoot, and without having Cuban security on our asses.

In the movies, surveillance is either a clown-fest of cars chasing each other through red lights and going the wrong way on freeways, or portrayed as an arcane art beyond the comprehension of the average human.

In reality, it is just another skill. There are certain key principles.

Good surveillance is like an NBA team, except that the pay is lower and the stakes are life and death. Millie's watchers were world class. Effective, professional, and virtually undetectable.

The Cubans were abundant and on their home court, but not in the same league. Which was not to say that they couldn't blow our OP sky high. We had to be totally free of ticks or the mission would fail.

The primary thing is to identify the target at an endpoint to initiate the surveillance. The trigger is the lynchpin. That's where most surveillance fails. If the trigger is exposed to the target, it's game over. Any trained operative would either abort or lead the tails on a worthless goose chase.

In my case, we could be sure the hotel manager sent out a trigger call when I left. In the case of Vinnie, most likely a trigger at the marina did the same. We'd already aborted once. Now we had to seem harmless and run CSRs until the watchers lost interest or made a mistake.

Once the target is acquired, the next step is simple. Cover all possible avenues of escape in what is called "the box." In this case, that box was layered and it extended to the whole bloody country. We had to operate inside the box and keep looking for seams and gaps.

It was a foregone conclusion that we'd have to shoot our way out. My primary goal was to have that high-risk event occur after our mission was successful. Next was getting my team out alive.

Fortunately, we were clear of ticks today. The problem with watching everyone, 24/7, year after year, is that the operators and guards get sloppy. Cuba's populace was docile. It was a police state.

The CIA didn't even have a presence here. America had enough Deep State leaks that Cuban security presumably knew that. America was a toothless tiger, and Cuba had an international role. One that the chaos in Venezuela and Mexico would enhance unless we took out their leadership.

Vinnie checked in. "Looks good."

I responded. "You are clean. Head back to the boat. Time the route."

Vinnie acknowledged. He was heading back and out of the game.

It was Terry's turn in the barrel.

I said, "Terry, head for YANKEE. Run CSRs. The rest to flex, intersect, and check him for ticks."

Everyone acknowledged. The rest was just me and Rudy. Pat was guarding the boat, and Vinnie was on his way back.

YANKEE was where our machine gun was cached. It would be where Terry would lay down the cover fire for our escape.

So far, so good. When Terry was good with YANKEE, the battle space was prepared.

We'd go kinetic on Sunday, early afternoon. It was the time window that Josie favored.

My plan was for our sniper, Pat, to make the hit. He was our best shot. Rudy and I would handle the close-in attack, and Terry would cover us with the machine gun.

As soon as both targets were down, our sniper team would egress. When they arrived at the boat, Rudy would already be on the way. He was the Captain. He'd head for the boat and get the engines warmed up.

That would leave two of us in the kill zone, me and Terry.

I'd egress and connect with him on the way out. With his machine gun and my MXT135 we'd discourage pursuit, hop on the boat, and make our run.

That was the plan. Like all plans, it was unlikely to survive contact with the enemy.

Forty Minutes Later, Havana

Rudy made the call. "Terry's got ticks."

I said, "Acknowledged. Describe the Tango."

"Blue Shirt. Jeans. Black beard. Dark glasses. Overweight. He's about a block in trail, on the opposite side of the street."

"Raven to Terry. Do not acknowledge. Slow down. Jog left one block, then get back on your CSR.

"Rudy, drop back and see if the Tango follows him. I'm coming that way."

Rudy said, "Copy that. Vinnie just peeled off."

I said, "We're going to feed the beast."

Several minutes passed before Rudy said, "Tango is following Vinnie. He's a tick for sure."

"Good. Let's run this for a while and see if he has a buddy.

"Terry, play dumb, quicken your pace, and roll into your next CSR. Divert. Do not go to YANKEE."

Terry came back, "Understood. Moving. Diverting. YANKEE is scratched."

I said, "I will intercept your route. Rudy, hang back. We'll see if your Tango passes Terry off or gives up."

Time passed and I moved into position.

Rudy said, "Tango is tiring. He's falling behind."

I said, "Copy. Terry pick up the pace a bit."

Rudy said, "First tick dropped off. A second one picked Terry up. Female. Tall, six feet plus. Dark shirt, jeans, and jogging shoes."

Shit.

I said, "Copy. Terry, slow down, but keep moving. Rudy, drop back further. Do not let her see you."

Two more clicks. I was thinking. *What now?*

Then I saw Terry, followed by Tango number two. She looked athletic. She had a spring in her step and was prancing along like a young deer. She was following close, apparently not caring if she was noticed or not.

I said, "All elements, we have a new plan. Terry slow down, lead her away from YANKEE, wander around, play dumb, like you're a tourist.

"Plan to stop somewhere for a cold drink. Let her follow you. Look harmless. Be unaware. Do not try to shake your tick."

Terry clicked acknowledgement.

Rudy came on. "What's the new plan, boss?"

An excellent question.

I said, "Stand by."

CHAPTER FORTY
JOSIE GOES OPERATIONAL

USS Gravely, International Waters, Off the Coast of Cuba

Josie and I had landed by helicopter. She didn't like the trip, but I thought it was perfect. A beautiful day and a Caribbean cruise. The views from the air were spectacular. The water was so clear you could see the bottom. It would be even better if Mike could join us.

Technically, it was the Gulf of Mexico. The Caribbean was on the other side, along with Jamaica and places like that. Here, the closest land was Florida to the North, famously "ninety miles away" for those who recalled the Cuban Missile Crisis. The Bahamas, James Bond country and the edge of the Bermuda Triangle, were a bit further, North and East.

There was a lot of history in these warm, clear, gorgeous waters, dating back to the days of sailing ships and pirates. What's not to like?

I soon found out....

Captain Hipp joined us in the wardroom. He was younger than I'd expected, perhaps mid-thirties, with blue eyes and sandy hair. He looked young, fit, and competent.

It was a small room. A Formica-like table, with nine chairs in brown leatherette, four on each side, and one at the end with a similar table, smaller, behind it, probably for coffee and food. The other end butted against the hull. I could tell that because there were two portholes covered by thin blue curtains, with the hot, bright, outside sun shining through.

Hipp sat at the end of the table, looking unhappy. He was scowling at Josie, seated next to me and across from a thin young man with gold wire-rimmed glasses and a walking cast on his leg, Lieutenant Commander Bromley.

Raven and Mike had spoken of Bromley favorably. He'd helped them with their boat. That was how he'd injured his leg.

"Is she the one we're taking care of?" The Captain asked Bromley, who nodded.

I said, "Her name is Josie."

Josie was watching the Captain. She didn't speak.

He turned his scowl to me. "You're another civilian? What's your role?"

I shrugged. "Yes, I'm a civilian. Gerry Mickelson. Retired NSA. I'm responsible for Josie's security. I guess in this case I'm also her interface to the military, which is to say, you."

"Are we on a first name basis, Gerry?"

"If you wish."

"Fine by me, Gerry. My first name is Captain."

I refrained from rolling my eyes. "If you wish."

"You are married to General Mickelson?"

"I am. Mike is retired. He is also now a civilian."

"He used to run Intel at Marine HQ in Washington?"

"Yes."

"Why are you here?"

I said, "Let's start at the other end, Captain. The fact is that we are here. What are your orders regarding Josie?"

Captain Hipp was silent for a long moment. He finally said, "I am to extend her every courtesy. She has a support role assisting a team operating in Cuba. I was not given any information on what they are doing, but I am ordered to assist and support them during their egress, subject to the safety of my ship and the requirements of international law.

"We have already provided some support to this team. That is how my weapons officer was injured."

"What are the requirements of international law?"

"In general, we are to stay 12 or more nautical miles off shore. That is where we've been patrolling. The details and protocols are complicated, contentious, and highly political. American warships are not welcome in Cuban waters"

"I presume you are allowed to access our base at GITMO?"

"Of course," Hipp said. "And to defend ourselves. We can enter Cuban waters with permission, though the protocols require prior paperwork. Like I said, it's complicated.

"The civilian boat we're assigned to protect – is it really called the *Busted Flush*?"

I nodded. "The card game, not the toilet...."

He did not smile. "The Cuba security zone requires non-public vessels less than 50 meters long that intend to enter Cuban territorial waters to receive prior Coast Guard authorization. Your vessel is U.S. registered, and it has a permit.

"There are twelve categories of visits allowed. Three are highly restricted: Tourism, family visits, and support for the Cuban people. Your vessel's stated purpose is category 10: Activities of private foundations or research or educational institutes."

The Captain paused and looked at me. Time passed. Finally, he said, "Well? What do you say?"

I shook my head, puzzled. "What do you want me to say?"

"What is your vessel doing?"

"You just told me, didn't you? Research, I would think. I don't know much about boats."

"You've never been on the boat?"

"No," I said truthfully. I looked at Bromley. He didn't speak. "What did Admiral Perkins say?"

"He did not say. He just ordered me to provide support. He said Busted Flush would be coming out at speed and that we were to support it, to protect it."

"To your maximum ability in accord with international law...."

"Yes, he did say that."

I shrugged. "Maximum ability. Perhaps you should ask for more specific guidance, Captain."

"I'm not going to mince words, so I'll get right to the point."

"Please do."

"I came up through the ranks under Obama. Our ships were under maintained, undermanned, and sent to sea with outdated, partially functional equipment. Several blue-water fighting ships lost lives and were damaged beyond their capability to be repaired at sea by damage control. That is a court martial offense, if I ever saw one.

"The USS Cole was a sitting duck in an Arab port, by orders from the Pentagon, or even higher. The sentries were not issued ammo by design. They were actually *ordered* to be defenseless."

None of us spoke. After a time, the Captain continued.

"Commanding a destroyer is a key job, ladies. Back in the day, we had the Gulf of Tonkin incident. On August 2, 1964, on a dark and foggy night, the destroyer USS Maddox, while performing a signals intelligence patrol, engaged three North Vietnamese Navy torpedo boats of the 135th Torpedo Squadron.

"A sea battle resulted, one in which the Maddox was hard pressed. She expended over two hundred and eighty 3-inch and 5-inch shells. It took air support to save her.

"This was a simple, low-risk, passive mission, one much like the one I've now been given. Cruise around in the ocean and monitor signals. The direct result was the Vietnam War."

I said, "Interesting history, but what's your point?"

"My point, Gerry?"

I nodded.

"My point is this. I'm a 30-year man, and I hope to retire as an admiral. That will never happen if my ship is severely damaged or if I wind up starting a war."

"You said there were ten categories of visits allowed to Cuba?"

"Yes."

"I presume one category that is not allowed is *starting a missile crisis*."

"I'm not amused, Gerry."

"Nor are we. May I speak freely and in confidence?"

The Captain nodded.

"This Sunday – we can give you a better time estimate when it gets closer – a small team of Americans might be egressing Havana's harbor in in a small, unarmed, civilian, fiberglass boat. They will be running for their lives.

Their egress might be resisted. They are faster than OSA boats, but they can't outrun missiles, and there may be other forces coming after them."

"I'm familiar with OSA boats. We can jam their radars."

"It may take more than that." I looked at him. "We're all on the same team, Captain. I am advised that both you and Commander Bromley have Top Secret DOD clearances. Is that correct?"

"Yes."

I looked at Bromley. He said, "I have a clearance."

"Good. I will share some restricted information with you, because I think you might want to share it with your Admiral. You must agree to discuss it only between yourselves and the Admiral.

"I offer this to help our mission success and save American lives. It might also help with your career decisions. Do you agree?"

"Yes."

Bromley said, "Yes. I also agree."

"Strict confidence, Captain."

"I said that I agreed. Please get on with it."

I looked at Josie. "Can you assess the probabilities for Sunday?"

She spoke for the first time. "Roughly. It will take more…."

"Roughly is good for now."

"These are fuzzy probability trails. They will become firmer as the time approaches."

"Understood. Just rough guesses."

"The **Busted Flush** is going to make it out of the harbor. 80% plus probability."

Bromley was smiling. The Captain looked stunned.

"Keep going," I said.

"This ship will become engaged in a firefight, a missile exchange. Better than even odds."

The Captain was staring at her.

I said, "What else?"

Josie's face dropped. "This ship may take major damage without fire support from the fleet. Perhaps 30% odds. That one is less certain, harder to predict."

"Thank you."

The Captain said, "What is this? Witchcraft?"

Josie said, "Tea leaves and computers, Captain."

I said, "The methods and sources are restricted. Let's just say that's what we do. Situation assessments. Josie just did you a favor. It's classified, and that's all I can say. We look at scenarios and figure the odds."

"What exactly do you expect me to do with this information?"

"Keep it in confidence, as agreed. What action you choose to take is entirely up to you."

"That's all?"

"For now, yes. We will need support from you to proceed. We'll know more as the time gets closer."

"What kind of support?"

"Not much. Josie will need periods of quiet time alone at the bow of the ship. Night is best, but also as the time of action approaches. We have some small secure COMs, and will need to go topside at times to communicate. The units will need to see satellites."

"No problem. What else?"

"When *Busted Flush* makes its run, we'll need to be on the bridge and to have normal commercial communications with the boat. They will be transmitting in the clear. You are to record and log that."

"What will you be doing?"

I said, "Assessing the situation."

The Captain shook his head. "Not on my bridge."

Bromley said, "How about in Fire Control? Would that suffice? You could hold my crutches."

I smiled and nodded. His crutches were leaning against the wall. He was clearly able to do his job in a walking cast, to handle fire control. "That would work, if your Captain allows it."

"Fine by me." The Captain looked at Josie. "Major damage to my ship?"

She looked glum. "I'm sorry. Your odds would improve with more fire support."

"That makes sense. Fire support always helps."

With that, the meeting broke up and we were dismissed. Bromley took us to the double room they had assigned to us. It was topside, so we could even use our COMs. I thanked him and he rushed off to rejoin his Captain.

I looked at Josie, "Are you all right?"

She shook her head. "No. I saw the ship burning. The Captain was dead. He's an asshole."

"He has a lot of responsibility, Josie."

"I know. He's afraid and doesn't want to show it."

"I hope he confers with his Admiral, but I don't want you to waste a viewing or worry about it. That's human free will. The Captain will return fire if his ship is engaged."

"Too late, maybe."

"It's his call, his command. We need to concentrate on saving Raven and his team."

Josie nodded. She looked sad.

"What?"

"The Captain is not worried about the Osas. There's still something I'm missing."

CHAPTER FORTY-ONE
ENGAGEMENT

Point YANKEE, Havana, Afternoon, Sunday

Raven was clear of ticks. It was a huge relief. *The first break we'd gotten in a long time.*

The city was quiet and it wasn't because of my superb CSRs. Cuban security seemed to be off duty today. Some big celebration last night, Josie said.

I'd found the YANKEE cache and checked its contents. A beautiful SIG Sauer MG 338, assembled, with its bipod and suppressor in place, a red dot scope that would automatically adjust for range, and six belts of ammo.

The *Santeria* had done their jobs. God bless freedom-loving Cubans. *Another happy outcome.*

It was almost show time. I'd traded places with Terry. From this shooting spot, he was shielded on three sides by trees and he had a direct view of the kill zone. He'd ranged it to be just over 800 meters, an easy range for this weapon. He could add to the fire support, an unexpected plus.

Terry and Rudy would handle the close-in work after Pat, our sniper, did his job. Rudy and the sniper team would scramble for the boat. Terry would join up with me and we'd leapfrog our way back, the last ones out. Rudy would have the boat ready and the engines warmed up.

I'd been in near constant contact with Josie. The Cuban government had moved their meeting to the late afternoon, and the good news was both of our targets would be there.

USS Gravely, Fire Control Center, International Waters, Off the Coast of Cuba

We were at alert, but not yet battle stations, so we'd not been locked down. Josie was topside, using her secure COM, doing a few last remote viewings and feeding update information to Raven.

Bromley looked at me. "The Cubans are running late, Gerry. Unfortunately, we're still doing this in daylight. Nautical twilight is about 20:00 hours. Sunset is about 20:30."

I said, "8:30 PM. Why is it so late?"

"You're in the tropics, Gerry. Long days. Everything is late. Solar noon is 13:27."

"What are you saying?"

"The Captain is as nervous as a long-tailed cat in a room full of rocking chairs. He's at high pucker. He met with the Admiral and came back looking unhappy."

"He wasn't happy when we talked."

"It's worse now. He's been running his officers through the details. Looking for soft spots."

I said, "Good."

"Not good. We own the night because of technology. If this extraction goes hot it will be a High Noon gunfight, one that favors the Cubans. It's clear, with no clouds or fog. They can get their target bearings with ordinary binoculars. We can't do a thing about that and the Captain knows it."

"Keep talking."

"Havana harbor is a bitch, Gerry. The only way out is a short, straight run of 1.5 kilometers, about a mile, with speed restricted to "no wake" and fortifications on both sides.

"No matter how fast *Busted Flush* can move, it will be crawling on the way out, running dead slow. America once lost a Battleship in there."

"That was in 1898, Commander."

"It's worse now. Cuba is a hard target. Your boat might not even make it out of the harbor."

"Raven's team is aware of that. The targets get to control our timing, Commander. Your Captain has orders to support us."

"He does and he sees his career at risk."

"More than that is at risk, including American lives. Will he support our mission?"

"He will follow his orders. So will I."

"That's all we can ask."

Josie came in, paused, and gave us both an intense look. "Are you all right?"

I nodded, not bothering to force a smile. I knew that I couldn't fool her.

"Not really. This is show time. We'll be all right after Raven and the team is out safe. How's it going?"

"Good. Our luck has finally turned. Cuban surveillance is lax and all the support gear made it. The team is moving into place. Both targets are on schedule.

"Tangos are estimated to arrive at 3:30 PM local."

Bromley said, "What can I tell my Captain?"

Josie said. "We can communicate securely and covertly with our COMs. I'm going to go outside where I get a solid signal. The team is going active.

"I will get five preloaded signals from Raven by text messages, in sequence. He will signal me 'Square One' through 'Square Five.' Mike and the others on our net will get copies.

"**One** means targets sighted. **Two** means targets engaged. **Three** means targets down. **Four** means heading for the boat. **Five** means they are making their run, heading out."

Bromley wrote all that down on a small yellow pad. "Check this."

Josie and I both did. She said, "That's it."

"What happens when they start out?"

I said, "What we discussed. *Busted Flush* is an innocent civilian boat, running for international waters. fleeing violence and internal Cuban problems. All communications will be in the clear. You are to record and archive them all."

Bromley said, "As will the Cubans and everyone else, including the media."

"Correct. You and the Captain can count on that. The world will be watching. Is there anything you want to tell me?"

"Just this. When *Busted Flush* makes it's run, we will probably be going to battle stations. Alarms will go off. This room will be locked down. You will be seated and strapped in for the duration. Do you understand?"

I looked at Josie. She nodded.

I said "Yes. We understand."

Bromley said, "Is there anything else you want me to tell the Captain?"

"Just that I'm glad that you said '*When Busted Flush* makes it's run.' Raven's team will do their part. After that, we are counting on you, on this ship and the U.S. Navy."

"Understood," Bromley said. "I'll be back in a few minutes. Stay close, please."

"I'll be here. Josie will be outside with her COM, just in case something comes in early."

His parting words were, "Damn the torpedoes...."

Point YANKEE, Havana, 3:45 PM, Sunday

Everyone was in place. I was waiting for the team to call our targets. It finally came. Rudy was the first to report.

"All elements. Tango one is in sight. His convoy has parked. He's getting out of his vehicle. Heading for the building with one of his security team. Moving slow."

Vinny said, "We have him. I confirm identity. Pat's on him. Call in when Tango two is visible."

I had my machine gun concealed under a blanket. I checked my area, confirming that I was still clear. I extended the bipod, inserted a belt, took the prone position, cocked the weapon, and looked though my sights.

There he was. Clear as day. I put the red dot on his chest.

"Raven confirms. Tracking Tango one."

Rudy called, "Second convoy is here. I have Tango two."

"Terry verifies Tango two. He's out of the car, heading in."

I said, "All elements. Take your shots, Pat. Follow up, Rudy. Terry, you are the backup for Tango two."

I heard a series of clicks. I had no view of Tango two.

I kept my sights on Tango one, slowing my breathing, waiting....

CHAPTER FORTY-TWO
KILL ZONE

Point YANKEE, Havana, Afternoon, Sunday

I was settled in, waiting. Tango one was in my sights, and I was waiting for Pat's shot. Time seemed to have slowed down, and then things happened in a blur.

The Tango's head exploded. I took up the pressure on the trigger and my SIG 338 bucked gently.

It was SIG's first machine gun, and the first time I'd fired it. *Talk about field testing*. The weapon had excellent recoil management and sound suppression, but I'd fired off three rounds before I could release pressure.

I think my rounds scored, but it was hard to tell. Rudy's follow up shot had also come instantaneously. His 35-millimeter HE round hit simultaneously with my bullets, a contact exploder. The target was shredded.

General Arnaldo Ochoa, the head of Cuba's Revolutionary Guard, was history. *One down. Overkill, but that kill alone justified our mission. We had removed the head of the snake.*

I heard Pat's voice on the COM. "Both Tangos are down."

Vinnie said, "I confirm two kills."

Terry said, "I confirm Tango two. We got him."

Hernando Cardoza, the Cuban Colonel in charge of the greatly-feared Colectivos, 100,000 strong, the thugs that had crushed resistance, who killed and tortured the citizens of Caracas, was no more.

Cuba still held the keys to Venezuela, perhaps, but the people holding those keys had been eliminated. It was a new ball game. Now all we had to do was clean up and get out.

I said, "Rudy and Terry, put fire into the kill zone. Clean it out."

There was a series of air bursts. I saw members of the Cuban security team falling. I was putting rounds down on them myself. We needed to discourage pursuit.

I started a timer going in my head and said, "Vinnie and Pat, good job. Time to egress."

Vinnie came back. "We need to leave our Chinese present. Three rounds. Get Rudy and Terry to cover."

I said, "Get it done. Rudy and Terry take cover."

Terry called, "Clear."

Rudy said, "Clear."

There were three air bursts over the kill zone. Antipersonnel rounds.

I could see shrapnel bouncing off the sidewalk and front of the building. Our little toy mortar seemed to work just fine.

I said, "Vinnie and Pat, move your asses. Don't wait for us."

"On the way," Vinnie said.

Rudy said, "Nothing is moving in the kill zone. They are all down."

I said, "Egress. You and Terry come to me. I'll cover you and we'll go back together."

"On the way."

I lay there taking deep breaths. Calming myself. Waiting for my shooters, Rudy and Terry.

It was time for another command decision. There was a loose end.

It was almost six miles to the boat. We'd lucked out and gotten a crappy rental car for our sniper team, from "Cuba Cars," located at the marina. Vinny came up with that, but it only solved half the problem.

He and Pat had good legends that gave them cover as locals living on the boat. For them to show up with more people, even if we could all fit, would attract notice. The place where we'd made our hit was the best option we'd found. Unfortunately, it was close to Havana's military airport, *Aeropuerto de La Habana Ciudad Libertad*. A bad place to linger, but so was the whole country.

The rest of us could scatter, leave our weapons, and fade away separately. I didn't like that. The alternative was for us to stay together and shoot our way out if necessary. My team also preferred the second option, but the vision of three foreigners, with or without weapons, jogging down the major road to the marina, *Avenida 5ta*, was unappealing.

We'd hoped to commandeer a Cuban vehicle, but the ability to do that was problematical. Plans were like that. In the end, when the shit turned real, you had to improvise.

Josie's viewings indicated that we could make it. I trusted her, but wondered. *Those shitty six miles could get us killed.*

USS Gravely, Fire Control Center

Josie entered, holding her COM up. "I just got four text messages from Raven, all at once. Good news. I need you to relay them to Mike."

Gerry said. "What happened? I don't have COM here."

"They did it. **Square One, Square Two, Square Three,** and **Square Four.**"

Bromley said, "This is mission accomplished? They got their targets and are on the way to the *Busted Flush*?"

Josie said, "Yes."

Gerry said, "Are you sure? They got both targets?"

"They did. Square Three was targets down. Plural. Both targets."

Bromley said, "Do we know when they're coming out?"

I shook my head. "Soon. A few minutes. Maybe an hour. We'll get the **Square Five** call when they are on the way out."

Gerry said, "Could you sense anything?"

"A lot of violence. People died. The kill zone was littered with bodies. I just got a glimpse. I dared not get too close. I can't shut down now."

"Right."

"The important thing is what I **didn't** sense, Gerry. Raven is okay. I'd know if he wasn't. He's alive. Not wounded. Doing what he does. Raven is coming back."

Bromley said, "Mission accomplished. I will inform the Captain. Thank you."

Gerry said, "I'll go with you. I need to get where my secure phone works. Mike and Goldfarb should be in the loop, on that COM channel, but I need to make sure."

USS Gravely, Bridge, International Waters, Off the Coast of Cuba

I made my report to the Captain.

"This is a mission accomplished? They are on their way to their boat?"

"Correct, Sir."

"We are picking up a lot of radio chatter from Cuba. Most of it is encrypted. What we get in the clear is confused, but they are moving their forces to a higher alert status. The messages are orders to report to duty stations and things like that.

"They have not locked down the country or closed Havana's Port, but they have declared a no-fly zone over Cuba. Whatever just went down, it got their attention."

"Yes, Sir."

"Get back to Fire Control. I'm going to report in to the Admiral before he calls me. We are not yet going to General Quarters, but I'm putting the ship on Air Alert after I speak with the Admiral.

"I want all our air defense systems powered up. Track anything inbound and all surface ships. Record all possible threats. If the Havana port or any ships go weapons hot, I want to know it."

"Yes, Sir."

The White House, Oval Office

President Peter Blager looked up when Goldfarb entered. "I only have a few minutes Aaron. I have a meeting with the Secretary of State. Something important."

"Excellent timing. This will be brief. It is 'mission accomplished' on **Square 1**. The Venezuela end of the invasion corridor now presents an opportunity, and the Mexico end is, effectively, a war zone.

"I have some late breaking news for you, Mr. President."

"You have my attention."

"General Arnaldo Ochoa, the head of Cuba's Revolutionary Guard, is dead. So is Hernando Cardoza, the Cuban Colonel in charge of the *Colectivos* in Caracas. They were both killed during an attack in Havana late this afternoon."

"You are certain of this?"

"Call it 95% certain, Sir. The team has not been debriefed, but that was the preliminary action report. Just a short text message of code words.

"Obviously, we can't be the first to know this, Sir. I suggest that you hold this in confidence until the world gets public confirmation and verification."

"Yes. I need to see the debriefing report."

"You'll get it as soon as we have it. We can't debrief until Raven's team makes it out."

"We still have Americans at risk in Havana?"

"They are on their way out, Mr. President."

"Did anyone make it out?"

"Not yet."

"Do we have casualties or KIAs?"

"Unknown, Sir. The signal was, 'mission accomplished.' I don't have any information beyond that."

The President looked at his watch. "Thank you. This is a game changer. Please contact me when you know more. Get me the debriefing. One copy, Top Secret, SI. My eyes only."

"Yes, Sir.

CHAPTER FORTY-THREE
SLIP SLIDING AWAY

Point YANKEE, Havana

Surprisingly, everything around me was still. No one was close. The city noises had faded.

Those out on the streets, sensing danger, had made themselves scarce. The distant explosions over toward the military airfield had gotten more attention than the suppressed fire of my SIG MG. Further away, toward downtown Havana, I could hear faint sirens.

I moved to a secluded location where I could see the street and waited for Rudy and Terry to show up. Time passed. Lingering in a hot zone was always the worst for me.

My gut screamed, "Get your ass out of here, Raven." My brain said, "Chill. They'll be here."

I heard a faint sound. It got louder, a low throaty rumbling. It was the sound of a large displacement engine, not well muffled.

Not good. A Cuban military vehicle?

I shifted my position, moving to concealment. Then I saw it. It took a long moment for the image to register. An old car with big tires, pastel blue with a white top, ponderous chrome bumpers, and a curved chrome strip going down the side, splitting the colors, blue above, white below. As it got closer, I could see the wheels, also chrome, and with white sidewall tires.

My brain clicked into focus. *An American Buick from the late 1950s, sparkling new, like it had just come out of a showroom. And then I saw Rudy at the wheel, the window down, his arm resting on the sill. Terry was next to him.*

I stood up and came out, both hands in sight. "Nice day for a drive."

Rudy grinned at me, "Need a ride, Raven?"

"Bet your ass."

He handed me a key. I unlatched the trunk and laid down my SIG MG in its covering blanket.

No automatic latches or access from inside. Such things hadn't yet been invented. Better than toting it around in the back seat, but nearly impossible to access. Their MXT 135s were both in there too. We all had hand guns, but most of our firepower was inaccessible.

I slammed the trunk. Terry hopped in back, I took shotgun, handed Rudy the key, and off we went. Slowly. Fast for Havana was about twenty-five. That's what we were doing. The speedometer even worked.

"Where the Hell did you get this?"

Rudy shrugged, "Found it on the street. Seemed useful. Last guy didn't need it anymore."

USS Gravely, Fire Control Center

Bromley came in, favoring his bad leg, looking concerned. "We have a problem, ladies. The people on the bridge are going apeshit. We are getting a flood of intercepts, many of them in the clear. Cuba is going to full military alert. All military forces have been ordered to report to their bases."

Josie said, "Isn't that what was expected? I reported the messages we got from Raven."

Gerry turned to Bromley, "Yes. Raven's mission was successful. That's why we're here, Commander."

"When do you expect that Raven will be coming out?"

"Soon. We'll know when I get his next signal."

"Let me rephrase that. There is a military airbase Southwest of downtown Havana. It's now on lockdown and it seems to be the focus of intense attention. Did Raven's team strike a Cuban military base?"

Gerry said, "Of course not. Raven's team only has five members, Commander. This was a limited, focused raid. They had two high value targets. They got them both."

"That's commendable, but why are the Cubans focused on that airbase?"

"Where Raven's team hit their targets wasn't far from the base. It was a few miles to the South, at a restaurant," Josie said. "Why are we discussing this?"

'Yes, I don't get that either. Raven's mission was successful."

"I hate to break the bad news, Gerry, but we don't think your team is coming out at all."

"Who, exactly, is we, Commander? Who thinks that?"

"My Captain. His chain of command."

Josie said, "Why do they think that?"

"Yes, why? We've been preparing for this. We expected a strong Cuban reaction. That's why Josie and I are here, why this ship is here, and why you are here."

"The geography doesn't work, Gerry. You didn't share that with us. This was a stupid attack. Your forces in Cuba are doomed. We are looking at an international incident, or worse."

Bromley rolled out a map. "Josie, can you put a finger on the place we just attacked?"

"I'm glad you said, 'we,' Commander. Josie and I were suddenly feeling lonely. Problem is, I'm not sure why you care or if you have a need to know...."

"It doesn't matter now, Gerry. The Cubans know, so why not the Navy?" Josie got up, walked over and put her finger on the map. "Right about here."

"About three miles to the Southwest?"

"Roughly. We have satellites. Don't you have an image?"

Bromley said, "Yes, we do. The area around the airbase is flooded with Cuban forces, including tanks and armored vehicles."

Gerry said, "And our team is long gone. So, what's the problem?"

"The problem is time and distance. You should have shared this with us."

"OPSEC, Commander. The targeting was set by our in-country team, based on the situation on the ground. Until now, I didn't know myself. Again, what's your problem?"

"It's basic logistics. Cuba has primitive infrastructure and is congested. Under normal circumstances it is about a three-hour drive from the location that you marked to the Havana harbor. Now, with checkpoints, it would be between much longer and no-way-in-Hell."

"Odd that you choose to bring this up now," Josie said.

"Yes," Gerry said, "Your mission was a simple extraction. Is that all, or do you have other problems?"

Bromley said, "My Captain has concerns about being able to complete our mission. Access to Havana harbor is a major choke point. Ships plan for an hour or more to make the transit, best case. The numbers don't work."

Gerry said, "So you are saying Raven's team has a zero chance of escape?"

"Exactly. I'm afraid so. The Captain doesn't want to risk an international incident over nothing. I'm sorry."

Josie was shaking her head. "Don't be, Commander. Thank you for your professional assessment and honesty. You have just vindicated Raven's planning."

Bromley blinked and looked at her. "I don't understand."

"Did I ever say that the *Busted Flush* was going to be coming out of Havana harbor?"

He was frowning. "You both asked me questions about Havana harbor. We ran simulations."

"True. But did either of us ever tell you that Raven would try to run that gauntlet?"

"I'm not sure...."

"The correct answer is, 'No.' We never did say that, did we?"

Bromley was frowning. "Maybe not. If you say so...."

"I do say so. *Busted Flush* is not in Havana harbor. It will be coming to you out of Marina Hemingway at speed, running for the open sea. I'm sure you can find that on your maps.

"It's right on the coast, to the West and South, and on the opposite side of Havana from where the Cuban forces are gathering."

He put a finger on the map. "Here?"

Gerry said, "That's what the legend on your map says, Commander. Marina Hemingway. If you task a satellite, you should be able to see them coming out.

"I didn't tell you that earlier, because I couldn't. I didn't know myself until now. You still don't have a need to know, but Josie was kind enough to share that information with you because the enemy already has it, because your Captain is about to make a huge mistake, and because he risks getting our team captured or killed. Is that clear to you, Commander?"

Bromley swallowed. "Yes, Ma'am. I get it."

"Good. My guess is that your ship will need to be in position to cover Raven's team in less than an hour. Is your Captain prepared to do that? Or is he going to leave them twisting in the wind?"

"To be honest, I don't know."

"So, go find out," Gerry said. "If you hurry, there might be time to get to the Bridge, prevent your Captain from considerable embarrassment, alert your chain of command, and persuade him to get his damned ship into position if he ever hopes to make Admiral, or even to keep his command."

"It is the Captain's decision. I'll see what he says." Bromley made his exit, moving fast.

Gerry was shaking her head, looking at Josie. "You made your point. His limp is a bit better. We got his attention."

"What a mess. I'm going topside. I'll be back when I have Raven's signal."

What that, she left. *The sailors and officers in Fire Control were totally silent. You could hear a pin drop.*

On Board the *Busted Flush*

Vinnie had started the engines and Pat had just gotten back from returning the car. They'd slipped the lines, except for one, and were ready to go. The sun was low and no one was around.

Those fishing generally left early and were back by mid-afternoon. A quiet Sunday.

Vinnie said, "Now we wait."

"Maybe not." A blue and white car was rolling slowly down the dock.
"What the Hell is that?"

Pat said, "Old Buick. My grandpa used to have one."

Vinnie said, "I see Rudy. White teeth, black face, big smile. He's having fun."

"It's them. You'll need to get down in the cabin. Rudy will take the helm, Raven's shotgun, Terry's local defense, and I'll take the long shots."

"What can I do down there?"

"Try not to throw up, you know how Rudy drives…."

"Other than that?"

"Wear a life jacket. Make sure you know where the exits are. There is one forward.

"Let Raven know if you see fire or water coming in. If one of us goes down, you bring him down there, patch him up if you can, and take his place. This thing is mostly fiberglass and gasoline. If it stops moving, get your ass out of there."

"Got it. Anything else?"

"Yeah. Enjoy your Caribbean cruise. People pay money for shit like this."

Rudy rolled up, the Buick's doors popped open, and they all piled out. Raven approached while the others got their kit out of the back. Weapons and ammo.

I said, "Nice ride."

Raven nodded. "Rudy has good taste. Are we good to go?"

"Roger that. Engines are good. All's quiet. Are you leaving the car on the dock?"

"Bet your ass. With the keys in the ignition. It won't be there long…."

Rudy took the Captain's chair. "I'll get the GPS and COMs up. Hop in, strap down, and hang on, people."

CHAPTER FORTY-FOUR
RUNNING FOR SAFETY

USS Gravely, Topside

Josie was holding her COM up where it could see the satellites, waiting for Raven's signal. The ship had changed course. It was increasing speed, rolling uncomfortably in a crossing sea, racing to be in position to intercept *Busted Flush* when she came out.

She was glad the crew left her a portable chair, lashed down in a sheltered location. Coming up, she'd stumbled and almost fallen. A sailor, Seaman Gomez, had helped her up the ladder and he was still standing by. A fall now would really complicate things.

He'd been concerned for her. "Remember the rule, 'One hand for you, one for the ship.' You have the right kind of shoes on, but it's easy to slip. We're running harder now. You'd be safer inside and strapped down."

Gomez was kind and gentle. She liked his aura. Josie smiled at him. "I'm okay, Sailor. Really."

He shook his head. "Need to keep you that way, Ma'am. It's my orders, but more than that. I have three sisters and mama raised us right. Orders or not, my job is to protect you. The whole crew knows this shit is about to get real."

Josie smiled. *Mama must not have minded vulgarity, and he is right. There is tension aboard the ship.*

She could feel it too. She could sense it. Forces were gathering. A nexus was approaching. Good and evil would collide. Some would live, and some would die.

Whatever conversations Bromley had with the Captain must have had an impact. Her paranormal senses indicated that Raven was OK. She didn't want to interrupt him or the team, but she had a job to do too.

Right now, her job was to wait. That was hard. She kept thinking of her scary viewings, those where *Gravely* was burning, the Captain was dead, and Raven and his team were dead or captured.

She was the one who had insisted that she needed to be closer to the action. Closer, and able to communicate in real time with Raven and those defending him if she was to do her job and keep him safe. The other part of her job was to not be fearful. Fear dulled her powers. It could even shut them down.

Fear is the mind killer. She needed her mind alert and her senses sharp.

On cue, the COM showed Raven's Ident and message. *Thank God, it is almost over.*

Josie looked at Gomez. "I need to stay up here. Would you please deliver a message to Commander Bromley?"

"Yes, Ma'am."

"Tell him, **Square Four**. Tell Gerry too. Raven's team is coming out of port."

Gomez said, "You need to stay right here till I get back. Ma'am. Keep one hand on the rail. I'll be back for you even if we go to General Quarters."

Josie looked at Gomez and nodded.

He said, "Promise me. Stay here. Hang on. I'll come back for you."

"I promise."

I hit my COM, acknowledged Raven's text, and sent, "Can you talk?"

He said, "Yes. All quiet, we're coming out slow and easy. No problems. Everyone is good."

"Seen the news?"

"Negative. Not for days."

"Pirates are working Cuban and Venezuelan waters."

"You are shitting me."

"It's the cartels. Mexico is a war zone and the border is locked down hard. Pirates are grabbing US registered boats to run drugs. Yours would be a perfect catch."

"Marvelous. What about Cuban warships?"

I said, "Clear so far. Keep coming. Gerry and I are on the *Gravely*. We don't detect any hostiles between you and us, but there is a lot of activity in Havana and there are patrol ships streaming out of the port there. There is also a lot of radio chatter and a no-fly zone up over Cuba."

"Got it, Babe. Twelve miles to International Waters. Flat out, *Flush* can do that in five minutes.

"We're running slow and innocent, waving at the fishing boats coming in. If it goes bad, we'll start calling for help in the open on the marine frequency."

I said, "Got it."

"Raven out. See you soon."

Gomez came back and helped me down the ladder. I was glad for his help. The ship was rolling more, moving around, and leaving a wake. I could hear alarm klaxons sounding.

USS Gravely, Fire Control Center

Gomez helped me to a chair and made sure I was strapped in. Everything was fastened down, and I could see a satellite image on a large screen display. It was overlaid with various markers and range indications.

Gerry said, "The green circle marks the *Busted Flush*. She's coming out slow. About ten knots."

I saw the indicator. The display changed as I watched. Fifteen knots. Then eighteen. They were running easy.

"Blue is commercial traffic. Red is hostiles. Yellow is unknown."

I said, "Got it."

A speaker came to life. I recognized Raven's voice. "*Busted Flush* is coming out of Cuban waters. We're a private vessel, US registered, bound for Miami. We're hearing about pirate warnings. Does anyone know what's going on?"

"This is the *USS Gravely*, on patrol off Cuba. At least two pirate vessels are known to be operating in Cuban waters. Give us an Ident, please."

"Wilco. Turning communications over to helm now. Stay with us, *Gravely*."

"We've got you, *Busted Flush*. We're close. Come left ten degrees, maintain speed, and we'll intercept and escort you as soon as you get into International Waters."

Rudy's voice came in clearly, "Wilco. I'm at the helm. We're coming to you, Gravely."

I heard the radioman acknowledge, followed by Bromley saying, "Oh, shit."

Bromley keyed his throat mike. "Fire control to Bridge, we've got a hostile. It just lit up and is moving to intercept the *Flush*. I'm activating our weapons."

He was pushing buttons and lights were coming on. One large button changed from green to red, from standby to battery armed."

The Captain's voice came over the speaker. "Do not engage. We're putting a drone up."

Bromley said, "Do not engage."

The satellite image zoomed in. It was a large vessel. There were men with weapons on deck.

The screen split. One half showed the Flush and its track to Gravely as a magenta path. There were now ID tags on the ships.

Flush was still moving slow. Gravely was up to twenty-five knots. There was an X where the two tracks intercepted, a point just outside the dotted line that demarked Cuban waters.

"Show me the hostile track," Bromley said.

A red line appeared. It intercepted the Flush's track in Cuban waters.

"I want an ID on the hostile."

"Stand by."

The image of the pirate ship suddenly got sharper. We could see every detail. There were several men on the deck with weapons.

"The drone's up. Sensors are active."

Bromley said, "Get me an Ident."

"We got it. It's the *Wild Goose*, a 78-foot Herman Turner out of Fort Lauderdale. She's been missing for three weeks."

"You got specs?"

"Negative. These are custom built. All steel. Long range. Built to handle weather."

"Confirm what we're looking at, Sensors."

"About fifteen men on deck. Most have AKs. I see two with RPGs, make that three, and...."

That screen went blank.

"What was that, Sensors?"

"It looked like a SA-7, an old shoulder-launched Vietnam era SAM. Our drone is down, Fire Control."

Bromley said, "Can see that, Sensors. Do we have another?"

"Negative."

The image shifted back to the lower resolution satellite image. The track vector was still there, in red. The tag said 25 knots.

"Fire Control to Bridge, that was a hostile act. Are we cleared to engage?"

The Captain said, "Negative. Not in Cuban waters, Commander."

Raven's voice came in on the open frequency, "We saw flashes. What's happening, *Gravely*?"

"Your hostile is a 78- foot shrimper, all steel. US registered as *Wild Goose*. Been missing for three weeks. They have men on deck with weapons and they just took out our drone. You should see her in a minute or two."

"Kill the bastard, *Gravely*."

"Negative, *Flush*. You can outrun her."

"Maybe, if we turn back towards Havana. Not going to do that. We're coming home."

A long moment passed and Raven said, "We have visual on the pirate, *Gravely*. She's got the angle on us."

"What are your intentions, *Flush*?"

"We'll try diplomacy, *Gravely*. Why not?"

Bromley was scowling. Gerry looked stunned. No one in Fire Control spoke. We watched the display.

I said, "What is he doing?"

"They are slowing down."

Busted Flush was turning, heading directly towards the pirate ship.

CHAPTER FORTY-FIVE
DEATH RUN

Onboard the Busted Flush

Raven yelled, "Slow down, Rudy! Five knots max. Steer for the pirate. Everyone listen-up."

The boat turned hard left and settled off plane into the water as Rudy yanked the power off. Vinnie stuck his head out the hatch below decks, and the roar of the engines softened to a purr.

"We're screwed, people. The pirates will either kill us, take us hostage, or turn us over to the Cubans. I'd rather go down fighting, but there's no point to getting you all killed for nothing.

"We've all got lifejackets. *Gravely* won't shoot, but they might do a rescue and I doubt the pirates will hang around. Does anyone want off?"

"Fuck no," Rudy said, prompting a chorus of similar answers.

"Hoped you'd say that. Here's the plan...."

Below Decks, the Busted Flush

Vinnie said, "We sure as Hell picked a good name for the boat, Boss."

Raven smiled grimly. He was checking the SIG MG and the special belt of ammo. One hundred rounds. He saw a mix of red-and-silver-tipped rounds. Incendiary and armor piercing.

No tracer. Good. He didn't much like tracer, because it worked both ways.

Raven said, "Here's the deal. The SIG has a low cyclic rate, 600 rounds per minute, to keep it light and controllable. It's well suppressed so it won't blow your ears out. Understand?"

"Affirm."

"The Tangos are going to have a lot of shooters on deck, mostly with AKs, but a few RPGs. Rudy's going to call out '*Hooah*' at 100 to 150 yards. You are going to pop the hatch open and I'm going to come out shooting with the SIG.

"You keep my belt clear. When I'm empty get your ass down. I'll be right behind you."

"Got it."

"We'll be bow-to-bow. I'll sweep any Tangos with their heads up over the rail and then do the wheelhouse. I don't know if these rounds can get through their hull or not. Maybe not, but I'll try. Our ability to put down suppressing fire is limited after I stop shooting.

"As soon my belt runs out, Rudy will turn hard right, go to full power, and run for the *Gravely*. I'll drop the weapon and head back for the shotgun seat. If any of us topside get hit, you are the backup."

"We hit them. I get out of the way. We run like Hell."

"Correct. And now we wait...."

USS Gravely, Fire Control Center

We were watching the satellite feed as Busted Flush slowly approached the pirate ship, which towered over the smaller boat.

Bromley said, "I see over a dozen Tangos on deck, five up at the bow, two with RPGs and the others with AKs. It's an impressive show of force. They can shoot downwards, like at fish in a barrel. There won't be any negotiations. He's going to surrender."

Gerry looked at me and I gave her a slight shake of my head. She nodded. We waited.

Flush's front hatch popped open. Raven popped out holding a machine gun, standing and firing. He raked the bow twice, left to right, and then back, short bursts. Another figure appeared, helping Raven, who now laid his weapon down on its bipod, firing longer bursts.

A stream of shiny brass was pouring out of his weapon. Shell cases.

The windows on the wheelhouse of the pirate vessel shattered. Men on its deck with weapons were crouching, rushing towards the bow. I saw two of them fall. There was a series of sparkles as rounds bounced off the steel hull, all across the bow, and then across the front of the wheelhouse. Even from the high angle, I could see holes appearing.

Gerry said, "Whatever he's shooting, some of the rounds are getting through."

Bromley said, "Nine Tangos, down."

Another one, coming forward with an RPG at a dead run, went down, losing his weapon, sliding on his face, and apparently pulling the trigger. There was a fireball on the bow of the pirate ship. Smoke was pouring out of the wheelhouse.

We watched as the *Flush* swiveled hard to the right, turning in its own length, pointing directly along the track line to our ship. Then it pitched up, water churned white, and it was suddenly moving fast. A shower of flares went up from its stern, along with chaff and smoke rockets.

A smoke trail came up from the pirate ship, an RPG.

"Fire Control to all stations. Pirate ship just fired an RPG at the **Busted Flush**."

We watched as the trail passed just behind the boat.

"Sensors to all stations, RPG missed astern of *Flush*. That boat is moving like a bat out of Hell."

The satellite view shifted away from the pirate, tracking the *Flush*. The tag said 45 knots, then 50, then 60, and it was still climbing. The boiling wake diminished. The boat was skipping along, flying, mostly out of the water.

"Sensors to Fire Control. We've lost radar on **Busted Flush**, it just frigging vanished. What's going on?"

Bromley looked questioningly at Gerry, but before she could answer there was another call.

"Sensors to all stations. Vampire, vampire, vampire. Missiles incoming."

There was a flash at the edge of the screen, and the pirate vessel disappeared in a fireball and billowing clouds of black smoke."

"Bridge to Sensors, what was that?"

"Sensors to all stations, that was a missile fired from a Cuban Osa boat out over the horizon. It's one of three coming out of Havana harbor. They possibly were shooting at *Busted Flush* and missed. Another missile is inbound.

"I repeat, Vampire, Vampire, Vampire. We have incoming missiles."

Bromley said, "Fire control to bridge. Request permission to engage."

"Bridge to all stations, permission denied. Defensive only. Stay alert. They are not shooting at us."

Bromley looked at Gerry. "That missile ignored the *Flush*. Raven's boat vanished from our radar. What the Hell is going on?"

"We have some experimental countermeasures systems we're testing, Commander. Apparently, they are working."

"Sensors to all stations. Vampire, vampire, vampire. There is a second missile about three minutes out, and it seems to be tracking us."

"Bridge to Sensors, are you certain?"

"Sensors to all stations. Negative. My opinion is it's headed for us, but *Busted Flush* is getting close and it might be after them. We can't say for certain, Captain."

Another screen lit up, showing a timer, an overhead view of Gravely, and a timer. The time was 2:48 and counting down.

Bromley said, "Fire control to Bridge, that missile has breached my inner defense circle. Speed is about Mach one. If it's coming for us, we may not be able to stop it."

"Sensors to all stations, we are showing two more missiles behind that one."

"Bridge to all stations, Fire Control, you are now Weapons Free. Signals, send in the clear to command and on the International Emergency Frequency, 'We are being fired on by Cuban Missile boats. Cease fire immediately or we will sink you.' Keep repeating the message. Put it on a loop."

Bromley ordered, "Kill the Vampires. All weapons to target the nearest one. Then engage the rest and the launch platform." His hand came down on a red button and a variety of sensors went live.

"Sensors to Fire Control, the SeaRAM you just fired was a miss. We're going to take a hit."

"Fire control to all stations, brace yourselves, we're going to take a hit. Vampire, vampire, vampire! It is in too close for SeaRAM. I'm activating the old Phalanx guns. Bridge, give me hard to Port, so both guns will bear. Expedite! We are out of time."

The ship immediately heeled over in a right-angle turn. A screen came live, showing a little dome that looked like R2D2 in Star Wars. It had a gun barrel, and it was spitting flame, swiveling as the ship turned.

Gerry said, "What are we looking at?"

Bromley said, "Obsolete now. Phalanx packs the M61 "Vulcan" 20mm cannon. Its six revolving barrels spray out a stream of tungsten sabot armor piercing rounds at a rate of over 75 rounds a second. Radar tracks the shells and the incoming missiles. Computers try to make them come together. Humans are too slow.

"They wanted to remove Phalanx when we upgraded, but I'm fond of it. The Cuban stuff is obsolete, so it might work against them. You never know...."

There was a flash and the screen went blank. There were crashes and thuds as *Gravely* took the hits.

"Damage Control to all stations. Taking shrapnel. The missile exploded before it hit."

The little screen came back up, and there was R2D2, blackened and singed, but still intact.

Bromley said, "Give me the status of SeaRAM."

"All green, Sir."

"Take out the other two Vampires. Can you engage the ship that fired them?"

"Yes, Sir."

"Excellent, put a Tomahawk on them."

"Firing now, Sir."

"Fire Control to Bridge, we barely got that one. We put SeaRAM on the next two and a Tomahawk on the launch platform."

"Bridge to all stations. Weapons remain free. Fleet is sending support."

"Sensors to all stations. Vampires are down, but we are still being painted by several Cuban Fire Control radars. *Busted Flush* is again painting on our radar."

"Bridge to all stations. Command advises other possible threats. Orders are to engage and neutralize threats. Stay alert. Good work, people."

"USS *Gravely* is calling on the emergency frequency. We've been attacked in International Waters by Cuban missile boats and are now weapons hot. Any further attacks will result in the destruction of the facility that initiated it. Diplomatic protests are being filed.

"Break. USS *Gravely* to civilian vessel *Busted Flush*, please acknowledge."

"*Busted Flush* copies you *Gravely*."

"*Gravely* witnessed you being attacked, *Busted Flush*. Do you have any casualties?"

"*Flush* is good, *Gravely*."

"*Gravely* requests you pull in close behind us, and follow. We'll be staying in International Waters.

"Warning. We are under orders to run up along the coast towards Havana and take a look. That may draw more fire, but you're probably safer with us than out here alone."

We heard Raven chuckle over the radio. "*Busted Flush* will comply, *Gravely*. The neighborhood seems dangerous. Thank you."

"Thank you, *Busted Flush*. *Gravely* will monitor this frequency."

CHAPTER FORTY-SIX
HYPERSONIC

Morning, Laurel Lodge, Camp David

We were sitting in the smallest of the three conference rooms of cabin Laurel. A small group, me, Josie, Goldfarb, plus Mike and Gerry. The senior person present was Joint Chief's Chairman Admiral Quigley, the only person here from outside my team and our control.

Mike told me the President was coming and said not to share that.

I'd met Quigley only once, back in the days of our now-defunct Covfefe committee, which had been dissolved as potentially getting too much press attention from an old Trump tweet that went massively viral, causing Fake News heads to explode and the code word to become unsuitable.

These days we were totally off the books. I liked that better, but I was surprised the Admiral was here.

Quigley was seated at the head of the table, with Goldfarb at his right and Mike and Gerry next to him. There was an empty chair on his left, and then me and Josie.

Laurel was up near the helipad and field house which were now surrounded by military hardware. There were four Apache helicopters on the pads, and two big Blackhawks parked out on the grass in the skeet range. The Marines on guard duty had M4s with live ammo and FIM-92 Stinger missiles.

Last time I'd been here – it seemed so long ago – there had been an attack, one of several that had targeted the President. This time, it seemed his defenders were taking no chances. Good.

Admiral Quigley looked at Goldfarb. "Aaron, would you please be so kind as to state the protocols and make the introductions. I know a few of the people here, but, since officially this isn't a meeting, we'll keep it loose."

"Right. The protocols are simple. First off, this meeting didn't happen. It is off the record and will not be logged. Secondly, anything may be discussed here, but nothing can be shared outside this group.

"There will be a meeting today, on the record, one held between myself, the Admiral, and President Blager, who will join us after lunch.

"At his option, some or all of you may be invited to stay. If so, you will attend as ghosts, advisors with no official presence. The rules are, 'no interruptions from outside,' and you will have noticed we have two Marines outside the door to enforce that. Any questions?"

Mike said, "Two questions, Doctor. You said, 'anything may be discussed.' Can you be a bit more explicit?"

Quigley said, "I'll take that. What he is saying is that I want you all free to speak your minds. I want candor. I will moderate and if it gets too off topic or lengthy, I'll cut you off. If you choose not to speak to a topic, I will honor that.

"Is that acceptable, Raven?"

He'd directed that comment at me, not Mike. "It is, Sir. I appreciate that."

That got a thin smile. "I've heard rumors that in a previous life, you were dismissed with prejudice by a certain agency for being, ah, unkind to a certain hostile nation with nuclear aspirations."

Goldfarb was frowning. "I'm going to flag that one as 'off topic' myself. Speculative and irrelevant. Best not to go there."

"Quite correct, Aaron. Strike that. What was your second question, Mike?"

Mike looked puzzled. "Actually, since you touched on this with Raven, that's what I'm going to ask. We work quite hard at keeping a low profile. It's how we function, how we survive. Security or not, we'll inevitably have been observed coming in and leaving Camp David. Do we have a plausible cover story, if asked?"

"We do, and it is even one that has the merit of being true. A private award ceremony.

"My official purpose, or excuse, is that certain people are of the opinion that your recent mission in Cuba rendered a great service to the Navy and to our nation. I'm here to recognize that. It's the first thing I wish to discuss with you."

Mike said, "Thank you, Admiral."

Goldfarb said, "It's your meeting Admiral."

"Good. As I said, this is off the record, but I do plan a short awards ceremony and will take a few vaguely general notes to justify my findings. Everything will be sealed and classified, of course. May I proceed."

Goldfarb nodded. "Please do."

"Good." Quigley looked at me. "I'll start with you, Raven, and ask others on your team to step in to flesh out the details. It seems that we came close to another Bay of Pigs, but this time with a happy outcome. "What the Hell happened in Cuba? I need a full debriefing."

We spent over an hour briefing the Admiral. In the end he said, "At great risk you and your team achieved a positive outcome for America and for our friends in the region. Is there anything you'd like to say about your interactions with the Navy?"

I said, "Commander Bromley was of great help in getting our boat equipped and my team trained in how to best put it to use. He is a fine officer. We might not have made it out without being allowed to have Josie and Gerry on the *USS Gravely*. You have my personal thanks and that of my team, Admiral."

Quigley looked at Mike.

"I concur with Raven's assessment, Admiral."

"Gerry?"

She blinked. "Sir?"

"I'm informed that you raised concerns about how well Raven's team was being supported. Would you care to comment?"

"No, Sir, not really."

Gerry and Mike exchanged a look.

Mike said, "We got the job done, Sir. God Bless America."

Gerry said, "I did have concerns for our mission. They were addressed. We had a few rough spots, but, in the end, everyone did their jobs and it turned out well."

Admiral Quigley said, "*USS Gravely* didn't go weapons free until a Cuban missile was well inside its defense perimeter, with two more close behind. Only the fact that the Weapons Officer had persisted in keeping an obsolete weapons system saved a billion-dollar warship and her three hundred and twelve officers and crew."

"I can't speak to that," Gerry said. "There were some awkward moments. *Busted Flush* almost took an RPG, but, fortunately, she did not."

Quigley nodded. "Yes. Some awkward moments. Captain Hipp said much the same. I'm about to have one now."

Goldfarb cleared his throat. "Yes, and I think I need to flag another 'off topic,' Admiral. Problematic command decisions are internal Navy issues.

"We had a successful mission. We appreciate the support the Navy gave us, and we thank you for it. Without the support of the fleet, it is unlikely that Raven and his team would have survived."

Quigley nodded. "Quite right, Aaron."

Mike raised his hand. "Can we stick with this for just a moment more? I think there is a possible learning moment."

Goldfarb frowned.

Quigley said, "I'd welcome your inputs, General."

"It's a Marine type viewpoint, Sir."

That got a grin. "I wouldn't have it any other way."

"It seems the Navy may have a hole in your Fleet defenses. If a threat gets in close, even your best warships are at risk. The Iranians have a strategy of swarming ships in tight waters with small, fast, expendable missile boats."

"Yes. Oil. The Straits of Hormuz."

"I've seen the results of the wargames. We lost."

"Sometimes we did."

"You might want to think about keeping some of the old systems. With minor modifications, Phalanx could kick ass against surface targets.

"Like Raven said, and I think you acknowledged, Commander Bromley may have saved your Destroyer. The modifications he suggested to us definitely saved the *Busted Flush*."

Quigley nodded slowly. "I like how you think, General."

"Thank you, Sir."

"To get back on topic, the Navy wanted to officially acknowledge your contributions, but it turns out that what you did doesn't fit well into our systems, or even into things that can be discussed."

"You got that part right, Admiral," Goldfarb said.

"Yes, well, here's how it turned out. We cannot, of course, give you an award for sensitive actions that might involve, ah, possible rule bending. Also, we had to find something that could be awarded to civilians by the Department of Defense."

Goldfarb said, "The highest civilian award has been the Presidential Medal of Freedom. Lately, it's been used by politicians to buy the loyalty of elites with fame."

"Sadly true. We studied and rejected that one. It is now awarded to celebrities, sports figures, political activists, and leftist politicians, often for actions that were not in America's national security interests, and, sometimes, even hostile to them. We rejected that."

Quigley gave a thin smile. "It seemed that you and your team might not want to be associated with that group, Raven."

I said, "Correct."

"Good. That left us with the Navy Distinguished Public Service Award. The problem, of course, was that we couldn't give a public service award for violent covert actions, nor even imply that kinetic operations in denied access regions might have an official sanction."

"Of course, not, Sir," Mike said. "We couldn't have that."

"Right. So, therefore, we narrowed your team's involvement justifying a commendation to heroically escorting the *USS Gravely* through disputed international waters in an unarmed civilian boat while being targeted by some of the most advanced and lethal weapons systems in the world."

Goldfarb said, "What about the encounter with the pirates?"

"What encounter? The *Wild Goose* was a U.S. registered civilian fishing boat. The Cubans sank it with a missile and there were no survivors.

"They may or may not have been allowing pirates to operate from their waters. In either case, the insurance company for the owners wants restitution. The State Department is adding that to a long list of complaints and claims."

Admiral Quigley looked at me, "Would that be acceptable, Raven? We are effectively giving you an award for using you as bait. The President didn't think either political party could object to that, even if they found out."

Now everyone was looking at me. I shrugged. *Politics.*

Goldfarb said, "The swamp is a dark, dismal place, Raven. All through our history. George Washington himself had horrible problems with Congress. I'd take the award for the team and move on."

I looked at Josie and Gerry. They both nodded, so I said, "We'd be honored, Admiral."

"Good. Normally, this award is presented by the Secretary of the Navy for specific courageous or heroic acts of substantial and long-term benefit to the Department of the Navy as a whole.

"It is the highest recognition that the Secretary of the Navy may pay to a civilian not employed by the Department of the Navy. In this case I am awarding it on his behalf to you, your boat team, and to those supporting your team from the fire control station of the *USS Gravely.*

He handed me seven leather cases. I opened one, saw my gold medal, nodded, and passed Josie and Gerry theirs. "Thank you, Sir."

"We can also provide a cash award for your team. This falls under complex rules for a 'Special Act Award.' My office is sorting that out, and it may take some time. When it settles out, we'll get you a check. You can disperse it to your team as you see fit."

The Admiral took a deep breath and shot a look at Goldfarb.

"It's all a lie, of course. You were not the bait, Raven. You had a different mission, one of great value. You got it done and we're grateful, but that is a separate issue. One that won't be discussed or officially acknowledged."

"Sir?"

"We were using the *USS Gravely* for bait. It made her Captain a bit nervous."

"I don't understand, Admiral."

"Have you ever heard of a Chinese missile system called the DF-26B?"

I shook my head.

"How about a hypersonic maneuverable reentry vehicle called the WU-14?"

"No, Sir."

"We call them 'carrier killers.' The 26B is a second generation ASBM, an Anti-Ship Ballistic Missile. There is now one of these in this hemisphere, in Cuba. It was tracking you all the way in. As you got close it was targeting *Gravely*. They were locked and loaded, ready to launch.

"We had an Electronic Warfare aircraft on station to monitor the radar emissions. We captured all that data and are now analyzing it. I'm told that the information obtained was of high value.

"We had a number of other assets deployed. Had that site actually fired a missile, an act of war, we would have monitored and tracked that as well. Our technical people want data on both the radar and the missiles. We don't know much about them."

Goldfarb said, "If they had fired, would we have lost *Gravely*?"

"We don't know, Doctor. She is one of our best Destroyers. I can say that if the Chinese had attacked and damaged or sunk *Gravely* in International Waters that particular missile site would no longer exist. It would just be a large smoking hole in the ground.

"The *USS Lincoln* attack group was about a hundred miles off shore with orders to take it out along with any air defenses or assets trying to protect it."

"Orders to hit Havana? To hit Cuba? To take action against the Chinese?"

Quigley shrugged. "If you want to get into that discussion, you can ask the President. He'll be here soon."

President Blager arrived in time for lunch. He dined privately with Goldfarb and Admiral Quigley in the conference room. They had 'Big Picture' matters to discuss. The tense military situation along the invasion corridor from Venezuela to Mexico and our southern border, had been helped, but also made more complicated, by the events in Cuba.

The rest of us took sandwiches and salad outside on the patio. It was a beautiful day, and, best of all, it was a safe, relaxing place. They'd call us back in when they needed us.

I looked at Josie. "The President is not going to be happy that we put you at risk, Babe. Did you know that the Chinese were going to use *Gravely* for target practice as a show of force?"

"It was likely for a time, but that awful future changed when he got us on the *Gravely*. I saw a myriad of disastrous possible futures, most of them resulted in the destruction of both *Gravely* and **Busted Flush**.

"With us on board, those futures all became low probability. So low that they didn't happen. If risk discussions come up, we should blame the Russians. The Chinese are working to replace them as the big dog, not just in Cuba but all down the invasion corridor. Right?"

I said, "Pretty much. The Chinese don't want a conventional war with America, not yet, but they would like to move Cuba into their sphere of influence and away from Russia."

"Correct," Mike said, "Blame me too, if it helps. We needed you there. Hell, if you and Gerry hadn't been there to intervene, we'd have lost Raven's whole team. That Captain was about to wet his pants."

Gerry said, "We need to get them both out of this hemisphere, Mike."
"Yes."

Josie said. "Great. We agree. Now can we talk about happier things? It's been a rough couple of days,"

"Sure."

And so, we did....

They didn't call us back in until almost three. We took the same seats, except this time with the President at the end of the table, Goldfarb at his right, and Admiral Quigley in the previously empty seat next to me. It appeared the President wanted to run the meeting himself.

He looked at me. "This will be brief, Raven. It seems that miracles occurred, because of you, Josie, and the rest of your team. What you've accomplished has a good chance of changing America's future history."

"Thank you, Sir."

"We can't give you public recognition, but Admiral Quigley and I are fully aware of your contributions, and also the extreme risk and difficulty you endured. You have transformed the geopolitics of the invasion route to our south. America owes you a debt of thanks, as does my administration."

I looked at my team. Except for Goldfarb, I saw puzzled looks. We'd expected an ass chewing and cautionary mention of our almost having started a second Cuban Missile Crisis.

Kennedy had publicly taken responsibility for the first one and his administration had never been quite the same. The Berlin Wall and Vietnam had followed, along with his assassination.

Goldfarb was watching me closely. "We need to say more, Mr. President. We need to tell them what they've accomplished. What we are now facing."

"Yes, we do. You tell them, Aaron."

Goldfarb said, "What I'm going to share goes far beyond any security classification we have. Hold it close. This is never to be written down. It is only to be discussed with the people present here, and only then in the most secure settings. I need to hear verbal acknowledgments."

Together, we chorused, "I agree."

"Good. One of the cleverest things you did was leaving that deceptive weapon behind in Havana, and having me get you a credible end-use certificate, a paper trail that links it directly to China."

I had to think for a moment. "Vinnie's little toy mortar?"

He nodded.

"Mike did that."

Mike said, "I did. At your request, Raven."

"Okay...."

"There is much tension between Russia and China in our hemisphere. You saw it in Mexico, where a cartel allied with China got a Russian diplomat assassinated. The Cubans, who control the Venezuela end, are being courted by China, who can offer them better weapons, and so forth...."

I said, "Russia has superior weapons. Better fighter planes. The best surface-to-air missile system in the world."

"True for the most part, but with exceptions. The DF-26 Missile is China's prized anti-carrier weapon. We have nothing like it, neither does Russia, and neither of us never will...."

I shook my head. "Never is a long time, Doctor. We can just develop one of our own."

"No," the President interrupted. "Actually, we can't, Raven."

Even Mike was shaking his head. I waited.

Goldfarb said, "A primary objective of all our major enemies is to take out our carriers. Do that, and we're vulnerable."

Mike interrupted. "We have the best mid-course anti-ballistic defense in the world, and are working on high powered lasers for shipboard terminal defense."

"We are," Goldfarb said. "Desperately. Because we have no counter to the DF-26. We don't know its capabilities, but we do know we can never deploy anything like it. Without doing that, we lack the expertise to develop trusted countermeasures, though the data we just got on their radar systems, thanks to Raven's team, is a big plus."

I said, "You're losing me, Doctor. Why can't we develop an anti-ship ballistic missile of our own?"

"Same reason the Russians couldn't. They put a lot of money into one, the R-27K – the K is for *Korabelnaya*, which means 'ship-related' – back in 1972. With a small nuclear warhead, it was a credible carrier-killer. It was going to win the Cold War for them."

"But it didn't."

"No, it did not. Turns out the Russians could not deploy it. I think that broke their spirit. We won the Cold War. That's your history lesson for the day, Raven."

"I already knew that."

"Ah, but you don't know why, do you?"

Mike interrupted, "Why not?"

"The SALT treaty, Mike. For every launch tube with an R-27K, the Russians would have to remove one missile from their strategic stockpile. It seems they preferred to kill our cities and airbases more than our carriers."

I was puzzled. "But the Chinese, knowing all that, have now developed and deployed a carrier-killer. That doesn't make sense, Doctor."

The President said, "The Chinese are not signatories of the SALT treaty. Nor are they ever likely to be, Raven."

"Why not? The Chinese have nukes."

"Of course, they do," Goldfarb said. "Advanced nukes."

The President said, "The Chinese say they don't need to sign. Instead, they've pledged never to use their nuclear weapons first."

I said, "The Chinese Communists have regular bioweapons 'accidents.' Dissidents and critics tend to disappear or have unfortunate deaths. Someone actually believes that crap?"

Mike said, "Of course they do. Many people. The UN. Fake News. Some of our own politicians. Most of the third world. All the nations that are obligated or loyal to China. Anyone who hates America."

Goldfarb was nodding. "Exactly."

The President said, "Your team's involvement in stressing, exposing, and neutralizing this Chinese aggression has been invaluable, Raven. We owe you, big time.

"My administration will now be working to see that missile system is removed from this hemisphere. The Russians and many others oppose a Chinese presence in Cuba. Sanctions and diplomatic action have been initiated. Protests have been filed.

"I will be announcing a blockade of Cuba tomorrow and reminding the world of the Monroe Doctrine."

"Interesting," Mike said.

Goldfarb said, "Many positive things are happening, because of what Raven and his team have done."

"I agree," the President said. "Take some time off, Raven. Stand down. You've earned it. If you need anything, have Doctor Goldfarb contact me."

I said, "Thank you, Mr. President."

Except for Goldfarb, as a group, we stood and made our exit.

Mike said, "I think we're dismissed. They're probably heading back to the swamp tonight."

Gerry nodded. "Yes. The President will need to be in Washington if all that is going down."

They both looked happy. Josie was quiet, almost somber.

I said, "Can you give us a few minutes alone? I'm going to take Josie over there to that shady corner of the deck, grab myself a beer, get her some cold white wine, and talk about happy things."

Mike said, "Sure. We'll see you at dinner and leave in the morning. Six?"

"Sure."

Josie nodded. "That's fine."

They left and we moved to the secluded corner. "Scary times, but we all came out the other side and this is one of the safest places on the planet, Babe. Are you Okay?"

"I hope so."

I came back with her wine. She took a sip, and smiled. "Nice. Thank you."

"What's wrong?"

"I'm not sure, Raven. I'm not even sure that I want to find out. I just have a sense of foreboding."

"Something close?"

"Not close. It is off at some distance, both in time and space."

"It won't mess up our vacation?"

"I don't think so. Not as far as I can tell, but I can't promise. It's just a feeling, like there is something out there, something vaguely forming, something way off down faint probability trails into the future.

"There is a lot of chaos in close. It doesn't directly impact us, but I can't see past it."

I said, "It's not a remote viewing or a vision?"

"No, just a vague feeling."

"Screw it, then. We'll deal with that, whatever it is, if it comes, when it comes, just like we always do. We deserve a vacation and I even know where you'd like to go."

She smiled for the first time. "Carate, Bungalow #7, Luna Lodge?"

"Yeah. What do you think?"

"Why there?"

"Because I miss the howler monkeys?"

She smiled. "No."

"Because no television or phones?"

Her smile was brighter. "Maybe."

"How about I just want to be alone with you, alone with someone I love, in a place that you love?"

"You love it too, don't you?"

"Maybe it's the snakes…?"

"Look at me."

I did. She stuck her tongue out, shook her head vigorously, and laughed. Her eyes sparkled and the gloom was gone. It was like a shadow lifted and the sun came out.

I said, "Well?"

"You're on!"

"Boy, am I ever, Babe."

I leaned over and kissed her.

THE END

EPILOGUE

Mexican Navy Ship ARM Isla Maria Madre (BAL-11), Three Months Later

Public Security Minister Genaro Santiago relaxed back into his chair and looked at me. "I do this trip several times a year and I must confess that you are the most unusual guest I've ever had, Colonel Giles."

We were seated in a small stateroom, one of the few private spaces on the small vessel. The ship was starkly functional, with modifications like a deck crane and an "accommodation module" for prisoners and their families.

I'd been passed through a scanner before boarding, as was everyone else, even the Captain and the Minister. I saw a sign in Spanish that said a maximum of 145 passengers. If so, they would be stacked like cordwood. Today there were about a dozen, plus the crew of seventeen

I shrugged, "I'm long retired from the military, Minister Santiago. And from industry, as well. I've been to many places over the years, and this is shaping up as one of the most unusual. Can you tell me anything about where we are going?"

"I'll trade with you. I have orders from President Obrador himself to see you get what you need, but I don't have any idea what you might want or how I might help you. We're not used to seeing Americans, though we do have two who work on the island. As long as I've been coming here, I've never been assigned one to escort."

"Fair enough," I said. "The literature I was sent is confusing. Some said Isla Maria Madre is a high security prison, but I also saw an article that said your President Obrador had closed it in 2019. Some said it was an eco-resort, a biosphere reserve, whatever that is. Some said it was a 'Club Fed' for nonviolent offenders."

Santiago nodded. "It's been all of those things at various times. The island was uninhabited until a high security prison was built in 1905 to house violent criminals and political enemies. For a time, there were over 29,000 prisoners. It was our equivalent of your Alcatraz, escape proof."

"Was it?"

"Pretty much. There were 70 escapes over 100 years, but few recent. Since my tenure, only one. One inmate has been missing. He could have escaped or died. Most think the latter, including myself."

"Why?"

"The only way on or off the island is this boat, which visits once a week, every Thursday. It arrives in the morning and leaves in the evening.

"Most here don't want to escape. There are only about 1,066 inmates, we call them 'colonists,' plus 275 non-inmate relatives, and 100 employees. It's the best life they've ever known. They are safe here.

"There are about 150 children and three schools. During free time, colonists can roam on their bikes, shop and visit with their families, who are encouraged to move to the island.

"At age 14 the children must go back to the mainland. That's the ultimate punishment, banishment from the island. The prisoner who disappeared was about to be released. I think he probably killed himself."

"This is the 'Club Fed' that people speak of?"

"It is. That model has a strong media appeal, but it doesn't work for Mexico. The eco resort couldn't be funded, and neither can the current situation, not long-term. It is being allowed to fade, because there would be upset in the world media if we tossed these 'colonists' back into our violent prison system.

"The last option is to go back to a high security prison, but that path totally lacks support."

"So, what's the solution, Minister?"

"There is none. The maximum-security model has not functioned in Mexico. La Palma, the maximum-security prison outside of Mexico City, was almost taken over from within by drug traffickers. It took tanks and the Army to restore order.

"The cartels run our prisons, Mr. Giles. The problem is human corruption that undermines the best-laid plans. We had to put El Chapo in your Super Max prison to keep him locked up.

"If we had cartel heads on the island, we'd have to allow them access to lawyers. Their lawyers would visit with their clients nearly every day – all day. Those lawyers, in reality, are narco messengers. They would demand secure communications, air transport, and more.

"At best, we'd be giving cartel heads safe havens from their rivals. At worst, we have paramilitary raids to spring them. Most likely, we'd have both. There would not be a happy ending."

Minister Santiago sighed and fell silent, looking off across the sea.

After a time, I said, "Thank you for the briefing, Minister. I appreciate it."

"Do you believe me?"

"Actually, I do, Minister Santiago. We in America suffer from corruption as well, the Deep State. We're coming back, but the swamp leads good people into very dark places."

"It does indeed, Mr. Giles. And I, of course, do know who it is that you wish to meet with. An American. We know him as 'Mr. Smith.' There is a price on his head placed by one of the cartels. He was being held by a different cartel, but your Government helped us purchase him and move him to safety. He is in the safest place we could find.

"America was most generous. The funding that we got from you helps keep our facility running. We've kept him safe, anonymous, and in good health."

"Thank you, Minister."

"Are you going to take him with you?"

"Not at this time."

"I can give you three hours alone with him. Is that sufficient?"

"More than sufficient, Minister."

"Are you going to kill him?"

I laughed. "Not likely. I just need to speak with him."

"You have support from high level people, but I can't figure out how you fit in. You are not State Department, FBI, or CIA. You showed me no government credentials."

"I'm just a civilian, Minister Santiago."

"Why did they pick you?"

"It is a long story, Sir. Part of it might be that I myself was abducted by Islamic terrorists from the United States. I was held in Bukhari for a time, but they transferred me to Syria before their government fell.

"I was imprisoned in Syria for seven years. Syria finally swapped me for another prisoner, one they wanted more."

"You might save Mr. Smith from the cartels?"

"It's possible. I don't know, but I do need to hear his story. Perhaps I can give him some options."

"Take another hour if you need it. I'll hold the boat, if necessary."

"I can't guarantee anything, Sir."

"Of course not. I'll ask the Captain to speed up a bit. You might need the time."

"Thank you, Minister."

Santiago took his exit. It was my turn to sigh and look out at the sea.

Everything I'd told the Minister was true. What I'd not told him was that his 'Mr. Smith,' in reality our missing Senator Ron Wyatt, likely was the same person who'd sold me out to the terrorists who abducted me from Oregon. What goes around, comes around....

Isla Marias, 230 Miles SE of Baja, Mexico

We were sitting outside, not far from the dock, under shade, watching the ocean. The view was stunning, with a climate like Puerto Vallarta, but visitors wouldn't get umbrella drinks or an open-air jeep for sightseeing. Most would be handed a shovel, a list of rules, and a housing assignment.

I was given private access to Mr. Smith, aka Senator Wyatt. Not in an interrogation room, but on a beautiful beach. I could not call the small island a prison, as Mexico's President Obrador had officially closed that on February 18, 2019.

The Hell-hole described in the José Revueltas book *Walls of Water* was ancient history. There were still a few cells for drug use or violence and there were three roll calls per day, but the focus was on tightly controlled communication, meetings, and access to the island. Inhabitants were scattered around the island in small camps.

Senator Wyatt looked nothing like his old PR pictures. I would not have recognized him. He was thin, bony, and shorter than I'd imagined, perhaps 5' 9" or a bit less, maybe 160 pounds. He had brown eyes and a big nose. He seemed happy and relaxed.

His signature dark, New York, custom-tailored suit, white shirt, and vivid-blue Democrat tie were gone. He wore a pale blue T-shirt, shorts, and leather sandals. His carefully-combed brown hair was now long, white, and scraggly. His tan partially hid a bad complexion.

To be sure, there were not a lot of barbers, tailors, or makeup artists on the island, but there was beauty and safety in abundance. No freedom, but peace. It was like the old Eagles song *Hotel California*, "*You can check out, but you can never leave.*"

Paradise or Hell? It was hard to say. I found it creepy, more like Orwell than the Garden of Eden.

Wyatt asked, "Who are you?"

I said, "My name is John Giles. I'm an American. I'm just a private citizen, but I've been sent to see you by people in Washington. I'm here to ask you a few questions."

"Why should I answer any questions for you?"

"Perhaps you shouldn't. You are still alive because the cartels don't **know** you're alive. You are here because we put you here. The amount of money on your head is, at least to me, rather impressive.

"Let's start with some easy questions. Do you recall the exact amount of cash that your group was bringing into Mexico for Los Serpientes?"

"I don't...."

"The correct answer is $25 Million in non-sequential $100 bills.

"What I find to be of interest is that the reward now posted for you is that same amount dead, but five times that if you are delivered alive.

"You are a very valuable person to the cartels, Senator. I'm tempted myself."

He blinked and turned a bit pale. "That's not possible. I was simply traveling with some colleagues from the House of Representatives.

They provided the money. I was there to observe and coordinate for the Senate."

"Do your recall the names of your colleagues in this endeavor?"

"That is none of your...."

"Let me help you. The Leader of your group was the House Minority leader, Nicia Volpe. I'm sure you remember her."

"She died during the transfer. When we delivered the money."

"Good for you, Mr. Wyatt. The first part of your statement is correct. The second is not."

"It is Senator Wyatt."

"You are mistaken. You are missing, presumed dead. The Governor of your State appointed a replacement. She will serve until your term runs out next Fall. Then there will be an election.

"Also, you failed to deliver the money you'd promised. The cartels are less than pleased."

Wyatt stared at me, but didn't speak.

"Ms. Volpe is dead. Do you recall who procured the money for her?"

"I can't recall. Some woman. She wasn't part of our group."

"That would be Jayne Whiteway. She was the minority leader of the House Finance Committee. There were some improprieties. She has since resigned from Congress and is now facing charges over misuse of funds."

Wyatt shook his head. "I don't think I ever met her...."

"How about Harry Schiff? He was, I believe, Ms. Volpe's #2 for your group. They were both from California."

"He's dead." Wyatt closed his eyes. "The money was missing. The pallet contained mostly paper, with a few bills showing in one open package. The head of the *Los Serpientes* cartel was very angry. Schiff kept saying he didn't know where the money was. He was screaming."

"The cartel head would be Miguel Trevino?"

"Yes. He was questioning Schiff. He had one of his thugs cutting on him, peeling his skin off. They made us watch."

"Carlos Gomez. A big man with a bad leg?"

"Yes. How do you know these things?"

"That doesn't matter. There was one more person in your group. Do you recall his name?"

"I'm not sure. He was from Texas. Bruno something...."

"Correct. Bruno Basso, from the Foreign Relations committee."

"Is he dead too?"

"That I do not know. I do know that he was less fortunate then you.

"The people I'm working with bought you from *Los Serpientes*. Basso was purchased by the *Sinaloa* cartel. For some reason they say it was their money that was stolen."

Wyatt was shaking his head. "Trevino was protecting us by then. He believed us after his man killed Schiff. He believed that we'd not taken the money and that we could get it replaced, which was true.

"Trevino thought that we had been betrayed."

"Trevino is dead, Mr. Wyatt. He can't protect you. He can't protect anyone."

"How did he die?"

"Poorly, I expect. The *Sinaloa* cartel posted images of his severed head on the Internet."

Wyatt was silent for a long moment. Finally, he said, "We were betrayed."

"It sounds like you are lucky to be alive."

"Why are you here Giles?"

"Because of my oath, I suppose."

"I don't understand."

"When I joined the military, I swore an oath to protect America from all enemies foreign and domestic. My oath has no time limit. When you were sworn in as a Senator, you swore a similar oath. The problems you face are because you broke your oath. You betrayed my country."

"You have no power to judge me."

"True, but America is finally draining the swamp. Corrupt officials in law enforcement have already been removed from office and prosecuted. The Blager Administration is seeking prosecutions of high-level elected officials for Broken Oaths. This will become a major focus after the election."

"Broken Oaths?"

"Yes, and in both political parties. Fixing that is a grave matter if we intend to keep our Republic. My guess is that many now in office will not be seeking reelection. Some, like you, are already gone.

"The Mexicans asked if I was here to kill you. I told them I was not. You get to live."

"You are going to bring me back and prosecute me?"

"No, I'm not. That's not my decision. I doubt that it is necessary in your case, but it is possible that you might choose to return to America and testify."

Wyatt's eyes narrowed. He was staring at me. "Again, what is your purpose here?"

I shrugged. "Mostly to have the discussion we just had, and to verify some loose ends. You have been most helpful."

"That's all?"

"For now. I can come back after the election in the Fall. The Mexicans can't keep you here forever, especially if we stop paying them, which we will, sooner or later. It might be time to cash in."

"What are you talking about?"

"You were one of the deepest, darkest, Deep State Senators. How long were you in office?"

"Almost thirty years...."

"Excellent. Someone will be back in the Fall, perhaps me. Then you have a choice to make. We can sell you to the cartels. That's the easy decision. Perhaps you can make friends with them again. We can get $100 million if we deliver you to the cartels alive."

"You said I have a choice."

"Yes, you do. Another option is that you stay healthy and start remembering things. Maybe even begin a diary. We could move you somewhere safe on American soil, perhaps GITMO, while we interrogate you and get information about various and sundry misdeeds in the Senate.

"If you know a lot that has value, I should think there would be a good possibility of a plea bargain. We'd likely credit the time you've served here, and then you could go free and into witness protection."

Wyatt was looking at me intently. This one was shrewd. In many ways it was sad he'd turned to treason.

"Is there a third option?"

I nodded. "Of course. There are always options. You could try to escape from here. If successful, that would make history."

"Why did they send you, Giles? Why are you qualified, instead of some DOJ lawyer or a diplomat?"

"I'm glad you asked. In a sense, I've been in your position. I spent seven years in a Syrian prison. I thought about suicide many times, but, in the end, I decided to live."

I looked at my watch. "Decide well, Mr. Wyatt. Perhaps we'll speak again."

I got up and walked to the dock. When I looked back, he was still sitting there, watching me.

Factoids and Fantasies

Long ago and far away (metaphorically), my nonfiction book *Engines of Prosperity* included a prescient mid-90s quote from Dr. Alvin Toffler, the futurist, "*The sophistication for deception is increasing at a greater rate than the technology for verification. This means the end of truth.*"

In today's world, there is a lot of truth in fiction, and a lot of fiction in truth. There are still First Amendment rights, but truth becomes buried under propaganda and plausible lies. Orwell warned us of this. So did the Bible. In Congress, lying is protected speech. "Thou shalt not lie," is long gone.

In contrast, even the FBI is now using perjury traps to convict and coerce innocent, honest men. *Thank you, James Comey.* Conversely, my novels, pure fiction, have tended to be predictive.

Raven's Run, featuring terrorists with Iranian nukes, came out before the Obama/Kerry "Iran Deal." That gave Iran a path to nuclear weapons and massive funding (~ $150 Billion) for terrorism. Iran is still chanting "Death to America," a goal which is embedded in their Constitution, and *Broken Oath* is now book #4 in my Raven series.

Privacy Wars predicted the NSA and IRS scandals. More recently, this novel foreshadowed what we now call #Obamagate. The hashtag has echoed around Cyberspace ever since January 2017, but only recently with the ongoing declassification of key documents can we begin to understand the dangerous impact of illegal government surveillance.

"There has been confusion about exactly what #Obamagate is, so let me summarize it: The weaponization of domestic and foreign intelligence against a presidential campaign from a sitting administration solely for political purposes to prevent the smooth transition of power."

George Papadopoulos 5/25/2020

"As one who helped to create and organize FISA and always a strong supporter, it must not be renewed unless substantially amended. The Obama administration abused FISA first to prevent the election of and then to overthrow, by fraud and deceit, the lawful election of a President."

Rudy W. Giuliani 5/28/2020

"The proposed Foreign Intelligence Surveillance Act (FISA) reflects a certain light headedness about the damage this will do to indispensable constitutional protections."

Robert H. Bork, WSJ, 3/09/1978

"What is overthrowing the government by illegal means? Treason."

Rudy W. Giuliani 5/28/2020

America has, for 243 years, been renowned for the peaceful transition of power. Up until now.

It is increasingly clear that America's intelligence and law enforcement agencies were weaponized for political purposes. At this writing, there have not yet been criminal indictments of those responsible, people at the highest levels of government in America's law enforcement and intelligence community.

Efforts to seek accountability continue. I'm with those who say this must never happen again. There has been more fear, confusion, and divisiveness than at any time since, perhaps, the Civil War.

Quarantine is when you isolate infected people. Tyranny is when you threaten healthy people with fines or prison if they don't stay home. Some now propose government "contract trackers," and even "tracking chips." Such things are better associated with Stalin's Russia than America.

Fake News is not trusted and neither is Congress. People are going back and reading novels like *1984*. My view is that the best fiction is NOT reality, but it is an image of reality.

Consider the Thrillers from major authors like Tom Clancy, Brad Thor, Michael Crichton, and Vince Flynn, among others. Their novels resonate with truth. My own novels tend to be predictive.

In a world where news resembles propaganda, novelists are again becoming the canaries in the coal mine. History tends to repeat. The names Rushdie, Solzhenitsyn, and Lorca come to mind.

Remote Viewing

The Intelligence Community had a number of active remote viewing programs during the Cold War, including Grill Flame, which was probably the most famous. These programs were officially terminated some time ago, and some of their relevant materials were declassified over the years.

Shortly after Hillary lost, January 2017, coincidentally the exact same time when #Obamagate started, the Brennan CIA effectively declassified my fictional character Josie's talent, remote viewing. The Central Intelligence Agency (CIA) released **13 million pages** of declassified documents detailing the agency's 1,864 investigations into the use of psychic powers.

The earliest document I saw there dated from about 1941. Few were recent, and the highest activity was at the peak of the Cold War. Shortly after Trump took office, this trove promptly disappeared, presumably reclassified. Poof.

Why? I have no idea. No matter. I do know there is now an interesting movie out on Amazon Prime called *Third Eye Spies*. Produced by some who were actually involved, it tells the story of remote viewing.

The character Josie in my Raven novels is a remote viewer. She is a national treasure.

As one reviewer said:

"It is Raven and Josie who are at the heart of this story and who form one of the most interesting romantic pairings in the thriller genre.

"Raven is a trained killer but also a patriot, a man on the order of the late Vince Flynn's character Mitch Rapp who will stop at nothing to destroy those he sees as a threat to his friends and country. In contrast, Josie abhors violence and is even physically and psychically sickened by it. Even guns disturb her. Josie's contribution to the team is as a remote viewer, a person who can through extra sensory perception sense people, objects, and, in Josie's case, future events from a great distance. Somehow the two manage to discover common ground, to blend darkness and light into a unique union in their relationship...."

The Chessboard and Invasion Route

Not many have thought deeply about it, but recent decades have seen a systematic "fundamental transformation" of Western Civilization. Trends have been toward socialism, rule by unaccountable elites, globalization, and decline of the Nation State. Sometimes this has been violent.

We all know about Benghazi and most have heard of the Arab Spring, but what was all that about? It was about the running of weapons from Benghazi (Libya, a failed state) through Turkey and into Syria.

Benghazi was the first bloody move in a plan to force massive migration, though few speak that ugly truth, and no one has as of yet been held accountable. The Deep State collapsed Libya, killed Americans, and ran weapons through Turkey into Syria, where ISIS was formed and trained.

The result was called the "Arab Spring" (aka, Islamic Winter) which saw genocide and the greatest flood of refugees in all of history. Most of Europe was "fundamentally transformed." This is still ongoing and, in many countries, (e.g., Britain who once saved the world from Hitler) it is a **crime** to speak about Fake News, Treason, or Islamic violence. In

America, we cling to our First and Second Amendments, and also to our guns and religion.

The focus and nexus of this global conflict (a new type of war) was centered on Syria. Benghazi led to ISIS, started in Syria with American support from the Obama Administration. ISIS prospered for a time. It rushed into Iraq, seized the weapons America left there, and soon dominated most of the region, even into Africa. This lasted until Trump took office, quickly destroying ISIS and curtailing Iran.

Military experts called Syria "the chessboard." Every major player in the world was there: America, Russia, China, Iran, all the Gulf States, the UN, George Soros, the New World Order, Israel, and more.

That fabric is a reality you've glimpsed in my Raven novels. What's new is that this tactic, this invasion, is here. It has reached the Western Hemisphere. It started, little noticed, with Eric Holder running guns into Mexico with "Fast and Furious." It expanded when Obama embraced Cuba.

Powerful forces are building a new chessboard in once-prosperous Venezuela. The invasion caravans were funded through there. Unnoticed, John Kerry abolished the Monroe Doctrine. It's now "fair game" to bring foreign systems of government to our hemisphere. Oh, Whoops!

In *Broken Oath* I send Raven and Josie down across the border to fight evil. The invasion route from Venezuela up to Mexico and our southern border is now by far the most violent place in on earth, the murder capital of the world. Mexico had more beheadings in 2019 than did the entire Middle East.

The old chessboard, Syria, never fell because of a long-time strategic Russian presence, but Venezuela is now a failed state. Cuba holds the keys to Venezuela, but it only gets the scraps. For a glimpse, check the *Jack Ryan* TV series, or the best-selling novel, *American Dirt*, which exposed cartel violence, but, written by an American expat, was soon trashed and stripped of an award for the sin of "cultural appropriation."

About the Author

John D Trudel has authored two nonfiction books and seven Thriller novels: *God's House, Privacy Wars, Soft Target, Raven's Run, Raven's Redemption, Raven's Resurrection, and this book.* He graduated from Georgia Tech and Kansas State, had a long career in high technology, wrote columns for several national magazines, and lives in Oregon and Arizona.

As an inventor and an instrument rated multiengine pilot, he has long loved aviation and technology. John had a pilot's license before he had a driver's license. He built and flew his own radio-controlled aircraft before they were called "drones" and programmed computers before PCs existed.

His popular "Freedom Writers" blog was selected by a Radio Host as one of the "top 8 in the Northwest." It has a mix of information about both real world events and novels.

http://blog.johntrudel.com

John's first six novels all won National awards. Two were finalists for the prestigious Eric Hoffer award. *Privacy Wars* predicted the NSA and IRS scandals, winning three Awards in the process. *Raven's Run* predicted the "Iran Deal," introduced the pairing of Raven and Josie, and has resulted in what is, so far, a four-book series. *Soft Target* discussed bioweapons. *God's House* was about corruption.

Details, links, interviews, and video trailers are posted on John's website. The first chapters of his novels are there too, free, as are audio clips.

https://www.johntrudel.com/

Dr. Jerry Pournelle, the late, world-famous SF writer and Star Wars scientist, described Raven's Run as a "Thriller on the bleeding edge of reality." General Paul Vallely, an expert on geopolitics, said of *Raven's Redemption,* "These things are already happening."

I would appreciate your writing a brief review on Amazon.com of any of my books that you have read. Twenty words is sufficient. My author's site has links that lead you and show you how.

THANK YOU ALL FOR YOUR INTEREST AND SUPPORT.

CPSIA information can be obtained
at www.ICGtesting.com
Printed in the USA
LVHW010940171220
674417LV00001B/21